Gray Area

Gray Area

KAY COVE

Page & Vine
An Imprint of Meredith Wild LLC

Editing by Michelle Morgan at Fiction Edit
Proofing by Judy Zweifel at Judy's Proofreading
Cover Design by K.B. Barrett Designs
Art by Aga Olario

Paperback ISBN: 978-1-964264-33-2

DEDICATION:

This one is for the women in the gray area—the ones caught between the life that fell apart and the one that hasn't taken shape yet.

For everyone who was told they were too old to start over, too late to begin again, too far gone to want something new.

Throw out the timeline. The best version of your life doesn't have a deadline.

EPIGRAPH

"Rock bottom is the end of what wasn't true enough. Begin again and build something truer."

– Glennon Doyle

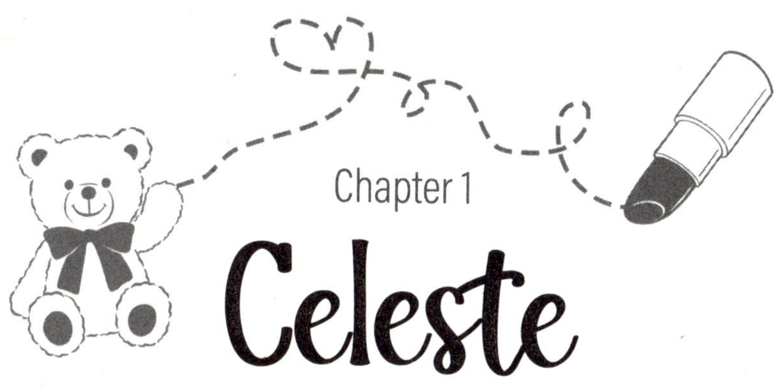

Chapter 1
Celeste

The textbook definition of a manchild.

The sketch isn't working.

I've been staring at this same page for forty-five minutes, my Caran d'Ache pencil hovering over what is supposed to be next season's statement piece—a structured jacket with asymmetrical lapels that I saw so clearly in my head this morning. Now it looks like a geometry homework assignment gone wrong. This is exactly the kind of drawing that would earn me a concerned note from my Principles of Design instructor.

Celeste, please see me after class.

Sixteen years later, and I can still see Professor Caplan's handlebar mustache twitching with disappointment every time I close my eyes.

I set down the pencil and push back from my drafting table, rolling my neck until it cracks in three places. Fed up with my creative block, I move to my desk to tackle emails and fully surrender to my administratively bogged-down Thursday afternoon.

My office is ostentatious—I'm aware. Twelve-hundred square feet of corner real estate on the forty-seventh floor of a building that has its own Wikipedia page. Floor-to-ceiling windows showcase Manhattan like a snow globe I can't shake hard enough. The Hudson glitters in the late-afternoon sun, ferries cutting white lines through gray-blue water, and somewhere down there, eight million people are living lives that don't involve staring at a blank page wondering where their talent went.

The rest of the space is a carefully curated chaos that took years and obscene amounts of money to perfect. Mannequins stand sentinel in the corners, half-draped with sample fabrics—a champagne silk charmeuse here; an experimental recycled wool blend there. The one nearest my desk wears a partially constructed bodice I abandoned last week when inspiration evaporated mid-stitch. She's half-naked and judging me intensely. I've named her Patrice.

And Patrice has *opinions* about my work output lately.

A Giacometti sculpture occupies the space near the window—elongated bronze figure, vaguely tortured, extremely expensive. Greg bought it for me on our tenth anniversary. He said it reminded him of me. I've never been sure if that was a compliment or a very pointed observation about my bone structure and general emotional state.

I still haven't decided if I love it or want to shove it right up his ass.

The walls hold my life's work in frames: original sketches from my first collection, magazine covers, a photo of me and Anna Wintour the very first year I could afford to purchase a table at the Met Gala. There's a Basquiat print I overpaid for at auction because I'd had two glasses of champagne and something to prove, and a series of black-and-white photographs from my debut show in 2004—models stalking down a runway I built in a warehouse in Brooklyn when I was twenty-three and stupid enough to believe that talent was enough.

It was.

For a while.

I pull my gaze from the window and look across the office to the sketch. The lapels really do look terrible. Unbalanced. Like I forgot how proportion works. Maybe I have. Maybe Greg is right, and my brain is starting to—

No.

I refuse to finish that thought. I'm thirty-eight, not eighty-eight. I've got at least three good decades of design left in me if I can just *focus*. If I can tune out the board meetings and the investor calls and the subtle way everyone's started looking at me like I'm a vintage piece they're not sure will hold value.

My phone buzzes. I ignore it. It's probably my assistant, Margot, reminding me about the dinner I'm supposed to attend tonight. Some charity thing for...children? Animals? Children who rescue animals? I genuinely cannot remember, which makes me a terrible person, but also, it's Thursday and I've already survived an endless week of overly long meetings that should've been one-sentence memos. I had to beg on both knees to renew our contract with our fabrics provider after Greg ruthlessly fired the company for a simple accounting error. Not to mention the condescending lecture I received from Accounting about my "creative materials budget."

Apparently "unlimited" has limits. Who knew.

I'm drafting email replies, determined to silence as much of the executive chatter as I can, when my office door swings open without so much as a knock.

Greg.

Of course.

My ex-husband strides in like he owns the place—which, technically, he does. Half of it, anyway. His Brioni suit, charcoal gray, hangs slightly askew on his frame, the wrinkles telling stories his calendar wouldn't dare record. I recognize that particular dishevelment—not the product of boardroom stress, but the hasty redressing after an "extended lunch."

"We need to talk," he announces, which is how Greg starts approximately ninety percent of our conversations. The other ten percent begin with "I've been thinking," which is somehow always worse.

I lean back in my chair and fold my arms. "Hello to you too."

"Sorry." He holds up both hands in surrender. "Good

afternoon, Celeste." He lifts his eyebrows expectantly, a silent plea to hurry up the niceties after the board begged us to at least pretend to be civil in the office. It's been over a year since our messy, public divorce. Everyone is over it and ready to move on like it didn't happen. Everyone except me and Greg, that is.

"Your shirt is untucked."

He glances down, noticing his sloppiness. Hastily, he tucks the tail of his dress shirt into his belt. "I got re-dressed quickly. I hit the gym over lunch." He pats his belly that has the slightest curve. He's inching toward a dad bod—minus the dad part. Not that I ever minded. Greg could be one hundred pounds heavier and I would've still loved him like I did when we were sixteen.

"By 'gym' do you mean your newest assistant?" I flash him a clipped smile before returning my attention to my sketch across the room. *Maybe it's leather. Would lapels work better in silk?*

"Celeste," he huffs out, rolling his eyes. But he doesn't deny a thing. "Don't start."

"I'm not starting anything. I'm *sitting*. In my office. Minding my business. *You're* the one who barged in looking like you lost a fight with a fitted sheet."

A muscle jumps in Greg's jaw as he clenches it, carving sharp angles beneath his skin. He's still handsome, I'll give him that. The bastard ages like fine wine while I'm over here scheduling preventative Botox appointments like they're dental cleanings. Silver threading through his dark hair, laugh lines that make him look "distinguished" while mine make me look "tired." The injustice of male aging never fails to astound me.

"Well, pardon me but I never know when you're here. I stopped by twice already to a locked, empty office. It's agitating trying to hunt you down. I'm the CEO of this company. I shouldn't have to beg to get on your calendar."

I lift my gaze to match his. "I'm sorry, are you complaining that your ex-wife, whom you cheated on, humiliated, then divorced, is no longer at your beck and call? Because as far as narcissism goes..."

He pinches the bridge of his nose, eyes clamped together to theatrically convey his irritation. "Fine. I'm the asshole. I get it. But I don't feel like taking your verbal lashings today. I stopped by to talk about the Monroe meeting." He pauses. "Care to explain?"

Ah. There it is. I was wondering how long it would take.

"Explain what?"

"I hired Hailey Monroe to study under you. She's practically been sleeping at the office, tirelessly working on her portfolio which you treated like a joke. She came to my office in tears right after your meeting this morning. I spent my entire morning comforting her."

"Oh." I nod in understanding. "So, Hailey was the gym session. Got it."

"Celeste, who I'm intimate with is none of your concern—"

"It *is* my concern, when all of a sudden your dick is making decisions for my company." I poke my chest so hard it hurts. "My designs. My brand. My name. You just go back to sleeping on the pile of money you made off the empire *I built*. Creative direction always has been and always will be *my* decision. Her designs were unimpressive. I gave her another chance for revisions."

He glances at the chair in front of my desk but knows better than to sit in it. "Are you sure you're making smart business decisions? Or petty ones?"

My nostrils flare as I take a deep, steadying breath. Now I glance at the guest chair. "Sit," I command.

He does, but so hesitantly, you'd think I lined the chair with invisible pushpins.

I pull Hailey's portfolio from my drawer, a once-pristine folder now transformed into a sea of neon Post-its. My handwritten critiques crowd each design like aggressive little islands, leaving only slivers of her original work visible beneath my surgical dissection.

"You eviscerated her," he mumbles, flipping through the folder. "Did you say anything nice?"

"The fact that this presentation isn't in the trash is the nice part."

"Celeste, you're so far up your own—"

"Ass?" I finish for him. "That's what you think? Because if it were up to you and all your favorite Gen Z acquaintances, my spring/summer collection would look like Avril Lavigne's closet from two thousand two. Since when does retro punk rock say, 'luxury fashion'?"

"Punk rock? That's what all these buckles are?" Greg continues to flip through pages. "I'll admit, it's a little juvenile. But surely there's something you could salvage. Instead of being a boss, how about you be a mentor?"

"*Mentor*?" I echo, then take yet another controlling breath. If Greg keeps popping into my office, I'll need a certified yoga instructor on-call to coach me through my rage-breathing. "Greg, we can sit here and debate my leadership style all day. But cut the shit for a minute. That's not why you're really here. What did you promise her when you hired her?"

His expression shifts. There it is—the tell. The slight flex of his nostrils, the way his shoulders creep toward his ears. He's not angry about my mentoring or design choices. He's angry that he got in trouble because I didn't roll over. Because I dared to have an opinion that contradicted something he's personally invested in.

And I do mean *personally*.

"I promised Ms. Monroe that at least three of her designs would be featured in our fall/winter collection. There's no time for her to work on a new set of ideas. Surely there's something in here that's workable." He stops on a page of the portfolio and tapes the simple white shift dress with the lace collar. "How about this? Plain but it's elegant. In fact, all of the designs from this section have good bones," he muses, leafing through the back half of the portfolio.

"Flip back, Greg. Did you read her marketing pitch for the spring line?"

"You're talking about the 'Only White' slogan," he surmises, like it's supposed to be a gotcha. "I'm aware. She explained the concept. It's about purity of design. Minimalism. The absence of color as a statement."

"The *absence of color.*" I let out a thick scoff. "Please tell me you're not that delusional. You realize how 'Only White' might be interpreted."

"It's fashion. It's art. Context matters."

"Context *does* matter. And the context is that we live in a world where launching a collection called 'Only White' would get us dragged across every social media platform in existence within approximately four minutes of the press release. And we'd deserve it for being tone-deaf and reckless." I shake my head. "I'm not tanking this company's reputation because someone was too myopic to consider the optics."

"Or maybe you're too old to understand the irony—"

"Careful."

It comes out sharper than I intend. Or maybe exactly as sharp as I intend. Greg stops and recalibrates, a stroke of worry crossing his features as we approach the subject of my age.

"I'm just saying..." His tone shifts to something smoother, more patronizing, "...younger consumers understand nuance. They appreciate subversion. Perhaps it'll take a younger designer to connect to their peers and encourage them to buy. Your generation isn't purchasing as much. Hailey would whip out the credit card to purchase a twelve-hundred-dollar Dior."

"Technically that *is* my generation buying, seeing as Hailey is twenty-two and the only credit card with a limit high enough to finance her expensive clothing taste is Daddy's...or yours, perhaps. Or is she calling you 'Daddy' yet?"

"Who I'm in a relationship with is none of your business."

"Relationship? Oh, please. You're plowing through twenty-somethings like Viagra is never going out of stock."

"Celeste—"

"What?" I snap, my temper barely under control. The microaggressions are crawling under my skin like fire ants and it's taking everything in me not to leap out of my chair and snatch his stupid Adam's apple that bounces up and down every time he swallows his words. I know Greg wants to unleash his temper too, but he's not a sociopath. At times I see the guilt behind his eyes for how he ended our marriage. He permanently lives in that damn doghouse he built two years ago.

"We have to stop letting our incompatibility as a couple interrupt our business partnership. We both want the same things."

The shock renders me immobile for a moment. *We want the same things?* No, that can't be right. Greg wants women with taut skin, full breasts, flat stomachs, and thick hair that has a fighting chance of recovering from all the chemical beauty treatments. He wants something I can't give him: the past. The only way he wants me is frozen, ten years ago, the time he still saw me as a woman he desired, and not simply the lynchpin of his company. As for me?

What do I want?

Maybe to stop being so bitter.

To stop focusing on what's behind me and have hope that the best parts of my life are yet to come.

Or maybe I should do what Elphaba did and just embrace the dark side—broom and all. I could play the jilted, bitter ex and haunt this office with my snarky comebacks and not-so-subtle lip-syncing of Sabrina Carpenter songs. Greg is indeed the textbook definition of a manchild.

"Look," he says, removing my sticky notes from one page in particular. The shift dress with white lace. Admittedly, my favorite of what Hailey created. "This is your taste and style. It's pretty, right?"

Reluctantly, I nod. "It has potential."

"Good. Then here"—he leans back in his seat and crosses his arms, gaze locked on mine—"I'm listening. How do we market this?"

I take one more deep breath, and this one feels less strained. "Air...light...simplicity..." I murmur mostly to myself, playing around with how the words feel on my tongue.

"What?"

I pull the folder closer to my side of the desk, reexamining the illustration I so quickly dismissed this morning. Fueled with fresh perspective, I examine the dress as my old friend—inspiration—who has evaded me for weeks now, decides to enter the meeting. "I like the neckline as is. Let's pull out the midsection and re-layer this lace around the rib area so it's sheer. I want to see two versions. Hemmed above the knee and then one to the ankles with a high slit, filled by the lace."

Greg releases a small hum of agreement and I steal a glance in his direction, catching the look of pride on his face. "I like that."

I reflect on my own disastrous sketch that's going nowhere fast. All the sharp lines look rigid and angry. I want light, soft, curves, flow. I want the models to be able to...

"*Breathe*," I say. "That's the marketing angle. The tension in the world is suffocating right now. I want this line to feel like relief after taking a deep breath. That's our inspiration."

Greg nods. He understands my creative process, and so to him, this isn't nonsense. It's gold. "Genius."

"Tell Hailey to sit with my notes. She has a week to deliver me new sketches—"

"A week?" he balks.

I narrow my eyes. "Three days if she works better under pressure."

"A week it is," he grunts, his gaze grazing the ceiling on its way back down. It was a nice moment of reprieve but our usual demeanors of casual resentment always quickly return. "Can I ask you an honest question?"

"Sure."

"I realize she needs time under your tutelage, but do you think Hailey has what it takes to be a creative director one day?"

We stare at each other across my desk. Patrice watches from her corner, silently rooting for me to go feral.

"A creative director of what in particular?"

"I don't know. I'm just thinking out loud about the future.

Celeste, you can't do it all by yourself. I know you're protective over your brand, but it's time for us to branch out. Home goods, fragrances, footwear, bags. You need a team—"

"I have a team," I insist.

"That you never use. Outside of your once-monthly luncheons, do you even communicate with your other designers? They are all sitting around, taking paychecks for work you won't let them do. Our company could be valued in the billions, but you won't let us scale because you refuse to take on investors and go public. The business makes a lot, but it spends a lot too. We're not going to sustain the way we're running."

"Your eyes are too big for your stomach. Isn't that how the saying goes? You're getting greedy. We should be grateful for what we've already built."

Greg's shoulders drop slightly—not surrender, just a tactical retreat. "All I'm asking is that you give the new designers a real chance. We need fresh perspectives if we're going to stay competitive."

I fold my hands together and place them in my lap. "Okay, I'll play ball. You want me to relinquish a little control? Fine. But I'll choose the designers working under me. Not you. Stop promising these coeds fresh out of college that they will inherit my business by crawling up under you. My design team will be built full of talent with experience, discipline, and culture."

"Hailey fits that. Start with her."

"Draping Barbie dolls with tissue paper and paperclips is not considered experience. And I want all my designers *over thirty*, at least. That way I know they are safe from your advances."

"Cheap shot."

"For a cheap man."

Greg's mouth thins. "You know, this would all be easier if you'd just accept reality."

"What reality is that?"

"That maybe..." He pauses, choosing his words like he's selecting a weapon. "Maybe it's time to let the next generation take the lead. You've had an incredible run, Celeste. Twenty years. That's more than most people get. But you're coming up on forty—"

"I'm thirty-eight."

"—and the industry is changing. Getting younger. Faster. More digital." He spreads his hands, a gesture of false reasonableness. "There's no shame in stepping back. Taking an advisory role. Letting fresh talent carry the brand forward while you enjoy the fruits of our labor."

The fruits of *my* labor. The labor he invested in with favorable terms that gave him controlling interest. The labor that made him rich enough to leave me for a succession of women young enough to be my interns.

"Women don't just die at forty," I say quietly.

"I didn't say—"

"We don't expire. We don't lose our value because some arbitrary number ticks over on a calendar." I meet his eyes, and I hope he sees the steel there. The years of swallowed pride and bitten tongues and tolerating his *bullshit* because I loved him once, because I believed in what we built together. "My biggest launches are ahead of me, not behind me. And if you can't see that, it says more about your vision than mine."

Greg opens his mouth to respond, but we're interrupted by a soft knock at the glass door.

A young woman peers in—blonde, wide-eyed in that way people are when they're new and still believe in things. She's wearing a messenger bag across her chest and holding a clipboard like a shield.

"I'm so sorry to interrupt," she says, glancing between us like she can feel the tension but can't identify it. "But I have a certified delivery for Celeste Prescott."

"*Brinley.* Celeste Brinley now," I correct, which earns me my third eyeroll from Greg. He's going to need Motrin from the sheer ache of overworking his eyeballs.

"I'm from Valcott and Finch. The front office sent me up. They said they messaged you. This legal document requires a signature."

I peer out of my office to see Margot has still not returned from her coffee run. Her desk—and by proxy, my office—remains unguarded.

"Come in." I wave her in, noticing Greg's gaze slide over her. Slowly. Appreciatively. Taking inventory of her youth, her freshness, her lack of wrinkles and cynicism. I want to throw Patrice at his head.

"Hello," he says and is met with a curt, dismissive nod that makes me want to buy her a coffee *and* scone. The girl approaches my desk, holding out the clipboard.

"Ms. Brinley, I just need a signature here. Blue or black ink is acceptable." She pulls two pens from her messenger bag, offering me an onyx option or an admiral blue. I choose the latter.

I scrawl my signature without really looking. "Thank you, deary." *Oh, fresh hell. Did I just say "deary?"* I meant it as cutesy, not cringey. I'll just go fetch my bifocals and retreat to my rocking chair now.

But she smiles so warmly at me anyway. Perhaps the way she smiles at her own grandmother. *Fuck.* "And then this is for you."

She trades me a thin tan envelope for the clipboard. It's intimidatingly thin. The kind that screams a very to-the-point legal issue without enough explanation. *Great.* What now? Another supplier lawsuit? A trademark dispute? Maybe someone's finally suing us for that time the runway collapsed at Fashion Week. In my defense, the structural engineer said it would hold.

It did not hold.

"Do you have any idea what this is...?"

She shakes her head. "Confidential of course. My job is just to make sure you received it."

I nod along, waiting for the shoe to drop. *Celeste Brinley, you've just been served!*

"Thank you for the delivery. There's usually a lunch spread on the main floor during this time. You are more than welcome to help yourself as a guest of ours today."

"I saw it on the way in. There's warm brie." She pumps her brows at me, and for some reason I immediately like her. "But I can't do soft cheese right now." She splays a hand over her belly. "I'm about fourteen weeks along."

The news of her pregnancy hits me like it always does—a physical sensation, as if someone has reached into my ribcage and gently squeezed. Not from jealousy. Not exactly. More like the feeling of pressing on a bruise you'd forgotten was there.

"Congratulations...I'm sorry, what is your name?" I ask.

"Raven."

"Congratulations, Raven. That's wonderful. Are you having a comfortable pregnancy so far?"

Greg shoots me a look before his eyes flicker to Raven's belly, then away, his interest visibly cooling like a burner switched from high to off.

"Sort of. Actually, no. I'm sick a lot. Everyone keeps telling me to suck on peppermint and ginger, but nothing works. I'd do anything for a little relief from the nausea."

"Vicks," I answer instinctively. "VapoRub. Just carry a small pot around and take a whiff when you need it. Resets the senses apparently. My friend is a senior editor at The Belly. She wrote an article about menthol or peppermint for nausea." I roll my wrist. "She told me a lot of women tried it and said it helped."

It's the most water-downed version of the story, but I'm not going to tell a total stranger that me and my best friend of twenty years had a massive falling out two years ago and haven't spoken since. It's time to call. It's well past time to call. One of us has to break the ice and considering the fact that I was the asshat in our last fight, it should be me.

"I read The Belly. What's her name?" Raven asks, with a peculiar interest that strikes me as unusual. "Your friend?"

"Whitney Trace. Although she writes under her pen name—Wren Tracie, if you want to look up the article. Ever heard of her?"

To my shock, Raven's face crumples for just a moment before she composes herself. "No. Sorry." Her voice wavers as tears well up and spill over, tracking silent paths down her cheeks even as she maintains a trembling smile.

"Are you okay?" I make a movement like I'm about to get up from my seat and comfort her, but perhaps that's too forward. "Do you want to sit down?"

Raven sniffles, wiping her nose with the back of her sleeve. "Hormones. I'm fine. I'm like this all the time lately." She points to a few CAD sketches I have framed and mounted to the wall. "You're very talented. And nice. I'm really glad I got to meet you. Both of you." She briefly glances at Greg in acknowledgment before practically floating out of the room, clipboard tucked under her arm. I wait until the door clicks shut before speaking.

"You're a pig."

Greg raises an eyebrow. "Excuse me?"

"You heard me." I lean back in my chair. "I saw you checking her out. That girl is young enough to be your daughter. She probably has student loans and a Pinterest board full of future career goals."

"Jealous doesn't suit you, Celeste." His jaw tightens, but he doesn't take the bait. "I have another meeting. We'll continue this later. I want to circle back to the expansion plans."

"Can't wait."

He leaves without another word, and I'm alone again with Patrice and the Giacometti and the weight of everything incredible I've built by sacrificing everything I ever wanted.

I look at the envelope in my hands. I'd almost forgotten about it.

Valcott & Finch. I know that firm—estate planning, trusts, wills, the kind of law that deals in death and money and the complicated intersection of both. Maybe someone left the company something. A former investor. A dead designer whose archive we're being offered.

I tear it open, expecting legalese and formality. Instead, I pull out two loose documents.

The first is a letter, brief and professional, requesting my presence at a reading of a last will and testament. I have been named as a beneficiary and my attendance is required at my earliest convenience. Standard legal language, nothing alarming.

It's the second document that stops my heart.

A funeral announcement. Heavy cream cardstock with an elegant black border. The kind of announcement you send for someone important, someone loved, someone whose absence will be felt like a missing limb.

The photograph in the center shows a woman with wild, curly red hair and a smile that takes up half her face. She's laughing at something off-camera, caught in a moment of pure, unguarded joy.

Whitney.

My best friend.

Was my best friend.

Before.

The words swim in front of me. *Beloved daughter, friend, and dreamer. Gone too soon. Memorial service...*

I can't read the rest. My hands are shaking. When did they start shaking?

Whitney is dead?

Whitney can't be dead.

Whit is *gone*?

This can't be real.

I would've known. We haven't spoken in almost two years. Not since that stupid birthday dinner. That ridiculous fight. The day I chose between the two most important people in my life... and I chose wrong.

"You're disappearing, Celeste. Every year, a little more of you vanishes into that marriage, into that man who doesn't cherish or respect you, and I can't watch it anymore. I love you too much to watch you become someone you're not."

I told her she didn't understand. That marriage was complicated. That Greg had his flaws but so did everyone. That she couldn't possibly judge my choices when she'd never had to make them.

She said: *"I'm not judging you. I'm mourning you. You're already gone."*

I stopped returning her calls after that. Changed the subject when mutual friends brought her up. Told myself I'd reach out eventually, when the dust settled.

I should've called right away, but I was too angry.

I should've called when Greg left me, but I was too ashamed.

I should've called the minute the ink was dry on my divorce papers, but I was too busy—determined to piece my life back together.

And now, I'll never get to...

How did this happen? What the hell? I'll never get to tell her...I'm...that I...

The room tilts. I try to stand, to get to the window that actually opens, to get *air*, to *breathe*, but my stilettos catch on something—the rug, my own feet, or my own fucking denial—and suddenly I'm falling, sideways, the world going diagonal in a way that doesn't make sense.

Strong hands catch me.

Greg.

He must have come back. Must have heard something, or forgotten something, or just had impeccable timing for once in his miserable life.

"Celeste? Celeste, what—"

He sees the announcement in my hand. The photograph. The name.

"Oh, dear God." His voice changes. Softens. His tone becomes something I almost recognize from a long time ago. "Oh, Celeste. Honey, no. I'm so sorry."

He pulls me into his arms, and I let him. I hate that I let him. I hate that he's here, that he's the one holding me, that after everything he's done and everything he is, he's still the person standing in my office when my world collapses.

The sob that tears out of me doesn't sound human. It's raw

and ugly and animal, the kind of sound you make when something fundamental breaks inside you. I'm crying into the shoulder of a man I despise, clutching his terrible rumpled suit, shaking so hard I can feel my teeth rattling.

Whitney is dead.

Whitney is dead, and I never called.

Whitney is dead, and the last thing I said to her was *I'll never forgive you.*

Whitney is dead, and I will never get to tell her that she was right about everything. About Greg. About me. About the slow, invisible way I lost myself and became everything I never wanted to be.

Greg holds me tighter. His hand rubs circles on my back, and it's such a familiar gesture, so ingrained from over a decade of marriage, that my body responds without my permission. I lean in, seeking comfort from the last person on Earth I should need.

"I'm sorry," he murmurs into my hair. "I'm so sorry, Celeste."

He means it. I can tell. Despite everything—the affairs, the cruelty, the way he's spent the last year trying to push me out of my own life—he knows what Whitney meant to me. He was there for all of it. The late-night phone calls. The girls' trips. The twenty years of friendship that survived distance and careers and life changes and everything...except him.

She was trying to save me.

And I chose him instead.

"I need—" My voice breaks. I try again. "I need you to go."

"Celeste—"

"Please." I pull back, just far enough to see his face. My mascara is probably running. My eyes are probably swollen. I probably look like exactly what I am: an almost thirty-nine-year-old woman who just discovered that regret is a painful, physical thing. A weight on your chest that smashes and reshapes your heart like Play-Doh. "Please, Greg. I need to be alone right now."

Or more accurately, out of respect for this woman who I loved with my whole heart, I need to not be with Greg right now.

He hesitates. For a moment, I see something in his expression—concern, maybe. Or guilt. Or just the awkwardness of a man who doesn't know what to say at a moment he's expected to be nothing short of eloquent.

"Okay," he says finally. "But if you need anything—"

"I know where to find you."

He nods and squeezes my shoulder once.

The door closes behind him with a soft click, and I'm alone.

Just me and Patrice and the Giacometti and the funeral announcement still clutched in my shaking hand. The photograph of Whitney smiling up at me, head slightly cocked, like she's waiting for me to speak.

I slide down the side of my desk until I'm sitting on the floor, legs splayed in front of me like a child's, designer dress be damned. The tears won't stop. I'm not sure I want them to. I want to drain every last drop so I don't have to hold the acid of remorse in my body.

Tears of guttural guilt and regret.

Twenty years.

Twenty years of friendship.

Twenty years of laughter and secrets and holding each other through awful parents, breakups, and job losses, and the kind of ordinary disasters that define a life. Gone. Because I was too proud to admit she was right. Because I was too scared to leave. Because I kept telling myself *later, later, I'll fix it later.*

There is no later.

There's just this. An office full of expensive things that suddenly mean nothing. A funeral I'll have to attend alone. A best friend I'll never get to apologize to.

And somewhere in that envelope, a will that named me as a beneficiary.

What could Whitney possibly have left me?

Was she angry? Or did she miss me too?

I sit on the floor of my ridiculous office, surrounded by the life I built on compromises and silence, and I cry until there's nothing left.

Patrice watches from her corner.

For once, she's silent. At a loss for judgment. All that's left is pity.

Chapter 2
Saylor

Gravity is the enemy. We resist.

The sun personally attacks my eyeballs the moment I step out of the subway.

I've been awake for twenty-six hours, give or take, and my body has moved past tired into that floaty, disconnected state where everything feels slightly unreal. Like I'm watching myself from three feet to the left. The guy shuffling down East 7th Street in yesterday's black T-shirt and jeans that smell faintly of cigarette smoke and spilled vodka? That's me. But also, somehow, not me.

Last night's gig was a private party in some finance bro's Tribeca penthouse—the kind of place with floor-to-ceiling windows and art that costs some people's entire 401k. I wasn't there as an escort. Just security. Standing by the door for eight hours, checking names against a list, politely redirecting the coked-up investment bankers who kept trying to bring plus-ones that weren't on the guest list.

It's not glamorous work, but it pays cash, and cash is the only language my landlord speaks.

I dig my keys out of my pocket as I approach our building—a crumbling, five-story in Alphabet City that's seen better decades. The lobby smells like mildew and someone's attempt to mask mildew with lavender air freshener. It's not working. The lift's been broken since the week we moved in, which means five flights of stairs that feel like fifty when you haven't slept.

By the time I reach our door, my thighs are burning and I'm reconsidering every life choice that led me to a fourth-floor apartment with no lift.

I pause with my hand on the knob, taking a breath. Resetting my face. Mum doesn't need to see how tired I am. She's got enough to worry about.

The door swings open before I can turn the key.

"There he is." Callie's standing in the doorway, her scrubs printed with little cartoon bunnies today. She's five-foot-nothing, with deeply tan skin, kind eyes, and the sort of smile that makes you feel like everything might actually be okay, even when it's demonstrably not. "I was starting to think you got lost."

"Traffic," I say, which is a lie. The truth is, the moment Callie texted me that she could bring Mum home this morning, I sat on a bench in Tompkins Square Park for twenty minutes, staring at pigeons and trying to remember what it feels like to not be exhausted.

Callie steps aside to let me in. "Your mom's in good spirits today. We just finished up."

Our apartment is small—two bedrooms, one bath, a kitchen that's more of a suggestion than a room. But it's clean, and the morning light coming through the windows makes it feel almost cheerful. Mum's favorite red, velvet reading chair dominates what used to be the living room, surrounded by the medical equipment that's become as familiar as furniture: the adjustable tray table, the shower chair we wheel in and out of the bathroom, the grab bars I installed myself after watching forty YouTube tutorials.

Mum is propped up against her pillows, her silver-streaked auburn hair freshly brushed and braided. Callie's work. Mum's hands shake too much these days to manage it herself, and my attempts at braiding look like something a drunk toddler would produce.

Mum's eyes find mine. "Morning, love." Her smile breaks across her face like sunrise—the same one she gave me when I won the Year Three spelling bee, when I graduated, when I helped her through her first steps of physical therapy. A smile that says I'm still her boy, her anchor, even though we're drowning in medical bills in a country where our slight accents mark us as outsiders.

I don't deserve it. But I'll take it anyway.

"Morning, Mum." I cross the room and drop a kiss on her forehead. She smells like the lavender soap Callie uses, clean and familiar. "How are we feeling?"

"Oh, you know." She waves a hand vaguely. "I'm vertical. That's something."

"Vertical is underrated."

"That's what I keep telling her," Callie chimes in from the kitchen, where she's packing up her bag. "Gravity is the enemy. We resist."

I perch on the edge of Mum's oversized chair, careful not to jostle her. The chronic pain is worst in the mornings, before her medications fully kick in. I can see it in the tightness around her eyes, the way she holds her shoulders. But she never complains. Never has.

It makes it all worse, somehow. Sometimes I think it'd be easier to handle someone who rages against their circumstances than someone who just...accepts them.

"Callie helped me wash my hair," Mum announces, touching her braid like it's a prize. "Feel how soft."

I dutifully run my fingers along the plait. Something catches in my chest when I feel how much of her has disappeared between my fingertips. The pills that dull her pain sharpen everything else into focus—the weight loss, the yellowing whites of her eyes, the tremor in her hands. Her medical chart tracks the shocking resilience of her organs, but it's this—this gossamer thread where rope used to be—that makes it impossible to pretend.

But I hide my fear and replace it with jovial optimism. "Very soft. Like a fancy shampoo commercial. You should charge for this, Cal."

"Please. Your mother's hair is a joy. Long and wavy like that?

Mine would never." Callie emerges from the kitchen, satchel slung across her body. "Okay, I've got her meds sorted for the next two weeks. Morning meds in the blue organizer, the afternoon in the orange. If she's having a particularly difficult day—"

"The red vial in the fridge. Twenty units, I remember."

Callie nods. "There are new syringes in the medical bag. And I left some extra anti-nausea in the bathroom cabinet, just in case." She hesitates. "I, um. I managed to get the Styrica at cost again. My contact at the pharmacy owed me a favor."

My chest tightens. The Styrica alone would be almost fourteen hundred dollars a month without insurance. With Callie's "contacts" and "favors," we pay maybe one-sixty. I don't ask too many questions about how she makes it happen. I'm too grateful to risk the answer.

"Cal..." I start, but she waves me off.

"Don't. Seriously. It's nothing."

"It's not nothing. It's—" I drag my fingers through my unwashed hair, searching for a way to express gratitude that doesn't sound hollow against the mountain of what I owe her. "You've been helping us for over a year now. The meds, the visits, the—" I gesture around at everything. "All of it. I don't even know how to begin to thank you properly."

"Then don't begin." She shoulders her bag, but something in her expression shifts. A flicker of something I've been pretending not to see for months now. "Actually, can we talk for a sec? In the hall?"

My stomach drops, but I keep my voice light. "Sounds ominous."

"It's not. It's just..." She glances at Mum, then back at me. "Private."

"I'll be right back," I tell Mum, who nods knowingly. She's not stupid. She's seen the way Callie looks at me. She's probably been waiting for this conversation longer than I have.

The hallway smells marginally better than the lobby, more like old carpet than active mildew. Small victories. Callie leans against the wall opposite our door, arms crossed, and I mirror her position because I don't know what else to do with my body.

"So," she starts.

"So," I echo.

"I'm moving."

The revelation lands like a punch I should've seen coming. "Moving where?"

"Paris."

"You're kidding—"

"No, not *that* Paris. The small town in Kansas."

"Oh...okay. Well, congratulations. This is a good thing, right?"

She tucks a lock of hair behind her ear, not quite meeting my eyes. "There's a hospice program out there, really progressive, and they offered me a lead position as a nurse practitioner. Better pay, better hours, amazing experience. It's kind of a dream job, honestly. Even if it is the wrong Paris."

"That's..." I swallow. "That's great, Cal. Really. You deserve it."

"I leave in three weeks."

Three weeks. That's twenty-one days to find a new nurse, a new source for discounted meds, a new everything. The mental math is already happening, numbers scrolling through my brain like a doomsday ticker. More escort shifts. More security gigs. Less sleep. Less time with Mum. Even less time for myself—

"Saylor." Callie's voice cuts through the spiral. "Breathe."

I realize I've been holding my breath. I force myself to exhale. "Sorry. Just...processing."

"I know. And I'm sorry. I wanted to give you more notice, but the offer came together fast and I had to make a decision and—" She stops herself, takes a breath of her own. "I'll help you find someone who can help you guys. I've got contacts, other nurses or CNAs who might be able to step in, at least part-time."

"Right. Yeah. Thank you. I hate to ask you for anything more, but that'd be helpful."

We stand there in the flickering hallway light, and I can feel the other conversation hovering between us. The one we've been dancing around for months. Callie's too kind to force it, and I'm too much of a coward to address it.

But she's leaving. And apparently that changes things.

"Saylor." She pushes off the wall, moving closer. Close enough that I can smell her perfume—something warm and slightly spicy, like cinnamon. "I'm going to miss you guys. I feel so guilty."

"Oh, hey, Cal." I gently squeeze the top of her shoulder. "You've done more for us than I could've prayed for. It's time. I can't even pay you properly. I don't know why you've put up with me this long."

"You really don't know?" Her voice softens, eyebrows ever so slightly arched. "Why I've stuck around so long? Why I keep finding ways to help, even when you won't accept it properly?"

In spite of her tone, the question hits like a sledgehammer. I open my mouth to deflect, to make a joke, to do the thing I always do when conversations get too real. But the words won't come. Callie reaches out and takes my hand. Her fingers are small and warm against mine, and she looks up at me with those kind eyes, and I hate myself a little for what I'm about to not say.

I know. Of course I know. I've known since the third month, when she started packing us home-cooked meals "because she made too much." Since the sixth month, when she started bringing Mum home from physical therapy appointments to spare me the drive into the city, always finding an excuse to linger and chat. Since the first time she touched my arm and I felt her fingers tremble, slightly, before she pulled away.

But knowing and acknowledging are different things. And acknowledging would mean having a conversation I'm not equipped for.

"Cal—"

"It's okay." She squeezes my hand once, then lets go. When she reaches up to touch my cheek, her smile is sad but not bitter. "I tried my best. But some walls don't come down, do they?"

"It's not—" I start, then stop. What am I going to say? It's not you, it's me? The most clichéd brush-off in history, except it's actually true?

"You don't have to explain." She pats my cheek gently, the way you'd comfort a child. "You've got a lot on your plate. More than most people could handle. I just thought maybe..." Her small shoulders lift in a shrug. "Anyway. I get it. No hard feelings."

"I'm sorry," I manage. "You've been so good to us, and I wish I could—"

"Don't. Seriously, Saylor. Don't apologize for not having feelings you don't have."

But that's the thing. It's not that I don't have feelings. It's that I can't afford them. Not when Mum needs me. Not when I'm working three jobs and barely keeping us afloat. Not when the idea of adding another person to my life feels less like companionship and more like another weight I'm not strong enough to hold.

I don't say any of this. I just nod, and Callie seems to understand.

"Okay." She takes a breath, squares her shoulders. "One more thing, and then I'll let you go get some sleep because you look like absolute hell, by the way."

"Cheers for that."

"Your mom's mobility—"

"Is improving," I answer, sounding accusing for some reason. "Sorry, I mean, she's getting around a little better lately. She barely touches the wheelchair. That's a good thing, right?"

Callie's face falls. "Saylor...your mom..."

"What?" I coax gently. "What about Mum?"

"I think it's important to Ada that you *think* she's improving, but the truth is her range of motion is getting worse, not better. The pain? Almost unbearable and she hates how the medication makes her feel."

The guilt sweeps me up like it always does. My mum lives in a prison of pain with only brief moments of relief when she's drugged out of consciousness. It's no way to live, but she has to because of me. She's like this...because of me.

"What about hydrotherapy?" I ask weakly.

Callie shakes her head. "I doubt it'd do much. The damage to her spine is so severe and none of the treatments we're trying are helping."

"Cal, I understand the prognosis. But seeing my mum walk one day without cringing from pain is sort of the only thing that gets me out of bed in the morning. You'll have to pardon me if I choose to hold onto hope."

Wearing a half-smile, she digs into her satchel and pulls out a sticky note—bright yellow, with handwriting so neat it looks typed.

"What's that?"

"Hope. A friend of a friend told me about this hotshot new neurosurgeon the hospital just drafted." She waves vaguely at the space between us. "Dr. Ali Yassa. He's running a research study on experimental spinal treatments—some new laser technique that's showing really promising results for chronic pain patients with little to no mobility."

I take the sticky note. The email address stares back at me: a.yassa.spinalstudy@mountsinai.org.

"I don't know all the details for participation," Callie continues, "but from what I've heard, it could be life-changing. They're saying this technology could put him in the running for a Nobel."

Hope is a dangerous thing. It's a lit match in a room full of gasoline, and I've been burned too many times to trust it. But I'm staring at this sticky note like it's a winning lottery ticket anyway.

"So what do I do?"

"Email him," Callie tells me. "You can use my name but it'd be pointless. He doesn't know me."

"I just email him, and say...what?" I look at her desperately.

Callie adjusts her bag strap. "That's the tricky part. I was able to get the email, but there's no official inquiry for experimental procedures. The hospital hasn't even announced his employment yet. So, your guess is as good as mine, but I would email him and ask for a meeting if you can get through. I wish I could do more—"

"You've already done too much, Callie. Thank you." I hold up the sticky note in wonder like it's the holy grail. "You are incredible." Abandoning my better sense for boundaries, I reach out to collect her hand as if I can press my gratitude deep into her palm.

Right when I release her, she steps closer, rises to her tiptoes, and presses a kiss to my cheek—quick, gentle, final. "It's wonderful how you take care of your mom, but take care of yourself too, okay? Even Superman had days off."

I smirk at her. "I don't think that's true."

"Oh, I'm sure of it." Callie gives me a wink. "Lois Lane would've insisted. All those big macho, mighty heroes are always kept in check by a woman."

Lost for a response, I duck my head and answer with a sheepish nod.

She starts toward the stairs, then pauses, looking back over her shoulder. "For what it's worth? Whoever eventually gets through those walls is going to be a very lucky girl."

And then she's gone, her footsteps echoing down the stairwell until I can't hear them anymore.

I stand in the hallway for a long moment, staring at the yellow sticky in my hand. The email address blurs slightly, and I realize my eyes are burning. From exhaustion, probably. That's what I tell myself.

When I go back inside, Mum is watching me with that look—the one that says she knows exactly what just happened and is waiting to see if I want to talk about it.

I don't.

"She's leaving," I say instead, moving to the kitchen to start the kettle. Tea fixes everything, according to Mum. It doesn't, obviously, but the ritual of making it helps. "Kansas. She got a big promotion."

"Ah." Mum's voice is carefully neutral. "That's a shame. She's lovely."

"She is."

"And she fancies you."

I busy myself with the tea bags. "Mum."

"What? I've got eyes. Broken spine, not blind." There's a smile in her voice, but when I glance over, her expression is more thoughtful than teasing. "You could've had something there, you know. If you'd let yourself."

"Could've, would've, should've." The kettle starts to whistle, and I pour the water with more focus than the task requires. "Doesn't matter now."

"It matters if you're lonely."

"I'm not lonely. I've got you." I bring her tea over—chamomile, two sugars, in the chipped mug she's had since I was a kid. "Besides, I'm too tired to be lonely. Loneliness requires energy I don't have."

Mum takes the mug with both hands, cradling it like a small treasure. Her fingers are gnarled now, the joints swollen from inflammation, but her grip is still steady. Small mercies.

"You work too much," she says. The same thing she's said every day for the past two years.

"Someone's gotta pay for this palatial estate." I gesture grandly at our cramped living room.

"Saylor." Her tone sharpens, just slightly. "I'm serious. You're running yourself into the ground. I see you leaving at all hours, coming back looking like death warmed over. The 'bartending' job, the 'security' job, the other job you won't tell me about—"

"There's no other job."

"Don't lie to your mother."

I freeze with my own mug halfway to my lips. She's watching me with those sharp blue eyes—my eyes, everyone always says—and I can see her doing the math. Putting together the late nights and the cash payments and the expensive clothes I sometimes come home in.

"Whatever it is," she says quietly, "I'm not asking you to explain. I just need you to know that I see you. I see what you're doing, what you're sacrificing. *And I hate it.*"

"Mum—"

"I hate that you're breaking yourself to take care of me. I hate that we lost everything because I believed a con man who promised he could fix me." Her voice cracks, just slightly, before she steadies it. "I hate that every day I watch my son disappear a little more, and I can't do anything to stop it."

The silence that follows is heavy. I stare into my tea, watching the steam curl upward, because I can't look at her face right now. I can't see the guilt there, the love, the helpless frustration, without wanting to collapse myself.

"And I hate that you're only in this situation because of me," I finally say.

"Oh, Saylor. For the millionth time. The accident—" She stops short.

My hand tightens on the mug. We don't talk about the accident. That's an unspoken rule between us—it has been since the day we left Sydney three years ago. But apparently today is a day for breaking rules.

"Callie told me about a surgeon, Mum—"

"No," she declares.

"It's *legitimate*. An experimental procedure—"

"I've heard that before."

"We're trying," I tell her.

"*Experimental*, Saylor. Do you know what that means? Out. Of. Pocket. Out of our budget. You need to start saving to get a new place."

"You're right about that," I answer before taking a short swig of my tea. "Clearly the lift is never getting fixed and we need to be on the first floor somewhere. Actually, my friend Taio's apartment is closer to your doctor's office. He's traveling indefinitely now, so I could ask him about a sublet."

Mum blinks slowly, patiently waiting for her turn to speak.

"No, *you*, Saylor. You need to get your own place and leave me to deal with the stairs. I'm the parent. You're my son. Not the other way around. You don't owe me your life, honey."

I stare into her big eyes, and despite the smile she's wearing, they look so sad. "Don't I though?"

"No parent wants to see their child like this. So busy surviving, you've forgotten how to live."

I don't have an answer for that. So I reach into my pocket and pull out the sticky note, smoothing it against my thigh. "We're not giving up. End of story."

"Fine. Email them," she relents. "But Saylor? Whatever happens...whatever this costs, whatever false promises they try to sell us...promise me you won't sell your soul for it. I'd rather live with the pain than watch you destroy yourself trying to fix me."

I just nod, and lean forward to kiss her forehead, and pretend the ache in my chest is just exhaustion. She reaches up to wrap her arms around my neck and hold me close, but her tender embrace causes her to screech in agony.

"Oh, *Mum.*"

"I'm fine, I'm fine," she whimpers, still shaking from pain. She hunches over, bent in an unnatural angle that's buying her some sort of temporary relief.

"I'll get the Styrica," I murmur.

"And the nausea medication, please? It helps but it makes me so sick."

"It's too much medication on an empty stomach. What would you like to eat? I'll whip up something."

"You just worked a double, love. Go lie down."

I ignore her protest. "Cheesy eggs? Hashbrowns? And some fruit with Cool Whip?"

"Okay," she acquiesces, a smile creeping onto her face. "That sounds really good. Maybe some sausage too? Callie kicked my ass with the stretches today."

"Coming right up."

As I head into the tiny kitchen, an intrusive image of hospital bills piling up and crushing our apartment until it falls on our head becomes a disturbing hallucination. I grab the eggs from the fridge, cracking two against each other before dropping them into a plastic bowl. My phone rings before I can collect a fork and begin to scramble the yolks into submission. I almost don't pick up until I see the Caller ID.

"Gimme a second," I answer without a hello, tracking through the living room. Wordlessly I point to my phone, then to the front door when Mum's eyes land on me. She nods at my charades, knowing it's impossible to have privacy in our cramped apartment.

The moment the door closes behind me, I press the cell to my cheek again. "A little early isn't it? I didn't know the Manhattan elite get horny at about nine in the morning."

"Hilarious. I need a favor," Rina, my boss, says in a huff.

"Where are you? It's loud."

"At the airport, trying to get home as quick as I can but I'm still in Paris."

"Kansas?" I ask cheekily.

"What? No—Paris in France. Are you high, Saylor?"

"No, I just... Anyway—what favor?"

"My friend, Celeste. The designer—"

"I remember. Forrest's custody hearing for Koda," I say too quickly. The details of that day blur together—the courthouse address, what month it even was—but Celeste herself remains in perfect focus, like a photograph burned into my retinas. Some people just leave that kind of impression.

"Right. She and Forrest are friends. *Platonic* friends. She'd typically just use him as armor against her sleazy ex."

"Speaking of sleazy exes—how's Sean doing?"

"Slimy as ever. Can we focus? Celeste just found out yesterday that her best friend passed away. She's headed Upstate for the funeral today and I don't think she can do this alone. Her crowd anxiety is also why she used to hire Forrest. But he's with Sora now and Celeste feels it's inappropriate to ask. Taio is taking some time off—"

"You mean bumping uglies with that pop star—"

"And so that leaves you."

"Your third-choice knight in shining armor."

"Oh, Saylor. You know you're my favorite."

I scoff, leaning back against the wall. "You're a skilled liar."

"It's called being an attorney. And all right, I'll give. This is really important to me. Obviously I'll cover any fees, but how can I convince you to accompany Celeste today?"

I sigh. "While a funeral does sound riveting, I can't. Mum's having a flareup and I can't keep making her nurse work for free. She needs me here."

"I'll pay you triple the normal rate. And you won't have to do anything besides provide emotional support. Believe me, Celeste wouldn't make a move on you if her life depended on it."

"Ouch."

"It's a funeral, Saylor."

"Triple?" I ask, glancing back over my shoulder. Triple is enough to pay Callie properly for a couple visits this weekend.

"Yes. Are you in?"

"Almost. I have a question for you. You and Sean bump elbows with a lot of the Manhattan upper echelon... Mount Sinai just hired a big-deal neurosurgeon—Dr. Yassa. Ever heard of him?"

"It's not ringing a bell."

"He's working on an experimental treatment but I'm not sure if Mum's a candidate, or if we can afford it..."

"All right, Saylor. I see where this is going. You go with Celeste. I'll make some calls or ask Sean too. He knows everybody in this city with a seven-figure salary."

"Fine. Good. Also, I'll need a suit."

"Celeste owns one of the most prominent fashion brands in the world. I'm sure they can rummage up something. I'll have her send a car for you. Can you be ready in two hours?"

I agree to the logistics and Rina swiftly ends the call, moving on to put plans in motion.

Celeste, huh? Not exactly the circumstances in which I was hoping to see her again, but I do remember wanting to see her again.

I walk in through the front door to see Mum's smiling face.

"Who was that?"

"My boss." I tuck my phone back into my pocket as if it's culpable. "I have to work this weekend."

"Aw, love. You're running yourself into the ground."

"It's okay. There's a bonus that'll make it all well worth it. Are you going to be okay for a couple days if Callie stops by a few times?"

"Of course, silly. No need to fuss over me." That would be far more convincing if her eyes weren't watering and she wasn't bent over like she's trying to attempt human origami.

I head back to the kitchen, returning to the bowl of unscrambled eggs.

For one moment, I let myself really go there.

What would it be like if Mum could walk pain-free again? If she could run a farm like she used to. If her smiles weren't forced, masking the excruciating torment. What if I were just a normal guy getting ready to go on a date with a woman he liked and knew it had potential to go somewhere?

What if...

I was anyone else. Anywhere else. In any other circumstance besides the one I created.

What if just for a moment...I really let myself have *hope*?

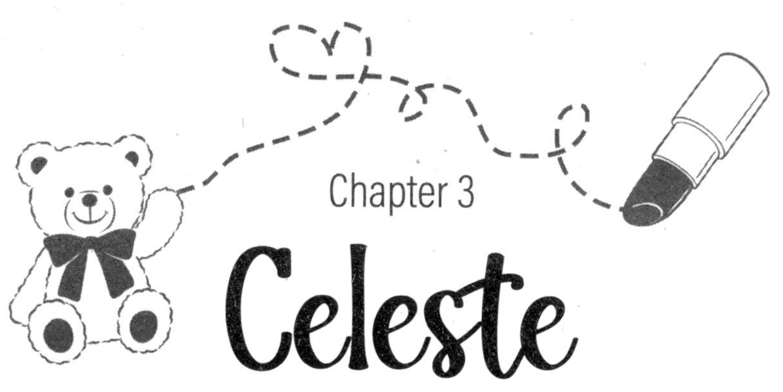

Chapter 3
Celeste

Twelve years my junior? He's a puppy.

I am going to die on this street.

Not metaphorically. Not in the existential, can't sleep, lying-in-the-dark-staring-at-my-ceiling-in-silence way I've been dying since I found out about Whitney's passing. I mean literally, physically, vehicularly. A woman in a sixty-thousand-dollar car is about to be taken out by a one-way street near Lower Manhattan, and the obituary will be humiliating.

Celeste Brinley, 38, fashion icon and peanut-butter-jelly sandwich enthusiast, met her untimely demise Thursday morning while attempting to wedge her Range Rover into a spot the size of Rhode Island. Her last words were reportedly "I think I can fit." She is survived by her dogeared Brené Brown books, seventeen half-empty La Croix cans scattered throughout her apartment, and her ex-husband, who is thrilled to take her hard-earned company public.

I yank the wheel left to avoid a delivery truck that materializes out of nowhere—I swear they just *spawn* in this borough—and the SUV lurches onto a street so narrow I can practically read the ingredient labels on the bodega products through the passenger window. My GPS has recalculated four times in the last six minutes. *Four.* I've been given the calm, robotic equivalent of *are you even listening to me* by a machine, and honestly, no. I'm not. I haven't been listening to anyone or anything for two days, wildly distracted by my sullen thoughts.

A cyclist flies past my window and screams something I can't make out but can infer from context.

"I'm *trying*," I mutter at no one.

Driving is an act of faith I've never possessed. You have to trust the other cars, trust the lanes, trust that everyone is operating under some shared agreement about physics and turn signals. I trust none of it. We're city people. If it's too far to walk, we don't go. I was forced to drive here and there when I was thirty-two because Maddox, my former driver, had a knee replacement and Greg told me I needed to "be less dependent." This from a man who once called me from our kitchen to ask where we kept the coffee mugs.

I got the license. I have used it exactly nineteen times, and each time has taken a year off my life.

But the alternative was three hours in the back of a town car with nothing to do but think, and I cannot think right now. Thinking is the enemy. Thinking means Whitney, and Whitney means the funeral, and the funeral means this isn't all a bad dream. She's really gone.

I spot the building. Green awning. The address Rina texted me after she assured me, as one of my closest friends, I could *not* handle this alone. Rina offered from the airport to hustle home and attend the funeral with me but I know what Paris means to her. I know why she's there. Looking for *him*. The him that's the entire reason her risqué agency exists. I don't want to add more to her mind at the moment. I considered texting Forrest, who, strangely enough, I consider a dear friend. But based on how we met, out of respect to the woman he now loves, he can't be my plus-one anymore.

I've met Taio before and he was a darling. And really tall. His frame alone could shield me from the judgmental stares of the people from my past, but apparently he's jet-setting across the country with the girl they are calling the next T. Swift.

Of Rina's favorite contractors, that leaves—

Shit!

I aim the car toward the curb the way one aims a prayer toward the ceiling—with great hope and very little precision—and the front right tire connects with something metal. A trashcan. It topples sideways with a clatter that echoes down the whole block, the lid rolling in a slow, accusatory circle before settling flat on the pavement like a cymbal crash at the end of a terrible performance.

I'm parked, but my foot stays pressed against the brake like it's the only thing keeping the world from spinning off its axis.

I should get out. Pick up the trashcan. I should do a lot of things. I should have returned Whitney's calls. I should have told her she was right about Greg the first time she said it, and the second time, and the fourteenth. I should have said *I'm sorry* when there was still a person alive to hear it.

The tears come so fast I don't even get a warning. One second I'm staring at a sideways trashcan through the windshield and the next I'm falling apart, my hands still gripping the wheel at ten and two like that's going to save me. My chest caves inward around something sharp that's been lodged there since I opened that damn envelope that left me raw and in denial. Surely I'll get to the Hamptons and Whit will be there to welcome me with open arms.

Her phone is only going straight to voicemail because she's busy.

Not because she's dead.

My brain scrambles to produce the last real memory I have of my best friend. The frustrated tears in her eyes. The tiramisu splattered across her red shoes. The way our shouting was bouncing off the bricks in the alley, echoing our rage. Never in a million years did I think that would be our last face-to-face conversation.

I press my forehead against the steering wheel and I cry the way I only ever do when I'm alone. Full body. Graceless. The kind of crying that would make the front page of Page Six and end my reputation as the woman who conducted a company-wide conference six hours after her divorce filing without a tremor in her voice, promising everybody nothing would change.

That woman is a performance.

This woman—mascara running, shoulders heaving, ugly-crying in a parked car in front of a tipped-over trashcan in Alphabet City—is much closer to the truth.

Knock, knock.

My head snaps up so fast my neck cracks. I swipe at my face with the back of my hand, which accomplishes absolutely nothing except smearing mascara in a wider radius, and turn to find Saylor standing on the other side of the glass.

Oh.

Oh.

I forget, for one suspended and wildly inappropriate moment, that I've been crying.

He's wearing the suit I sent over. The charcoal Tom Ford, and either my tailor is a genius or God spent extra time on this man's shoulders, because the jacket fits like it was stitched onto his body. White dress shirt, no tie—I sent a navy silk tie and he apparently made an editorial decision, which under normal circumstances I would find sloppy, but with the top button undone and the collar open against his neck, I'm forced to admit the edit was correct. His hair is freshly cut, tapered on the sides, and a leather overnight bag hangs from his shoulder like it weighs nothing. He stands there with the easy confidence of a man who's never had to practice his posture in a mirror.

I roll down the window. The warm May air hits my wet face and I feel every inch of the disaster I must look like.

Saylor's expression shifts as he takes in my face. It's a quick read, the kind of adjustment you'd miss if you weren't watching for it. But he doesn't ask if I'm okay. He doesn't tilt his head or soften his voice into that careful register people use when they think you're fragile. He just looks at me like I'm a person having a rough morning, which is the kindest thing anyone has done for me all week.

"Celeste. What a nice surprise. I thought I was meeting you there," he says, easy, warm, like we're picking up a conversation from five minutes ago. "I was expecting a driver with a fancy hat. Maybe a little sign with my name on it. Perhaps some champagne in the back of a limo."

I let out a sound that's somewhere between a laugh and a hiccup. "Sorry to disappoint."

He smiles and for a fleeting moment, I feel all right. Not good. Just...sturdier. A touch distracted.

"Are you kidding?" he asks. "This is definitely an upgrade."

"What's an upgrade? The Range Rover, or the crying woman driving it?"

"The company," he clarifies. "We're headed to the Hamptons?"

"Yes."

He clasps his hands together with a boyish excitement, grinning from ear to ear. "Please tell me you like road-trip games."

"I've never played one." I shrug. "To be honest, I didn't want to sit in the back of a car for three hours alone with my thoughts. I actually hate driving. I risked it out of desperation."

His eyes slide past me to the trashcan lying on its side by the curb. The corner of his mouth twitches—not a full smile, just the beginning of one trying to escape. "And how'd that go?"

"Don't start. Believe me, I'm already aware I am a horrible driver."

"No, I believe you." Now he's fully smiling, and it does something inconvenient to my chest—a small crack in the ice, warmth leaking in where I wasn't ready for it. "You have to watch these trashcans. Vicious little things pop out of nowhere and attack innocent luxury vehicles."

"Hardy-har-har."

I want to be annoyed, but the absurdity of the moment is settling over me like a blanket someone draped across my shoulders without asking. The trashcan. My ruined face. The impossibly handsome escort in his perfect suit, smiling at me through my car window like nothing about this scene is strange. Yet it's the first human interaction I've had in days that hasn't felt forced.

He taps the window frame twice with his knuckle. "Unbuckle

and unlock the door."

I do, and he opens it from the outside then offers me his hand. His fingers are warm, his grip steady and sure, and I let him guide me out of the driver's seat like I'm being extracted from a small disaster, which I suppose I am. I'm in heels—black Louboutins, because even in grief I am constitutionally incapable of not dressing like myself—and the pavement is uneven. Instinctually, his other hand goes to my elbow to keep me from wobbling. He is tall. I knew he was tall, I registered it when I first saw him at Forrest's custody hearing months ago, but standing next to him on a Brooklyn sidewalk with my hand in his, it hits differently. I come up to his chin. I am wearing four-inch heels.

He lets go of my hand, reaches into his breast pocket, and pulls out the navy kerchief I included as an accessory.

"There was a tie that matched this."

He pats his back pocket. "I will absolutely put it on if you'd like...but also, please don't make me. I have a thing with ties. They are like fancy nooses."

My lips twitch, but the smile doesn't fully land. "I'll spare you this time."

With a gentleness that doesn't match his size, he uses the handkerchief to dab at the skin beneath my right eye, then my left. I stand very still. His face is close enough that I can see the flecks of gold in his blue eyes, which is information I absolutely do not need to focus on right now.

"I want to be honest with you," he says, still dabbing.

"Okay."

"This isn't going to cut it." He pulls the kerchief back and examines it. Black mascara is smudged across the linen like a tiny Rorschach test. "We have a situation." He folds the kerchief neatly and tucks it back into his pocket like he's preserving evidence. "Did you bring makeup?"

"I have a bag in the trunk."

"Great. Because right now you look like a very beautiful raccoon, and I say that with the deepest respect."

A laugh cracks out of me—short, surprised, almost painful. The kind of laugh that sneaks past grief when you're not guarding the door. Saylor grins, and it's the grin of a man who knows exactly what he just did. He reached into the wreckage and pulled out something small and light and handed it to me, and I took it, and for three seconds the world didn't feel like it was ending.

"How about you let me drive?" he says, already moving toward the trunk. "I have street cred with the trashcans. They never jump out to attack me."

There's a click-clack against the asphalt as I follow him. He pops open the trunk, and after depositing his overnight bag next to my Hermès Togo Travel Bag. To my shock, he opens it and starts fishing with a level of comfort that should not have been earned in five minutes. Before I have a chance to react to his audacity, he finds my emergency kit—the leather case with the Tom Ford foundation, the Charlotte Tilbury concealer, the Dior mascara, the Chanel blush, the Pat McGrath eyeshadow palette, and the Hermès lipstick—the arsenal that normally lives in my purse because Celeste Brinley does not exist in public without a contingency plan.

He hands it to me. "Is this what you need?...What's wrong?"

"You opened my bag. I have...intimates in there." I cradle the leather bag in my hands.

He sucks in his lips in an attempt to hide his smirk. His attempt fails. "I'm sorry. I wasn't thinking and I wasn't after your intimates. Fetching things is second-nature for me. My mum is..." he trails off. "Never mind."

Instead of pushing the automatic button, he closes the trunk manually with the easy physicality of someone whose body is a tool that simply *works*, no vanity required, and moves around to the passenger side. I hurry after him, my Louboutins clicking against the pavement like tiny exclamation points.

"Why never mind?" I ask, surprised by my sudden curiosity. "What about your mom?"

He opens the door for me.

It's such a small thing. His hand on the frame, a step back to give me space, the briefest touch at the small of my back as I step up into the seat. I was married for fourteen years to a man who stopped opening car doors for me approximately three weeks after our first date.

"Sorry, small slip," he says. "When I'm with a client, it's all about her. I keep my baggage all locked up." He juts his thumb toward the trunk, emphasizing his pun.

"You can tell me what's on your mind. It's a welcome distraction."

I'm reaching for my seatbelt when I notice he's paused. He's standing in the open door, one hand on the frame, and he's looking at me. Not staring. Not the way men in clubs look at women, or the way Greg looks at the twenty-two-year-olds in our office. It's more involuntary than that. Like a person rounding a corner and catching a view they weren't prepared for. Something crosses his face, quick and private, and then he blinks and redirects his gaze to the seatbelt buckle, his jaw tightening almost imperceptibly.

"Are you checking me out?" I don't mean to sound as shrill and uptight as it comes out.

"I'm sorry," he says. Quietly. Like he means it. "I just—" A small shake of his head. "It's impossible not to notice you. *Sorry.*"

Something warm sparks in a region of my chest that has been in cold storage since Greg told me, during our last real fight, that the market for women my age was "niche at best." I feel it flare, brief and bright, and I extinguish it immediately.

"How old are you?" I ask, even though I already know. *Too young for him to be smiling like that.* But I need to hear him say the number. I need it to fall between us and do its job.

"Twenty-six."

Twelve years my junior? He's a puppy.

"Cool," I answer. The word feels rusty in my mouth, like I've pulled it from some linguistic time capsule buried in two thousand five. My God, am I really trying to seem hip to a twenty-something?

"And how old are you?" he asks, because he apparently didn't take that training course informing him that it's practically a misdemeanor to ask a woman her age after her twenty-first birthday.

"Way too old for you to be looking at me like that."

I let it land. Then, because his face has gone slightly uncertain and I don't want to punish him for being honest—not to mention, there's something in me that's dangerously close to being flattered and I need to shut that down before it gets ideas—I add, more gently, "This weekend, I'm not expecting anything from you except friendship. Think of yourself as a very supportive little brother."

Saylor cackles.

Not laughs. *Cackles.* His head tips back against the car frame, and the sound is bright and unguarded and completely unselfconscious, and for a disorienting second I want to bottle it.

"Little brother," he repeats, tasting the words. Finding them hilarious. "Okay, *cool,* Celeste. I can do little brother. I'm very supportive."

I'm almost certain he's teasing me with that word, but I don't give it more attention. "Good."

"Do little brothers get to pick the music, or—"

"Don't push it."

He's still grinning as he closes my door and comes around to the driver's side. He adjusts the seat, sliding it backward until his long legs have room—a silent commentary on our height difference. He handles my car the way he handled me on the sidewalk: easily, naturally, like it doesn't require his full attention.

I find that both reassuring and mildly offensive.

"It must be hard to drive in shoes like that." He glances over to the passenger side floorboard. "But they're pretty. Forrest told me you're a high-end fashion designer. Did you design your shoes and that bag in back?"

"No. We only do clothing." I lift my foot to show him the red bottoms. "These are Louboutins. My travel bag's a Birkin."

"Your dress? Is that Celeste?" Saylor asks casually as the

engine purrs to life.

I chuckle to myself, looking at my plain black funeral dress. "Target."

He looks at me, puzzled. "Forty-thousand-dollar bag, forty-dollar dress?"

"Roughly," I admit, looking ahead because I don't like the way my stomach flips when we make eye contact.

"Why not wear one of yours?"

It's a fair question. But it's too difficult to convey the complexity of emotions. I don't just have guilt. I have *layers* of guilt. "It's hard to explain."

"Try me."

I stare forward at the trashcan I assaulted, at the trash bag half-splayed on the sidewalk and road. A cornucopia of candy wrappers is visible beneath the veil of plastic. "Whit was my best friend for twenty years, and I'm just now realizing how much my business and ambitions dominated our conversations. So today, out of respect, I didn't want it to be about me. I don't want to be *Celeste* today. Just Lessi."

"Lessi?" Saylor asks, his tone dropping to soft and warm, a dangerous pairing with his slight Australian accent.

"Her nickname for me, since our freshman year as roommates." I smile. "It makes me sound like a mythical lake creature, and I hated it. Except when she used it."

"Ah. I would've thought maybe Cici or something," Saylor says.

"Cici is my mother. My grandma, my mom, and me—all Celeste. Most people don't know this but technically my company is named for my grandmother. She's the one who inspired me to be an entrepreneur."

"I see. That's a sweet sentiment." He pulls up the GPS, punches in the address I give him, and studies the route for a moment. "About two and a half hours with traffic. Could be closer to three. So Whit lived in the Hamptons?"

My throat tightens. "No. She lived in Jersey."

"So why is the service in the Hamptons?"

Air leaves my lungs in a slow, controlled leak, like I just dislodged a nail from a tire. I reach for the glove box. Inside, nestled in a matte-black presentation case, is the watch. I pull it out and set it on the center console between us.

Saylor looks down at it. Then at me. "What's this?"

"A Rolex Datejust. Silver dial." I keep my voice even, businesslike, the voice I use in boardrooms and with fabric suppliers and with anyone I don't want to see me trembling. "Would you mind putting it on?"

After taking his hands off the wheel, he opens the case carefully. The watch catches the morning light through the windshield, and I watch his face cycle through several things—surprise, appreciation, the quiet resistance of a man who isn't accustomed to receiving things that cost this much. Maybe he's not used to receiving anything at all.

"Celeste, this is—"

"Necessary." I stare forward through the windshield, at the brownstones across the street, at someone's fire escape holding a dead plant that nobody's bothered to throw away. "I have to warn you, we're about to walk into the lion's den."

I can feel him looking at me. Waiting.

"Whitney's mother arranged the funeral," I say, and I hear my own voice go flat, the way it does when I'm holding something toxic at arm's length. "Eleanor Montgomery-Trace from Scarsdale Traces. That's why the service is all the way in the Hamptons."

"I don't understand."

I let out another breath, one that tastes bitter. "Whit came from a world where everything is a performance of wealth. Even grief. *Especially* grief. Eleanor and Whit were estranged, but that's not going to stop her from throwing the most beautiful funeral East End has ever seen. Every person there will know exactly how much it cost." I pause. "That's the point. Everyone in attendance is going to talk money without words. Without that watch, you look like an escort I hired to accompany me because I'm too alone, and too much of a coward to let these people know just how alone I am. It's the first time I'm seeing them since my divorce."

Saylor is quiet, processing. He puts on the watch. It looks good on him—the silver face against his wrist, the weight of it settling naturally, like he was always supposed to be wearing something that expensive. I file that observation away in the part of my brain marked *absolutely not* and keep going.

"The Rolex isn't a gift. It's armor. Everyone at this funeral will be wearing armor." I jazz-hands at my own expensive shields—the Cartier Love bracelet stacked against my grandmother's vintage Tiffany diamonds, the Van Cleef & Arpels earrings that are disturbingly expensive. "This isn't an outfit. It's a costume. We're going to a performance, and you need to look the part."

"For a funeral, shouldn't looking the part be looking...sad?" he asks mildly.

"Yeah, Saylor. To people with a soul."

He raises an eyebrow. "Are you sure you want to go to this? If this isn't the way you want to remember your friend, maybe we mourn in a different way."

"Don't tempt me," I plead. "But I *have* to attend. I wrote a speech for Whitney." I tap my pocket because this dress is from Target and it has *pockets*. The beautiful irony of fashion is the cheaper the dress, the more functional it is. Not one of the dresses from my favorite Celeste line has pockets. Probably because the women who can afford to buy them can also afford an entourage to follow behind, bearing the responsibility of her belongings.

His mouth twitches, but he lets it go. "Fair enough. So these people. What should I expect?"

"Old money. Or people who've spent thirty years pretending they have old money, which is somehow worse. They're going to look at me and calculate. What I lost in the divorce. Whether I've aged. Whether the rumors about the company are true." I curl my fingers into my palms. "I haven't seen most of them since Greg and I split. To tell you the truth, I haven't seen Whitney since before Greg and I split." My voice cracks. A hairline fracture. I try to keep going because stopping feels more dangerous than breaking, but no words come out.

"Oh, hey now." Saylor reaches over the middle compartment, and cradles my shoulder with his palm—warm through the thin fabric of my dress. It's not a squeeze or a pat. It's gentle and firm, his fingers curving around the ridge of my collarbone, thumb pressing lightly into the hollow beneath it. Like he's trying to hold that one piece of me in place while he watches the rest of me concave, my spine wilting forward, my chest collapsing inward around the vacuum where my composure used to be. "People lose touch, Celeste. It doesn't mean you didn't love her."

I shake my head, desperately trying to convince him of my culpability. "You don't understand. We had a fight. It was my fault." I wave him off. "Sorry, it's too much to dump on someone for one weekend. I only want you to understand where the judgmental glares will be coming from. I don't want you to feel uncomfortable."

"Celeste." The way Saylor says my name summons my gaze. I turn my head, meeting him eye-to-eye. "It's not too much to dump on me. This is my job. Grabbing your makeup bag for you, driving, giving you an escape plan—it's part of the package. I've been hired for a few funerals and in my experience you need a boyfriend, a partner. Not a nervous first date. So don't worry about how I'm feeling. Just focus on how I'm making you feel."

And good at his job, he is. The sentiment sinks deep into me and I speak before thinking. "You're making me a little too comfortable. Loose-lipped."

"Good. Say what you need to. I'll listen."

"I'm not even sure she'd want me there," I whisper. "I fucked up so badly."

The car is very quiet. Outside, Brooklyn carries on—someone honking, a dog barking, the distant hydraulic sigh of a garbage truck. But inside this car, it's just my breathing and the space Saylor is holding without filling it. There's a steadiness to his silence that makes me think he's held grief like this before. For someone else. Someone he loves.

I realize my eyes are wet again. I press my fingertips beneath my lashes and they come back black.

"My makeup," I murmur. "It's a disaster."

"Well, I wouldn't say it's red-carpet ready," Saylor agrees, and something about his honesty—the absolute refusal to do the polite thing and pretend I don't look wrecked—makes me settle right into his presence. This is exactly what I needed. Raw honesty. Someone who says exactly what he means. "But I'll help you fix it. Or maybe just take it off entirely. You'd look just as pretty without."

I peel my gaze away and stare forward again. "Is that a line?"

"Oh yeah. Strap in. I've got an arsenal full of compliments that'll keep you blushing or at least distracted during what I'm sure will be a difficult weekend for you. I'm here for whatever you need."

"Thank you, Saylor. But let's keep these compliments platonic and little-brother appropriate, yes?"

He purses his lips, smirking with all sorts of guilt written on his face. "In that case my arsenal is significantly less impressive."

I chuckle and hate myself for it. "Don't do that. Don't make me laugh the week I found out my best friend passed away."

He reaches over to place his hand on my knee. All these gentle touches—now I know they are strategic. Or are they? I can't tell if I'm being handled or held. "Tell me about her. Whitney sounds like an artsy name. Was she creative?"

I nod, warm memories flooding me, smoothing out the goosebumps on my legs. "Whit was good at everything. Art, writing, cooking, sports, you name it. I have never known anyone who sampled life like she did."

Her laugh echoes in my brain, like a beautiful haunting. I try to focus to place the right visuals with the right soundtrack in the labyrinth of my memories of Whit. That laugh...from the time she got her hair stuck in that defunct curling iron. It burned a whole chunk of hair off. We had to cut off six inches to make it look even. That hot tool committed a felony terrorist attack on her beautiful red curls. It'd be enough to send any reasonable woman into a spiral, but Whit? She laughed. *Hard.* With me. At herself. She took a disaster and somehow found joy. And yes, her hair looked damn good short.

Saylor releases my knee and collects my hand, weaving his fingers into mine.

Not in a romantic way. Not the way men reach for women in movies, all loaded glances and meaningful squeezes. He just takes it. Like it's the most natural thing in the world. Like he noticed my hand sitting there empty and cold and decided to fix that particular problem the way he'd right a knocked-over trashcan—simply, without fanfare, because it needed doing. Which reminds me...

I nod toward the sideways metal can in front of us. "I should pick that up."

"Nah, I left it on purpose. Belongs to our neighbor who never picks up after his dog which is why our street always smells like shit. Maybe this'll force him to pick up something for fuck's sake."

His hand is warm and enormous around mine. My rings press into his palm and he doesn't adjust his grip.

"Our neighbor?" I ask. "Do you live with a...colleague?" I cringe. Damn, why did that sound like I was accusing him of living in something akin to a brothel? "I mean it's hard to live anywhere near Manhattan these days without a roommate."

Saylor gives me an obvious once-over that makes me feel unsettlingly vulnerable. Like I'm being judged, naked...after binge-eating Cheetos, orange dust still coating my lips.

"I meant *my* neighbor."

I nod emphatically, taking his subtle hint not to ask.

Saylor straightens in the seat and checks the GPS. "This address?" He waits for my confirmation then checks his mirrors before pulling smoothly into the street—unlike me, he does not hit anything. All the tension in my body has relaxed as I watch Saylor merge into traffic with the relaxed confidence of someone who trusts the physics. I wiggle my ass in the passenger seat. Yes, this is best. This is where I belong—nowhere near a steering wheel.

"So why don't you tell me about Whitney," he says.

And it's the way he says it. Not *what happened with Whitney* or *why did you two stop talking* or *are you going to be okay*. Just: *tell me about her*. Like she's still a person worth knowing. Like the story matters not for context or preparation, but because he wants to understand what I lost.

I look out the passenger window. The city is sliding past—bodegas, laundromats, a man walking four dogs who are each pulling in a different direction. Normal life. Ordinary Tuesday-morning life. And I'm in a car with a twenty-six-year-old man I barely know, heading to a funeral I'm terrified to attend, wearing four-inch heels and ruined mascara and a grief so enormous I can feel it pressing against my ribs.

This time I reach for his hand, pressing my palm tightly against his.

"She had the best laugh. Completely unrivaled," I tell him. "And she would have *loved* this. Me, showing up to her funeral with a hot twenty-six-year-old in a Tom Ford suit." I wipe my eyes with my free hand and let out a wet, broken laugh. "She would have absolutely lost her mind."

Saylor squeezes my hand. "Hot? Now is that any way to talk about your little brother? Kind of creepy, Celeste." He pulls his eyes away from the road just long enough to wink at me.

I shoot him a scowl that's also kind of a smile. "Shut it."

He chuckles. "All right, Lessi, tell me more. I want to know everything about her."

The floodgates open. The tears flow again. And I start talking.

Chapter 4

Saylor

All great meet-cutes are generally unhinged.

I've been to some dodgy venues in my line of work. Warehouses converted into "experiential galleries." Rooftop bars with forty-dollar drinks that taste like someone emptied a perfume counter into soda water. A retirement party on a yacht that hit a sandbar. But I have never, in my twenty-six years on this planet, attended a funeral with valet parking.

The bloke opens Celeste's door before I've even fully stopped the car. He's wearing a pressed black polo with gold embroidery on the chest—some logo I don't recognize—and he's got the careful, neutral expression of someone trained to look at extremely wealthy people without actually seeing them. A second attendant appears at my window and I hand over the keys, resisting the urge to ask if the trashcans around here are friendlier than the ones in Brooklyn.

Two women in black cocktail dresses intercept us at the entrance with flutes of champagne on silver trays. The bubbles catch the afternoon light, tiny golden explosions climbing the glass.

"Welcome," one of them murmurs, like we've arrived at a spa retreat and not a memorial service.

Celeste takes a glass without looking at it. I watch her jaw tighten as her gaze sweeps the venue—a converted estate hall with floor-to-ceiling windows overlooking a manicured lawn that rolls toward the ocean. White hydrangeas spill from every surface. A string quartet is warming up in the far corner, and the air smells like lilies and money. Nothing about this says *a woman died.* Everything about it says *look how much we can spend on the fact that she did.*

"Champagne," Celeste says flatly. "At a funeral."

I take a sip of mine. "Decent champagne, at least."

She shoots me a look. I raise my glass in a small, guilty toast.

"If Whitney could see this—" Celeste's fingers tighten around the stem. She doesn't finish the sentence, but I've spent the last two and a half hours listening to stories about Whitney Trace, and I can fill in the blank. Whit would've hated every square inch of this. The hydrangeas alone would've sent her into a rant.

Celeste squares her shoulders. The transformation is immediate—the softness from the car, the tears, the wet laughter, all of it disappears behind a wall so polished I can almost see my reflection in it. She is, in the span of a breath, someone else entirely. Someone armored.

"I need to find Eleanor," she says, scanning the room. "I wrote a speech for Whitney, and knowing her mother, she's planned every second of this program down to the bathroom breaks. If I want a slot, I'll need to ask in person." She reaches up to fiddle with one of her earrings—ones I probably couldn't dream of affording, the kind of jewelry that comes in a velvet box with a certificate. "It's better if I approach her alone. Eleanor and I have...history."

"Are you sure?"

"No. But I'm choosing to spare you. Eleanor has the warmth of an ice storm." Celeste glances at me, and for half a second the armor slips. Something uncertain flickers beneath. "Will you be all right on your own?"

"Celeste, I'm a grown man at a weirdly fancy funeral with free booze and hors d'oeuvres everywhere. I'll manage."

The corner of her mouth lifts. "Avoid the truffle brie bites. I promise they will turn your stomach into an active volcano."

"How do you know they will have truffle brie bites?" I scan the room as if Celeste has seen something I haven't noticed yet.

"Because they always do. They always have white hydrangeas, staff dressed in black-tie, bottles of Dom Pérignon and Belvedere on ice. The pomegranate sorbet as a palate cleanser. These events are rinse and repeat. She couldn't even switch up her playbook for her own daughter's funeral." Celeste mutters something more under her breath that I miss. But it sounds bitter.

"Hey, I forgot to say this in the car."

"What?" she asks.

I pull her into a hug, my arms circling her shoulders gently. Her spine stiffens beneath my touch, and for a heartbeat, she's frozen against me, like a deer caught in headlights—this small act of comfort apparently more startling than anything the day has thrown at her so far. "I'm really sorry for your loss, Celeste."

She looks up, and once our eyes are locked I swear I see a flicker of something. Nothing indecent. Maybe just...hope that tomorrow will feel more normal. The next day even more so. It seems like Celeste, with one look, is asking me if everything is going to be okay. I don't know if that's what's really going through her head, but it feels right to answer her unasked question. "Everything is going to be okay. You'll get through this."

"Thank you." Nodding, she touches my cheek. It's quick, almost reflexive—but before I can allow myself to enjoy the graze of her fingertips against my jawline, she's free of my embrace, cutting through the crowd with the practiced stride of a woman who has been walking into hostile rooms her entire career.

I watch her go. She moves like she's on a runway even when she's not, which is either a professional habit or a survival mechanism. Probably both.

A man in a windowpane suit catches my eye from across the room and gives me a slow, assessing once-over—shoes, watch, shoulders, face—before returning to his conversation. I've been on the receiving end of looks like that before, but usually I'm working security at the door, not standing inside holding champagne.

I drain my glass, set it on a passing tray, and go looking for the restroom.

The hallway leading away from the main space is quieter, all dark wood paneling and recessed lighting. My dress shoes click against marble floors and I catch my reflection in a gilded mirror hanging between two oil paintings—a sailboat, a horse. Rich-people art. The kind of stuff that exists solely to fill wall space in buildings where the walls cost more than the art.

I stop.

The mirror shows me exactly what I suspected: a bloke playing dress-up. The suit is perfect. Celeste has an eye, I'll give her that—but the man inside it is still the same kid who grew up in a fibro house in Wollongong, who learned to shave from a YouTube video because his dad was already gone, who eats cereal for dinner three nights a week because groceries are a luxury after Mum's prescriptions. The Rolex catches the light and I twist my wrist, watching the face glint. It's beautiful. It's also a lie strapped to my arm.

Celeste and I spent the whole drive up here talking like equals. She told me about Whitney—about their freshman year in adjoining dorm rooms, about the road trip where Whit's car broke down in Delaware and they hitchhiked to a gas station singing Destiny's Child's "Survivor." I told her about Mum's garden, how she grows tomatoes on the fire escape because she misses having land, how she talks to them in the mornings like they're pets.

For two and a half hours, the twelve-year age gap and the several-hundred-million-dollar net worth gap didn't exist. We were just two people in a car, being honest.

But standing in this hallway, surrounded by paintings and polished marble, I can feel the gap opening back up like a fault line. This is her world. These are her people. Even if she hates them, she speaks their language. I'm a tourist with a borrowed watch and a borrowed suit and a return ticket to Alphabet City, where the trashcans fight back and nobody gives you champagne for showing up.

So stop it, mate. Stop replaying the way she tucked her hair behind her ear during the drive. Stop thinking about how she laughed—really laughed, open and startled—when I told her about the time Mum accidentally FaceTimed Forrest while wearing a mud mask and he nearly called an ambulance. Stop cataloging the exact shade of her eyes, which is a color I'm fairly certain doesn't have a name but should, because the world is worse off without one.

She's a client. She's twelve years older. She's grieving.

And she called you her little brother.

So act like one.

I push through the men's room door and the marble-and-mahogany theme continues. Individual stalls with actual wooden doors, not the gapped aluminum slabs, and a countertop with rolled hand towels arranged in a basket. There's a small dish of mints. A candle is burning. It smells like eucalyptus.

I approach the sink and run cold water over my wrists, a trick I use for calming down. The water hits the Rolex face and I pull back instinctively, shaking my hand. *Right.* Borrowed watch. Probably shouldn't drown it.

Then I hear it.

Retching.

The sound is unmistakable—violent, full-bodied, the kind that comes from the gut. It's coming from the last stall, and whoever's in there is having a genuinely terrible time.

Another heave. A low, miserable groan then a soft, "fuck my life."

I freeze, water still running. This is the men's room. I'm certain of it—I checked the sign twice because the font was so ornate I thought it might be decorative Latin. But regardless of what the sign says, that was most certainly a woman's voice.

"Oi," I call out, shutting off the tap. "You all right in there?"

The groaning stops. Silence. Then the woman's voice again, thin and hoarse: "Shit. This is the men's room, isn't it?"

"Yeah, it is."

"Of course it is." A pause. More groaning. "Can you just go... and pretend I'm not here?"

"Uh, I absolutely cannot do that. Are you sick? Do you need help?"

"I need a time machine to get me out of this mess."

"Hangover?" I ask.

"Sort of. But it's kind of a nine-month hangover from one risky afternoon."

Despite the circumstances, I almost smile. I move toward the stall. The door is unlatched, hanging open a crack. I push it gently with two fingers. "I'm coming in, all right? Don't throw anything at me."

She's on her knees in front of the toilet—a young woman, early twenties maybe, in a black dress that's bunched up around her thighs. Her blond curls are swept to one side, pinned loosely with a clip that's losing the war against gravity. Her skin is pale and flushed, and mascara tracks run down both cheeks. One hand grips the porcelain bowl while the other clutches a tiny beaded bag like it's a life raft.

She peers up at me with watery blue eyes and lets out a short, defeated breath. "I look unhinged."

"All great meet-cutes are generally unhinged." Damn, I've already seen a lot of mascara running today and the funeral hasn't even started.

She manages a weak laugh, which immediately triggers another wave of nausea. I drop to one knee beside her and gather her curls away from her face without thinking—muscle memory, years of holding Mum's hair during her bad days, when the pain medication hit her stomach wrong and she'd spend an hour on the bathroom floor while I sat next to her reading aloud from whatever novel she was halfway through.

"Thanks," she mutters between breaths. "Very chivalrous. Very weird that a stranger is holding my hair."

"I've done weirder things for people I've just met."

"How many meet-cutes have you had?"

It doesn't seem like an appropriate time to confess to a stranger that one of my professions is fabricating romance for money, so I simply shrug.

She sits back on her heels, wiping her mouth with the back of her hand. Her shoulders sag with the slow, cautious relief of someone who thinks the storm might've passed but isn't ready to commit to the diagnosis.

"So by a nine-month hangover, you meant you're—"

"Pregnant," she says, matter-of-factly. "Four months. This is morning sickness. Which is a lie by the way. A filthy fucking lie. It's not *morning* sickness. It doesn't care what time of day it is and it doesn't care that I'm at a funeral. It's mean and relentless." She braces one hand against the stall wall. "Help me up?"

I grip her elbow and guide her to standing, keeping my hand steady until she's got her balance. She's small—five-three, maybe—and also wearing flats. She barely reaches my shoulder. I guide her to the sink and turn on the cold water before grabbing two of the fancy rolled towels. I soak them then wring them out.

"Here." I hand her one for her face and press the other gently against the back of her neck. "Cold compress. Helps with the nausea."

She holds the towel to her face and lets out a sound that's part relief, part surrender. "I would've settled for 'not a serial killer' but it seems my luck with men has improved. You're a downright hero. Why are you so good at this?"

"Lots of practice."

She peeks at me over the towel. "Lots of pregnant women in your life?"

I chuckle. "No."

The woman eyes me up and down. "Okay. But I'm assuming looking like you do there are lots of *women* in your life?"

"Wow. Bit judgy of you."

She nods in agreement. "Yes, but that was a positive judgment. A compliment."

"Compliment adjacent," I clarify. "You just basically called me the male version of a slut."

Her jaw drops. "That's a little sexist of you."

"What?" I'm genuinely floored and confused.

"There's no male version of a slut. A slut is a slut. Slutty is not gender exclusive."

I blink at her. "Say slut one more time," I deadpan.

She flashes me a wicked smile. "Slut."

We both break face at the same time, letting free our hearty chuckles. Hers light and melodic. Mine, like a gorilla grunt echoing off the bathroom walls.

I lean against the counter, giving her space. "My mum has severe chronic pain and has to take a lot of medication. If she put her pills in a bowl, it'd look like she was eating cereal. It's hard on her stomach. I've held more hair than a salon and I'm a whiz at making a cold compress out of anything."

"Anything?"

"Soak a small nappy under the sink and freeze it. Works across the forehead or behind the neck like a charm."

"A nappy, like a diaper?" Her face twists up in disgust and a wave of nausea crosses her expression.

"Nah, yeah. But to clarify, I meant a *clean, unused* nappy."

"That seems more reasonable."

Her expression softens. She lowers the towel and dabs carefully at the mascara streaks. "I'm sorry about your mom. Why is she in so much pain?"

"Car accident. She was thrown through the front windshield." I leave it at that because this is not my day to break down. "She'd like you. She loves anyone who makes her feel less alone in the vomiting department."

That gets a real laugh. She extends her hand. "I'm Raven by the way."

"Saylor." I shake it. Her grip is firmer than I expected. "How'd you know Whitney?"

The question lands differently than I intend. Raven's face shifts—the humor draining, replaced by something raw and tender.

She turns back toward the mirror, pressing the towel against her cheeks, but I can see her reflection. Her chin is trembling.

"Whit was..." she trails off, blinking rapidly. "I didn't know her *that* well. I worked for her in a sense. We talked about once a week over the phone and met once a month outside of my appointments. She was...a really good person." Raven means to tap her heart I think, except she crosses her chest with her left hand, patting the wrong side. "Good to her core. Nothing about this makes sense. She should be here. She promised me she was going to make it."

I don't say anything. Some moments need space, not words.

Raven sniffs hard and straightens. "What about you? How did you know her?"

My mouth opens and then immediately shuts, because in the two and a half hours Celeste and I spent in that car, we talked about Whitney's childhood and Celeste's guilt and my mum's tomatoes and whether rest stops off the Long Island Expressway are a viable food source. Spoiler alert—they are not. What we did not discuss at all is what I'm supposed to say when someone inevitably asks how Celeste and I know each other. Are we together? Friends? Colleagues? Lovers? Did we meet at a gala or a gallery or a goat yoga retreat?

We didn't cook up a single word of backstory. Brilliant.

"Friend of a friend," I say, which is technically true. "I'm here with someone who was very close to Whitney. Celeste Brinley."

Raven goes still.

Not the normal kind of still, where a person pauses to think. The kind of still where every molecule in the body locks into place. Her hand, still holding the damp towel, stops mid-dab. Her eyes fix on mine in the mirror, wide and searching.

"Shut the actual fuck up. You're here with Celeste? She is in the building?"

I keep my lips closed and Raven gives me the universal look for "well, explain yourself."

"I'm sorry, do you want me shut the fuck up or answer your

question?"

Raven rolls her eyes and I take my cue.

"Yes, Celeste is here. She's off finding Eleanor to ask about speaking during the—"

"Oh my God." Raven presses both hands to her face. "Oh my God, it worked. I want you to know you're speaking to an actual genius. Not on paper or anything, I barely passed high school algebra. But when it comes to schemes, I'm your girl." She holds up her hand, begging for a high-five.

Something about the way she says it—not relieved, not surprised, but *validated*, like a gamble she'd been holding her breath on just paid out—trips a wire in the back of my brain. "I'm not congratulating you until I know what scheme you're talking about."

She drops her hand, looks at me, then looks at the bathroom door like she's calculating whether she can make a run for it.

"Raven. What worked?"

"Okay." She grips the edge of the sink with both hands, steadying herself. "Okay. This is going to sound insane."

"Lucky for you, my bar for insane has been significantly raised in the last ten minutes."

Another laugh—this one nervous, almost manic. She turns back to the mirror, fidgeting with her clip, not looking at me directly. "The baby I'm carrying. It's not mine."

The bathroom goes very quiet. The eucalyptus candle flickers.

"I'm Whitney's surrogate," she says. "This baby is Whitney's."

I stare at her reflection. She blinks back. The information settles into my chest with the slow, heavy weight of something that's about to rearrange everything.

"Whitney's," I repeat.

"Whitney's. She wanted a baby more than anything. And she chose me to carry it." Raven's hand drifts to her stomach, protective and automatic. "We'd been planning it for a while. She had everything figured out. The nursery, the name shortlist, the—

" Her voice breaks. She swallows it back. "But then she died. And now I'm four months pregnant with a baby whose mother is being eulogized in the next room by a woman who I'm pretty sure she hated for her entire life."

"Eleanor."

"Eleanor." Raven's jaw clenches. "Who is already trying to contest Whitney's will. Who didn't even want to invite—" She stops. Presses her lips together.

"Didn't want to invite who?"

The stall door behind us swings lazily on its hinge like a ghost just finished and exited from it. Raven flinches at the sound and goes quiet, her fingers white-knuckled on the countertop. For a moment I think she's going to be sick again. But she steadies herself with a long breath, the kind that requires a conscious decision.

"Whit was getting better, but she was still sick. So, she drew up the will the moment we conceived. She told me she left her baby to the person she loved most in the world," Raven says carefully. "Her best friend. The person she trusted more than anyone. But earlier this week, Eleanor told me she would be taking custody. I'm not in the will, so I can't see it or do anything about it. But I swear on my life Celeste is in there. *I know it.*"

The puzzle pieces are aligning in my head faster than I want them to. The champagne in my stomach turns.

"Eleanor wants this baby," Raven continues. "She's already assembled her lawyers. She's claiming Whitney wasn't in her right mind when the will was drawn up, which is *bullshit*—Whitney was sharper than anyone I've ever met, even at the end. But Eleanor's got so much money and connections and..." She stops again, squeezing her eyes shut. "She wasn't going to tell Celeste about the baby. She wasn't even going to invite her to the funeral."

I feel like I'm watching the final scene of a horror movie. The part when you realize the call was coming from inside the house the entire time.

"I don't think that's true, Raven. Celeste told me that the

Traces' lawyers sent the information to Celeste's office. That couldn't have happened without Eleanor knowing."

"Technically..." Oh, I don't like that guilty tone one bit. She meets my eyes in the mirror. Hers are red-rimmed and defiant and scared.

"I might've posed as a legal messenger. I googled some legal documents online and wrote up a memo that looked official enough to pass. I included the funeral invitation. I needed Celeste to come because Whitney wanted *her* to have this baby, not Eleanor, and if Celeste didn't even know—" Her voice cracks. "I never met Celeste until I gave her that envelope. But the way Whit talked about her...I just thought Celeste should know. It's my job to make sure this baby is delivered safe and sound to the *rightful* mother. I didn't have Celeste's personal number and I didn't realize she was a sort of celebrity. All I had was her company's address. So I faked a delivery from an estate attorney and prayed she'd show up."

Footsteps approach, and I brace for the interruption. I'm gripping the countertop now too, standing next to Raven like two people bracing for turbulence. But whoever is passing by is unmistakable in high heels as they head down the hall, likely to the women's restroom that Raven never made it to.

"Does Celeste have any idea?" I ask, even though I know the answer. "About the baby?"

She shakes her head. Slowly. "I didn't want to tell her something and it not be true. Like I said, I haven't seen the will. I just needed to get her *here*."

"So you lured Celeste to a funeral with forged legal documents, and now she's standing in the next room with no idea she's about to possibly inherit the child of her deceased best friend whom she had no idea had a baby on the way."

Stated aloud, it sounds absolutely mental. Raven, to her credit, winces.

"When you say it like that—"

"There's not a great way *to* say it, Raven."

"I know." Her eyes are filling again. "I know. But you've been with her. You drove here with her. Is she..." She searches my face for something she can use. "If she is named as guardian of little blob, is she the kind of person who would—"

"She spent the last two and a half hours crying over Whitney," I say quietly. "She wrote a speech. She flew through New York City in a car she can barely drive because she couldn't stand to be alone with her grief. She's terrified that Whitney wouldn't even want her here." I pause. "Yeah. She's the kind of person."

Raven's whole body sags with relief. She fumbles open her beaded clutch and pulls out a small, battered tub of VapoRub. She unscrews the cap, holds it under her nose, and takes a deep, shuddering inhale.

I watch her, baffled. "Is that—"

"VapoRub. Kills the nausea. Sort of. I just started trying it after reading an article." She holds it out. "Want some? You look like you might be sick too."

"I'm processing."

"Process faster, because now I need to pee."

"I believe your restroom is down the hall."

She rolls her eyes. "I'm already here alone."

I tap my head, then shoulders, ending with my chest. "Just making sure I'm physically here and therefore you can see me, right?"

Raven pouts. "My feet hurt and the women's bathroom is probably ten years away."

I push off the counter. "Okay, fine. I need to go find Celeste anyway. Are you sure you're going to be okay on your own?"

She nods emphatically. "I'm already feeling better. We have about twenty minutes until the funeral starts. Plenty of time for a couple more preemptive pukes to get me through the service."

"Great. Also, gross. Hang in there. I'm sure we'll be seeing you again when this Pandora's box you've handed out is opened up and all our faces melt off."

She squints at me. "I think you're confusing movies right now." But she shifts her weight from one foot to the other, the universal dance of someone who can't wait much longer to relieve their bladder.

"Right, I'm going. Don't leave until Celeste gets a chance to talk to you today, yeah? Promise?"

Raven promises by holding up her pinky. I awkwardly twist it in mine. I can't remember the last time I pinky-promised anyone anything. "See you on the other side," she says.

With that, I exit the men's room, heading for the main hall, my borrowed shoes clicking against marble, my borrowed watch ticking against my wrist, and a conversation in my chest that I have absolutely no idea how to start.

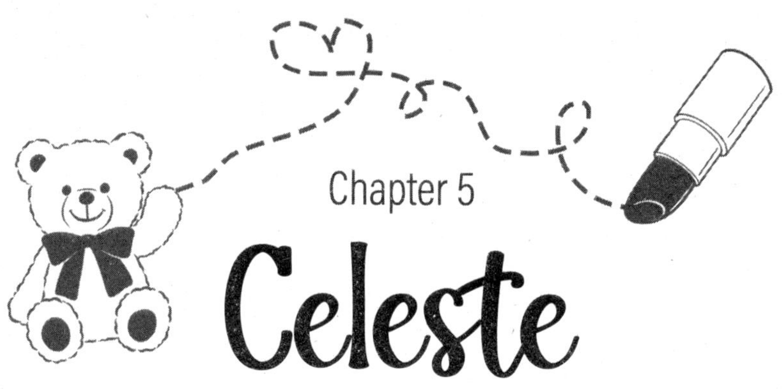

Chapter 5
Celeste

This is an odd take on grief.

The sound of Eleanor's voice carries down the hallway before I even reach the kitchen, her crisp consonants slicing through the air like knives through butter. I pause at the doorway, watching her gesture at the counter with the controlled movements of a surgeon.

This is an odd take on grief. She's not sitting quietly in a chair somewhere, staring at a photograph of her daughter, letting the loss wash over her in waves the way normal people do. No. Eleanor Montgomery-Trace is standing in the middle of a catering kitchen the size of my apartment, pointing at a tray of hors d'oeuvres like it owes her money.

"The crostini are uneven," she says. "They look homemade."

"They are homemade, Mrs. Trace. That was the directive," the woman next to her explains.

"The directive was rustic-elegant. These are just rustic. There's a difference."

I retreat from the kitchen doorway and flatten myself against the hallway wall, safely out of sight but close enough to hear. It smells like roasted garlic and fresh flowers—an unsettling combination that rockets me backward to dinner parties Whit and I used to dread. Back when Whit and I were still in college, my parents were aloof. Eleanor was tyrannical, performing the role of doting mother for the crowd, but bullying Whitney in private.

Her clothes, her hair, her grades, her body—all weaponized. How many events did we leave with Whitney in silent tears, me, her dutiful plus-one, trailing behind in silence knowing no words of encouragement could save her from her mother's chronic criticism and condescension?

Those dinners always smelled just like this. Garlic. Flowers. And an undercurrent of tension so thick you could spread it on the crostini. Whitney used to prep me in the car beforehand like a cornerman before a boxing match.

"Avoid mentioning anything remotely political. That'd be entering a gun fight with a knife. Never say a word about the new curtains unless you want to hear the entire saga of their selection. And please, for the love of God, if she starts with any comments about my size, stomp on my foot before I lunge at her."

God, I miss her.

I peek through the archway to catch a cook passing Eleanor with a tray. She stops him with a single raised finger, the way a traffic cop stops a semi. She lifts a napkin, inspects something beneath it, replaces the napkin, and waves him on without comment. The cook exhales like he's been released from a hostage situation.

The woman standing next to Eleanor must be the event coordinator. Or at least I'm assuming she is because she's wearing a headset, holding a clipboard, and is radiating the specific brand of patience reserved for people who manage other people's catastrophes for a living. She places a hand on Eleanor's arm.

"Mrs. Trace. Everything is under control. I've done over two hundred events in this space, and I promise you, the crostini are beautiful. Why don't you take a few minutes? Get some air. Let me handle this part so you can focus on getting through the day."

Eleanor doesn't respond right away. Her face twists up in that familiar expression that makes my skin restrict around my bones—a practiced pause she deploys when someone tells her something she disagrees with but she doesn't want to argue about it publicly. But make no mistake, she'll corner you later and rip you to shreds in private. I know, because this is the same look she gave me ten years ago when I told her Whitney's engagement was off and Whit no longer wanted to speak to her mother.

"Fine," Eleanor says. The single syllable carries enough frost to chill the hot trays.

After a single sharp inhale, I force myself to step around the corner and trespass into the kitchen.

It's all stainless steel and organized chaos—caterers in black aprons moving between stations, steam rising from covered pans, trays of champagne flutes lined up like soldiers. Eleanor stands at the center of it, impeccable in head-to-toe black Chanel. Her auburn hair is pulled back so severely it seems to be holding her face in place, and her pearls sit against her collarbone with the quiet authority of heirlooms that have attended more funerals than I have. She looks exactly the way she's always looked: expensive, controlled, and slightly terrifying.

Her eyes land on me and something flickers behind them—surprise, calculation, then nothing. She irons her expression flat in under a second.

"Celeste."

"Hello, Eleanor."

We regard each other across ten feet of kitchen tile like two women who've both been in love with the same person and lost. Which, we have. We just lost her differently.

"I'm surprised to see you here. How'd you find out about the event?"

I want to screw up my face and call out the obvious, which is that obviously she invited me. Did she really think I'm so cruel I wouldn't attend Whitney's funeral? But I don't feel like throwing the first punch on today of all days. "I just got the information on Thursday. I tried to call you but the number wasn't in service."

"Or perhaps you're blocked," Eleanor offers, her lips in a tight line.

"Fair." I look around the bustling room. "Could we have a word?"

"Go ahead."

"I meant privately. Maybe a walk? The courtyard looked—"

"Oh, yes, please. What a great idea." The event coordinator materializes beside me with an eagerness that borders on desperate. She wants Eleanor out of her kitchen the way sailors want storms off their horizon. "The courtyard is gorgeous. The wisteria is in full bloom. I'll make sure everything here stays on track."

Eleanor regards the coordinator the way one regards a fly that's landed too close to one's wine. But she doesn't argue.

I pivot to the coordinator before we leave. "I'm sorry, I'm Celeste Brinley. I was wondering if there'll be a chance during the service for people to speak? I've prepared something for Whitney and I'd like—"

"There is, but the speaking portion is typically reserved for family," she says gently. Apologetically. Like she's delivered this line before and knows it stings.

"I am family."

"Oh, well in that case—"

Eleanor's voice cuts in from behind me, cool and precise. "Celeste and Whitney hadn't spoken in years. That hardly qualifies as family."

The kitchen goes quiet. Not silent—pans still clank softly; someone adjusts a burner—but the words stop. The caterers develop a sudden, intense fascination with their cutting boards and mixing bowls.

I turn to face Eleanor. I spit out what's burning the tip of my tongue before I can soften it, "How many years were you and Whitney estranged, Eleanor? Over a decade? So based on your own logic, are you the appropriate person to deliver the eulogy?"

Dammit. There it is. Not the first shot. But I definitely delivered the most lethal.

The air between us crystallizes. A cook near the stove accidentally scrapes a spoon against a pot, and the sound is deafening in the silence.

Eleanor surveys the room—the frozen caterers, the

coordinator clutching her clipboard like a shield—and her mouth curves into something that isn't quite a smile. She eyes me like a cobra, waiting for the perfect moment to strike.

I drop my head, shaking it in shame. "I'm sorry. That was uncalled for—"

"Nonsense. Grief brings out heightened emotions." Her voice is warm, measured, public. Which means the real storm is brewing for later. "I apologize for the disruption, everyone. Please continue."

She touches my elbow before striding past me. "Let's walk," she hisses under her breath.

We exit through a side door into the courtyard, and the late-May air wraps around me like a shawl I didn't ask for. The Hamptons in spring is obscenely beautiful—the kind of beauty that feels like an insult when you're this miserable. Wisteria drapes from a wooden pergola in heavy, violet clusters. A stone path winds through manicured hedges toward the lawn, which rolls out in an unbroken sheet of green toward the ocean. The water beyond is flat and silver under a pale sky. Somewhere, a bird is singing. It doesn't know that Whitney is dead. None of this knows. Nothing here cares. Nothing about this feels right.

The moment we're out of earshot, I reach for Eleanor.

"I *am* really sorry," I say, pulling her into a hug. "I shouldn't have said that to you, especially not in front of your staff."

Eleanor does not hug back.

She stands inside my arms the way a mannequin stands inside a dress—present but uninhabited. Her body is rigid, her hands at her sides, and she gives off the faint, powdery scent of Chanel No. 5, which she has worn for as long as I've known her and which I will now forever associate with being held at an emotional distance.

I release her and step back.

"I'm also very sorry for your loss, Eleanor. You know how much I loved your daughter."

The breeze catches a cluster of wisteria petals and sends

them drifting between us like confetti at the wrong party. Eleanor watches them fall, then lifts her gaze to mine.

"How did you find out?"

Not *thank you for coming.* Not *I know you loved her.* How did you find out. Like the answer matters more than the sentiment.

"I received the letter from Valcott and Finch," I say. "Something about Whitney's will. And the funeral invitation was included."

Eleanor's forehead tightens. The movement is subtle—a fraction of tension above the brows—but I've been reading faces for twenty years. It's my job to notice when fabric pulls wrong, when a seam sits a millimeter off. Faces are no different.

"Valcott and Finch," she repeats. Flat. Testing the words.

"Yes."

She turns and begins walking along the stone path, and I fall into step beside her. The ocean breeze pushes my hair across my face and I tuck it back, wishing I'd brought a clip. Eleanor's neat, shellacked bun doesn't move.

"I'll be having a conversation with them." Her tone has shifted—still controlled, but there's a wire pulled taut beneath it. She's angry, but I can't tell if the anger is directed at me, the lawyers, or something else entirely. "That was not how I intended for this to be handled."

"How did you intend what to be handled?"

She doesn't answer. A gardener kneeling near a hedge of boxwoods glances up at us, then drops his gaze and returns to his pruning with the studied indifference of someone who's learned that rich people's conversations are none of his business and nothing but trouble.

We walk in silence for a few more paces. The path curves around a rose garden—pale pink and white blooms, meticulously pruned, not a single dead head in sight. I wonder if Eleanor chose this venue specifically so she'd have beautiful scenery to hide behind during difficult conversations. It's her specialty. Stage the backdrop so thoroughly that no one notices what's happening in the foreground.

The ocean opens up before us as the path reaches a low stone wall at the lawn's edge. We stop there, side by side, not quite touching, both looking out at the water. Two women who loved the same person, standing at the lip of the Atlantic, unable to bridge three feet of distance.

"Why here, out of curiosity? Whitney hated the Hamptons," I muse. I meant it as an observation, but it triggers Eleanor. Her eyes narrow to pins.

"What do you want?" Eleanor asks, all sharp edges now. A blade sliding out of a drawer. "You, who already have so much. A billion-dollar company. Properties. Resources most people can't imagine." She glares at me sidelong. "My daughter hasn't heard from you in two years, and you show up the moment there's something to collect?"

The accusation hits me square in the sternum. "What are you talking about? I'm not trying to collect anything. I don't even know what she left me." My voice cracks like thin ice, rising an octave as I press my fingernails into my palms. I take a deep breath, counting silently to three. "Eleanor, I don't want money. I don't want possessions. I'm here because Whit was my best friend for twenty years and I want to say goodbye. I'm not here to take anything away from you."

"Aren't you though?"

I stop walking. The roses blur. I blink hard, pressing my thumbnail into the pad of my index finger—a trick my therapist taught me, pain to redirect the spiral before it starts.

"I'm here because she's gone," I say, "and this is the closest I can get to telling her I'm sorry."

The words leave me and immediately I wish I could pull them back, reshape them into something less raw, less naked. But they're out now, hanging between us in the salt air, and I can't unsay them any more than I can unsay the last thing I told Whitney in that alley behind the restaurant—both of us crying, tiramisu on her shoes, my voice so loud it bounced off the bricks.

"I'll never forgive you, Whitney. I'll never forgive you for making me choose."

She wasn't making me choose. She was trying to save me. I didn't understand the difference until it was too late to matter.

Eleanor stops a few steps ahead of me. She doesn't turn around. The wind lifts the hem of her jacket and the wisteria petals keep falling and the ocean keeps doing its beautiful, indifferent thing against the shore.

"You can't apologize to someone who's gone, Celeste. The damage is done."

I stare at her back—spine like a ruler, not a single auburn hair escaping its lacquered prison, shoulder pads cutting perfect right angles beneath dove-gray wool that whispers couture in the way only fabric worth seventeen thousand dollars can. She looks villainous. And I can't decide if she's cruel or just so broken that cruelty is the only shape her grief can take.

"I only came early and found you to say I wrote a speech. For Whitney. It's the only thing I have left to give her, and I'd like the chance to deliver it. That's all."

Eleanor studies me. Her eyes are dry but the skin around them is thin and papery in a way it wasn't five years ago, and I recognize—with a jolt that feels like touching a live wire—that she's aged. Not just years. The kind of aging that happens when something essential gets pulled out of you and doesn't get put back.

"The Hamptons grew on Whitney," Eleanor says. "We spent a lot of time here together before the end."

I bite my tongue to keep from challenging her outright. Whitney in the Hamptons with her mother? The Whitney I knew would sooner swim with sharks. What seismic shift could have possibly driven her back into her mother's orbit?

"I'm glad you got time with her." My eyes are burning. I press my thumbnail harder into my finger. "When did you two reconcile?"

"When she got sick."

"Sick?" I parrot. It's an essential question that I don't yet have the answer to. Maybe I'm old-school and I didn't want to google an obituary to find out what happened to my best friend. I figured I'd get answers today, but I didn't really want them from Eleanor.

"Colon cancer. She got better for a while. No one expected..."

Cancer? The news sits like a stone in my throat. Whit kept this from me—the first and last secret between us. I search Eleanor's face for answers I'm afraid to ask for: why my best friend turned to the mother she'd spent decades avoiding instead of me. My lungs seem to collapse inward, as though someone has reached inside me and pulled a pin from the center of my chest causing me to internally unravel.

"Was she suffering all this time?" Asking is too much, but not asking would be unforgivable.

Eleanor is quiet for a long time. The string quartet inside has started playing something I almost recognize—Debussy, maybe. The notes drift through the open windows and settle around us like weather.

"She lived fully," Eleanor says. Softly. So softly I almost miss it beneath the wind. "Until her very last day, she was herself. Stubborn. Funny. Absolutely impossible to argue with." The ghost of something crosses her face—not a smile, but the memory of one. "She went in her sleep. Peacefully. We had hope. She was close to remission, but then everything turned, and it happened too fast for any of us to—"

She stops. Swallows. Looks toward the ocean.

"She didn't suffer," Eleanor finishes. "Not at the end."

"I'm so terribly sorry I wasn't there for her. Or for you. I didn't know."

"On the contrary. I'm glad you didn't know." Eleanor's chin lifts—a small, defiant motion. "Because when she lost you, she needed me again." A pause, deliberate as a held breath. "And for that, I'm grateful."

The image of a stiletto heel impaling a champagne flute crosses my mind. The glass holding as much pressure as it can before it shatters around its aggressor. I'm not livid at her statement because the words are cruel—although they are. It's because they're true. I abandoned Whitney, and in the wreckage of that abandonment, she rebuilt a relationship with the mother she'd spent a decade avoiding. My absence became Eleanor's gain. My failure became her second chance.

I don't have a response to that. There's nothing to say to a woman who is simultaneously thanking you and eviscerating you with the same sentence.

Eleanor straightens. Whatever softness surfaced during the last sixty seconds—the quiet voice, the ghost-smile, the tremor in her hands I pretended not to notice—disappears. She smooths her jacket, adjusts her pearls, and becomes, once again, Eleanor Montgomery-Trace, hostess of the most expensive funeral on the East End.

She pulls me into a hug this time. It's stiff and brief, all architecture and no warmth, like being embraced by a brick building. Chanel No. 5 nearly suffocates me.

"Since you're here," she says, releasing me, "enjoy the service. But I wouldn't fuss over a speech, Celeste. I can't imagine you of all people want to stand in front of two hundred guests and speak." Her eyes hold mine for a beat too long. "That's never really been your strong suit, has it?"

The anxiety hits before the anger does. A cold, liquid thing pooling in my stomach, spreading through my limbs like ink in water. Two hundred people. Two hundred sets of eyes, belonging to people who knew me as Greg's wife, as the woman who built a fashion empire and then watched her marriage implode publicly, as the friend who vanished from Whitney's life without explanation. Standing at a podium in front of all of them, cracked open, with nothing between me and their judgment but a speech I wrote at three in the morning while sobbing onto my laptop keyboard.

Eleanor knows exactly what she's doing. She knows about my crowd anxiety which has been prevalent since Whitney's twenty-first birthday where I fumbled my toast miserably. It's only gotten worse since Greg and I divorced. He was at least good at that, being a pillar to lean against when I was on the brink of collapse. And now Eleanor is right. I have nothing to lean on, hide behind, or run to. Especially now that Whitney's gone.

I hold her gaze. "I'll be fine."

"Of course you will." She pats my arm the way you'd pat a dog that's performed a trick you didn't ask for. "I should check on the caterers. Make sure those crostini survived my absence."

She strides back toward the building, her heels clicking against the stone path with the metronomic precision of a woman who has never once in her life been uncertain of her next step. The side door closes behind her. The instrumental music swells briefly then muffles back to nothing.

I'm alone in the courtyard.

I grip the stone wall with both hands and breathe. In through the nose. Out through the mouth. Count to three. Hold. Release. The exercises my therapist taught me, the ones I practice in bathroom stalls before events and in the back of town cars and in my office with the door locked while Margot fields my calls. The exercises Whitney used to talk me through over the phone when she could hear the ragged edge in my breathing, before I even had to say a word.

"Match my breath, Lessi. In, two, three, four. Hold. Out, two, three, four. There you go. You're okay. You're always okay. It's just people. They aren't that scary."

Shit. I am not okay.

My chest is tight. Not grief-tight—anxiety-tight. The kind of tightness that starts in my ribs and radiates until my fingers tingle and the edges of my vision go soft. I know this feeling. I've known it since I was twenty-four, standing backstage at my first runway show, hyperventilating into a paper bag while my seamstress told me to count backward from ten. I've known it at galas and award ceremonies and every social event where the spotlight wasn't on my clothes but on me. It's the reason I started hiring escorts to accompany me to events years before Greg and I split—having someone beside me, someone whose job it was to make me feel less alone in a room full of people, was the only way I could walk through the door.

Behind a podium at my company, I'm untouchable. That's *my* stage. My kingdom. I can command a room of five hundred executives because the conversation is about fabric and vision and business, and in that arena, I am fluent. But a eulogy is personal. A eulogy strips the brand away and leaves only the woman, and the woman is the part of me I've spent my entire career learning to hide.

Whitney knew this. Whitney was the one who used to stand in the wings at events and give me a thumbs-up before I walked out, who'd whisper *you've got this, Lessi* through my earpiece when she could hear my breathing change. She was the one who told me, on my worst day, that bravery isn't the absence of fear—it's the decision to speak anyway.

And now I'm about to eulogize her without a net.

I release the wall and flex my fingers. They've left pale impressions in the stone's dusty surface. A wisteria petal has landed on my wrist and I flick it off, watching it catch the breeze and tumble across the lawn toward the ocean.

I pull my phone from my pocket—my Target dress pocket, that I'm eternally grateful for—and type a text to Rina.

Friend, I need your help. Legal stuff. Call me when you're back from Paris.

I hit send, then stare at the screen. Rina will know what to do about the will. If Eleanor is this hostile about my presence, it's because there's something she doesn't want me to find. It has to be money. Maybe it's property. Maybe it's something Whitney left me that Eleanor thinks she deserves more. Whatever it is—I don't want it.

I don't want Eleanor's fight. I don't want a legal battle with a grieving mother. I don't want to sit across from lawyers in a conference room and argue over the possessions of a woman I failed while she was alive. If Rina can help me forfeit my claim to whatever Whit left me, I'll sign the papers today. I came here with one purpose, and it wasn't to collect an inheritance.

I came here because my best friend is dead and the last thing I ever said to her was *I'll never forgive you*, and I've been carrying those words in my chest like shrapnel ever since, and the only surgery that might help is standing at a podium and saying the things I should have said when she was alive.

You can't apologize to someone who's gone. Eleanor was right about that.

But I can stand in a room full of people who loved her and tell them who she really was. I can give them the Whitney I knew—the one who could've joined Destiny's Child, she sang those songs so well; the one who burned her hair off with a curling iron and laughed about it; the one who wrote articles about life and love as if it were divine poetry. The Whitney none of us deserved, but were privileged to experience anyway.

That's not an apology. It's not forgiveness. It's the only offering I have left, and I'm going to deliver it even if my hands shake and my voice breaks and two hundred people watch me come undone.

The courtyard is empty now. The wisteria sways in the breeze. The ocean crashes against the shore with the steady neutrality of something that has been here long before any of us and will be here long after.

I tuck my phone away and walk back toward the building. Somewhere inside, Eleanor is terrorizing caterers. Somewhere inside, Saylor is navigating a world that isn't his with the kind of grace I've never been able to manage in my own. Somewhere inside, two hundred people are settling into their seats, preparing to mourn a woman most of them probably didn't really know.

And somewhere inside me, beneath the anxiety and the guilt and the grief, a small stubborn voice that sounds suspiciously like Whitney's says: *Get your ass up there and say what you need to say, Lessi. That's all you owe me.*

She's wrong of course.

I owe her so much more.

But this is where I'll start.

Chapter 6

Saylor

I'll stop, smell the roses. I'll choose glitter polish,
even if I'm too old for it.

By the time I find Celeste, the service is minutes from starting.

She's standing near the entrance to the main hall, arms crossed, one hand gripping the opposite elbow like she's physically holding herself together. Her lips are redder than when we arrived, like a fresh coat of paint. She must have found a bathroom and touched up her makeup again because although the rest of her looks put-together, her eyes betray her. Red-rimmed. Slightly swollen. The face of a woman who's been crying and then carefully pretending she hasn't.

"There you are," she says, and the relief in her voice catches me off guard. Like she wasn't sure I'd come back. "Where did you disappear to?"

"Got turned around." The lie tastes sour. "Big venue."

I want to tell her. The words are right there, stacked behind my teeth like cars in a traffic jam—Raven, the surrogacy, the baby, the forged documents, Eleanor's legal maneuvering. All of it pressing against the back of my mouth, demanding to be spoken.

But the funeral attendants have begun herding everyone toward their seats. The string quartet has shifted from warm-up noodling to something deliberate and somber. And Celeste has a folded piece of paper sticking out of her dress pocket—her speech, the one she wrote at three in the morning, the one she is so determined to deliver for Whitney's sake.

I can't drop a bomb on her and then send her to a podium.

It will just have to wait. A delayed truth for the sake of mercy.

"Ready?" I ask, offering my arm.

She threads her hand through the crook of my elbow. Her fingers are ice cold. "No."

"Fair. Should we go in anyway?"

"Definitely."

We enter the hall. Two hundred chairs are arranged in precise rows facing a raised stage, and nearly every seat is occupied. The hydrangeas are all over—lining the aisle, framing the stage, clustered around an enormous portrait of Whitney that sits on an easel surrounded by white candles. She's laughing in the photo. Mid-laugh, actually, caught in the act of finding something hilarious, her red curls wild around her face. She looks alive in a way that makes the rest of the room feel like a museum exhibit.

A staff member guides us toward the back rows, gesturing to two open seats near the aisle. Celeste nods and starts to sit, but then someone official looking with a clipboard and headset intercepts us. She gently touches Celeste's arm.

"Ms. Brinley, I'm sorry. Please, come with me. I have seats near the family closer to the front."

Celeste stiffens beside me. She opens her mouth—probably to decline—but the coordinator is already moving, and we're trailing her up the center aisle like two people being led to the principal's office. Every step takes us deeper into the room, past rows of straight-spined people with stoic faces, most of them dressed in the kind of understated black that communicates wealth without trying. A few heads turn as we pass. I catch whispers.

"Celeste's new husband?"

"Doubtful. I heard she's barely divorced."

"Probably just some arm candy."

My stomach churns at their audaciously accurate commentary. Except I don't think I'm here to be candy. More like...decoration.

The coordinator deposits us in the second row, just behind a cluster of people I assume are family or inner circle. She gives Celeste a warm, conspiratorial smile. "Whitney would want her best friend up close."

She disappears before anyone can intervene—but the woman who I'm assuming is Eleanor, Whitney's mother, has noticed. She's seated at the far end of the first row, and her gaze finds us with the precision of a guided missile. Red hair pulled tight. Pearls. Chanel. She looks exactly like the woman Celeste described in the car, except worse in person, because photographs can't capture the particular quality of a stare that makes you feel like you've been weighed, measured, and found insufficient.

Her eyes move from Celeste to me, and the assessment is slow and thorough. Shoes. Trousers. Watch. Shoulders. Face. It's not attraction; it's inventory. She's cataloging me the way you'd catalog evidence, filing me away for future use.

I meet her gaze and hold it, because I'm Australian at heart and we don't look away first. After a beat, she turns to face the stage.

Celeste hasn't noticed the exchange. She's staring at Whitney's portrait, her jaw locked so tight I can see the muscles working beneath her skin. Her hands are folded in her lap. Her printed speech sits on her knee, slightly crumpled where she's been gripping it.

I settle into my seat and try to focus.

The service begins with a priest who speaks about Whitney with the careful generality of a man working from notes he received that morning. He mentions her kindness, her creativity, her love of life. He does not mention anything specific—no stories, no details, no evidence that he ever met her. It's a eulogy built from adjectives, and it floats through the room without landing on anyone.

Next comes the montage. A screen descends behind the stage and the lights dim, and for three minutes the room watches Whitney Trace grow up in photographs. Baby pictures. Childhood.

Graduation. I scan the images as they cycle—Whitney in a field of sunflowers; Whitney at what looks like a book signing; Whitney on a beach with her arms thrown wide. But what strikes me is how after the high school graduation picture, Celeste appears in nearly every frame afterward. Suddenly it's like I'm watching two lives unfold in tandem, two stories so tightly interwoven they've become a single narrative. The epiphany sweeps over me and the magnitude of the situation stretches as wide as the ocean outside. This is more than friendship. This was Celeste's twin flame.

Which is maybe why I'm watching Celeste watch the screen as if she's in a trance. One by one the memories fill the room, haunting her.

Then one image slides into frame that makes my chest tighten. Whitney and Celeste, young—maybe late teens—sitting on the hood of a car, legs dangling, both mid-laugh. Whitney's red curls are enormous and Celeste's hair is pulled back in a messy bun and they're wearing matching university sweatshirts and the photo radiates the kind of joy that only exists when you don't know yet how much you have to lose.

Beside me, Celeste makes a small sound. Not a sob. More like the sound of something cracking that was already under pressure. I find her hand in the dark and hold it. She doesn't look at me, but her fingers lock around mine.

Another photo: Whitney, trying on wedding dresses, showing off the massive diamond on her left hand. The image is there and gone in four seconds, dissolving into a shot of Whitney blowing out birthday candles. The last photo is a family portrait of Whitney, Eleanor, and a man in a suit that must've been her father. An entire montage of Whitney's life—Celeste present for the thick of it, but cut out at the end. It's uncomfortably symbolic.

The short film ends. Polite applause. The lights come back up.

Eleanor is on stage. She must've slipped up there while we were distracted with the presentation I'm certain she prepared. She grips the podium with both hands and delivers a eulogy that is technically perfect and emotionally vacant. She speaks about Whitney's accomplishments—her career at The Belly, her volunteer work, her "zest for life." She doesn't cry. She doesn't pause. She doesn't tell a single story that couldn't have been pulled from a LinkedIn profile. It's four minutes long, and when she finishes, the applause is respectful and measured, the kind of applause that acknowledges effort without being moved by it.

She returns to her seat. The room settles into an expectant quiet.

The event coordinator who escorted us up to the apparent VIP section of this funeral clicks across the stage, her heels punctuating the silence. She adjusts the microphone with manicured fingers, the silver bracelet on her wrist catching the light as she leans forward. "Before we close the formal portion of our service, Whitney's dearest friend, Celeste Brinley, would like to say a few words."

She gestures toward our row. Two hundred heads turn.

And Celeste doesn't move.

Her hand is still in mine and I feel it happen—the sudden, total lockdown. Her fingers go rigid. Her breathing, which had been shallow but steady, stops entirely for a beat before restarting in short, rapid pulls. Her eyes are fixed on the stage like it's a cliff edge she's been asked to jump from.

I lean close. "I think that's you."

"I realize. My legs won't move." Her voice is barely audible. Thin. Stripped of every ounce of the wit and composure I've come to associate with her in the six hours I've spent with this woman.

"That's all right. We'll get them moving."

I stand first, keeping hold of her hand, and ease her up beside me. She rises like someone surfacing from deep water—slow, unsteady, blinking against the light. I place my other hand on the small of her back and guide her toward the aisle, matching her pace, which is glacial. Her heels strike the floor—tap, pause, tap-tap—like a metronome petering out, each step threatening to fold beneath her.

We reach the short staircase leading up to the stage. I walk her to the bottom step. She's gripping the railing with one hand, my hand with the other, and for a moment we stand there. Two hundred people watching. The portrait of Whitney laughing behind the podium. The one billion white hydrangeas. The ocean light pouring through the windows.

"You wrote this," I murmur, low enough that only she can hear, "because you loved her. That's all this is. Just talk to Whitney."

She nods. Releases my hand. Climbs the stairs.

I go back to my seat and realize my palms are sweating. I wipe them on the Tom Ford trousers, which feels like a crime against money, but Celeste isn't in a position to judge me right now.

She reaches the podium, dutifully unfolds her speech, then flattens it against the surface with both hands. She's silent, smoothing the creases, buying time. The microphone catches the sound of the paper rustling.

"Good afternoon." Finally. Her voice is steady. Almost normal. Probably boardroom boss Celeste, showing up in the nick of time. "My name is Celeste Brinley, and Whitney Trace was—"

She stops. Swallows. Tries again.

"Whitney Trace was my best friend for twenty years. And I—"

Her voice fractures. Not dramatically—just a hairline crack, the kind of break that starts small and spreads. She clears her throat. Looks down at her speech. The paper is trembling in her hands.

"I'm sorry. I—" She swallows again. "We met our freshman year on the very first day of school. She was my roommate when I wasn't supposed to have a roommate. But um...it..." She forces out a steadying breath. "Sorry. That's not particularly relevant. Anyway, the first thing she said to me was..."

But the words aren't coming. I can see it from my seat—the moment when the muscle memory of public speaking collides with the reality of what she's actually saying, and the armor that got her to the podium disintegrates. Her shoulders curve inward. Her chin drops. The speech flutters in her shaking hands like a white flag.

"I'm sorry." She presses a hand over her mouth. The mic picks up everything—her ragged breath, the muffled sob, the raw edge of a woman who is coming apart in front of everyone she was terrified to face. She looks up to the ceiling. "I'm so sorry, Whit. I'm trying. I can't—I can't do this. I'm sorry...I love you so much..."

The room is silent. Not the polite, attentive silence of Eleanor's eulogy. The held-breath silence of two hundred people watching something real happen for the first time today.

And I think to myself...this is how someone should be acting at a funeral. This is the only honest thing that's happened in this building since we arrived. The champagne...the over-the-top flowers...Eleanor's eulogy. It all seemed so out of place.

This fits. Celeste, shaking at a podium with mascara threatening to run again, is the only person in this room who is actually grieving. And they're all just sitting there, watching her drown.

I'm on my feet before I've made a conscious decision.

I take the stage stairs two at a time and then I'm beside her. She's so small next to me—even lifted in her heels, even cradled in her tens of thousands of dollars' worth of jewelry. Nothing can protect her right now. *Except me.* I wrap my arms around her and pull her into my chest. She resists for half a second, her body rigid with the instinct to perform, to recover, to handle it. Then she folds.

I press my lips to the top of her head. Her hair smells like something I recognize. A distinct mix of jasmine, maybe, or gardenia and citrus. Like this morning Celeste washed her hair with Head & Shoulders. How fantastically simple. Shampoo. Just regular-people shampoo. Celeste, beneath all the luxury layers, is just a person.

"I'm here," I say, quiet enough that the mic won't catch it. "Let's do this together, yeah?"

She tilts her face up. Her eyes are puffy—red, wet, terrified—but somewhere beneath the wreckage, I see it. Trust. Not earned over months or years, but forged in hours of honesty and utter desperation.

She nods.

She hands me the speech.

I release her gently, keeping one hand on her shoulder as I step up to the podium. The paper is warm from her grip and damp at the edges where her palms have been sweating. Her handwriting is neat, precise, architectural—the penmanship of a woman who draws for a living.

I adjust the microphone. The faceless crowd fixates on me, but I'm not intimidated. I glance at Celeste, who has stepped to the side of the podium, arms wrapped around herself. She gives me the smallest nod.

I look down at the page and begin to read.

"Whitney Trace was the bravest person I ever knew. Not in the way people usually mean when they say 'brave'—not the loud kind, not the kind that announces itself. Whitney was brave in the ways that actually matter. The quiet ways. The costly ways."

My voice carries through the room, steadier than I expect. Celeste's words feel solid in my mouth, carefully chosen, weighed.

"She was brave enough to tell people the truth when lies would have been kinder, brave enough to love with her whole heart when the world had taught her to hold pieces back. She was brave in that devastating way that changes you forever—choosing herself even when the gravity of everyone else's expectations was crushing. A lot of us talk about freedom, but I really think Whitney experienced it. She loved me through my darkest days, and when I became nothing but a shadow, she was brave enough to tell me."

I pause. Not for effect—because the words hit me. She's writing about herself and Whitney, but she could be writing about my mum. About anyone who's ever loved someone enough to let them go.

"I met Whitney on September third, two thousand five. I'd insisted on having my own dorm room because of my social anxiety. I couldn't fathom the idea of sharing a room with someone.

But there she was, unpacking a box of books in our double and she looked up at me and smiled—" I squint at the next line. Celeste's handwriting has gotten slightly unsteady here, like she was crying when she wrote it. "I told her I wanted a single, and she admitted she was a last-minute addition that year. She was supposed to go to Oxford and selfishly I'm so glad they screwed up her paperwork because Whitney was the best thing to happen to my life. I figured that after a while at school I'd eventually make friends, but the universe knew I needed something bigger than that. I needed a sister. And I got one that very first day of college. It took a while for Whitney to realize she committed too fast and she's the one who got the short end of the stick. But I stuck to her like a barnacle. Luckily for me, our unspoken contract was the forever kind. She should've read the fine print."

A ripple of soft laughter moves through the room. Surprised laughter—the kind that catches people off guard at funerals, the kind that reminds them the person they're mourning was a person, not a tragic saint.

"Whit had this beautiful way of looking at life. She was so fearlessly present. Every mistake propelled her toward a deeper truth. Every regret taught an important lesson. See, what Whit did, that maybe we should all do, is celebrate every single version of ourselves. The versions that stumble, make messes, and embarrass us along the way. Whit knew how to laugh at herself, forgive herself, and expect great things from herself."

My throat tightens. I glance at Celeste. She's standing perfectly still, tears streaming down her face, not wiping them away. Letting them fall.

"Whitney had this gift," I continue. "She could walk into any room and find the person who needed her most. Not the most important person. Not the most interesting. The one who was quietly falling apart. She'd find them and she'd sit beside them and she'd stay. That was her superpower. She just stayed. And my biggest regret in life is not getting to say this to her today..."

I have to stop for a second. I clear my throat, pressing my

thumb against the edge of the podium.

"Whit, thank you for choosing me. Thank you for seeing me. Thank you for lending me your bravery when I had none for myself. I didn't deserve you. None of us did. But you do deserve the truth which is this: from my bones, I'm sorry that I let time and distance steal precious years. You were, as you always were, *right*. About everything. And even though it'd make me feel so much better to live the rest of my life suffocating with guilt, I know that's not what you'd want for me. If you were here, you'd tell me to take that next step, and embrace the next chapter, the new version of me. So that's what I'm going to do. That is my promise to you. I'll stop, smell the roses. I'll choose glitter polish, even if I'm too old for it. I'll never cut out carbs again. In fact I will exclusively live on the bottom layer of that food pyramid. I will live like life is supposed to be enjoyed. Like you always wanted me to."

The room has shifted. I can feel it—a change in the quality of the silence, from respectful attention to something deeper. People are leaning forward. A woman three rows back is pressing a tissue to her mouth.

My voice nearly breaks as I begin again, the immensity of Celeste's pain so vivid on this page it's almost unbearable to speak aloud—like reading someone's diary to a room full of strangers, except she asked me to, and that trust is the only thing keeping me upright. And I have to finish. Just one more line to go.

"And I'll be counting down the days until I get to see you again. I love you, Whitney Trace. Until the end. *Past* the end."

I lower the page.

"Rest now, Whit. You more than earned it, my friend. My best friend. *My sister*."

The silence that follows is vast. Not empty—full.

Full of two hundred people sitting in the wreckage of their own composure, undone by the words of a woman they'd been prepared to judge.

Then, the applause. Not the polite, golf-clap applause that followed Eleanor's eulogy. This is different—raw, uneven, building from scattered claps into something sustained and genuine. People are wiping their eyes and clapping simultaneously, which is an awkward physical act that somehow communicates more sincerity than any standing ovation I've ever seen.

I glance toward Eleanor. She's sitting very still, hands in her lap. Her face is unreadable—but her lips look glued into a thin line, and her chest rises and falls with the deliberate rhythm of a woman who is working very hard not to feel something in public. Whether it's grief or fury or shame, I can't tell. Maybe all of it.

My eyes sweep through the crowd and find Raven. She's near the back, standing because she probably couldn't sit for that long with the nausea, and she's beaming at me through a face full of tears. Her hand rests on her stomach. She mouths two words I can't quite make out, but I think it's *thank you.*

I fold Celeste's speech carefully—along its original creases, the way she'd want—and turn to her.

She hasn't moved. She's standing where I left her, arms at her sides now, face wet, but her makeup by some miracle, still in place. She looks exhausted and emptied out and strangely, impossibly beautiful—the kind of beautiful that has nothing to do with clothes or makeup or anything you can buy. The kind that only shows up when every wall has come down and there's nothing left but the person.

I step toward her and take her hand.

Her fingers latch onto mine so tight it almost hurts—a grip that says *don't let go, don't let go, don't you dare let go*—and I squeeze back with equal force. A silent covenant that passes between our palms like a current.

I'm right here. I'm not going anywhere.

We walk off the stage together. Down the stairs, up the aisle, back to our seats. It's not long after that before the service closes with a final prayer from the priest. Celeste launches out of her seat the moment we're dismissed, and as we hurry down the aisle, past the hundreds of faces looking at us, I notice something I didn't expect in a room full of Eleanor's guests.

Warmth.

We keep walking. Through the main hall, past the champagne station and the hydrangeas and the string quartet that has resumed playing something gentle and solemn. We don't stop until we reach the courtyard, where the flowers are still blooming and the ocean is still indifferent and the birds are still singing for no one.

Celeste releases my hand. Takes a breath. Turns to face me.

And for a long, quiet moment, we look at each other. Two people who met this morning and somehow ended up here—standing in a courtyard at the edge of the Atlantic, holding a speech that made a room full of strangers cry, bound by a secret I need to tell her but can't find a good time to.

She opens her mouth to say something.

My phone buzzes in my pocket. I ignore it.

"Saylor," she says. Just my name. Like she's testing whether it still means the same thing it meant this morning, before I held her on a stage in front of everyone she was afraid of.

It means more.

"Yeah?"

She reaches up and straightens my collar—the one she sent, on the shirt she chose, part of the suit she picked. Her fingers brush the side of my neck and I stop breathing for exactly one second.

"Thank you. For reading it when I couldn't."

"Thank you for writing it when no one else could."

She nods. Wipes her eyes. Squares her shoulders. And just like that, the armor starts going back up—piece by piece, brick by brick—because that's what Celeste does. She rebuilds.

But I saw what's underneath now. And I'm not going to forget it.

"I was planning to stay the night but maybe we should head back to the city," she says. "I did what I needed to do. You said what I came here to say. Time to go home." She takes another deep, fortifying breath and I hate that I'm about to be the one to shatter her world again.

But what choice do I have?

"I think we should stay, Celeste. There's something I need to tell you. And it's big."

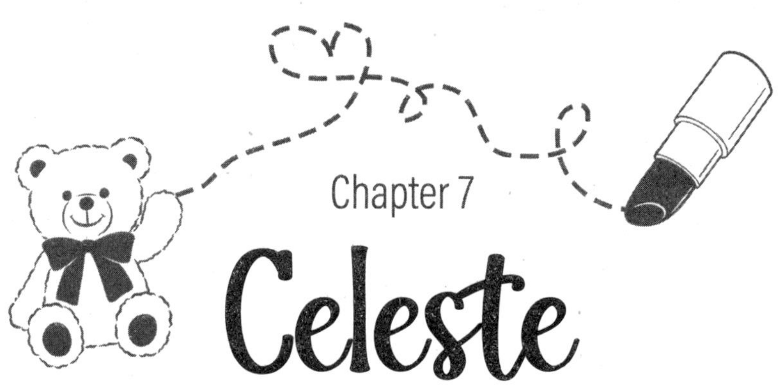

Chapter 7
Celeste

Somewhere between peanut butter and pickled jalapeños, we made sense.

"There's something I need to tell you. And it's big."

I stare at Saylor. The courtyard is quiet around us except for the rhythmic whoosh of the ocean waves, cresting and breaking. I watch his face cycle through something I can't quite read. He's not nervous, exactly. He's careful. Choosing his words the way I choose fabric—feeling the weight of each option before committing.

My mind does what it always does: races ahead to the worst possible scenarios and ranks them by devastation level.

Eleanor said something to him. Cornered him during the service and told him I'm unstable, dramatic, not worth the trouble. Handed him a check to disappear or worse, out me as a desperate old lady who hired an escort for a funeral.

Perhaps he's quitting. The day has been too much between the crying, the panic attack, the speech, the full-body clinging on a stage in front of two hundred strangers. Maybe he's decided this isn't worth what he's getting paid.

That last thought hits differently than it should. Sharp and low, like a paper cut in a place you didn't know could bleed. I've known this man for less than a day. The fact that losing him already feels like something worth fearing is a problem I'll need to address later, likely with my therapist and a very large glass of wine.

Saylor glances back toward the building. Through the windows I can see the dinner setup taking shape—long tables draped in white linen, more hydrangeas, silver candelabras. Eleanor's staff moving with military precision. A butlered dinner. At a funeral. Because apparently we've run out of ways to avoid actually grieving, so we're going to sit down and eat a five-course meal while a string quartet plays pretentious classical music, and everyone pretends this is normal.

Nothing about this is normal. Nothing about this feels okay.

"Not here," Saylor says, to my great relief. He turns back to me and his expression settles into something resolute. "Would you be open to leaving early? Eating somewhere that doesn't serve champagne and truffle brie?"

I look at the estate hall. I look at the ocean. I look at the man standing in front of me in the suit I picked out, asking me to leave my best friend's funeral to go grab a bite like we've known each other for years.

"Promise me something."

He nods, unbothered. Unintimidated. As if he's been waiting to make this promise all day.

"If I die," I say, "you are personally responsible for ensuring there is no catered, black-tie dinner at my service. No hydrangeas. No string quartet. No pomegranate sorbet."

"What do you want instead?"

"Potluck. Crock-Pots. Paper plates. That awful-looking seven-layer dip from the grocery store with the avocado layer that's neon green. No one here will admit, but that stuff is delicious. I want warmth, love, and people telling stories, and absolutely none of—" I gesture at the building behind us. "None of whatever this is."

Saylor's mouth curves. "Sure, Celeste. I've got you. Potluck, cheap dip, and casual attire. I'll show up in socks and sandals, just to show you how committed I am."

Despite myself, despite today...I smile. "Thank you. How about you? How can I give you the funeral of your dreams?"

He points to his chest. "Oh me? No, I don't plan on dying. I would like something in exchange though."

"What do you want then?"

His gaze sweeps over my lips. "Obviously not this weekend, but when you're ready, could I see you again? Outside of work, I mean."

"For what?"

His eyes lift to the sky, then drop back down. "To discuss your funeral arrangements in more detail, obviously."

"Obviously," I echo, still not understanding. "Wait...what?"

"Celeste, this is me, asking you out...at the most inappropriate time and location possible. But clearly, I love a challenge."

"A challenge?" I erupt with laughter—the kind that starts deep in your belly and takes over your whole body. Even as I watch Saylor's face crumple with dismay, I can't rein it in. The sound keeps spilling out of me, beyond my control. Rising to my tiptoes, I place my hands on his shoulders, placing a quick kiss on his smooth cheek.

I get a faint whiff of his aftershave and visions of bright lightning striking the ocean at sunset come to mind. This is how creativity approaches me. It's a dance that starts with an invitation—a visual, smell, a taste. It's really the only superpower I have as a designer. My brain loves to set a scene. My Willow line was inspired by the cattails in bloom in a scorching summer, the dandelion debris floating through the air like snow on a sunny day. My Scarlett line was inspired by a London rainstorm at night. Thick, angry droplets pummeling into the ground, exploding like grenades. That line was all dark hues, sharp, sexy angles, leather mixed with lace. I'm used to the visuals, but this is odd. Never once has inspiration started with this—a small, innocent kiss to the cheek.

"Saylor, you're sweet, but I used to have a Blockbuster card. Do you understand that? Whit and I grew up in the era where we rented DVDs and thought Bluetooth would give us radiation poisoning when they first introduced it. So, thank you very much for the compliment of asking me out but, I'm way too old for you. Not to mention, I have no interest in a romantic relationship right now."

What does he expect? Does he think I'm hiring escorts to be swept off my feet? No, I'm only trying to appear, at least to the outer world, as if I'm not Greg's leftovers and slowly succumbing to my inevitable fate as a childless spinster who has a hand-knitted blanket draped over her favorite creaky rocking chair.

He stares at me for a while, like he's actively composing a Plan B in his mind. "What the hell is a Blockbuster?"

"Exactly." God, I love it when people prove my points for me. I wear my smug smile proudly while I tuck the giddy school-girl excitement of a man like Saylor looking at me *like that* deep down into the pits of my gut. "Anyway, what did you need to tell me? You look stressed out."

"Let's go eat," Saylor says. "Do you mind staying right here? If you're okay with it I'm going to go find a friend and see if she can join us."

Did this man just suggest a threesome after I turned him down? That's quite the leap. "You made a friend? At a funeral?"

"Well, I'm very likable. Not to you, clearly. But to some women."

"Ah, so now the pouting begins?"

"Brace yourself," he says, his grin spreading ear to ear. "But no, there's a situation I think she can explain better. Most definitely a conversation we should have away from all of this."

I can't argue with that. "Fine. Let's go before Eleanor discovers I'm skipping her dinner and dispatches the catering staff to drag me back in a straitjacket to 'enjoy' the same five-course meal I've eaten at least sixty times in my adult life."

"There. I see her. She's near Eleanor though." Saylor points toward the main building where guests are gathering in the foyer behind the floor-to-ceiling glass. "Why don't you sneak around back. I'll touch base with my friend and grab the car. Wait for five minutes, then meet me out front, okay?"

"Sure." I don't bother to hide the skepticism in my voice. But I am too emotionally drained to argue. And starving now that Saylor mentioned it. He hustles away and I absolutely *do not* check out his behind. I'm blissfully unaware of how muscular his ass looks as he jogs out of sight and into the crowd. As instructed, I wait a few minutes then take the stone path around the building to the front entrance. I must be moving at a glacial pace because by the time I climb the hill in my very pissed-off Louboutins—Christian did not design these for exercise—Saylor is there waiting, my Range Rover already pulling around the valet station.

The closer I get, the more I hear. The more I hear, the more I'm horrified. Saylor lies with the ease of a spoiled house cat.

"It really was a nice speech. Such a shame you have to run out early," the valet attendant says.

"Agreed. All Celeste's words, not mine. She wrote such a beautiful message, and we hate to leave, but as it goes, she's spewing from both ends, so it's probably safer and more hygienic for everyone if we make our way out now."

"Poor darling. Any idea what did it?"

"I'm thinking the truffle brie bites?" Saylor says. "She only had a couple, but their wrath was fast and furious. There's a janitor's closet on the second floor you just do *not* want to go in."

By the time I'm standing next to Saylor, my jaw is dropped and all I'm seeing is his faceless silhouette against a backdrop of angry red.

"Feel better, Ms. Celeste. Take care," the attendant says, depositing the keys into Saylor's hand. Saylor smoothly slips him a bill I can't see before he scuttles away. Very suave, very masculine. Very above his years. Very much not important at the moment because the man just told a stranger I had explosive diarrhea.

"What the *fuck*, Saylor? What exactly are you accusing me of doing in a janitor's closet?"

He places his hand across his chest. "I was planting the seeds of a backstory. Now, if anybody notices your absence, at least the valet team knows you weren't feeling well."

I hold up one finger. "Emotionally overwhelmed." Another joins. "Family emergency." I lift the third. "Searing migraine." I wiggle three fingers in his face. "All better options to accomplish the *same thing* without telling people I was *spewing from both ends*!"

Saylor nods, trying to hold in his smile. "Oi, now I see it. I think I got stuck on your notes about the truffle brie and kind of ran with it. I should've went with migraine."

I smack his arm with the back of my hand as his laughter breaks free.

Still chuckling, he opens the passenger door of my vehicle for me. "Your chariot awaits. Unless you want to drive?" he teases.

Rolling my eyes, I hoist myself into the seat, aggressively buckling like I've got a bone to pick with the seatbelt. My car smells a little unfamiliar. The blend of mine and Saylor's scents—shampoo, soap, perfume, aftershave, a touch of fresh laundry. It all melts together to create something totally foreign. Something pleasant actually, borderline intoxicating.

Before he puts the SUV in drive, Saylor pulls out his phone, thumbing a quick text.

"Who are you messaging?" I ask as if it's my business.

"The friend I told you about. She suggested a burger place about twenty minutes from here. Riptide, I believe."

I can't help my smile. "Riptide is still here?" I laugh, settling into my seat and my own glee, which is a nice momentary reprieve from the pain of this day.

"You know it?" Saylor asks.

"Oh yeah. Me and Whit spent a couple obligatory summers here. There's probably still grease in my veins from their burgers and fries because we ate there so much. They have the weirdest, best burgers. We'd always order the same thing then swap halfway through."

"Great," Saylor says, flicking on the blinker for nobody. We're alone here, the only car trying to make a getaway. "What a perfect way to honor Whitney today. What's the usual order?"

"Oh, I'm sure the menu's changed."

"Tell me anyway. Call it one more Whitney story." At the bypass, he checks left-right-left-right with exaggerated caution, like someone who's borrowed something valuable and is terrified of damaging it.

"Whit would get the spicy Hawaiian burger with barbecue sauce and pickled jalapeños, and I'd get...a different one." I catch myself, remembering how weird this sounds to other people.

"A different one? Care to elaborate?"

"Not particularly."

"Celeste. You asked me to plan your funeral. We're way past bashful. Come on, out with it."

"You'll judge me."

"Are you a lettuce-leaf bun kind of girl?"

"Woman," I remind him. "And no."

"Then, spill. I promise no judgment. Probably."

Air leaves my lungs in a slow surrender. "It's...a burger with a brioche bun, slathered with a bacon-and-berry compote, and a drizzle of a creamy peanut-infused reduction."

Saylor is quiet for a long time. Just the sound of the blinker as he passes a red Hyundai going ten under the speed limit. When he's safely reset into the right lane, he steals a glance in my direction. "Did you just try to make a peanut-butter-jelly burger sound fancy?"

Heat rises in my cheeks. "I said what I said."

He bursts out in laughter. "Maybe I didn't lie to the valet. With half a spicy Hawaiian burger, and your weird Frankenstein mash-up, we might both end up spewing from one end or the other."

"We?" I ask, lifting a brow.

"Oh, yeah. I'm in this. Pickle for pickle. Oh wait, gross. You don't put pickles on the peanut butter burger, do you?"

"What? That's crazy." My awkward laughter is an obvious confession. I tried pickles on it once. I didn't hate it as much as I should have.

When our laughter fades, Saylor reaches across the center console and grabs my hand just for a moment before releasing it. "I'm sorry I asked you out earlier. I got swept up in the moment and it wasn't the right timing."

"It's fine, Saylor. There's been a lot of heightened emotions today. It's natural to want to feel close to someone. I am not upset. We can just forget about it."

"Yeah, maybe, but still. And I'm sorry for the future too."

My head whips around. "What do you mean?"

"I mean a preemptive apology."

"For what?"

He looks ahead at the road with feigned nonchalance. I swear I see the corner of his lips twitch into a smile. "For when I ask you out again."

Riptide looks exactly the same.

That's the first thing that hits me—not nostalgia, not sadness, but the sheer stubbornness of a place that has refused to change. The same sun-bleached wooden sign with the wave logo. The same screen door that doesn't close all the way. The same neon beer signs glowing in the window, one of which has been flickering since two thousand six, and evidently will flicker until the sun explodes.

The memories come at me next, wrapped up in the enduring smell of grease and salt and something sweet—the buns, maybe. They bake them in-house, or they used to. The aroma itself throws me into a time machine, and suddenly I'm twenty-one years old, sitting across from Whitney in the corner booth, splitting a basket of fries and arguing about whether Orlando Bloom or Viggo Mortensen was the superior *Lord of the Rings* love interest. Whitney was team Viggo. Rugged, broody, tortured. Of course he was the finer hero. We eventually agreed I was wrong, and she never let me forget it.

"You okay?" Saylor asks, holding the screen door open.

"Yeah." My voice comes out thicker than I intend, like I'm shouting underwater. "I just haven't been here in a long time."

The interior is small—maybe fifteen tables, vinyl booths along the walls, a counter with swivel stools. The lighting is warm and slightly yellow, the kind that makes everyone look like they're in an old-timey film. There's a chalkboard menu above the register with items written in colored chalk, and someone has drawn a surprisingly talented cartoon burger wearing a cowboy hat in the corner.

I scan for the corner booth with the only round table—mine and Whit's favorite—and it's open. Of course it is. The universe has a sick sense of humor today.

"That one." I point. "If you don't mind."

Saylor nods toward the "Seat Yourself" sign planted at the hostess station like a scarecrow in an empty field. As I remember it, this sign is code for: *I'm out back smoking. Don't rush me.*

The vinyl protests as we slide into the booth. I spot the familiar wobble in the table—the same one I've stabilized with folded napkins a hundred times before. My fingers automatically reach for a napkin, folding it precisely. Before I can wedge it under the uneven leg, Saylor's elbow bumps the table, sending ripples across the surface. He grips the edge and rotates the entire table with surprising force, like a parent trying to launch their kid on a playground carousel. When he presses down, the surface holds firm. I test it with a little shake—nothing. Whatever Saylor did, the wobble's gone.

Eventually a waitress appears. Right around the time my hunger has devolved into hanger. I haven't had much of an appetite, but the last thing I ate was a mini Kind bar on Friday morning and the grief distraction has run its course. My stomach is trying to digest itself, and I'm about three minutes away from becoming feral.

The waitress is not the teenager I expected, but a woman around my age with sun-streaked hair and a pen behind her ear.

She sets down two waters and a basket of warm rolls with their famous sour-cream dip.

"You guys know what you want, or you need a minute?"

Saylor doesn't even look at the menu. "Do you have a weird peanut-butter-jelly burger? And then a spicy Hawaiian one?"

The waitress looks over her shoulder and screams toward the kitchen. "I need a Sweet Nut and a Burnin' Love." She looks back at Saylor. "Circles or sticks?"

His eyebrows lift. "Sticks?"

"It's diner talk. Sticks are fries. Circles are the house-made kettle chips," I say, looking to the waitress who gives me a single, validating nod. I can physically feel the memories. The soft vinyl melding to my ass, the clink and clank of a bustling kitchen. Fryer grease, wood smoke, the sweet undercurrent of homemade ice cream—these smells could transport me back a decade in an instant. Back when everything seemed simpler, when laughter came easier, when aging was something that happened to other people. Back when Whit was still here. Back when I still recognized myself.

"One with circles, one with sticks, and we'll share? Is that what you and Whitney would do?"

I grin. "Yes. That sounds great."

It's such a sweet sentiment, I will never ever tell him how Whitney had an aversion to potatoes of all types. We'd get our burgers without any accompaniment.

"Anything else?"

"A milkshake?" I ask Saylor. "We can share. They are huge. Whatever flavor you want."

"I get to pick?"

I nod emphatically. *Please say chocolate, please say chocolate.*

"Vanilla with fudge on top?" he more asks than orders.

Fudge is chocolate. He almost got that right.

"Two cups or two straws?" The waitress's gaze bounces between me and Saylor, trying to make it make sense.

"Two cups, please," I say.

"Straws," Saylor answers at the same time.

She scribbles and disappears, apparently making the final call on that herself. I settle back into the booth and for a moment, I let myself just be here. In this place that Whitney and I claimed as ours during summers that felt infinite.

There are no paper menus at Riptide. Instead, you have to order by squinting at the giant wraparound whiteboard on the far wall of the restaurant. Regulars don't mind. Tourists hate it. But that's half the fun. There are so many options, you have to panic-order in a pinch and most often the thing you thought you'd hate, turns out to be a masterpiece. Hence my love affair with the Sweet Nut burger. The menu looks much the same except for the addition of a new section called "TikTok Famous" which is an uncomfortable reminder of inevitable evolution. But the counter. The stools. The wobbles. The bones are all the same, and I needed that today. I needed familiar.

The front door screeches open, as the bells on the door protest their disturbance loudly.

"Saylor!" a voice I vaguely recognize calls out.

I turn. And I know her immediately.

The blond curls. The blue eyes. The small frame, barely five-three, now unmistakably pregnant in a way that her black funeral dress couldn't quite conceal. The last time I saw this woman, she was standing in my office doorway holding a tan legal envelope, tears welling in her eyes, telling me she was really glad to meet me.

Raven. She spots us and makes a beeline for the booth, sliding in next to Saylor with the easy familiarity of someone who has decided they belong here and isn't interested in waiting for an invitation.

"Hi." She beams at me across the table with an intensity that borders on unhinged. "Oh my God, Celeste, your speech was incredible. I was sobbing. Like, full ugly-cry. Whitney would've loved every second of it. She would have been so proud of you."

I look at Saylor. His expression is carefully neutral, but his shoulders rise almost imperceptibly before settling back down, like he's bracing for impact and hiding it badly.

I look back at Raven. The woman from my office. The legal courier from Valcott & Finch. The one who handed me the envelope that brought me here. Who is now sitting in Whitney's booth, at Whitney's restaurant, talking about Whitney like she knew her.

"Raven," I say slowly. "You delivered the documents to my office."

"Yes!" She reaches for a roll, dunks it in dip, and pops it in her mouth with the enthusiasm of someone who has been nauseous for four months and is currently experiencing a window of tolerance. "I can't believe you remember me."

"I've got a knack for remembering names. I thought you didn't know Whitney. Yet, you attended the service?" I don't say it unkindly. But I am aware, suddenly, that something is very wrong with this picture. Or very right with it. I can't tell yet.

"Right. Yeah. That was—" She waves a hand. "A lie."

She ends her sentence as if it needs no further explanation. She is very incorrect.

"I'm sorry. How do you two know each other?" This time I'm pointing between her and Saylor like a detective connecting pins on a board.

"We just met. At the funeral," Saylor answers. Carefully.

"And you're already this chummy?" I silence that quiet bitch named jealousy. First Greg, now Saylor. I remember when men so quickly wanted to be my *friend* too. Roughly more than a decade ago.

"We bonded aggressively," Raven adds with zero carefulness. "He held my hair while I threw up in the men's bathroom. So we have just met, but I'd say our friendship intensity is at least a year old."

"The men's bathroom?"

"The signs were very confusing," Saylor adds.

I file this away. Something is building in the air between the three of us—a pressure change, like the deceptive warmth mere minutes before a hellacious storm breaks. Saylor is too still. Raven is too animated. And the thing Saylor has been trying to tell me all afternoon—the big thing, the thing that required a separate location and a third party—is sitting across from me with blond curls and a slight baby bump.

"Raven," I say. "What do you do? At Valcott and Finch?"

The roll Raven helped herself to freezes halfway to her mouth. She glances at Saylor. He gives her the smallest nod.

"Okay." Raven sets down the bread and takes a breath that seems to require her whole body. "I don't work at Valcott and Finch. That was one of the lies."

"*One* of them?"

"One of many," Saylor chimes in. Raven shoots him a pointed look that seems to say: *don't you dare throw me under the bus, buddy, because I'll take you with me.*

"I don't work there. I've never worked there. I just was familiar with that firm because of the Traces."

The booth feels very small. The chalkboard burger with the cowboy hat grins at me from across the room.

"Then who are you?" I ask. Calm. Too calm. The kind of calm that precedes either an epiphany or a felony.

Raven's hands drift to her stomach. That gesture again—protective, automatic, the same one she made in my office when I asked her how her pregnancy was going. She looks at me and her light eyes fill with tears, and for the first time since she sat down, her energy shifts from manic to something raw and frightened and desperately honest.

"My name is Raven Pecker. And I'm a surrogate."

"Pecker?" Saylor whips his head toward Raven, his brows narrowing in concern. "That's your actual last name?"

Raven returns to her prior chirpy demeanor. "Oh, it sucks. And, my mother's maiden name is Drews. After my parents got divorced she insisted I hyphenate, so for the longest time everyone made fun of me because my last name was—"

"Drew's Pecker. Oh that sucks, Raven." Saylor releases a

sympathetic chuckle. "I'm sorry."

Okay, this is bizarre. I realize Saylor flirts for a living, but no way he went to a funeral with me, found a stranger, struck up a whirlwind romance, mere minutes before asking me out all earnest and adorable. None of this is adding up. Why is Saylor suddenly so invested in...

Oh.

My eyes land shamelessly on Raven's stomach as a thought scuttles into my mind. But there's no way...right? No fucking way.

"Raven." I say her name like a full sentence, effectively silencing her and Saylor. "Whose baby are you carrying?"

She exchanges a nervous glance with Saylor, further confirming my suspicions.

"Whitney's. Well, Whitney and Donor Zero-two-five-three-three-seven." She examines my expressionless face, frozen in place as if her words are Botox. She apparently feels the need to fill the uncomfortable silence. "I just made up the donor number. That's probably not accurate. I only mean to say there's no official dad. So, it's just Whitney's. Well, and yours."

"I'm sorry?" I barely recognize the pitchy, strained sound that squeaks out of my throat, like someone's stepped on a deflating balloon.

The world tilts.

Not dramatically—not a fainting, cinematic swoon. More like the moment on a boat when you realize the dock is moving and you're standing still, and everything you thought was stable is actually floating.

Whitney's baby.

Whitney was having a baby.

Whitney—for whom motherhood was never a question of if but when, who would wake me up with midnight texts about whether "Juniper" was too hipster or "Matilda" too old-fashioned, who carried a small notebook just for jotting down DIY nursery ideas. The Whitney who was already trying to master the perfect after-school chocolate-chip cookie. She was already a mother, she just didn't have her baby yet.

I thought that ship had sailed for her.

How is this possible?

Whitney was going to be a mother. And I didn't know.

"She wanted to tell you," Raven says, as if she can hear my internal thought. "She talked about you all the time. Almost every time I saw her. She'd tell me stories about you—how talented and smart you are, how beautiful and kind. I didn't realize you guys weren't talking. No one would've ever gotten that impression based on the way she talked about you. She said she was going to surprise you with the baby news soon when she officially asked you to be her godmother—"

"Raven." Saylor's voice is gentle but firm. "Slow down. Let her breathe."

But I don't need to breathe. I need to understand.

"Whitney left the baby to me," I say. It's not a question. The pieces have been assembling themselves since the moment Raven sat down—actually, since before that. My first red flag was in the courtyard when Eleanor asked *what are you here to collect*, since the kitchen when she looked at me like I was a threat she hadn't anticipated. "Does Eleanor know about the baby?"

Raven nods.

"Does Eleanor know Whitney wanted me to take the baby if something happened to her?"

She nods again. "You're in her will, Celeste. Whitney told me the day we conceived. She said if anything happened to her, there was only one person in the world she trusted with her baby." Her chin trembles. "She said that person was you. She told me specifically the paperwork was already drawn up."

"Raven, if that were true, the executors would've sent me a copy of the will. Maybe Whitney told you that, but she changed her mind. It's possible in the end, Whitney chose her mother. That's okay."

But Raven's head whips side to side with such vehemence that her blond curls become a blur. "Eleanor is playing dirty. You're in the will, Celeste. Eleanor is trying to hide it from you."

"That's illegal," Saylor says. "She could get in big trouble. I doubt she'd do that and risk the consequences."

"She's not risking anything," I muse to myself. How do I explain to Saylor and Raven that at a certain net worth, you start thinking you can operate above the law?

Saylor reaches across the table and collects my fingers in his. "You okay?"

I nod, but my fingers tell a different story as they grip his hand like it's the only solid thing in a tilting world. "So I wasn't actually invited to the service?"

Raven shrugs innocently. "I mean, I invited you. I don't know if carrying Whitney's baby gives me that authority, but I did it anyway."

No wonder Eleanor looked like she saw a ghost when I appeared in that kitchen. She was trying to gauge if I knew what she knew. If I wanted what she apparently wants. *But Eleanor? With a baby?* That can't be right. Eleanor approaches motherhood like a surgeon performing an appendectomy with an oversized oven mitt—technically possible, but fundamentally disastrous for everyone involved.

I stare at the table. The scratch I was tracing earlier suddenly looks like a river on a map—a path carved into the surface by years of plates and elbows and half-eaten burgers. How many times did Whitney sit in this exact spot? How many conversations did we have at this table, laughing with our mouths full, stealing each other's fries, complaining about boys and bosses and the impossible weight of being young women in a world that wanted us to sit down, shut up, and look pretty?

She sat right here. She ate these burgers. She dreamed about this baby. And when it was time to choose who would raise her child, she chose the woman sitting across from her in this booth—even after that woman abandoned her.

What does that kind of faith feel like from the other side? What did it cost Whitney to write my name in that will, knowing

I might never see it?

"How long have you known?" I ask Saylor. My voice is steady. Flat. I'm holding it together the way I hold together a garment during a fitting—pins, tape, tension, and the knowledge that if I let go, the whole thing falls.

"Since right before the service. Raven told me in the bathroom."

"You knew when you read my speech."

He holds my gaze. Doesn't flinch. "Yes."

"Why didn't you tell me?"

"Timing. Because you needed to give that speech. If I'd told you before, you never would have made it to the podium. And that speech was the most important thing you did today."

I close my eyes. "I didn't even do it. *You did.*"

"Hey," he says, catching my gaze in a way that makes the whole world melt away. "I was a mouthpiece. Your heart. Your words. That's what matters."

He's right of course. If I'd known about the baby, I would have either shattered completely or gone nuclear on Eleanor. The speech would have died in my pocket, and with it, the only apology I had left to give Whitney.

He protected the moment. He let me have it.

I look at the man who held a secret that could have unraveled me, who stood at a podium reading my words while knowing we were on a countdown before my entire world detonated, who made the impossible call to wait—and got it right.

When is the last time a man didn't just do what I said, but anticipated what I needed? When's the last time I trusted anyone to *know what I needed*? It's been so long.

"Excuse me," I mutter. "I need a minute."

I slide out of the booth and walk to the bathroom on legs that feel borrowed. The bathroom is tiny—one stall, a sink, a mirror with a surfboard sticker someone tried to peel off and gave up on. I lock the door, grip the porcelain, and look at my reflection.

I look like a woman who's been through a war and lost and

won simultaneously. Mascara—still holding, somehow, the one victory I'll claim today. Eyes swollen. Lips faded. The Target dress wrinkled from a day of sitting, standing, breaking down, being held.

Whitney left me her baby.

The cry comes from the basement of me. Not the podium tears—those were grief and shame and public agony. This is something else. This is the sound of a door opening that I thought was permanently locked. The door marked *Mother*. The one Greg nailed shut and I wallpapered over and pretended wasn't there.

I think about fourteen years of "we'll revisit." Of Greg patting my hand across dinner tables and saying let's focus on the brand, honey, kids will come later. And later became next year, and next year became maybe, and *maybe* became his affair and my silence and the quiet, suffocating death of a dream I was too afraid to fight for.

Whitney fought for it. Whitney, who was sick, who was dying, who had every reason to give up—she found a surrogate, she planned a pregnancy, she worked hard to get better, and wrote a will in case she didn't. She did every brave thing I was too scared to do. And then, in her final act of bravery, she handed the dream back to me.

"It's okay to be a feminist icon, and want to be a mother, Lessi. You can have it all if you want. Don't let Greg or anyone else make what you want not matter anymore."

I press my forehead against the cool mirror. My breath fogs the glass.

Eleanor wants this baby. The same Eleanor who controlled Whitney's body and hair and choices through mean-spirited commentary and backhanded compliments. Who told her to forgive a cheating fiancé because that's just what women do. Who only got her daughter back because I left first, and is now trying to steal her daughter's last wish.

I think about Raven—twenty-something, probably terrified, four months pregnant with a baby that she doesn't know who to deliver to, forging legal documents and driving to Manhattan because a dead woman trusted her to do the right thing.

I think about Saylor—twenty-six, eating fries in a borrowed suit, holding secrets that don't belong to him, running up stairs two at a time because a woman he barely knows was drowning and he couldn't watch.

I think about Whitney—brave, stubborn, impossible Whitney—who loved me enough to leave me everything and trusted me enough to believe I'd fight for it.

I run cold water over my wrists. Count to four. Hold. Release.

Three minutes. I give myself three minutes. Then I put myself back together, because that's what I do, and that's what Whitney would want me to do, and that's what this baby is going to need from me—a mother who falls apart and gets back up.

I dry my hands. Straighten the dress. Walk out.

Raven and Saylor are sitting in tense silence when I return. Raven's been crying—she left the rest of the rolls untouched, which might be the most alarming sign of distress I've seen from her. Saylor looks like he's been holding his breath since I left the table.

I slide back into the booth. Fold my hands.

"When are you due?" I ask Raven.

"October."

"Okay. And you haven't seen the actual will?"

"No. But I swear Whitney told me."

"Has Eleanor formally filed to contest?"

"I don't know the legal details. But she's been requesting copies of the surrogacy agreement. She has also been watching my diet like a hall monitor after I told her the baby's been craving Flamin' Hot Cheetos. She's acting like it's already decided." Raven's fingers curl into fists against the table. "*Whitney* decided. She just didn't ask Eleanor's permission."

I absorb that. Think about Rina—my text from the courtyard. *Friend, I need your help. Legal stuff.* I didn't know what the legal stuff was when I sent it. Now I do. And Rina, who has never lost a fight she believed in, is going to lose her mind when she hears this.

The burgers arrive. The waitress sets them down between us—the peanut-butter-bacon monstrosity I've been dreaming about for the past hour, and the infamous spicy Hawaiian, both steaming, both absurdly large. The milkshake appears with two straws, exactly as Saylor ordered.

Nobody moves to eat. I just realized how rude it was for us to not wait for Raven to order. Then again, it was kind of rude to barge into my office, masquerading as a legal messenger, to effectively turn my life upside-down with the mountain of secrets she was squatting on. So, I'm going to call it even.

"What do you want to do?" Saylor asks quietly.

I look at the two burgers. Mine and Whitney's. Side by side, the way they always were. We'd eat halfway and swap—her spice for my sweetness, my weirdness for her heat. A trade we made a hundred times without ever acknowledging it was a metaphor for our entire friendship. She gave me courage. I gave her softness. And in the middle, somewhere between peanut butter and pickled jalapeños, we made sense.

I pick up the Hawaiian. Whitney's burger. Lift it to my mouth. Take a bite.

It's perfect. Messy and spicy and overwhelming and exactly right.

I set it down. Wipe barbecue sauce off my chin with the back of my hand, in the most un-ladylike *fuck it* style I can manage.

I look at Raven. Then at Saylor.

"It's not about what I want. If it's true, and Whitney left me this baby, then I'm going to honor her wishes. If Eleanor wants a fight," I say, "*she's got one.*"

Not loud. Not dramatic. Said with teriyaki sauce on my fingers and a milkshake between us, in a booth where my other half used to sit, in a restaurant that smells like the best years of my life. Said with the quiet, irreversible certainty of a woman who has just found something worth fighting for.

Raven's face crumples with relief. She reaches across the table and grabs my hands—sticky sauce and all—and holds them like they're the only solid thing in a world that's been spinning for months.

"Thank you," she whispers. "Thank you, thank you, thank you."

"Don't thank me. Thank Whitney. She always had better taste than me." I squeeze Raven's hands. "Except in burgers. My burger is superior and I will die on that hill."

Raven laughs—wet, messy, the kind of laugh that's sixty percent crying. "Yeah, what the hell is that abomination anyway? Who puts peanut butter on a burger?"

My throat closes. I hold on tighter.

Across the table, Saylor is quiet. I glance at him and find that expression again—the one I saw in the courtyard after the speech, the one I don't have a name for yet. It's not the look Greg used to give me, which was always about ownership, or appraisal, or the performance of caring. It's not the look clients give me when they're pleased with a design.

It's the look of a man who seems fascinated watching someone go from a caterpillar to a butterfly. One earth-shattering truth. Whitney has a baby. She wanted me to have this baby if she couldn't. Therefore, the mission is clear. My purpose set. Never in the history of history has someone evolved and spread their wings this quickly. That's the Whitney magic.

The part of my speech I couldn't quite put into words. Whitney made people realize themselves. The good, the bad. She was a mirror, and the reflection was always the quiet truth.

I pick up the peanut-butter burger. Hold it up.

"To Whitney," I say.

Saylor picks up his half of the Hawaiian. Raven snags a roll, inviting herself into my toast.

"To Whitney," they echo.

We eat. And for the first time all day, the grief doesn't feel like drowning.

It feels like the beginning of something.

Chapter 8

Saylor

Do you think I'm too young for you, or do you think you're too old for me? Because those are two different things.

After dinner, Celeste, who had been debating, decided she didn't want to drive back to the city after all. She offered to get Raven a room at a nice hotel, but Raven insisted on driving back to Jersey City before dark settled. Celeste bit back her concern, but I saw the space between her eyes crinkle in anguish. Already, she feels protective over this baby. *Now, her baby.*

After saying our goodbyes and see-you-soons, Celeste and I climbed into her vehicle with nowhere to go. I suggested a Motel 6 that I spotted on the drive up. She looked at me as if I'd suggested she bathe butt-naked in toxic waste. Instead, with one phone call, Celeste conjures up a suite at the Hampton's most exclusive bed and breakfast—a place that according to their website mere mortals couldn't book with six months' notice and a personal connection.

Actually, that's a slight exaggeration. It was two calls. The first was to her assistant to carry out said task, and when that flopped, Celeste called her contact personally. Judging by the way Celeste's nostrils are flaring as she tries to keep calm, her assistant, Margot, needs to be very concerned about her job.

According to Celeste, Margot is getting a six-figure annual salary to consistently drop the ball. She's always leaving work early for mental health reasons and even tried to use petty cash for her weekly mani-pedi. Margot has set very clear boundaries about her work-life balance which apparently is a ninety-ten split the wrong way. Look, if you're making six figures to be someone's right hand, sometimes that hand needs to answer the phone on a Saturday when your boss's life is imploding. That's the job you signed up for. That's what the extra zero in your paycheck is for.

"Thank you, Dianne. You are so very kind. Please don't worry about dinner service, we already ate... No need for champagne... Yes, I attended the service, thank you for asking... Flat water is perfectly fine."

I can only hear Celeste's part of the conversation, but whoever is on the other end is asking enough questions to renew a passport.

She ends the call and types an address into the GPS which instantly demands I make a U-turn.

We drive in silence for a bit. Through the car window, the Hamptons blur into a mirage of manicured hedges and mansions that probably have names instead of addresses. I try to enjoy the scenery, but eventually the silence between us stretches thin, pressing against my chest like the last seconds before breaking the surface after diving too deep.

"So, Tidewater House?" I glance at the GPS.

"For privacy. It's highly unlikely any of the funeral guests are staying there. You'd need a reservation months in advance."

"How'd we get in with such late notice?"

She bites the inside of her cheek until a small hollow appears beneath her carefully applied blush. "In my world, making a call means pulling a favor. The inn owner's daughter is an up-and-coming runway model. I might've hired for a few shows in exchange for—"

"A room that's always ready for you."

Celeste turns her head, looking out the window. "Saylor, can I ask you an honest question? Don't spare my feelings."

"This feels like a trap, but I'll bite. Please continue."

"I don't really come off maternal, do I?"

"Sorry?" I steal a glance away from the road to study her face. Nothing there to read. Just the perfect profile of a woman lost in a thought beyond the glass. "What is maternal to you?"

She pauses. "That's the thing. I don't really know. Whit and I were both raised by parents that saw us as investments. With all the money in the world, they sent us to the best private schools, we had name-brand clothes, got brand-new cars on our sixteenth birthdays. But none of that felt...warm. And every generous thing they did for us was laced with expectations. We were dividends yet to be paid out. That's not the kind of mom Whit wanted to be. That's not the kind of mother I want to be. But how can I be something I've never known?"

The question hangs in the car like smoke from a fire neither of us started but both of us feel responsible for putting out. It's not the kind of fire you smother right away—the kind you watch to see how long it glows.

I think about Mum. About the way she'd pack my school lunches with little notes folded into the napkin—not inspirational quotes or anything precious, just simple observations. *Thank you for feeding Red this morning. You're so responsible, Saylor. I'm proud of you. Thought you should know.* Or: *You are so loved, my sweet boy. I'll have cookies waiting when you come home.* I'd unfold these in the cafeteria and roll my eyes because I was twelve and resisting all forms of affection from your mother was the entire job description. But the memory has lingered this whole time. It planted something deep in the chasms of nostalgia, and all these little seeds was my mum planting a happy childhood. I never felt lonely or lost, even without my dad around. She was my everything.

"You didn't have to come to this, Celeste," I say. "Who could possibly hold you accountable?"

"Me." She turns to look at me. "Of course I had to come. Of course I had to be here. She was my closest friend."

"Sure, but nobody at the funeral would judge you. You don't speak to someone for two years, space is natural. Sometimes you can't go back."

She's still not looking at me, but I register her jostling her head in disagreement. "I didn't do it for the people at the funeral. I did it for Whit. Because I loved her. *Love her.*"

"I figure that's motherhood. Loving someone past your own comfort. Showing up even if you're not sure they'll see you. Doing the right thing, even if it matters to no one but you and your kid. All the puzzle pieces are there, Celeste. You're going to make a wonderful mother."

I can feel her gaze on me now. "Are you sure?"

I keep my eyes on the road because if I look at her right now, I'll lose the thread. "Definitely. Maternal isn't some gene you're born with. It's not a personality type. It's the willingness to carry something that matters more than you do and try your best even when you're terrified. You've been doing that all day."

The silence that follows is different from the one before. Warmer. Less pressure. Like the surface broke and we're both breathing now.

"Whitney used to say I'd be a great mother if I could get out of my own way," Celeste says quietly. "I told her that was a big 'if.'"

"Sounds like Whitney knew you better than you know yourself."

"That was kind of her gift. She'd hold up a mirror and you'd see yourself the way she saw you—which was always more generous than the version you were carrying around." Celeste's voice has the particular quality of someone talking to a memory instead of a person. Soft at the edges. Present tense slipping into past. "She made people realize themselves."

Tidewater House rises through the trees like something out of a catalog that Celeste's company would shoot—stone and cedar, tasteful landscaping, the kind of lighting designed to make you exhale the moment you step out of the car. The GPS announces our arrival. Once we're parked, I grab my bag and Celeste's, refusing her help like the dutiful pack-mule that I am.

The lobby smells like cedarwood and white tea and money that's been around long enough to stop being loud about it.

A woman at the front desk greets Celeste by name—well, Ms. Prescott, which earns her a pointed look before Celeste clarifies *it's Brinley*—and walks us to the suite personally, narrating the amenities like she's guiding us through a small museum. The complimentary robe closet. The espresso machine. The fact that turndown service includes lavender on the pillow, as if the pillow needed a personality.

The suite is absurd.

Not gaudy absurd. Square-footage absurd. A living room with a sectional that could seat a football team. A bedroom through French doors with a king bed that looks like a cloud applied for a job in furniture. A bathroom with a freestanding tub and one of those rain shower heads that makes you feel like you're being gently baptized. A kitchenette with a marble countertop and a fresh-fruit bowl which will probably only ever be decoration. What a waste. I'm eating that papaya before we go.

There's a balcony overlooking the ocean. The waves are invisible in the dark but I can hear them—steady and stolid, like the sound of the world breathing.

"This is..." I turn a full circle. "More square footage than my apartment, and all of the apartments on my floor. *Combined.*"

Celeste surveys the suite with the flat appraisal of someone who exists in spaces like this regularly. "It'll do." She winks at me. "The couch pulls out into a queen-size. There are extra blankets in the closet if you get chilly."

I point through the French doors. "Want me to check the closet for monsters first?"

"Cute."

She snags her luggage from where I set it down and disappears into the bathroom. The door clicks shut and a moment later I hear the shower start, and beneath the sound of expensive plumbing and old stone walls, the muffled cadence of someone letting the day out in the only private space she has left.

I don't go to the door. I don't call out.

Instead, I sit on the sectional and pull out my phone.

Hey. Weekend went well. Long story. How are you feeling?

Mum responds before I've set the phone down. She's always near it—her portal to the world beyond the apartment that has the nerve to trap her in her home by three flights of daunting, concrete stairs. I wonder if she's needing anything right now and refusing to ask for it. Refusing to bother anyone or take up the space she rightfully deserves.

Mum

I'm fine, love. Callie stopped by for stretches. We watched a cooking show after. How was the event?

You know. Work. Met some interesting people.

Mum

Interesting people or Interesting person? Unrelated, I'd love to be a grandmother before I die. *Winking face*

I stare at the screen. Mum can read subtext through a phone the way seismologists read tremors—subtle shifts in language that most people would miss, picked up instantly and filed away for future interrogation.

People, Mum. Plural.

Mum

Mm-hmm. Are you eating? You've been looking thin lately.

I literally just ate two bizarrely delicious burgers.

Mum

Good boy. Come home safe. Love you to the moon and back. And a few more trips. xx

Love you, Mum. Call me if you need anything.

I sit with the phone in my hand and think about the conversation that just happened, the one that looks identical to every other exchange we've had for years. Her pretending she's fine. Me pretending I'm fine. Both of us fluent in the same warm, careful lie.

After what seems like an entire season of random TikTok videos of food-eating competitions, Celeste finally finishes her shower. The bathroom door hinges release a nearly imperceptible sigh as it swings open, releasing a cloud of lavender-scented moisture into the room.

Celeste emerges wrapped in one of the hotel robes—white, enormous, swallowing her frame so completely she looks like a very elegant ghost. Her face is scrubbed clean. No makeup. No jewelry. No armor. Without the foundation and the mascara and the architectural precision she applies to her appearance like structural engineering, she looks different. Not younger, exactly. Unguarded. Like a rough sketch where all the essential lines are visible but none of the polish.

Her eyes are red but she's steady. The crying is finished. Tucked away in whatever compartment Celeste stores the things she doesn't want anyone to witness.

She cinches the robe higher. "Do I look like I just escaped a hospital ward?"

"A very exclusive, fancy hospital ward."

"Thank you. That's exactly the energy I was going for." She peers over at the kitchenette. "Please tell me there's wine."

I investigate. The minibar is stocked like a small, curated liquor store—the kind that charges by the adjective. I find a bottle of something French and red and pour two glasses, feeling mildly fraudulent because I couldn't tell you the difference between a table blend and a Malbec if my life depended on it.

Celeste accepts the glass, settles into the far corner of the sectional, and tucks her legs beneath her. The robe fans out around her like a wedding gown. She takes a sip, closes her eyes, and lets out a breath that seems to originate from her toes.

"Do you want to talk about it?" I ask, taking the opposite end of the couch. "Or do you want to not talk about it?"

"I want to not talk about it. But if we sit in silence, I'll spiral, and spiraling in a bathrobe feels especially bleak." She opens her eyes. "TV?"

Mounted above the fireplace, angled toward the sectional, lies the perfect distraction. I find the remote on the coffee table and click it on. A streaming menu appears.

"What are we watching?" I ask.

"Something with zero emotional depth. Something where the biggest problem is whether the popular girl gets asked to prom."

I scroll, and with the enthusiasm of a toddler receiving a popsicle, she suddenly shrieks.

"Stop. *That one.*"

My thumb pauses on the down arrow. "This one? *She's All That*?"

Celeste's face transforms. The grief, the exhaustion, the worry lines that have been etched into her forehead since approximately six o'clock this morning—all of it vanishes, replaced by the expression of a woman who has just been reunited with something she loves.

"Oh my God. Yes. You've never seen *She's All That*?"

"No. Is it an older movie?"

"Not *that* old," Celeste answers. "It's a masterpiece of American cinema. Freddie Prinze Jr. in overalls at the prom? That is a cultural moment. That transcends generational divides."

I shrug as I flip over to the button that says, more information. "It was released in nineteen-ninety-nine. The year I was born."

Celeste's smile collapses through a series of reactions. Her jaw drops, eyes widening with the stunned recognition of someone who's just been ambushed. Then her features contort into something more visceral—eyebrows pinching together, mouth twisting sideways—as if she's just discovered an uncomfortable truth about herself that can never be unlearned.

"Right. Ninety-nine," she muses.

"Okay, Celeste, tell me the truth. Do you think I'm too young for you, or do you think you're too old for me? Because those are two different things."

She locks onto my gaze, challenge dancing in her eyes, her smirk guiding me to the metaphorical edge of my seat. But "let's watch the movie" is all she says.

I press play. The opening credits roll and I realize immediately that this movie is exactly as dated as advertised. The fashion alone is a time capsule. We enter the realm of chunky highlights, cargo pants, platform sandals. The soundtrack sounds like the inside of a store that went out of business. I have no idea what's happening and I am deeply invested.

Celeste provides context. It starts as quiet observations on culture, as if she's a historian trying to walk me through a different era. "Back then that haircut was considered sexy, by the way" is just the beginning. Eventually, Celeste's commentary escalates into full narration. She knows every scene. She mouths certain lines before the actors say them. When Freddie Prinze Jr. removes his sunglasses and does the slow-motion head turn, she clutches her chest like a woman receiving medical news.

"This was it," she whispers. "The swoon."

"He took off sunglasses. Indoors."

"Yeah." She shoots me a look. "And it changed my life."

I'm laughing. Not the measured, strategic laugh I've trained myself to deploy at work events and client dinners. The real kind—the one that starts in my stomach and ambushes me like an intrusive thought, the one that sounds like it belongs to someone who laughs all the time, which I don't. Celeste watches me with the satisfied expression of a woman who intended exactly this, and I realize this might be the first time I've laughed like this in months.

The movie plays. We drink the wine. She narrates the prom montage and a scene involving a hacky sack that she insists was "athletically groundbreaking." By the time credits roll, she's already queuing up the next one.

I'm so exhausted. I was hanging by a thread when I got home this morning. Stretching out the sleep-deprivation is almost physically painful. I most definitely should not be operating heavy machinery at this point, but there's no way I'm going to sleep on this precious opportunity to see Celeste giggling like a school girl. It becomes my instant life-mission to stay the hell awake.

"*Ten Things I Hate About You*. Nonnegotiable. Let your education on good cinema continue."

"You mean my education on guys you thought were hot in the nineties. Is this the one with—"

"Heath Ledger. Yes. And if you say a single negative word about Heath Ledger in this room, I will make you sleep on the balcony."

"Understood."

Now this one I've seen—or at least, clips. *The Taming of the Shrew* in a high school. The paintball scene. The bleachers. Heath Ledger singing on the stadium steps, which is one of the most genuinely charming things I've ever watched a human being do on film. It's right up there with the dude holding the boombox over his head, serenading that girl from her bedroom window.

This is actually fun. A nice escape from the monotony of helplessness.

Somewhere during the second act, the geography of the couch shifts. It happens the way shorelines change—so gradually that you only notice when you look up and the landscape is different. Celeste started in the far corner. Now she's in the middle, her feet tucked under the throw blanket, her shoulder three inches from mine. I don't remember either of us moving. But here we are.

"Can I tell you something?" she says during a quiet scene.

"Of course."

Celeste looks at me. Her eyes are wet but she's smiling. "Whitney would really like you."

"I think I'd like her too."

The credits roll. She doesn't start another movie. I expect her to—the third pillar, *Clueless*, the completed trinity as she explained—but instead she just sits there, wrapped in her robe and the blanket and the quiet, looking at the dark screen like she's watching something the rest of us can't see.

"One more?" I ask.

"I'd like to, but I am operating on approximately four percent battery."

"Is that why you stopped chattering through the whole movie?" I tease.

"Yes, the commentary function has shut down to preserve core operations. Aren't you tired?"

She's scooted at least a few more inches closer. I look her right in the eye. "Not anymore." And it's the truth. For some reason, this is invigorating.

She queues it up. Alicia Silverstone appears on screen in a plaid skirt, and Celeste exhales into the couch like a woman who has finally found the one place in the world where nothing is expected of her.

Twelve minutes in, her head finds my shoulder.

I don't move. I don't adjust. I don't do the thing I should do, which is shift slightly, create a buffer, maintain whatever boundary existed between us before this weekend burned it to the ground. Her hair is still damp and smells like the fancy hotel shampoo—not the Head & Shoulders from this morning, something botanical and French—but underneath it, there's just her. Soft and close and leaning against me like I'm a wall she trusts not to move.

I've been leaned on before. Professionally, personally, physically. I have been the shoulder and the wall and the steady thing that holds while other people fall apart. That's the role. That's the function. That's the reason I'm in the room.

But this doesn't feel like that.

This feels like the opposite of that. This feels like someone leaning into me not because they need something, but because they want to be near. And the difference between those two things—need and want, function and choice—is so vast and so unfamiliar that I don't know what to do with it except sit very still and let it happen.

Her breathing changes around the twenty-minute mark. Slower. Deeper. Her hand has come to rest on my forearm, fingers loosely curled, and the weight of her against my shoulder is slight and warm and devastating in its simplicity.

She's asleep.

I reach for the throw blanket and pull it over both of us without moving her. On screen, Cher is arguing about something in a debate class and I've lost all track of the plot. My eyes are heavy. The sectional has magic powers of sedation because it feels impossible to move at the moment, trapped under this cozy haze.

I should carry her to the bedroom. I should sleep on the opposite end of this enormous couch, or on the floor, or on the balcony she threatened me with. I should maintain some version of the professional distance that stopped existing approximately nine hours ago when I ran up a set of stairs and held her while she fell apart in front of two hundred people.

Instead, I tip my head back against the cushion and close my eyes.

Tomorrow I'll go back to Alphabet City. Back to the cramped apartment and the medication schedule and the sticky note on my nightstand with Dr. Yassa's email that I still haven't sent. Tomorrow I'll return the suit and slide back into the life that was waiting for me before this weekend—the one where I tend bar, guard doors, take bookings from Rina, and sleep four hours. The life where I take care of everyone except myself.

But tonight, on a couch in a suite I could never afford, in a suit I didn't pay for, with a woman who asked me if she seems maternal and doesn't realize that the question itself is the answer—tonight, I'm not carrying anyone.

And someone, whether she knows it or not, is carrying me.

I fall asleep to the sound of Celeste breathing and Alicia Silverstone explaining something about the federal mail system, and I don't dream about anything at all.

Chapter 9

Saylor

We slept. We were together.
What part of this are you struggling with?

I'm not sure what I've been waiting for. But I've waited patiently for *nine days*.

Nine whole days since the funeral. Nine days since the Riptide booth. Nine days since I fell asleep on a couch next to Celeste who is now taking up a greedy amount of space in my brain. But it's obvious Celeste isn't thinking about me.

I've heard absolutely nothing. I didn't even grab her number which seems ludicrous now. She dropped me off at home the morning after we fell asleep on the couch like she was eager to get rid of me, which didn't feel great, but she had a lot on her mind.

Which is fine. *It's fine.* She doesn't owe me updates. She's not my girlfriend. She's not my friend. She's a client I spent a weekend with, and the weekend is over, and whatever happened between us—the trauma bond, the effortless way she let me hold her when she was about to collapse—that's finished. Filed under "memorable experiences" right alongside the time I watched a man cry over *Hamilton* from the third row and the night I talked a stranger through her divorce at a bar in the West Village.

Except it's not filed. It's not anywhere close to filed. It's loose in my brain like a marble in an empty room, rolling into every corner every time I tilt my head.

I know the basics through Rina when I not-so-casually asked how Celeste was doing with the baby. Rina gave me a tight-lipped, attorney-like reply. What I gathered between the legal jargon is that Rina put Celeste in touch with the best family attorney in the Tri-state area. Eleanor is indeed contesting the will, that absolutely did name Celeste as guardian to the baby. Raven's pregnancy is going well, and she has an upcoming ultrasound to find out the sex of the baby. But that's it. That's all I'm allowed to know because even though I feel like I started this quest, I've been kicked off the great trek to Mordor.

The details—the legal strategy, the caseworker, whether Celeste is sleeping or spiraling or pacing back and forth in her living room at four in the morning, whether she's missing me—those, I don't know. Because I don't have a right to know. Because the funeral is over, and the appropriate thing to do is return to my regularly scheduled life and stop checking my phone like a teenager who's been left on read.

My regularly scheduled life, for the record, is not cooperating with this plan.

Monday through Wednesday I pick up shifts at the bar. Thursday I spend the morning with Mum, reorganizing her medications, fixing the loose grab bar in the bathroom that's started wobbling. By Friday, I've run out of tasks and chores to keep myself busy, so I sit in my room alone and stare at my phone. I scroll, but not even dancing chicken videos or food-eating competitions are entertaining enough to hold my attention. Usually on Friday nights, I see if Rina has work. I make so much more as an escort than a bartender or bouncer, but after last weekend, it seems impossible.

It's hard to explain, but I already feel the distance between me and Celeste. Literally. Physically. I don't want to take any more steps in the wrong direction. I need a change. I can't keep going like I have been. It's sprinting in place, my bones ache, my muscles are stripped, and I'm getting *nowhere.*

I close the app. Pick up the Rolex case from my nightstand.

Turn it over in my hands.

The watch is worth thirty, maybe forty thousand dollars. It's sitting in my apartment like a ticking time bomb with a price tag. I can't keep it. I can't pawn it. And I can't pretend that the only reason I want to return it in person is because I'm ethically opposed to FedEx.

I want to see her. That's the truth, stripped of every justification I've been constructing for nine days. I want to see Celeste. I want to know she's okay. I want to sit in whatever room she's in and feel that thing again—the recognition, the frequency, the sense that someone else speaks the language I've been speaking alone.

Before I can stop my thumbs, I'm googling Celeste's headquarters. An impressive building in the ritzy part of Manhattan populates on the image search. It's only fifteen minutes away.

Oi, this is fucking crazy.

But I've already swung my legs around the edge of my bed. Already rummaging through my small closet for a shirt with a collar. I've already decided I'm getting answers today. After nine days, two hours, and roughly four hundred phone checks since I last saw her—I put on the nicest things I own, tuck the Rolex case under my arm, and take the subway to Midtown.

The building has a security desk. Two guards, one turnstile, the kind of badge-access system that says you either belong here or you don't. I do not. I also do not have a plan for this, which I probably should have considered during the subway ride instead of staring at my own reflection in the dark glass and rehearsing opening lines like an understudy.

A woman in a pencil skirt and headphones is walking toward the turnstile with her badge already extended. I fall in two steps behind her, close enough to seem like we're together, far enough to not seem like I'm following her. She badges through. The turnstile clicks. I slip through in the gap before it resets, angling my body so the Rolex case looks like a delivery and my collared shirt looks like a uniform and my entire vibe says I do this every day, I'm bored of this building, please don't look at me.

Neither guard looks at me.

Full ops success. I'm in.

The lifts are a wall of polished steel. I press the top-floor button because if you're Celeste Brinely—if you've built an empire from a sketchbook and a name you inherited from your grandmother—you don't sit on the third floor. You sit at the top. Where the view matches the altitude of your standards.

The doors open on forty-seven and the guess pays off.

It's chaos. Beautiful chaos—the productive kind, where everyone is moving with purpose and nobody has time to question the man in the collared shirt who just stepped off the lift holding a box. Garment racks line the hallway. Fabric bolts lean against the wall like colorful drunks. Someone speed-walks past me carrying a mannequin torso under each arm, which is a sentence I never expected to witness in real life.

I keep walking. Down the main corridor, past open workrooms where sewing machines chatter and designers pin things to forms and a woman argues passionately into a phone about something called a "hand feel" which I'm choosing not to investigate. Everyone is too busy to notice me, which is the beautiful thing about creative environments—if you walk with enough confidence, you become part of the scenery.

A sign on the wall catches my eye. Sleek, minimal, the same font as the logo on the building's exterior. It reads 'Celeste.' It's only in this moment I realize how freaking confusing it is to have your company name be your name. Because where am I headed right now? Celeste's office? Or a boardroom?

I follow the arrow anyway. The hallway narrows, the noise dims, and the energy shifts from workshop to executive. Quieter. Cleaner. The air smells different up here—less fabric dust, more ambition.

There's a desk outside a glass-walled corner office. An executive assistant's station, clearly—dual monitors, phone console, a small orchid that's somehow both alive and resentful. The chair is empty. No assistant. No gatekeeper. Just an unguarded threshold between me and the woman I've been thinking about for nine days straight.

Through the glass, Celeste is at her desk. Head down. Reading something with the kind of puzzled intensity that suggests the document is written in hieroglyphics. Her hair is pulled back. Black blazer. Glasses I haven't seen before—reading glasses, thin-framed, making her look like a very stylish professor who's about to fail your entire thesis.

Oh, shit. Not good. This naughty-professor look is doing things beneath my belt, and I want my presence here to be a pleasant surprise, not predatory.

I knock on the glass.

Her head comes up. And for one unfiltered second—before the composure kicks in, before the armor slides back into position—her face does something I wasn't prepared for. Her lips part. Her eyes widen. Her hand freezes over the document mid-turn. It's not surprise, exactly. It's something rawer than that. Recognition. Relief. The look of someone who's been waiting for a knock they didn't believe was coming.

Then she blinks, and Celeste, CEO, returns to the building.

She stands. Walks around the desk. Opens the glass door herself, and stands there looking at me with her arms not yet crossed but clearly considering it.

"How did you get up here?"

"Charisma and a collared shirt."

"Security didn't stop you?"

"Security was...busy."

"Busy?" she echoes in disbelief. "That's concerning, Saylor. Security is here to make everyone feel safe at their place of work. No strangers."

"And they're doing a great job. I feel very secure. I haven't seen even one stranger on the way up."

Her mouth twitches. She steps aside just enough to let me through, and I walk into her office. It's everything I imagined and nothing like I've seen before—enormous windows, sculptures in the corner catching the light, sketches pinned to a corkboard behind her desk, the faint scent of something expensive that I can't identify but that my brain has already filed under her. There's a mannequin in the corner wearing what looks like a half-finished dress, draped in muslin with pins catching the sun and glowing, like tiny lightsabers.

Celeste closes the door. The lock clicks behind me.

Now she crosses her arms. "Why are you here, Saylor? Is Rina okay?"

The question hangs between us in the glass-walled office, forty-seven floors above a city that keeps moving even when the people in it are standing completely still. Through the windows, Manhattan does its thing, cabs and cranes and a million people going somewhere, and none of it matters because Celeste is looking at me with those doe-like brown eyes and I've forgotten every reasonable answer I rehearsed on the subway.

"I came to see you."

Her fingers press to her temples as she tilts her head, studying me like I'm a design flaw in an otherwise perfect garment. "But why?"

"You know why." I beg her to understand the sentiment so I don't have to awkwardly explain it. But she stands stoically, like she's frozen in place, waiting to thaw out.

She holds my gaze. I hold hers. The silence is a living thing—it breathes, it expands, it takes up residence between us like a third person in the room who knows more than either of us is willing to say. I can see her jaw working, the almost-imperceptible clench and release of someone who is deciding, in real time, how much of herself to reveal.

She obviously decides: not yet.

"I don't know why. It's why I asked," she says, but the edge is gone from her tone. What's left is quieter. Curious, maybe. Or tired of pretending.

I lift the Rolex case. "I only came to return this." It's a cop-out, but I'm reading the room. And everything in here is saying I really don't belong. This was a bad idea. Impulse control is a skill I clearly lack.

"I meant for you to keep it. As a thank-you for being such a lovely date, Saylor. Actually, you were so much more than that. An instant friend and confidant. I appreciate it."

Damn she built the walls up high in just over a week. I might as well be on my tiptoes trying to look over the Great Wall of China.

"I'd have no use for it besides pawning it. Something this beautiful shouldn't end up at Fast Jerry's on Eighth Avenue."

"Who is Fast Jerry?"

"He's a loan shark who owns a pawn shop that you should only go to out of pure desperation. He pays decent but you're lucky to make it out alive."

Her left eye squints. "What? Do what you please with the watch, Saylor. But please don't go to Fast Jerry's anymore. There's a reputable used jewelry exchanger on Fifth. Very honest and *legal*. Would you like a card?"

"I can't accept a gift like this from a client. You know it's too much." I hold up my thumb and forefinger, pinching the air. "And it makes me feel about this big."

"I didn't mean to—" She sighs. "Just keep it. *Please*."

I set the case on the edge of her desk. She looks at it. Looks at me. Neither of us moves it.

"I bet you I'm more stubborn than you are," I say.

"I highly doubt that—"

A knock on the glass door startles us both. Through the glass, a woman is pressing her face close to the door with the confused urgency of someone who has just discovered that her own office is locked against her. She's young, brunette, holding a smoothie in one hand and her phone in the other, wearing an expression that suggests she's never encountered a locked door in her professional life and isn't sure this is real.

Celeste closes her eyes. A deep breath enters through her nose and exits through her teeth in a controlled stream that could strip wallpaper.

She unlocks the door.

"Margot."

"Hi! Sorry, I was just—the door was locked? I didn't know it locked. Did you know it locked? I brought you a smoothie."

"Yes, Margot. I'm aware my office locks. And I didn't ask for a smoothie."

"I know, but I passed by this place and stopped for a boba tea. This is way healthier than coffee..."

"Well thank you for watching my waistline, but I specifically sent you out for a cortado. I need a boost. I'm going to be here all night working on the fall line."

"Which is why this is better. It's brain food...it's green...it has spirulina." Margot holds it out like a peace offering from a country that doesn't understand the terms of the war. I'm the outsider here, and even I want to tell her to zip her lips and stop digging her grave.

"Did you call the linen mill?"

"I left a voicemail."

"A voicemail."

"Two voicemails, actually."

"And the Bergdorf meeting?"

"Still on the calendar for next Tuesday."

"Which Tuesday slot? The two o'clock in Midtown or the two thirty in Chicago? Because last I checked, both are on there, and I haven't yet figured out how to split myself into two separate women, though at this point I'm considering it."

Margot blinks. Looks at the smoothie. Looks at Celeste. Looks at me, as if I might offer a lifeline. I offer nothing. This is between a woman and her assistant and the deep, abiding chasm between them.

"I'm not sure if the meeting is at their office or yours."

Celeste closes her eyes, grimacing like she's chewing on glass. "Could you find out please?"

"Uh, yes. I'll...go check on that," Margot says, retreating with the smoothie still extended, like someone backing away from a bear while holding a picnic basket.

"Margot," Celeste calls after her. "If the meeting is at their office, can you please arrange my travel?"

"Yes." She nods enthusiastically. "Totally can do that. Where are you going, and what days?"

Celeste catches my gaze, steam coming out of her ears, wordlessly asking me if I see what she has to deal with.

"You know what, Margot? Don't worry about it. Just confirm the meeting location."

Margot sets the smoothie down by the side table toward the front of the office. Only when she's on the other side of the door and out of sight does Celeste hurry to the table to collect the smoothie. "This is art. Hand-sculpted pottery by the apprentice to the pope who said throwing clay is how he has his spiritual epiphanies. This is the last piece he made before he fully joined the church. And now...there is a green smoothie ring on it."

Celeste stares at the ceiling for a long moment. When she looks at me again, there's something almost funny in her expression—the dark humor of a woman who is fighting for custody of an unborn baby, battling her dead best friend's mother in court, and yet somehow her most persistent daily crisis is a six-figure assistant who can't operate a calendar.

"She's my biggest problem," Celeste says. "I'm in a legal war with Eleanor Montgomery-Trace, I'm trying to prepare for a caseworker who's going to evaluate every corner of my life to justify to everyone why I'm not fit to be a mother, my new fall line is refusing to come together even well past its deadline, and somehow the thing that's going to break me is Margot and her fucking spirulina smoothies."

Celeste buries her face in her hands and it takes everything in me not to cross the space between us and wrap her in my arms. I'm not on the clock today. Am I even allowed to touch her anymore?

"What's she not doing? Besides everything?" I ask.

Celeste crosses the room, sets the smoothie down on a coaster on the coffee table, then sits on the edge of her desk. The executive posture loosens—just a fraction, just enough for me to see the exhaustion underneath. "The personal things. The things I can't delegate to my legal team or my design team. The things that require someone to actually show up and do the work." She rubs the bridge of her nose beneath her glasses. "The attorney warned me that Eleanor has a strong case. This is no longer about what Whit wanted. This is about what's best for the baby. She thinks it'll help my case if I look less like a Manhattan CEO who lives in a high-rise and more like someone who's prepared to raise a child. Eleanor's already told the court that my lifestyle is incompatible with motherhood. My apartment is a glass box in Tribeca. It screams 'childless career woman.' It doesn't scream 'nursery.'"

"So you need a different space."

"Well I *have* a different space. My parents left me their house in Westchester when they relocated to Milan. It's been sitting empty for six years. It has a yard. It has a neighborhood with good schools. It has everything a caseworker would want to see." She pauses. "It also hasn't been touched since my parents left. There are rooms with sheets over the furniture. The kitchen hasn't been updated since the early two thousands. There's a loveseat in the master bedroom in French Script."

"French Script?"

"You know, with all those calligraphy letters printed all over cream linen in no sensical fashion, like a fabric printer's machine had a nervous breakdown. It isn't dangerous to a child, but it is miserably outdated. I swear the only thing worse than my mom's cooking is her taste in textiles."

I snort, then try to cover it with a cough. "You need someone to fix it up."

"I need someone to make it look like a home instead of a time capsule. And I need it done before the caseworker's visit, which is"—she checks her phone—"two weeks away. There's too much to coordinate, and you know how contractors are. About five years into our marriage, a renovation nearly broke me and Greg." She shrugs. "In hindsight, I wish it would've. I could have saved myself some wasted years."

"I can do it."

Celeste's eyes snap to mine. "You can do what?"

"The house. I can get it ready in time. I'm good with my hands—I've been maintaining a building with a broken lift and a landlord who thinks 'responsive' means returning a call within the same fiscal quarter. Painting, repairs, light renovation, furniture assembly—I've done all of it for my apartment and a couple neighbors, too. And I work fast."

"Saylor, this isn't a small apartment. This is an entire suburban house. Five thousand square feet. Five bedrooms. Four full bathrooms and two half-baths. An entire backyard with a deck that's falling apart. It would take a small army to make that house presentable in time."

I lean against the wall, smiling at her smugly. "You just said you don't have time to vet contractors and manage a rapid renovation while running a company and fighting a custody battle. But you've got me. And I've got nothing but time and a really strong opinion about wallpaper."

She's studying me. I can practically see the calculations running behind her eyes—the risk, the logistics, the fact that letting me into her childhood home is a different kind of intimacy than letting me read her eulogy. One is public. The other is closets full of old photographs and rooms where she grew up and the particular vulnerability of showing someone the place where you became yourself.

"Why?" she asks. Not confrontational. Genuinely curious. "Why are you so insistent on being a part of my life?"

I point at her. "I promise you, when I figure that out, you'll be the first to know. All that matters is right now, *I do*...want to be a part of this. I want to help."

The office is quiet. Through the glass walls, the forty-seventh floor continues its choreography—designers moving, machines humming, Margot presumably googling "how to operate a Google calendar." But in here, it's just us and the Rolex on the desk and the question of what happens next.

"I'd pay you," Celeste says. "For the work. Contractor rates."

"You don't have to—"

"I'm not going to let you renovate my house for free. This isn't a favor. It's a job. You'll be compensated, and we'll keep it strictly professional."

"Professional. Right. Like the funeral."

"The funeral *was* professional."

"I mean...we did sleep together."

Her face flushes and she looks around the office as if there's anyone besides the faceless mannequin to hear us. "We did not."

"You fell asleep on my shoulder watching *Clueless*."

"That's not sleeping together."

I blink at her. "We slept. We were together. What part of this are you struggling with?" It takes Herculean effort to keep my smirk from breaking free.

"Saylor, I want to make something clear."

I roll my wrist, gesturing for her to continue.

"My divorce was really hard on me. And unfortunately, Greg and I can't seem to escape each other's orbits. I'll admit, Rina and her agency helped me feel less like a loser. That's why I brought Forrest to a few weddings and ceremonies. That's why I brought you to the funeral. I'm not proud of it; it was a survival mechanism. But I'm knocking on the door of forty, okay? A hot and heavy romance with a guy that's way too young for me is not a destination, it'd only be a detour. And I don't have time for detours. So when I say professional, *I mean it.*"

I let the silence do its dance, too afraid to disturb the thick tension growing between us. I love the way she's staring at me like she wants me to look away first. To prove I see her truth and understand it. But I don't. "So what I'm hearing is you think our romance would be hot and heavy?"

"Saylor," she snaps.

I grin. She doesn't—but she wants to. I can see it in the fault line forming at the corner of her mouth, the tremor before the quake.

"Fine," I say. "Contractor rates. Pay me whatever you like. I'll start this very weekend if you give me the address and a key."

She sighs. "I'll drive you out there tomorrow morning. You'll need to see what you're working with before you commit. I have an early Zoom meeting I have to take from my office. Can you meet me here right after, at ten?" She slides her glasses off and sets them on the desk, and without them her face is the one I remember from the couch—open, unshielded, the version of Celeste that exists after all that pretty armor comes off. "And Saylor?"

"Yeah?"

"I'll have a badge made for you, in case you plan on breaking into my office again. Please scan in properly and don't sneak past my security."

I look at her—glasses off, arms uncrossed now, sitting on the edge of her desk in her corner office forty-seven floors above a city full of people who would kill for five minutes of her attention. And I think about telling her exactly what's going through my mind. *This feels big. Earth-shattering big. Like a meteor crashing into a planet. The entire ecosystem of our lives is about to change. I can feel it.*

But she's not ready for that. And maybe I'm not ready to say it in a glass office where anyone walking by could see the moment it lands.

"Yes ma'am."

She reaches across the desk to snag a simple black business card with the Celeste logo on it. "This has my cell and my office number if you need anything." She points to the watch box. "Don't forget the watch."

"Nope. Leaving it. I will take this though." I snag the green smoothie. The condensation racing down the thin, plastic cup instantly soaks my hand.

"Gen Zs," she mutters under her breath. "Obsessed with drinking your vegetables."

"You millennials," I answer. "Always commenting on Gen Z behavior. Do I detect a hint of bitter jealousy, Ms. Brinley?"

"Absolutely. I'd kill for your birth year. I'm tempted to kiss you just for a taste of youth."

I'm sure she meant it as a joke, but she's got my attention. "I'm right here. Try it out."

Yes, she rolls her eyes. But she also blushes, so I'm calling it a win. "Goodbye, Saylor. I have work to do. See you tomorrow?"

"You got it. Ten o'clock."

Sipping on the fresh and creamy green smoothie that Celeste is most definitely missing out on, I leave the Rolex on her desk and walk out before she can argue. Down the hallway, past the mannequin in the corner wearing half a dress and looking better in it than most people look in a finished one. Past the workrooms and the garment racks and the woman still arguing about hand feel. Into the lift. Down forty-seven floors.

The lobby. The turnstile. The guards who still don't look at me.

Manhattan is bright and loud and exactly the same as it was forty minutes ago, and yet I am not the same at all.

I'm walking back toward the subway when I pass a kitschy, boutique coffee shop with a giant decal of the Eiffel tower on the front window. I don't know if this is where Celeste wanted coffee from, but this place reminds me of her, so I walk in.

The smell of fresh bread, lined with a rich sweetness, makes me want to stop, sit, unwind, and bask. But I'm on a mission. I head straight to the line-less counter and ask for a cortado.

"That all?" the barista in the brown apron asks.

"Yes, but can you have it delivered? Right across the street."

"To the Celeste building? Sure, we have a group order heading out in about five minutes. So no charge for delivery. Which floor and office?" She holds up a paper cup, wielding a Sharpie in her other hand.

"This needs to go to Celeste Brinley. CEO's office. Can you also throw in a pistachio muffin? I have to make sure my boss is fed." I pull out one of the last twenties in my wallet and hand it over.

The barista smiles at me. "Oh, you're the new assistant? I'm not surprised, the last one was useless. Ms. Brinley is here more often than not, getting her own coffee."

My chest swells with pride knowing this must be a regular spot for Celeste. It makes me weirdly proud that I already seem to know her better than either of us thinks.

"No, Margot's still around...for now. I'm a contractor." I shrug it off. "Keep the change."

With that, I'm on my way, back to the subway, back to home. But newly equipped with hope and excitement.

Tomorrow. I'm going to see her childhood home. I'm going to strip wallpaper and paint walls and fix whatever needs fixing in the house where Celeste grew up. I'm going to build something. Not for a client. Not for my mum. For the first time in as long as I can remember, I'm building something that I actually want to see finished.

I take the subway home and I don't check my phone once.

I don't need to. I know exactly where I'm going.

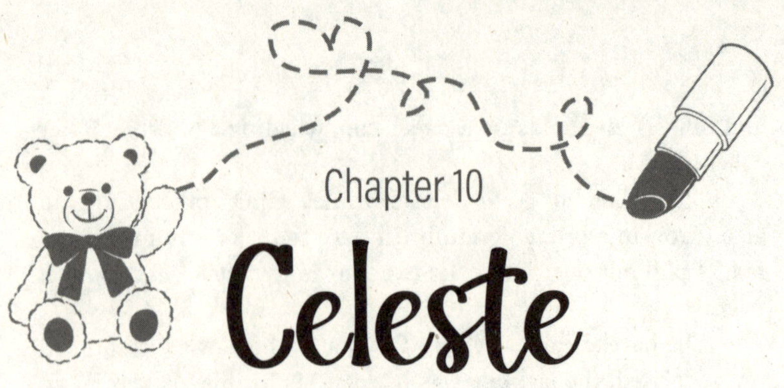

Chapter 10

Celeste

A Pollock painting in espresso and mascarpone.

My alarm goes off at six and I am already awake.

Not the productive kind of awake—not the kind where your eyes open and your brain is already three steps ahead, running the day's agenda like ticker tape. This is the other kind. The kind where your body woke you at four thirty and you've been lying here since, staring at the ceiling, cataloging every crack in the plaster like a woman conducting a structural survey of her own disintegration.

The Valencia call is at seven fifteen. Milan office, fabric development team, the final sign-off on the silk organza for the fall collection. I've been chasing this particular silk for three months—a weight and luminosity that doesn't exist yet, that I've been describing to increasingly frustrated Italian textile engineers as "moonlight caught in motion." They think I'm being pedantic. I think they're being unimaginative...and lazy. We've reached an impasse that can only be resolved by me, on camera, in a blazer, with swatches fanned out on my desk at a time when most of Manhattan is still asleep.

I cannot miss this call. This is the call. If I miss it, the fall line stalls, production timelines collapse, and the Bergdorf exclusive I've been nurturing for eight months dissolves like sugar in rain. My entire team has been building toward this moment. Margot, in a rare act of competence, actually ironed out the scheduling mishap and I'm expecting my most important partners in my office well before I'm prepared for them.

I sit up.

The room tilts.

Not dramatically—not a movie swoon, not a hand-to-the-forehead collapse. Just a slow, nauseating rotation, like the apartment has been placed on a turntable and someone is adjusting the speed, up and down, mercilessly. My head is pounding. Not a normal headache—the kind that spawns behind your eyes and radiates, turning every source of light into a personal assault. The kind that says: you haven't slept properly in two weeks, you've been surviving on cortados and adrenaline, and your body has decided, without consulting you, that today is the day it collects the debt.

I lower myself back against the pillow.

The ceiling is still cracked. The light through the curtains is pale and thin and gray, the color of a city that hasn't committed to morning yet. My Tribeca apartment—the glass box, as I described it to Saylor—is perfectly climate-controlled, perfectly silent, perfectly empty. Two thousand square feet of Italian marble and custom cabinetry and not a single person to hear me if I screamed.

This is the part they don't put in the profiles. The Forbes features and the Women in Business roundtables and the magazine spreads where I'm photographed in my atelier looking purposeful and backlit—none of them capture this. The six a.m. version. The woman coated in anti-aging night creams and serums from a twelve-step beauty routine to fight her cruel fate of aging, lying in a bed designed for two and occupied by one, trying to calculate whether she has enough structural integrity to get vertical.

I think about Eleanor, and the calculation fails.

Eleanor, who has a legal team and a Scarsdale estate and the particular confidence of a woman who has never once questioned whether she deserves what she's asking for. Eleanor, who looked at me across a courtyard and said *what are you here to collect* like I was a debt she didn't want to honor instead of a person. Eleanor, who is at this very moment building a case that I—Celeste Brinley, CEO, designer, the woman who can identify thread count by touch—am not fit to raise a child.

And the worst part. The part that keeps me awake at four thirty and drills holes in my skull at six. She might be right. Not about the custody. About me. About the glass box and the empty apartment and the eighteen-hour workdays that leave no room for anything soft. I built this life on purpose. I designed it the way I design a collection. Every element intentional, every choice deliberate, every vulnerability eliminated at the pattern stage. And now I can't let a caseworker walk through this apartment and see exactly what I built: a showcase. Beautiful, cold, and utterly inhospitable to a child.

I think about Whit, and the headache deepens.

Whit, who wanted to be a mother more than she wanted anything. Whit, who chose me out of everyone in her life, including the mother who raised her, to protect the thing she wanted most. Whitney, who I hadn't spoken to in two years because I was too proud, too scared, too busy choosing the wrong man over the right friend.

I think about Greg, and I want to throw something. Right off my penthouse balcony.

Greg, who is somewhere in this city right now, probably sleeping soundly in whatever apartment he's renting with whatever portion of my company's revenue he's siphoning, unbothered by custody battles or caseworkers or the particular agony of being a woman who is expected to perform competence in every arena simultaneously and without complaint.

My phone buzzes on the nightstand. A calendar reminder. *Valencia—fabric sign-off—seventy-five minutes.*

I pick up the phone. My hand is trembling, which I resent. My hands are the steadiest part of me. They cut fabric and sketch and gesture and hold—they are the instruments of my entire career, and right now they are shaking like I've had seven espressos, when in fact I've had nothing, because getting to the kitchen requires standing and standing requires a version of me that hasn't reported for duty.

And I don't think I'm in control of it.

My head is throbbing, the intrusive, depressing thoughts ricocheting off my brain like a pinball machine that launched too many balls at once. It's debilitating chaos and I can't form a single coherent thought for the world of fashion this morning. I have no choice.

I do something I never do.

I open my email and type a message to my VP of production.

From: C. Brinley, CEO
Subject line: URGENT AS ALL HELL

Maria,

Sorry for the late notice, but I need you to take the Valencia call alone this morning. I trust your eye. Sign off on the organza if the hand is right. If it's not, tell them I'll call Monday. I'm unwell.

-Celeste

The word looks foreign on the screen. Unwell. I've worked through fevers. I've taken calls from hospital beds. I've shown up to a fitting twelve hours after my divorce was finalized, pinning a hemline with hands that had just signed away a decade of my life. Unwell is not a word in my vocabulary. It's not in my brand guidelines.

Still, I press send.

Then I open my texts. Saylor's name is there—a new contact, added from the business card exchange that somehow became the most loaded moment of my week. I type with the trembling hands of a woman admitting defeat:

I'm sorry, Saylor. I need to reschedule our drive to Westchester. I'm not feeling well today. I'll reach out when I'm back on my feet.

I send it before I can revise. Before I can add qualifiers or professional padding or the three additional sentences I'd normally include to ensure no one worries, no one reads too deeply, no one sees the cracks. Then I turn the phone off. Not silent. *Off.* The screen goes black and the room goes quiet and I am alone in the most complete way a person can be alone—by choice, by necessity, by the specific cowardice of a woman who would rather disappear than be seen like this.

I pull the duvet over my head. The darkness is immediate and total and warm in a way that feels like permission.

I close my eyes. And the dream comes, except it's not a dream. It's a memory wearing a dream's clothes—perfectly preserved, mercilessly clear, playing behind my eyelids with the fidelity of something that never stopped happening.

La Fondue Douce on a Saturday night. And we have the whole restaurant to ourselves. I admit, it's over-the-top but turning thirty-six felt like the kind of thing that deserved melted cheese and privacy. It's tucked on a side street in the West Village—exposed brick, copper pots, the kind of candlelight that makes everyone look like a Vermeer painting. There are twenty guests. My favorites. Rina, a new friend, a few designers from the atelier, college friends who still text the group chat. Greg is at the head of the table because Greg is always at the head of the table, even when it's not his table, even when it's not his night.

Whitney is beside me. She's wearing a dress I made for her—a deep emerald silk with a bias cut that follows her frame like water.

I finished it two weeks ago, specifically for tonight. The neckline took three iterations. The hem is hand-stitched. It's one of the best things I've ever made, and watching her wear it feels like watching someone read a letter you wrote them—your work, her body, the collaboration of love and craft.

Her red curls are down. Her freckles are showing because she stopped wearing foundation six months ago and announced, with the conviction of a woman discovering religion, that "covering freckles is a hate crime against your own face." She looks beautiful and restless, and I should be paying closer attention to the restless part, but I'm not, because the fondue is perfect and the wine is a Sancerre that Whit picked specifically because it was the wine we drank the night we graduated, and I am thirty-six years old and in love with my life.

That's the version I'm telling myself, anyway.

Next to me, Greg is telling a story. He tells stories the way he does everything—louder than necessary, taking up more space than the content warrants. This one involves a golf trip and a celebrity I'm supposed to be impressed by. The table is laughing in that polite, wine-lubricated way that could mean anything. I'm half-listening, dipping a cube of bread into the Gruyère, when I notice Greg lean toward our waitress—a brunette, mid-twenties, the kind of effortlessly pretty that makes you feel like you're working too hard at your own face—and murmur something near her ear while touching the inside of her wrist.

It's three seconds. Maybe less. His thumb grazes her pulse point and she smiles—not a service smile, a real one—and he holds the contact a beat too long before pulling back and returning to his story like nothing happened.

I dip my bread. I chew. I swallow.

Whitney's hand finds my knee under the table and squeezes.

I don't look at her. I know what I'll see if I look at her, and I am not interested in seeing it tonight. Not on my birthday. Not in this restaurant that I rented and this life that I chose and this marriage that I am holding together with the same meticulous attention I bring to a seam that's starting to fray—steady hands, even pressure, the quiet belief that if I just keep stitching, nobody will notice the fabric is coming apart.

But thirty minutes later, right after my birthday cake is served, Whitney is missing. My birthday candles still giving off wisps of smoke when I notice she's gone.

And I mean gone-gone. Her clutch is missing. The vintage Chanel jacket that she found at a consignment shop in SoHo and considers her greatest material achievement—is no longer draped over the back of her chair. A cold draft from the front of the restaurant tells me the door has been opened recently, and so I take a chance and leave the table while my guests are lost in small talk and surface-level conversations.

Rina notices me rise, and gives me a concerned look. I smile and nod, a charade of: it's all fine. I just need some air. I grab a to-go box and stuff a slice of the cake in the square, plastic container. It's tiramisu—my favorite, to most of my guests' chagrin. But it's my birthday. Whit special-ordered from that place in Carroll Gardens because "regular cake is a betrayal of the Italian people." She didn't even stay for dessert which is very un-Whit-like. I pack her a piece as either an offering or a hostage. I'm not sure yet.

As I suspected, I find Whit on the sidewalk. She's pacing, which is what Whitney does when she's trying not to explode—short, tight laps, heels clicking, arms crossed, the emerald dress catching the streetlight and throwing it back in shards of green.

"Whit."

She stops pacing. Turns. Her face is flushed and her eyes are bright with something combustible.

"Don't," she says.

"Don't what? I just came to see if you're okay."

"I'm fine. Go back inside. Enjoy your party."

"You are clearly not fine."

She presses her fingers to her temples—a gesture I realize, with a jolt, is one I've stolen from her. Or she stole from me. After eighteen years of friendship, the plagiarism runs both ways.

"I can't do this anymore, Celeste."

"Do what?"

"Sit in there and pretend." She gestures toward the restaurant, toward the warm glow of the windows and the muffled laughter and the man at the head of my table. "Pretend I don't see what's happening. Pretend Greg isn't—" She stops. Breathes. Starts again. "The audacity. It's your birthday and he's shamelessly hitting on other women right in front of you."

"Oh, he's just a flirt when he's drunk. You're making a mountain out of a molehill."

"Lessi! Wake up. The waitress inside is the tip of the iceberg. What about the fact that he has two phones—"

"Two work phones. Two totally different businesses—"

"The plane ticket receipt you found which was to a city he never told you about."

"Because we don't babysit each other! That's called trust. Without it, we have nothing."

"It's called gaslighting. Greg has officially made you feel like you deserve the way he treats you."

Her voice cracks the quiet of the street like a rock through glass. A couple walking their dog across the street glances over. Whit doesn't care. Whit has never once in her life modulated her volume for the comfort of strangers.

"I've been keeping my mouth shut," she says, lower now but no less intense. "For years, Celeste. Years. Because I kept telling myself it wasn't my place. You're a grown woman, you make your own choices, and it's not my job to stand between you and your marriage. But I can't—" Her voice catches. "There is no way you aren't seeing this. He's not even trying to hide it. The late nights. The way he guards his phone like a Rottweiler with a bone. The way he looks at every woman in a room that isn't you. And the jokes, Celeste. About your age. 'My vintage wife.' 'The classic model.' It's not charming. It's not banter. He's reminding you—and everyone else—that in his eyes, you've expired, and he thinks that gives him permission to shop around."

"Whitney, stop it. Stop it right now."

"No. You stop. Stop pretending this is normal. Stop telling yourself this is what marriage looks like after a decade, because it's not. It's what happens when one person has checked out and the other person is too scared to admit it."

I feel the anger before I understand it—a hot, sick wave that starts in my stomach and rises through my chest and hardens in my throat like concrete setting. Not at Greg. At her. At Whitney, who is standing here in the dress I made her, telling me truths I've been folding into smaller and smaller squares and hiding in drawers I lock shut.

"It's not my fault you don't know what marriage looks like," I say. My voice is level. Controlled. The voice I use in boardrooms when someone has miscalculated and I need them to know it without raising my volume. "You've never stayed with anyone longer than a year. You collect relationships like frequent flyer miles and then cash them in the moment things get uncomfortable. So forgive me if I don't take marital advice from someone who treats commitment like a seasonal trend."

The words land. I watch them hit. Whitney's face absorbs the impact the way fabric absorbs a stain, the damage spreading outward from the point of contact, darkening everything it touches.

"That's not fair," she says quietly.

"Neither is ambushing me on my birthday."

"I'm not ambushing you. I'm trying to wake you up. But you're not sleeping are you? You're pretending. Acting out your life instead of living it." She stops. Her jaw works. I can see her choosing between the safe thing and the true thing, and I know which one Whitney always picks. "You're turning into my mother."

The street goes silent. Or maybe it doesn't. Maybe the cabs still honk and the dog still pants and the city keeps doing its indifferent thing. But in my ears, there is nothing. Just that sentence, hanging in the cold air between us like smoke from a fire she just lit in the center of our friendship.

"I'm sorry," she says, softer now, but the damage is done. "That came out harsh. But, Celeste. My mother spent her entire marriage looking the other way because the alternative was admitting she'd built her life around someone who didn't deserve it. And you're doing the same thing. Tolerating a man because you're afraid of what you'll lose if you leave. My mother chose money and status. She said the emotional trauma was worth estates with manicured lawns, private yachts, and black-tie dinner parties that nobody likes to go to. My mom chose a lie instead of choosing herself. Instead of choosing me. Now, you're facing the same decision. What do you want?"

I stare at the to-go container. The tiramisu sits in its plastic shell like something precious trapped in something cheap. I hold it still for a moment. Then I open my hand and let it drop.

It hits the sidewalk and splits open. Cream and cocoa and ladyfingers splatter across the concrete, across the toes of Whitney's heels, across the hem of the emerald dress I spent three weeks making. A Pollock painting in espresso and mascarpone.

"How dare you. How dare you compare me to the woman you hate most in the world."

Whit looks at the cake on her shoes. On her dress. She's slathered in the mess I made. When she looks up, the fire has gone out. What's left is something worse—sadness, heavy and deliberate, the expression of someone who knew this was coming and chose to come anyway.

"I don't hate my mom," she says. "I grieve for her. Because she's brilliant and strong and she let a man convince her she was neither. And I don't want that for you, Lessi. I don't want you to wake up at fifty and realize you spent your best years performing a marriage with a man you resent."

My hands are shaking. Tiramisu is on my shoes too. We match—stained, standing in the wreckage of dessert and honesty.

"When you're ready to walk away from him," Whitney says, "I'll be right beside you. When you're ready to be brave and face what's actually happening, I will face it with you. But until then—"

Her voice breaks cleanly, like a thread snapping under tension. "I can't watch you do this to yourself. I can't sit at that table and smile and clink glasses while the person I love most in the world disappears into a marriage that's killing her."

"So you're giving me an ultimatum," I say. "Greg or you."

Whitney doesn't answer. She stands on the sidewalk in the emerald dress with tiramisu on the hem, and her silence is the loudest thing I've ever heard. It's louder than the cabs and the dog and the couple who are definitely pretending not to watch. It's louder than the laughter still leaking from the restaurant behind me where twenty people are eating fondue and none of them know that my life is splitting apart on this curb.

"I'll never forgive you for this," I say. My voice doesn't sound like mine. It sounds like someone reading from a script they found on the ground—flat, rehearsed, belonging to a woman I don't recognize but am choosing to be. "For making me choose."

I turn around. I walk back into the restaurant. The warm light swallows me. The door closes behind me and the cold air and the cake and the emerald dress and Whitney—my Whit, my twin flame, my eighteen years of someone who knew me better than I knew myself—are on the other side of it.

I sit down. Greg asks where I went. I tell him I needed air. He pours me more wine and goes back to his story about the golf trip and the celebrity, and I drink the wine and I laugh in the right places and I never once look at the empty chair beside me where the person I love most in the world was sitting ten minutes ago.

The chair stays empty for two years.

Six months later, I catch Greg with his hand on someone else's wrist. Not a waitress this time. An intern from our company. In our bedroom. And Whit's voice echoes through me like a bell I can't stop ringing: When you're ready to be brave. When you're ready to face it.

I face it. I file for divorce. I do the brave thing, finally, too late, after the woman who begged me to be brave got tired of waiting and walked away.

I never call Whit. I mean to. Every day, I mean to. But what do you say to the person who told you the truth and got punished for it? What do you say to the friend who offered to hold your hand through the fire and got told I'll never forgive you? I keep meaning to call. I keep rehearsing the words. I keep telling myself: next week. When the divorce is final. When I'm ready. When I've earned the right to apologize.

And while I'm stalling, Whitney gets sick. While I'm being a coward, Whit finds a surrogate. While I'm lost in my own life, Whitney dies.

She dies on a Tuesday in May two years later...

And I'm still rehearsing.

I wake up with my face wet and the duvet twisted around me like a cocoon that failed at its one job. The apartment is bright now—mid-morning light, aggressive and specific, the kind that exposes every smudge on every surface. My phone is off. The Valencia call happened without me. The world kept turning while I lay here drowning in memories of a restaurant that closed after Christmas last year after a grease fire that got out of control.

It's all just gone now. The building, the people, all moving on to their inevitable fates, the memories burned to ash.

I roll onto my back and stare at the ceiling. The cracks are still there. The apartment is still empty. And somewhere across this city, Saylor is checking his phone and seeing my cancellation text and probably thinking I'm fine, because I wrote *not feeling well* instead of what I actually am, which is broken open, gutted, lying in the debris of a friendship I destroyed with my own cowardice.

I picture the baby. I do this sometimes—close my eyes and try to imagine her, even though I don't know if it's a *her* yet, even though Raven's next ultrasound hasn't happened. I picture a girl anyway, because Whitney would have a girl. Red curls. Freckles. Whitney's face in miniature—those eyes that always saw too much, that always knew the truth before you said it, staring up at me from a bassinet with the quiet, devastating expectation of someone who is counting on me to be better than I've been.

One day, this child with Whit's eyes will look at me and I will have to be the woman Whitney believed I could be—not the one who walked back into the restaurant. Not the one who chose Greg. Not the one who spent two years rehearsing an apology she never made.

The brave one. The one Whit kept waiting for. The one who was always in there, somewhere underneath the high-end pantsuits and the executive boardrooms and the perfectly structured life, too afraid to live until it was too late.

I can't be too late again.

I sit up. The room tilts, but less. The headache pulses, but quieter. My hands are still trembling, but I realize in perfect timing, my hands have trembled before and still cut fabric, still sketched, still held a pen steady enough to sign divorce papers. Trembling is not the same as broken. Trembling is what happens when something inside you is trying to move.

I don't turn my phone on. *Not yet.* The world can wait another hour. For now, I sit in the bright, empty penthouse and let myself feel all of it—the grief, the anger, the guilt, the terrifying hope—without folding any of it into squares, without locking it in drawers, without designing my way around it.

For now, I just sit with it.

It's the bravest thing I've done all week.

Chapter 11

Saylor

You're about as romantic as a cactus, know that?

Forrest drives like a man who learned on dirt roads and never fully adjusted to the concept of lanes. His left hand is loose on the wheel of the rented pickup, his right elbow hanging out the window despite the fact it's fifty degrees and the wind is turning his knuckles pink. The truck bed is loaded with everything Home Depot had to offer at seven in the morning on a Wednesday—paint rollers, drip cloths, a power drill, three different grades of sandpaper, wood filler, a shop vac, and a cooler full of water bottles and gas-station jerky because Forrest insisted that "you can't renovate on an empty stomach, that's how people lose fingers."

"So let me get this straight," Forrest says, merging onto I-87 with the casual aggression of someone who genuinely does not see other cars as obstacles. "You met Celeste two weeks ago. At a funeral. Where you were her hired date. And now you're renovating her childhood home?"

"Contract work. She's paying me."

"Contractor rates."

"That's what I said."

"And you called me at six in the morning to help because—"

"Because you're my friend and I asked nicely."

"You said, and I quote, 'Hawk, get up. I need your hands.' And then you hung up. That's not asking nicely. That's a hostage negotiation without the negotiation."

"And yet here you are."

"Here I am." He reaches into the cooler wedged between us and pulls out a stick of jerky. Tears it with his teeth. "Because I'm a good person and also because Koda is with her mother, and Sora kicked me out of the house so she could write in peace. Apparently I'm a distraction."

"Because you can't keep your hands off of her," I say. "Hard to write a book when you're on your back with your legs in the air."

"That's the love of my life you're talking about."

"Hey, don't get me wrong. I'm on her side. Leave that poor girl alone and let her work. It's exhausting being your girlfriend. Or...wait. Fiancée now?"

Forrest smiles. "I got the ring. Mr. Cooper, sort of reluctantly, gave me his permission. I just have to figure out how to ask her."

"Will. You. Marry. Me. Four words, mate. Not that complicated."

"You're about as romantic as a cactus, know that?"

Forrest has the grin that made him one of Rina's most requested escorts before Sora came along and retired him—easy, warm, the kind of smile that makes people feel like they've been friends with him for years when they've known him for minutes. He's wearing a flannel with the sleeves rolled to the elbows and work boots that actually have mud on them, because Forrest is the only person I know in New York City who owns work boots with real mud. Ranch kid from Wyoming turned fancy law student. Spent his childhood moving cattle and mending fences before trading it all for Manhattan, which, when you think about it, involves a similar skill set—reading the herd, keeping things calm, knowing when to get out of the way.

"So what exactly are we doing when we get there?" he asks.

"Assessing. Cleaning. Starting whatever we can. She described it as a time capsule. Apparently her parents left the country six years ago, nobody's touched it since. I'm not sure if this is a light decorative facelift, or an episode of *Fixer Upper*, but we're about to find out."

"And this needs to be done by when?"

"Next week. Celeste is still fighting for custody of her friend's unborn baby. A caseworker's coming to evaluate the home to determine if Celeste can take care of a child."

"What the hell? Kind of intrusive, isn't it? Nobody did a home visit after Koda was born."

"Your dead best friend's mother wasn't trying to take the baby from you. It's a battle between two women and two legal teams at this point, and to be honest..." I hate the words I'm about to say. "On paper, Celeste and Eleanor are kind of replicas. Wealthy, every amenity and resource at their fingertips. It's not a question of providing for the baby, now it's a question of who is better suited. Eleanor had a baby. She's done this before. Eleanor lives in the suburbs. Eleanor doesn't travel much—"

"So Celeste is screwed."

I nod. "That's the gist of it. We need an edge. This house might be that edge."

Forrest lets out a low whistle. "Wow, man. You're in deep already. You're fixing up a whole-ass house in under a week for a custody case you're not involved in?"

"No. *We're* fixing up a five-thousand-square-foot house in under a week for a custody case *we're* not involved in."

Forrest grumbles. "I need new friends. Ones that ask for fewer favors."

The highway opens up north of the city, the skyline shrinking in the rearview as Westchester spreads out around us—greener, quieter, the kind of suburban sprawl that looks like someone designed it specifically to make Manhattan feel like a mistake. The houses get bigger. The lawns get wider. Each driveway showcases vehicles that look collectible.

"How's Celeste doing with all of this?" Forrest asks. "I've been meaning to check in on her, but Sora and I have been flat-out with work, and Koda's been with us every other week, so—"

"She's struggling. She canceled on me Saturday and has

barely been responsive since. I think the weight of it finally caught up."

"That tracks. She's always been a keep-it-together-until-she-can't type. One of those people who runs at full speed and then just stops." He pauses. "When I'd take her to events, she'd be perfect all night—charming, funny, totally in control. Then she'd get in the car after and go completely silent. Like she'd used up every drop of energy performing and had nothing left."

"That's exactly it. Like every conversation drains her battery, and she's operating on fumes. I keep asking myself what could help her relax. She appears to only take breaks from work to attend funerals."

"Celeste doesn't relax. How can she with her ex breathing down her neck?"

I take a deep breath, trying not to sound too inquisitive. "Yeah, what do you know about the bloke? Is he a problem?"

"I only met Greg once. The night I met Sora, actually. We were at a wedding of one of their mutual friends."

"What's the verdict?"

"Total prick." Forrest's jaw tightens. "He's the kind of guy who diminishes you in a room full of people and then acts confused when you're upset. He probably jacks off to his clever one-liners that he thinks makes people feel small. The ego on the guy, I swear."

"Why'd they divorce?"

Forrest glances my way. "Why do you think?"

"He cheated?"

"He made cheating a sport. Qualified it into the Olympics. Won a fucking gold medal."

A kindling of rage begins to smoke inside my chest. I'm glad Celeste is no longer with Greg—for more reasons that I can admit to at the moment. But the fact that he hurt her pisses me off. I'll let that fire simmer and then explode in due time.

"*Geez.* Do you think she's still hung up on him?"

Forrest glances at me. A slow glance, the kind that takes a

detour through amusement before arriving at the point. "Why are you so concerned with who Celeste is hung up on?"

"Professional curiosity."

"Professional curiosity. Right." He chews his jerky with the deliberate patience of a man who has all the time in the world to watch me dig this hole. "I think Celeste is someone who's always trying to keep pace with Greg. He gets a new girlfriend, she books one of us. He shows up at an event, she has to show up looking better. It's not love. It's competition. And she's losing because she doesn't realize the game is all in her head. And Greg doesn't help. He has this weird possessive thing over Celeste. He doesn't want her, but he doesn't want anyone else to want her. It's crippling. She needs to get away from him, except they co-own her company together."

"You got all of this from like four dates you went on with her?"

He shoots me another look. "You're renovating her home after one date with her. And that was a date to a funeral no less."

"Fair. So you think she doesn't love him, she's just stuck, unable to move on?"

"She's not stuck. She's moved. Just not on. More like sideways." Another bite. "Why? You're that interested?"

"I'm renovating her house, Hawk. That's all you need to know."

"That doesn't tell me much."

"Exactly."

"You called me at six a.m. on a Wednesday to help you renovate a woman's house. A woman you are asking about with the specific intensity of a man who is definitely not just renovating her house." He looks at me flatly. "I've seen that look before. In my mirror. About eight months ago, when I was telling myself the exact same lie about Sora."

I let that sit for an entire mile of silence.

"Celeste's nervous about the whole thing," I say, shifting the subject slightly. "The baby. Being a mother. She told me she doesn't know what maternal even looks like because her parents were kind of absent."

Forrest nods slowly. "Hannah and I weren't exactly planning on parenthood either. You know that. I was twenty-two and terrified and had no idea what I was doing."

"What made you ready?"

"Nothing. You're never ready. That's the whole trick. Everyone's out here waiting to feel qualified and the feeling never comes. You just start doing it and figure out the rest while you're knee-deep in diapers and existential dread." He smiles—not the easy one, the deeper one. The one that shows up when he talks about Koda. "But the thing is, the fact that it scares you? That's the qualification. If it didn't scare you, you'd be a sociopath. Celeste being terrified of motherhood is the most maternal thing about her."

"That's basically what I told her."

"Great minds." He tips the jerky stick at me like he's toasting. "Seriously though—Celeste is going to be a good mom. She's intense and she's a perfectionist and she'll probably have this baby dressed for the red carpet by the time it can crawl. But she loves hard. You can tell. Anyone who's spent ten minutes with her can tell."

Hawk is right. I can most definitely tell.

The highway thins to two lanes. We're deep in Westchester now, past the strip malls and the commuter stations, into the part where the trees outnumber the people and every driveway is longer than my block.

"How's your mom doing?" Forrest asks, like he can sense I've been circling something.

"Same. Good days and bad days. Callie's leaving next week—moving to Kansas. So I'm sorting out a replacement for the meds and therapy work." I watch the trees blur past. "But there's something else. I emailed this surgeon, Dr. Yassa. He's Mount Sinai's new neurosurgeon who specializes in repair and rehabilitation. He's doing these experimental laser treatments.

Like nerve regeneration."

"Uh-oh, Saylor. I'm sorry man, but this story sounds scary familiar."

Forrest is right. He knows my backstory, why Mum and I are stuck in America while we call Australia home. About four years ago a different surgeon sold us a similar story. A life-changing experimental procedure that could give my mum her life back. We sold everything. Our house, the farm, my truck. We bet everything on this one lottery ticket...and we lost. Not because the procedure didn't work. But because it never existed. Gullible and stupid, I got scammed, and we were stranded in New York City with nothing and no home to return to. It was the second time I ruined Mum's life, because apparently once wasn't enough.

"That's why I got Rina involved this time. She can smell blood in the water a whole ocean away. She vetted it. It's legit. There's only one problem...well two."

"Being?"

"They've done about sixty successful procedures with mind-blowing results. Patients who were stuck in wheelchairs were taking their first steps in decades."

"That's amazing, man. Like a miracle."

"Aye, but there were two cases—one full paralysis. One death."

"That's above a ninety-six-percent success rate," Forrest says without thought, using mental math to inadvertently remind me how smart he is. Sometimes I forget he graduated top of his class at Columbia Law.

"Right but neither death or full paralysis is a risk I can take. On the other hand...the treatment is showing real promise. The laser therapy—whatever they're doing with the nerve pathways—even the early results are strong. Really strong. I keep picturing how happy Mum looked when she was training. Imagine if she could run again, y'know?"

Forrest is quiet for a moment. He knows what running means to my mum. I've told him about Red, about the mornings in

Wollongong, about the woman who ran five miles every day before she started her farm work. Mum really lived...until she couldn't.

"Are you asking for my advice, Say? Because I can't make this decision—"

"It's not that, mate. I'm thinking out loud. Even if all the stars aligned and we were accepted as patients, the risks were next to nothing, it's also one hundred and sixty thousand dollars. Minimum. Out of pocket because it's experimental, so insurance won't touch it."

"You'd have to take out a loan."

I swallow. "I don't even know if I have credit. And if I do, it's bad. I've been getting paid under the table for years. A loan isn't an option."

The revelation sinks into the truck cab like a stone dropped into still water. We both just watch it sink.

"Does your mom know?" Forrest asks eventually. "What does she think?"

"I'm not telling her until I figure out the money situation. And the risk situation. And the—all of it." I lean my head against the window. The glass is cold. "She walks through pain every day, Hawk. Watching her climb the flights of stairs to our apartment is like watching someone tortured. One time I had to carry her, it was so bad. She leaves the apartment less and less because I don't think she wants me to see her *like that*. Mum never complains and she never asks for help and she never, not once, feels sorry for herself. If I tell her there's a chance and then I can't make it happen—or worse, if I make it happen and it goes wrong—"

"Hey." Forrest's voice is steady. The ranch-kid voice, the one that's calmed horses and children and one very overwhelmed escort who is trying to dive headfirst into a situationship with a client. "One thing at a time. Figure out the money. Research the risk. Talk to the doctor. And when you're ready, talk to your mom. But don't carry this alone. That's not strength. That's just stubbornness with a martyrdom complex."

"You sound like a therapist."

"I sound like a dad. Same skill set, terrible pay. Like...no pay."

I laugh. It comes out more like a pressure release than actual humor, but Forrest takes it for what it is and lets the silence fill back in, comfortable and undemanding, the way silence works between people who don't need to perform for each other.

"Do you think she's out of my league?" I ask, after a while. We've turned off the highway now and the houses have upgraded yet again—stone facades, circular driveways, the kind of landscaping that requires a full-time staff.

"What league?"

"Mate, look around." I gesture at the neighborhood—wrought-iron gates, hedgerows taller than me, a BMW parked in front of a house that has a name on the mailbox instead of a number. "She grew up around here? She's basically Alicia Silverstone from *Clueless*."

Forrest gives me a look that's equal parts confusion and concern. "What the hell is *Clueless*?"

"Are you serious right now? It's a movie. A classic. American cinema history."

"Never seen it."

"You are such a Gen Z."

"We're both Gen Z."

"Yeah but I'm a cultured Gen Z. You're a ranch Gen Z. You probably think cinema peaked with *Yellowstone*."

"*Yellowstone* is a television show, and it's a masterpiece, and I won't hear otherwise." He points the jerky stick at me. "But to answer your question—no. Nobody is out of anyone's league. That's some made-up bullshit guys tell themselves so they don't have to risk getting rejected. If your heart's in the right place and you treat her right, the rest is just geography and tax brackets."

"That's surprisingly wise for a man eating gas-station jerky at eight in the morning."

"Wisdom and jerky are not mutually exclusive." He chews. Swallows. Gets serious in the way Forrest gets serious—quietly, without announcement, like a sky going from blue to gray while you're not looking. "But Saylor. If you're really into Celeste—and I'm not saying you are, because you clearly haven't figured it out yet even though literally everyone else has—maybe stop taking jobs from Rina for a while."

I crack my knuckles one by one. *Yeah, way ahead of you, buddy.* "I haven't taken one since the funeral," I admit.

"Good. Keep it that way. At least until this crush passes."

Crush? Dear God, I'm offering manual labor for a crush? Imagine if I loved this woman. I'm scared I'd volunteer to move a mountain. Although...if Celeste asked me to, oi, would I be tempted. I don't know what it is about her. I've never seen so many layers to a person. Every time I encounter her it's a new mystery revealed. A new challenge, accepted. A new adventure, begging for my attention. With the burden on my back and an impossible destination ahead, it takes a lot to stop me in my tracks. Celeste is...a lot. In all the right ways. But hearing all this from Forrest, who walked the same path and came out the other side with someone who loves him, makes it feel less ridiculous.

"No more jobs," I say.

The GPS leads us off the main road and through a gate—actual gate, stone pillars, a security booth with a guard who checks our names against a list. Celeste called ahead. Even mid-breakdown, even barely answering texts for five days, she made sure we could get through.

The guard waves us through and the neighborhood shifts again. If the houses before were impressive, these are architectural declarations. Set back from the road on half-acre lots minimum, each one different—colonial, Tudor, a modern glass thing that looks like it was designed by someone who hates walls. Old trees line the street, the kind with trunks wider than this truck, throwing shade patterns across lawns so green they look Photoshopped.

"There," Forrest says, slowing. "That's the number."

The house sits at the end of a curved driveway behind a row of mature oaks. My first thought is that Celeste's description was either incredibly humble or deliberately misleading, because this isn't a house that needs fixing up. This is a house that needs a documentary crew and a historical preservation grant.

It's Colonial. White clapboard, black shutters, a covered porch that wraps around the front and disappears around the side. Two stories plus what looks like a finished attic with dormer windows. The yard is enormous—not estate-enormous, not Eleanor-enormous, but the kind of big where a kid could run until they got tired and still have room left. There's a detached garage, a stone path leading to a back garden that's gone to seed, and a deck off the back that's visible from the driveway and is, as advertised, in rough shape. A few boards are warped. The railing leans.

But the bones. The bones are stunning.

"Shit," I say quietly.

"What?"

"She's definitely out of my league."

Forrest puts the truck in park and kills the engine. "I literally just told you—"

"I know what you said. But you said it before I saw the size of this house."

We get out. The air is different here—thinner, cleaner, carrying the smell of cut grass and something floral I can't identify. No sirens. No garbage trucks. No upstairs neighbor running the dishwasher at midnight. Just birds and wind and the enormous silence of a place where people have enough space to not hear each other.

The front door has a keypad. I punch in the code Celeste texted me. She reset it as her birthday, which she either chose for convenience or as an unconscious act of intimacy that I'm choosing not to read into—and the lock clicks open.

The foyer hits me first. Double-height ceiling, a staircase curving up to the second floor, hardwood floors under a layer of dust so thick our footsteps leave prints. A chandelier hangs overhead, crystal, enormous, wearing a veil of cobwebs like a bride who's been waiting at the altar for six years. The air is stale and cold and carries that particular smell of a house that's been breathing its own air for too long—closed rooms, settled dust, the ghost of whatever cleaning products were used last.

"Wow," Forrest breathes, standing in the middle of the foyer and turning a slow circle.

I'm already moving. Through the foyer into the living room—high ceilings, crown molding, a fireplace with a marble mantel. The furniture is draped in white sheets, giving the room the look of a very sophisticated haunted house. I pull one back and find a grand leather, burgundy sofa in great condition, spared from years of arses using it as a landing pad. But it also looks like the kind of furniture that belongs in Dexter's lab, if you know what I mean.

The kitchen is next. Large by any standard but horrendously dated—oak cabinets from the era when oak was the height of sophistication, granite countertops yellowed slightly, appliances that work but belong in a museum that highlights the wayward design choices of the early two thousands. The fridge is unplugged, door propped open. The sink is dry. But the window over it looks out into the backyard, and the view is something else. No wonder Celeste wanted the caseworker to come here. The deck, the garden, an old oak tree with a tire swing still hanging from a low branch—it's exactly the kind of backyard you'd place on the cover of a family magazine.

We continue to move through the house. Past a coat rack by the back door with hooks at different heights—two high ones for adults, two lower for a child. Pencil marks on the doorframe between the kitchen and the hallway, faded but legible: *Celeste, age 7. Celeste, age 8. Celeste, age 9.* Each one slightly higher, the handwriting changing from year to year—a parent's careful print giving way to a child's own letters, then to a teenager's rushed scrawl before the marks stop at *Celeste, age 14*. Fourteen. The year she outgrew the ritual, or the year she stopped wanting to be measured, or maybe both.

I press my thumb against the mark at age nine and something in my chest rearranges itself.

"You good?" Forrest asks from behind me.

"Yeah. Just looking."

Upstairs. Five bedrooms. The master is the largest—king bed under a sheet, ensuite bathroom with double vanities and a soaking tub. And the loveseat. I see it immediately, pushed against the wall beneath the window, upholstered in that French Script fabric Celeste mentioned. She was right. It's not dangerous to a child. It's just aggressively outdated, the kind of fabric that says *I decorated this room in two thousand three and I will dutifully die on this hill.*

The third bedroom is smaller, painted pale yellow, with built-in shelves and a window overlooking the backyard. A nursery. Or it could be. With fresh paint, a crib, the right touch—this could be the room where the baby sleeps.

The fourth bedroom stops me cold.

It's Celeste's old room. I know it immediately—the specific energy of a space that shaped someone you're trying to understand. The walls are lavender. There's a desk under the window with a lamp shaped like a cat. A bookshelf crammed with paperbacks and sketchbooks. And on the wall above the desk, pinned directly to the plaster with thumbtacks that have gone rusty, are fashion sketches. Dozens of them. Pencil on paper, some colored in with markers, some just outlines. Dresses, coats, a jumpsuit that looks surprisingly modern for something drawn by a teenager. The lines are unsteady in places—an inexperienced hand learning its future language—but the instinct is already there. The eye. The vision. The specific way Celeste sees art before it exists.

I stand in the doorway and feel something I wasn't prepared for. Not attraction—that's been simmering since the funeral and I've made my peace with it. This is tenderness. The kind that comes from seeing where someone started and knowing where they ended up and understanding that the distance between those two points is made entirely of work and courage and loneliness and a thousand choices nobody else witnessed.

She was always going to be extraordinary. Even at fourteen, when the height marks stopped—she was already becoming.

"Saylor." Forrest's voice from the hallway. "Come look at this."

I follow him to the last bedroom—storage, mostly. Boxes stacked floor to ceiling, old furniture, a treadmill with a coat draped over it indicating this exercise equipment has transformed into a backup coat rack. But Forrest isn't looking at the boxes. He's looking at the wall, where a family portrait hangs in a gilt frame above a dresser.

Three people. A man—tall, silver-haired, distinguished in the European way that suggests good tailoring and moderate wine consumption. A woman—dark-haired, elegant, wearing a silk blouse that even I can tell is expensive and a smile that doesn't quite reach her eyes. And between them, maybe ten or eleven, a girl with brown hair and brown eyes and the serious expression of a child who is already paying closer attention than the adults realize.

Little Celeste. Hands folded in her lap. Chin lifted. Already composed. Already watching.

"Am I crazy or does she look exactly the same?" Forrest muses. "Same exact eyes."

"Yeah. She does. Wild." It's odd to note that Celeste is so concerned about her age, where I just don't see it. I look at her and see *woman*, and sophistication, and sexy glasses, and sweet tears. I see...what I think I want.

We head back downstairs. I stand in the kitchen, looking out the window at the tire swing and the overgrown garden and the deck that needs new boards, and I make a list in my head. Not a contractor's list, not yet. A different kind of list. The list of what this house needs to become in six days so that a caseworker walks in and sees what I see: a place where a child could grow up knowing they are loved.

"Righto." I turn to Forrest. "We have days to get this place breathing again. Beautiful and lived-in. It needs to sell a story—a family home. Not a museum. Not a showcase. A place where a kid runs through the hallway and gets her height marked on a doorframe."

Forrest leans against the kitchen counter and folds his arms. "I say this with full sincerity, Saylor."

"What?"

"You fucking suck."

I chuckle. "Come on. It's nothing two former farm boys can't handle."

"Ranch," Forrest corrects, pushing off the counter. "I grew up on a ranch. I'm a cowboy. Cowboys are significantly cooler than farm boys. There's a whole genre of music and books about us. I don't see a romance section in Barnes and Noble about boys who feed chickens."

"Oh please. You're a pretty-boy jackaroo. I could work circles around you and still kick your arse."

"Outwork me? You're Australian. My dad's ranch is the size of your entire country, buddy. You don't have my stamina."

"It's a continent, actually, and—"

"Okay, are we going to stand here debating geography, or are we going to fix this woman's house?"

I look around the kitchen. At the dated cabinets, the yellowed granite, the window with the view that could sell a dream. I think about the girl who grew up here and left and is now trying to come back, not for herself, but for a baby who doesn't exist yet and already needs a home.

"Let's fix the house," I say.

Forrest rolls up his flannel another notch. "Where do we start?"

"Deck first. It's structural—can't have the caseworker falling through a board. Then the nursery. Paint, shelves, make it look like someone's expecting a baby and is genuinely excited about it. Kitchen after that—deep clean, new hardware on the cabinets, replace the appliances if the budget allows. Then clean up, room by room, until we run out of days or energy, whichever comes first."

"And that heinous wallpaper?" Forrest points toward the living room where ugly floral patterns have accosted the walls.

"That wallpaper dies tonight."

Forrest nods, grabs two water bottles from the cooler we brought in, tosses me one, and heads for the back door. I follow him out onto the deck, which groans under our weight like a bloke getting out of a chair after sitting too long, and I look at the backyard—the oak tree, the tire swing, the garden that's one good weekend away from being beautiful again—and I think about a girl with brown eyes who used to live here. Who drew dresses on her wall and measured herself against a doorframe and grew up to build something extraordinary from nothing but vision and stubbornness and a refusal to accept the world as less beautiful than she knew it could be.

I'm going to make this house worthy of her. Worthy of the baby. Worthy of the woman Whitney believed Celeste could be.

Six days. Two guys. One truck full of power tools and gas-station jerky.

We've handled worse.

Probably.

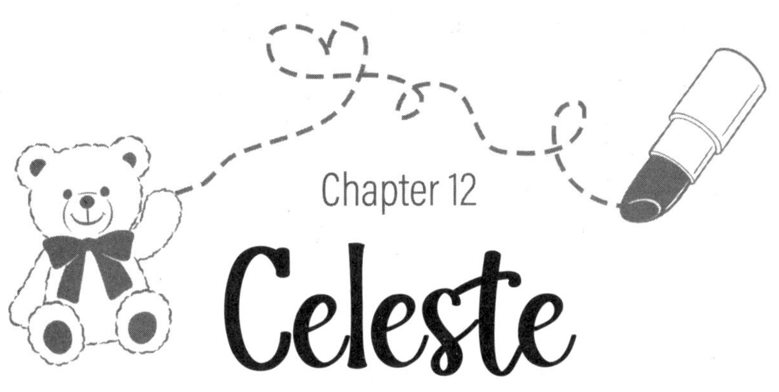

Chapter 12 Celeste

If it were for sale, I'd make sure it was yours.

I am driving forty-nine in a thirty-five, my left blinker still flashing from three turns ago, and the speedometer needle twitches higher every time I remember I'm supposed to be slowing down. I am chaos. I am chaos incarnate. And I don't fucking care.

My new attorney called eleven minutes ago while I was standing in my closet in underwear and pantyhose, holding a blouse that I'd already rejected twice, trying to decide if my first functional day back at the office warranted silk or cotton. The answer, it turns out, is irrelevant, because Denise Bilch—my new, sharp, expensive, mercifully blunt attorney—said the words "they moved it up" and my entire morning plan to head to work detonated.

Two days. The visit was supposed to be Friday. I had two more days to pull myself together, to drive up to Westchester and see what Saylor had done, to walk through the rooms and rehearse answers and build the version of myself that a caseworker would trust with a child. Instead, the caseworker is arriving at eleven a.m. today because apparently the court's calendar shifted and nobody thought to give me more than a sneeze of a warning.

Denise said Eleanor's team requested the acceleration. Of course they did. Eleanor wants me unprepared. Eleanor wants me to scramble. Eleanor has been playing chess while I've been lying in bed for four days staring at ceiling cracks and crying into a duvet like a woman auditioning for the saddest perfume commercial ever made. The black-and-white kind, where she's stuck in a French noir scene after some Don Juan broke her heart. But that's okay—this perfume is magic elixir and with one spritz she's young, alive, and everything is in color.

I have no such magic elixir.

What I have is sheer determination, and a deep-rooted desire to send Eleanor straight back to the twisty maze of Pan's Labyrinth from where she emerged.

I texted Saylor before I got into the car, not wanting to add yet another risk to my morning. Me, having to drive, is dangerous enough. I shot off a message, thumbs shaking. Autocorrect mangling every other word.

Caseworker visit got moved to today. 11am. I'm driving up now. Before you ask, I am not okay. Please tell me the house is somewhat ready.

His response came in under thirty seconds.

Saylor

Breathe. Hawk's busy today but I've been here since six. We have enough done. It's going to be okay. I'm ready. Are you?

No.

It's the last text I send before I slam on the gas, peel into traffic amidst a symphony of protesting honks. At least it was honest. I am very, very not okay.

Breathe. He tells me to breathe like it's a skill I should have mastered by now, like oxygen is something I simply forgot about in between the panic attack in my closet and the moment I got in the car wearing a blouse that is technically ruined because I did not heed the "Dry clean only" warning, which is basically a sin against my own religion.

The Saw Mill River Parkway stretches ahead of me—trees, guardrails, the occasional minivan carrying someone to a life that makes sense. Definitely not my life. My hands are tight on the wheel. My hair is in a low bun that I assembled in the rearview mirror at a red light, which is apparently the signature style of a woman whose life is held together by bobby pins and spite.

My blouse is cream. Wool black dress pants. The Louboutins flats—authoritative but not aggressive, the shoe equivalent of "I am a serious person who is also prepared to chase down a fleeing child before they find the road." I put on the reading glasses even though I don't need them to drive because they make me look thoughtful, and then I took them off because I realized I was costuming myself for a role instead of showing up as a person. But then I put them back on because the costume is all I have right now.

The real Celeste has been in bed for four days. The real Celeste doesn't have her shit together. The real Celeste is a thirty-eight-year-old woman driving to her childhood home to convince a stranger she'd make a good mother while privately wondering if Whit made a terrible mistake.

She was so focused on who she thought I was, maybe she overlooked who I actually am. It's possible she didn't realize how hard it would be to turn me into a mother worthy of her daughter or son.

The exit comes up fast. I take it too sharp, the tires complaining, and then I'm on local roads—the tree-lined, hedge-trimmed, absurdly manicured roads of the neighborhood where I grew up believing everyone's house came equipped with a home office, two spare bedrooms, a guesthouse, pool, and of course everyone's mother wore silk to the daily full-spread breakfast.

I practically blast through the security gate, the tiny sensor in the upper-right corner of my Range Rover triggering. The guard waves through the rearview mirror, holding his walkie-talkie to his lips. Possibly warning other security members that a crazy lady is coming through at the speed of light.

As I near my destination, the oaks close overhead like a cathedral ceiling, dappling the windshield with light.

And then I see the house.

I haven't been here in over a year. The last time, I drove up alone on my birthday—my first birthday divorced from Greg. I sat in the driveway for twenty minutes, then drove back home without going inside, realizing my childhood was just as lonely as my current adult reality. I couldn't face it. The house felt empty, even when we inhabited it. I didn't hate my childhood. My parents weren't cut from the same cloth as Whitney's, but there was something hollow about the way I grew up. I don't have warm memories, just transactional ones. I was fed well, medically cared for, got a great education, but to this day, I bet my life my parents couldn't tell you what my favorite food or color is. They don't really know me. They never felt they needed to.

When they gifted me this house, I think they thought they were handing over my childhood in some grand gesture. They didn't understand I saw this place as a museum, and I was on display. There was nothing warm about it. No warm chocolate-chip cookies after school. No beaming faces staring back at me from the talent show audience. They weren't there to help me get ready for my junior prom. I wasn't even excited about going with Greg. I was proud to be wearing a dress I designed. It was all endless missed opportunities to get to know me.

But the house I'm looking at now is not the house I left.

The porch has been swept. The shutters—the black shutters that were peeling so badly they looked leprous—have been repainted. The front path, which was cracked and weed-choked the last time I saw it, has been cleared and edged. The garden beds flanking the entrance have been weeded, the dead plants pulled, the soil turned. Someone—Saylor—has placed two potted mums on either side of the front door. Yellow. Cheerful. The kind of detail that says *someone lives here and they give a damn.*

I pull into the driveway and park behind the rented truck that appears to have become Saylor's mobile workshop. My hands are still shaking. My blouse may or may not be clean. And there is a dark gray sedan pulling in behind me that I am choosing to believe is a neighbor but know, with the certainty of a woman whose luck has been on an extended sabbatical, is the caseworker. Shit, *shit*, I hope she didn't clock my manic driving. That can't look good on my motherhood application.

I get out of the car at the same time as she does.

She's younger than I expected. Mid-thirties, maybe. Natural hair pulled back, a navy blazer over a printed blouse, sensible flats, a leather portfolio tucked under her arm. She has the calm, observant energy of someone whose job is to notice everything and say very little, which is essentially the opposite of my entire personality.

"Ms. Brinley?" She extends her hand. "I'm Janet Lundy. Court-appointed family services evaluator."

"Janet. Thank you for coming." I shake her hand with the firm but warm grip I reserve for people who hold my fate in their portfolio. "I apologize I'm a little disheveled. I barely made it in from the city in time. There was some confusion with the scheduling—I only learned about the change this morning."

"It's purposeful. We find that flexibility is actually part of what we're evaluating." She smiles—professional, practiced, giving nothing away. Her eyes are already on the house. "Shall we?"

That was swift. Did she just admit to pulling the ol' bait and switch to catch me off guard? I instantly hate her.

The front door opens before I reach it and Saylor is standing there like he owns the place. Which, in some ways, after days of labor, he does. He's wearing jeans and a white T-shirt—clean, I notice, like he changed into something presentable before I arrived—and his sandy-blond hair is pushed back, still damp from what I suspect was a sink-wash five minutes ago. There's a smudge of paint on his forearm that he either missed or left intentionally because it says *I've been working* in a language that caseworkers probably speak fluently.

"Hey," he says, looking at me. And the way he says it—soft, steady, a single syllable that carries the weight of five days of barely answered texts and a house he rebuilt while I was falling apart—makes something inside me crack along a fault line I didn't know existed.

"Hey," I say back, and it comes out smaller than I intended.

He turns to Janet with the easy, open smile of a man who has never once in his life been nervous around a stranger. "G'day, ma'am. I'm Saylor. Come on in."

We step inside, and I have to physically stop my mouth from falling open.

The foyer. The foyer that was dusty and cobwebbed and smelled like six years of stale air is...gleaming. The hardwood floors have been cleaned and polished. The chandelier is lit, every crystal clear, throwing prismatic light across the walls. Fresh flowers sit on the entry table in a ceramic vase. The staircase railing has been wiped down and oiled. It smells like lemon cleaner and fresh paint and something warm underneath—cinnamon, maybe, as if someone has been baking, which is insane because the kitchen didn't even have a functioning oven last week.

"We've been doing some work on the house," Saylor says to Janet, leading her forward with the proprietary ease of a man giving a tour of his own home. "Celeste felt like the suburbs would be a better environment for the baby. More space. A yard. The kind of neighborhood where kids ride bikes and people wave at each other." He gestures toward the living room. "We're still in the middle of renovations, but the main living spaces are coming together beautifully. Don't you think?"

We. He said *we.* Like this is ours. Like this is something we're building together.

The living room stops me for the second time. The sheets are gone. The burgundy sofa has been cleaned and repositioned around the fireplace with throw pillows—where did he find throw pillows?—and a soft blanket draped over one arm. The mantel has been dusted and arranged with candles and a framed photo that I recognize from the upstairs hallway. It's my parents and me at the shore, me maybe six or seven, mid-laugh, sand on my knees. Saylor chose that photo. Out of everything in this house, he chose the one where I look happiest.

Janet is taking notes. Small, efficient marks in her portfolio. She doesn't comment, which I'm learning is her style.

The kitchen. I barely recognize it. The cabinets have new hardware—brushed nickel, modern, a ten-dollar fix that transforms the entire room. The countertops have been scrubbed until the yellowed granite almost passes for intentional. The appliances are the same but they've been cleaned to glistening, and the window over the sink—the window with the view of the backyard—is framed by new curtains. Simple. White linen. The kind of curtains I would have chosen, which means Saylor was paying attention to something I said or didn't say, and I don't know which possibility undoes me more.

The fridge is running. I open it reflexively and find it stocked—milk, eggs, fruit, vegetables, juice. A container of something labeled *leftover pasta* in handwriting that is not mine. Saylor's been eating here. Probably sleeping here. Living here, practically.

"The yard is a work in progress," Saylor says, guiding Janet toward the back windows. "But we've got the deck stabilized and the garden's going to come back. I don't have a green thumb...I have a whole green hand and I'm picturing tomatoes, peppers, eggplants at least." He opens the back door and the three of us step onto the deck which, last I saw, was warped and leaning and dangerous. Now, it's solid. Level. New boards where the old ones rotted, the railing straight, the whole structure sanded and sealed. He did this. With his own hands.

Sweet. Enormously generous and kind. I focus hard on those friendly adjectives, because my brain is doing this thing all of a sudden where I'm picturing Saylor in weathered jeans, shirtless, sweat dripping down the six-pack that you just *know* this man has.

"Celeste, are you okay?" Saylor asks, waking me from my fever dream right before fantasy Saylor pours a whole glass of water down his chest and starts running like he's auditioning for a Baywatch feature.

"Huh? Yeah. Fine." I am positive I am blushing.

Janet looks at the tire swing hanging from the oak tree. Writes something down. Then, she swivels around, facing the house, using body language to tell us it's time to move on.

Saylor leads us up the stairs. Instead of the miserable wail I usually hear when I climb the third highest step, there's nothing but a solid thud when my foot lands. He skips the second door on the left and moves past it with the smooth redirect of a man who's been conducting tours in his head for days. The master bedroom is clean and staged. The French Script loveseat is gone—replaced, somehow, with a simple upholstered bench in cream linen that makes the room look ten years newer.

"Where's the—" I start.

"Garage," Saylor murmurs near my ear, low enough that Janet doesn't hear. "Couldn't burn it. Thought about it."

My laugh surprises me. It escapes before I can catch it—short, bright, a sound I haven't made in days. "Burn it," I mutter. "I hate that thing."

Janet glances over. I press my lips together.

"What's next?" Janet asks.

"The nursery," Saylor answers matter-of-factly.

The door to the third bedroom is closed. Saylor opens it and steps aside, and I walk in. I'm allowed one small inhale before my throat closes, cutting off my airway. The most aggressive, vicious form of stealing a woman's breath.

The walls are pale sage green—soft, warm, gender-neutral. The built in shelves have been sanded and painted white. A small crib stands against the far wall—simple, wooden, assembled with care. There's a small dresser with a changing pad on top. A rocking chair in the corner by the window, angled so that whoever sits in it can see the tire swing and the oak tree and the garden below. On the shelf above the crib, a row of children's books—spines bright, uncracked, new.

And on the wall beside the window, painted in small, careful letters: *You are so loved.*

I can't breathe.

I can feel Janet watching me. I can feel Saylor watching me. I'm standing in a room that didn't exist a week ago, a room that a man I've known for three weeks built for a baby who doesn't exist yet, and I am trying very hard not to cry in front of a court-appointed evaluator because crying might look like instability when it actually is the most overwhelming act of kindness I have ever received from another human being.

"This is lovely," Janet says. She writes in her portfolio. "You've clearly put a lot of thought into this. I think I've seen enough up here. Is there a restroom I could pop into?"

Saylor cringes. "The powder room on the first floor right by the entrance is clean." Judging by the look on his face, by clean he means functioning. I know for a fact this house has plumbing issues.

The moment we hear footsteps descending stairs, I release the breath I've been holding. "Saylor, how in the world—"

He holds up his hands in surrender. "I'm not saying this is the stuff you'll use. These are hand-me-downs from Forrest's daughter, Koda. We raided his storage unit and put whatever we could in here."

"How much if I want to keep it all?" My voice catches. I clear my throat to distract from the sniffle I can't help. If I'm sick of me crying, I'm sure Saylor is too. But then again I did just lose my best friend of two decades and inherited her unborn baby. Someone has to cut me some slack.

"How much?" Saylor parrots. "I don't think it's for sale, Celeste. Forrest let us borrow all these, but it has sentimental value. He probably wants it back. These are memories of Koda, you know?"

Suddenly a truth about parenting becomes crystal clear. It's not just about creating memories my child will remember. It's about creating moments that even I want to hold onto.

"That makes sense. I'm sorry. That was insensitive of me to ask."

"Oh, hey now. No. Not to give myself too much credit, but the room looks great. I'd want to keep it as it is, too. If it were for sale, I'd make sure it was yours."

I nod. "I know you would. Thank you."

We move through the rest of the upstairs while Janet pokes around the main floor. She's snooping, clearly. I heard the toilet flush at least five minutes ago. But I'm too lost in Saylor's narration to care—casually, confidently, pointing out the bathroom renovations, the storage plans, the guest room that could serve as a playroom later. I most definitely prefer the private tour, because he's talking about this home like he's a part of it.

He talks about the neighborhood—the schools, the parks, the fact that the family next door has a daughter who's two. He talks about the house like he's lived in it his whole life, like its history is his history, and I realize, standing behind him in the hallway while Janet spies downstairs, that he learned the house the way he learns everything—not by being told, but by paying attention.

Downstairs again. The living room. Janet is already settled on the edge of the sofa with her portfolio perched on her knee. This is the interview portion, and I can feel my armor assembling—the executive posture, the measured answers, the woman who has sat across from investors and buyers and board members and never once let them see her sweat.

But Saylor sits next to me. Close. Not touching, but close enough that I can feel the warmth radiating off him, can smell the paint and sawdust and soap, and his proximity does something to my armor that no boardroom has ever managed. It loosens. Not all the way. But enough. Just enough to make it ineffective.

Janet dives in without mercy, asking immediately about my work schedule. I explain the flexibility I've built-in—remote days, a VP who can run operations, the ability to restructure my calendar, pull back on travel, and ensure I'm around for a child's needs, especially in their infancy. She asks about support systems. I list Rina, my parents—which is a stretch, I admit, the attorney. It sounds weak. My backup babysitter is my lawyer? Yikes. But what am I supposed to say? Don't worry, I can afford a legion of nannies? That doesn't sound very warm.

And then Janet looks at Saylor, and at me, and at the sliver of space between us on the sofa.

"I have to say," Janet begins, pen hovering over her portfolio. "And I want to be transparent—my role is to observe and report, not to advise. But I will share that in cases where the court is deciding between two single guardians with similar financial profiles, the presence of a stable partnership can be significant." She pauses, choosing her words with the care of someone who knows they'll be remembered. "A two-parent household isn't a requirement. But it is definitely noted that you two are together."

I'm sorry...did she just say 'together'?

Are we not giving off lady-of-the-house and hired-contractor vibes? Is it because Saylor has been giving me puppy-dog eyes since I arrived and I keep having hallucinations about him doing very sexy things to me in the back of that pickup in the driveway?

Her sentiment is rolling around the three of us like a grenade with the pin still in. Saylor's posture shifts beside me—not a flinch, not a stiffening, but something more alert. Like a frequency change. Like he heard the same thing I did: *if you're together, you have an edge over Eleanor.*

I should correct her. I should say: we're not together. He's a contractor I hired. He's someone I've known for three weeks who happens to be extraordinarily kind and confusingly dedicated and sitting too close to me on a sofa in a nursery-green house that he painted with his own hands. I should say all of this because I am an honest person and because lying to a court evaluator is probably illegal and definitely inadvisable.

But I don't. Because I look at the framed photo on the mantel—the one of me laughing at the shore—and I think about the nursery with the baby board books on the shelf and the words on the wall, and I think about Whitney standing on a sidewalk in an emerald dress asking me to be brave, and the truth is I am brave enough to accept the gift of advantage Saylor is giving me. I'm brave enough to fight dirty when it comes to Eleanor.

So I say nothing. And my silence draws a line that I can't uncross.

"It's clear you two have a strong dynamic," Janet continues, glancing between us. "But I'll note that in my experience, the court does take into account the perceived stability of the relationship." Her eyes move to Saylor, then to me. "The age difference, for instance—and forgive my frankness—can sometimes read as, well, transitional. Especially to a judge who's evaluating long-term suitability."

Transitional. The word hits me like a slap. Not because it's offensive—it's clinical, it's measured, it's the word I've been using in my own head. Detour. Temporary. A hot and heavy romance that isn't a destination. Janet just said out loud the thing I've been telling myself since Saylor walked into my office with a Rolex case and a collared shirt, and hearing it from someone else's mouth exposes what it really is: a defense mechanism dressed up as wisdom.

"If transitional means fooling around...that is not us. We're um, definitely end game. Yeah." Saylor gives me a lunatic smile while pumping his eyebrows. "In it to win it." His hand lands on my knee.

I feel the contact the way you feel a change in altitude—pressure, warmth, the immediate recalibration of every nerve in your body. His palm is broad and takes up the entire span of my knee. Beautiful, strong, callused working hands. Hands that could never belong to Greg because the only thing he knows how to work is a phone, calling somebody else to do the job he can't.

"So you obviously plan to be a big part of the baby's life."

He glances at me, seemingly asking for permission. I give him a quick nod. Saylor lies under pressure much better than I do. Let's call that an orange flag, not red. At least he's lying *for* me?

"Absolutely. Celeste and I are already arguing over baby names. I like Reed Bailey—gender-neutral, a little distinct. Celeste of course will want to name our baby something more regal and French—Sandrine, Fleur, Vivienne...the vetoes go on and on."

"What's wrong with Vivienne?" The question breaks free like word vomit. Me, getting defensive over names I didn't come up with, momentarily forgetting we're not actually naming this child together.

"Well, you get it," Saylor says. "Typical lovers' quarrels. How do you feel about Vivienne, Janet?"

She gives an odd smile. Like she's trying to be kind, but she smells something sour. "Vivienne is a nice name in my opinion. But that's not my bigger concern. Just for clarity on my report, what exactly are you guys? Casual? Boyfriend-girlfriend? Planning a future?"

"Which of those options helps our case?" I ask pointedly.

"What would *not* help your case is fabrication," Janet says, emphasizing her words. "But it'd be notable in my report if you two were in a committed relationship. Obviously you're not married, but knowing this is a serious relationship is a distinction I could make."

"Well, then, *sweetie*, I think for the sake of clarity, it's time we share the news." Saylor makes big, cartoon eyes at me. "Where's your ring? Is it in the car? You should go put it on."

My heart literally stops beating. I know this because I hold my breath, sit perfectly still, and I wait for the soft knock inside my chest cavity which doesn't come. Holy shit. Am I having a heart attack right now?

"My...my...ring?" I stutter out.

Saylor sighs with ease. "Okay, this is a little embarrassing. I'm not bringing much to the table financially. Everything we have is from this beautiful woman's hard-earned success. But, she insisted, if and when I ever proposed that she wanted something sentimental. Something I bought for her with my own money, even it was a peanut glued to a piece of twine. Not materialistic, this one. So I bought the best diamond I could afford, but when I gave it to her, it looked so dinky. I feel bad, this woman deserves a whole damn skating rink, you know? So I asked her to keep it to herself until I can afford something worthy of her pretty fingers."

Why is this man such an elaborate storyteller? First, the diarrhea in the Hamptons. Now, the most made-up story about a pauper trying to propose to a princess. Has Saylor never heard of a minimal response in his life?

"I'm not embarrassed," I add. "I love my ring. It's just that we haven't told anybody we're engaged *except for you, Janet*," I say through gritted teeth.

"The point is...you two are engaged?" Janet asks, her pen frozen in air, waiting for its next commandment.

Saylor turns to me, and I see it in his eyes—the flicker of *oh God, what have I just done* immediately overridden by something brighter and more reckless. Conviction. The same look he had when he showed up at my office uninvited. The same look he had in the Riptide booth when he told me I wasn't alone.

"Yup," he says with his full chest. "We are getting married. Wow, it feels so good to say that out loud. We've been keeping this secret for so long. In fact..." He wraps his arm around my shoulders, pulls me into him, and kisses me.

It is not a careful kiss. It is not a staged kiss or a strategic kiss or the kind of kiss two people plan in advance to sell a lie. It is the kiss of a man who has been thinking about this for three weeks and has finally been given—or has created—an excuse to do it. His mouth is warm and firm and he kisses me like he knows exactly what he's doing, which is infuriating because I cannot say the same. I am being kissed on a burgundy sofa in my parents' living room by a twenty-six-year-old Australian contractor-slash-escort in front of a court-appointed family services evaluator, and my brain has left the building.

My body stays.

For two seconds—maybe three, maybe a century, time has become unreliable—I kiss him back. Not because of Janet. Not because of the custody case. Because his mouth is on mine and something inside me that has been clenched for years, possibly decades, releases. A fist opening. A seam letting go. The specific surrender of a woman who has been holding herself together so tightly that she forgot what it felt like to be held by someone else.

Then I pull back. Compose my face. Smooth my blouse. Become Celeste Brinley, CEO, again—or some approximation of her that can function while her lips are still tingling and her knee is still warm where his hand was.

"Engaged," Janet repeats. She smiles the first genuine smile I've seen from her. "Congratulations." She writes something in her portfolio. Something long. Something that I desperately want to read and absolutely cannot ask to see. "That's wonderful news. I'll make sure to include that in my report."

"We're continuing to keep it quiet for now," Saylor says smoothly. "With everything going on—Whitney's passing, the custody proceedings, Celeste's company, the renovation it's just so much at once. Our engagement means everything to us. We want to give the news time to breathe until we're all really ready to celebrate."

"Of course. Completely understandable." Janet closes her portfolio and stands. "I have everything I need for today. The home is beautiful already. Once the renovations are done, I'd say this is a perfect home for a child. The nursery especially—it's clear a great deal of care went into it. That's what we love to see."

She shakes both our hands. At the door, she turns back.

"I should mention, my next visit won't be scheduled. The court prefers at least one or two unannounced evaluations to observe the family in their natural environment. The next one could be anytime in the next few weeks." She says this pleasantly, the way you'd mention a weather forecast, but the subtext is unmistakable:

I'll be back. Without warning. And whatever I find needs to match what I saw today.

"We'll be here," Saylor says, his hand on the small of my back.

Janet leaves. Her gray sedan reverses down the driveway, turns onto the road, and disappears behind the oaks.

The front door closes.

Saylor's hand drops from my back.

And the house—this gleaming, painted, staged, impossible house—goes silent around us like a theater after the audience has gone and the actors are left standing in the set they built, trying to remember which parts were real.

I turn to face him.

He's already looking at me with an expression I can't categorize—something between triumph and terror—the face of a man who just jumped off a cliff and is still calculating whether there's water below.

"What," I say slowly, "have you done?"

"I improved our odds."

"You told a court-appointed evaluator that we're engaged."

"I did."

"We're not engaged."

"We're not."

"You kissed me."

"I did."

"In front of a government official."

"She seemed to enjoy it."

"Saylor." My voice is shaking and I hate it. I hate that it's shaking because I'm not sure if it's shaking from anger or fear or the fact that I can still feel his mouth on mine, still feel the exact pressure of his lips, the roughness of his jaw, the way his hand tightened on my shoulder when I kissed him back. Because I did. I kissed him back. In front of another person, an important person and her leather portfolio and her efficient little notes. I kissed him back, and I would do it again, which is the most terrifying realization I've had since the phone rang this morning.

"Saylor, this isn't a game. If she finds out we lied—"

"Then we don't let her find out." He says it simply. Not flippantly. There's no mischief in his voice, no smirk on his face. He looks serious. More serious than I've ever seen him. "She's coming back unannounced. Which means someone needs to be here. Living here. Making it look like a home and not a stage. I can move in. If you don't mind, Mum can come with me—the ground floor has everything she needs, no stairs necessary. We can keep the house warm and alive. We can be here around-the-clock, prepared for Janet's next visit. And once you get awarded custody, and when the baby comes, we'll be on our way."

My brain is doing the logistics. Everything makes sense... except the emotional math. How can I play house with Saylor without letting my mind wander from fantasy to real-life infatuation? He's twenty-six, hotter than hell, and keeps making his intentions abundantly clear. How long can I resist this?

"Okay, that's a start," I say slowly until another thought dawns on me. "Wait, what do you mean your mom has to stay on the ground floor? You guys are doing me a huge favor. Give her the master for God's sake."

Saylor's gaze drops to his boots. "My mom was in a really bad car accident. Her spine is so twisted up, it's basically braided. She has intense chronic pain, and major difficulties walking. We live on the fourth floor—stairs are the enemy."

"Oh my gosh, Saylor. I'm so sorry to hear that." I ignore the boundaries I just told myself need to go back in place. I grab his wrist, move my gentle squeezes up his forearm until I'm caressing his elbow. "And you take care of her?"

He shrugs. "I'm kind of her problem and her solution, I guess."

I stare at him. He stands in my parents' foyer—this boy, this man, this impossible person who broke into my office and rebuilt my childhood home and just kissed me on a sofa and called it strategy—and I want to scream at him. I want to shake him. I want to tell him that he has no idea what he's gotten us into, that this is fraud, that this is reckless, that this is the most irresponsible, impulsive, potentially catastrophic thing anyone has ever done on my behalf.

But the look in his eyes when he talks about his mom... All my sensible rage dissipates. There is a warmth spreading through my chest that I cannot name and cannot stop and most definitely don't want to.

"Celeste," he says, and his voice is quiet now. The performance is over. Janet is gone. It's just us and the house and the silence and whatever is building between us like pressure behind a closed door. "I know this is crazy. I know you didn't ask for this. But I'm not going to let Eleanor take this baby from you. And if that means moving into your parents' house and pretending to be your fiancé for a few weeks, then that's what I'll do. No hesitation."

"Why?" It comes out as barely more than a whisper.

He holds my gaze the way he held it in the office. The way he held it at Riptide. The way he held it on the couch at Tidewater House, when I fell asleep on his shoulder and he pulled a blanket over both of us and didn't ask for anything in return.

"You know why," he says, which I'm learning is his catchphrase.

And I do. That's the problem. I know exactly why, and I'm not ready for it, and it's here anyway—standing in my foyer, smelling like paint, looking at me like I'm the answer to a question he's been asking his whole life.

I press my fingers to my lips. They're still warm.

"Move in," I say. "You can move in as soon as you'd like. Bring your mother. I'm going to give you my black card. Buy any and everything you guys need to be comfortable."

He shakes his head but I glare at him and he reluctantly shrugs. We just had our first, silent, power struggle. Adorable. I won.

"And Saylor?"

"Yeah?"

"This is still professional. If you ever kiss me in front of a government official again without warning—" I search for the appropriate threat. My brain, still vibrating from the kiss and the lie and the enormity of what we just set in motion, offers nothing useful. "—I'll think of a consequence later. But it will be severe."

He grins. That grin. The one that started all of this.

"Noted."

He walks past me toward the kitchen, presumably to resume whatever work he was doing before my life careened off a cliff. And I stand in the foyer of my childhood home, in my wrinkled cream blouse and my Louboutins and my carefully constructed bun, and I press my fingers to my mouth and feel the ghost of a kiss that was supposed to be fake and wasn't, that was supposed to be strategy and was something else entirely, that changed everything and left me standing in the wreckage of my own composure wondering how, exactly, a woman who designs things for a living ended up in a situation she didn't see coming.

Whitney would laugh. Whit would throw her head back and howl and say, *"finally, Lessi. Finally. You're living now, girl."*

I almost smile.

Almost.

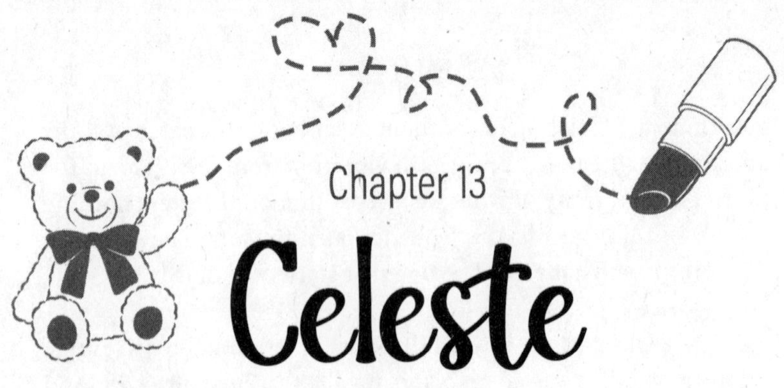

Chapter 13
Celeste

This man is building you Barbie's dream house, Celeste. And I hate to break it to you, but he thinks he's Ken.

The silk is wrong.

I've been staring at the same swatch for forty minutes—pinned to the dress form under the track lighting in my studio, rotating it a quarter inch every few minutes like I'm trying to crack a safe. The weight is right. The drape is right. The color—a muted copper that I've been calling "rusted dawn" because naming fabrics is sixty percent of my job and I refuse to call anything "brownish orange"—is almost right. But the hand is off. There's a stiffness to it, a reluctance, like the fabric knows what I want it to do and is choosing not to cooperate.

Had I chosen to be on that call with Valencia a few weeks ago, instead of surrendering to my emotional breakdown, I wouldn't be having this problem. Maria, my VP of production, probably didn't yell on that meeting. No good. You must yell at Valencia to get their attention, otherwise they won't listen. I swear I put that in our SOPs.

The fall line is due to my production team in three weeks. I have eleven pieces finalized out of twenty-two. I have a Bergdorf exclusive hinging on a collection that is, at best, half-finished and, at worst, actively resisting me. I have sketch after sketch pinned to my corkboard that looked brilliant at two in the morning but looks like the fever dreams of a woman who's forgotten how to design in the sober light of ten a.m.

This doesn't happen to me. I don't stall. I don't stare at fabric and wait for it to speak because fabric has always sung to me—in textures and possibilities, in the specific language of what a body could become if you dressed it with intention. But for the past week, the fabric has gone quiet, and I'm standing in my studio like a woman waiting for a phone call that she knows isn't coming.

The phone calls that are coming, for the record, are all from people I don't want to hear from. Amy from accounting, reminding me that production is at least twenty percent over budget and we need to use more cost-effective material. *Not happening.* My publicist, asking why I haven't confirmed the Vogue feature. *Mostly because I have nothing to say at the moment.* Denise Bilch, asking for documentation—something from mine and Greg's divorce I don't feel like digging up—that I should have sent three days ago. And Margot, asking if I want a green smoothie, because she has learned nothing, evidently.

What I want is to be in Westchester. Away from all of this.

The thought arrives uninvited, the way all the dangerous thoughts have been arriving lately—without permission, without context, wearing the casual clothes of something harmless when it is, in fact, the most destabilizing thought I've had all day. I want to be in the house. I want to see what Saylor's done to the kitchen. I want to sit in the rocking chair in the nursery and look at the tire swing and feel, for even five minutes, like the person Janet Lundy thinks I am: a woman with a partner, a plan, and a home that smells like cinnamon and fresh paint.

Instead, I'm here. Staring at copper silk that won't behave. Being exactly the version of myself that Eleanor described to the court in her statement—a career-obsessed CEO who doesn't know how to stop working long enough to raise a child.

There's a knock on my office door. I ignore it as if I'm invisible through these walls of windows. Instead, my office landline beeps loudly. The call comes from Margot's desk. I answer before I look up.

"Margot, if that's a smoothie, I swear on everything—"

"It's a bánh mì and it's from me, so put the claws away."

At my office door stands the most pleasant surprise for a Friday afternoon. I wave Rina in, rising from my seat, preparing my apology for being rude.

She walks in carrying a brown paper bag and two iced coffees, looking like the only functioning adult in my life, which she may in fact be. She's in a charcoal pantsuit with red heels—power outfit, which means she either came from a meeting or is heading to one, or both, because Rina operates at a frequency that makes my eighteen-hour days look leisurely, and that's even after she quit teaching.

"You haven't eaten," she says. It's not a question.

"I had coffee."

"Coffee is not food, Celeste. Coffee is a coping mechanism that you've promoted to a food group." She sets the bag on my coffee table, nudging a pile of swatches aside with the precision of a woman who knows better than to wrinkle anything in my studio. "Eat. Then tell me why you look like you haven't slept."

"I've slept."

"You've slept the way I've slept, which is four hours with one eye open and your phone charging six inches from your face." I make my way to the sofa, and she sits on the stool across from me, crossing her legs. "How's the line coming?"

"The line is plotting against me."

"That bad?"

"Eleven of twenty-two. Three weeks to deadline. And the hero piece—the copper gown that's supposed to anchor the entire collection—is currently giving me the silent treatment, with two middle fingers erect in the air." I gesture at the dress form. "I can't find the movement. It should cascade. It should feel like liquid metal. Instead it feels like—"

"A curtain."

I stare at her. "Yes. Exactly like a curtain."

"Sometimes you just need fresh eyes. Step away. Eat the sandwich. Come back to it tomorrow."

"I don't have tomorrow. I have three weeks and a Bergdorf buyer who will not hesitate to replace me with whatever twenty-four-year-old designer is trending on Instagram this month." I unwrap the bánh mì anyway because Rina brought it and Rina is usually right about the things I need, even when I'm committed to refusing them.

I take a bite. It's perfect. Pickled daikon, cilantro, jalapeño, the bread crisp and warm. I hate that it's perfect because it means Rina was right and I was hungry and I didn't even know it, which is becoming a theme—people around me identifying my needs before I can.

Rina sips her coffee and watches me eat with the patient satisfaction of a woman who has completed a mission. Then, casually, the way she delivers all her most significant information: "Saylor quit."

I stop chewing. "Quit what?"

"The agency. Officially. Called me four days ago, thanked me for everything, and said he was done."

The bánh mì sits in my mouth, un-chewed. I force myself to swallow even though it hurts. "Wow. Did he say why?"

"He said he had other things he wanted to focus on." Rina's expression is carefully neutral. It's the face she wears in negotiations, the one that says 'I know more than I'm telling you and I'm waiting for you to figure it out.' "So that's three. Forrest, Taio, and now Saylor. My three best guys, gone in six months. All because of love." She sips her coffee. "I'm starting to take it personally."

"Saylor is not in love...well, with me. It's possible he's in love with someone his own age. Someone who's not—"

"Hey. Careful. We're the same age. Whatever you say about you, you're saying about me."

I cringe. "The point is, Saylor didn't quit because of me."

The words leave my mouth with the conviction of a woman

reading a teleprompter. Rina doesn't even dignify them with a response. She just looks at me over the rim of her iced coffee with an expression that roughly translates to: *sure, Celeste. Whatever helps you sleep at night. Assuming you're sleeping, which we've established you are not.*

"He said he's living in your parents' house. He moved his mom in? He's helping you with the custody case? Do these sound like neighborly, platonic favors?"

"It's not a favor. I'm paying him as a contractor."

"Yeah, so was I."

"What are you getting at, my friend?"

Her smile is sly and cocky. "I'm simply saying if it looks like a duck, quacks like a duck, waddles like a duck, loves water like a duck..." She raises her eyebrows. "How long do I have to keep going?"

"You have it all wrong. I mean, sometimes we text," I say, because apparently I've decided to defend a position I didn't take. "He sends me updates on the house. Photos of the progress. What he's working on, what supplies he needs." I pause. "He sent me a photo a few nights ago of the kitchen backsplash he's tiling. Asked me to choose between two patterns. I spent twenty minutes deciding before I texted back, so he called. And yeah, we talked a bit. But it's all very platonic."

Except that kiss. Definitely not platonic. Definitely not going to bring that up.

"Talked about what? Backsplash, huh?"

"It's a significant design decision."

"This man is building you Barbie's dream house, Celeste. And I hate to break it to you, but he thinks he's Ken."

I set the sandwich down. "That's not what's happening."

"What is happening?"

What's happening is that every night around ten, after Ada's gone to bed and the house is quiet, Saylor texts me. It started as logistics—measurements, paint colors, whether I wanted to keep the old dining table or replace it. But somewhere around day three, the texts got longer. He told me Ada had him rearrange the living room furniture because the sofa was facing the wrong direction for afternoon light and she was right, the room looks better now. He told me he found a box of my old Halloween costumes in the attic and that I apparently went as a "fashion designer" three years in a row, which tracks. He told me the neighbor's daughter, the two-year-old, wandered over while he was fixing the deck railing and sat in the sawdust watching him work for fifteen minutes before her mother came looking for her, and that the little girl called him "hammer bang-bang man," which he now considers his official title.

He asked me about my day. Not performatively, not as a segue to talking about himself. He asked, and then he listened, and then he responded with something thoughtful, and then we kept going until midnight, and I fell asleep with my phone on my chest and woke up with a message that said: *Goodnight, Celeste. The house misses you. So does the backsplash.*

So, no, Rina. I'm not getting a lot of sleep. But it's not for the reason you think.

"Do you know Ada well?" I ask, redirecting.

Rina's face softens. "Not very well. But enough. Definitely enough to care about what happens to her, Saylor, and their whole situation." Rina pauses, and the softness shifts into something heavier. "I worry about her. And I worry about Saylor carrying all of it."

"Carrying all of what?"

Rina sets her coffee down. Studies me for a moment, the way she does when she's calculating whether a piece of information will help or harm. "How much did Saylor tell you about his mom?"

"I know she was in a bad car accident. Chronic pain. Trouble walking. He takes care of her."

"That's the headline, honey. The article is worse." Rina leans back on the stool. "Ada was a marathon runner. Competitive. Ran track in college, trained every morning, it was her whole identity. She and Saylor lived on a small property outside Wollongong—

south of Sydney. Beautiful area. She ran a little hobby farm, raised Saylor on her own. He stuck around even after he was of age. He was twenty-two when they got into the accident."

"They? I thought *Ada* was in a car accident. Saylor never mentioned he got hurt."

"Because he didn't. Miraculously. But he *was* driving. He was okay, but Ada was thrown through the front windshield. The poor thing crumpled like a piece of paper. Saylor said when he came to, he saw his mother's body by the side of the road and thought for certain she was dead."

"And the other car?"

"Walked away, unscathed. Everyone was okay, except for Ada."

I place my hand over my heart and exhale with measured control like I'm trying to cool a hot beverage. "This all happened in Australia? Then how did they get here?"

"About a year after the accident, some doctor—or someone posing as a doctor—sold them on an experimental procedure. He told them it could restore her mobility and stop the pain. Saylor believed it. He sold everything. Their house, the farm equipment, a truck. They put every dollar they had into this treatment. They wrote a check, and moved to the United States."

My stomach drops. "And? It didn't work."

"It didn't work because they didn't do it. It was a scam. The procedure didn't exist. The money was gone. They had nothing—no house, no savings, no way to get home. Saylor somehow scraped together enough for a rent-controlled apartment that would accept cash payments. He thought if he could just get Ada to the right doctors..." Rina trails off. "He was twenty-two, barely a man. He moved his disabled mother to a foreign country with no money, no contacts, no plan. Just the hope that someone in this city could help her."

"And that's when he found you."

"Actually, that's when Taio found him. Bartending, barely making rent, taking extra shifts as a bouncer. Taio recognized the hustle—a good-looking kid working himself to death for very little pay—and brought him to me. A little more money changed everything. He could afford to fix up their apartment, he got Ada into pain therapy, got her medication. But nothing will ever absolve the guilt..." Rina shakes her head. "He blames himself for the scam. He blames himself for selling the farm. He blames himself for the fact that his mother lives on the fourth floor and can barely make it to the street some days. Every dollar he makes goes to her. He keeps nothing for himself."

I'm not eating anymore. The bánh mì sits on its paper wrapping, untouched, growing cold. I'm thinking about Saylor in my foyer saying *I'm kind of her problem and her solution.* I'm thinking about him fixing my mother's staircase while his own mother can't walk up them. I'm thinking about the Rolex he wouldn't keep because forty thousand dollars felt like someone else's money when his mother needs help that probably costs four times that.

Is that honorable? Or martyrdom?

"There's hope though," Rina adds. "A new experimental treatment, but I vetted this lead myself. A Dr. Yassa—Mount Sinai's new walking billboard for medical advancement in neurosurgery." Rina rolls her eyes. "Does it ever bother you how saving lives has to be commercialized?"

"It gets donor attention," I say. "You know how this game works."

Rina knows money. I know money. We're friends because more often than we'll admit, we detest it. Not because money doesn't open doors. It's just that once you walk through, it traps you in small, stuffy spaces, locking you into a facade that's hard to walk away from.

"The experimental treatment. The one at Mount Sinai with Dr. Yassa. How hopeful is it on a scale of throwing darts in the dark, to shooting fish in a barrel?"

"That's a weird scale, Celeste, but I guess somewhere in the middle? Some case studies had remarkable results. But it's expensive, insurance won't cover it. And there's risk. And even if there wasn't, Saylor just doesn't have the money." She looks at me with an expression I recognize—the one she wears when she's placed all the pieces on the table and is waiting to see what you build. "He won't accept help. You know that by now."

Oh, do I. I know it the way I know the thread count of Egyptian cotton by touch—instinctively, completely, without needing to be told.

I pick up the sandwich. Take another bite. Chew slowly because it's lost its luster as my appetite fades. I say nothing, getting lost in my own thoughts.

There's a primal urge deep in my gut to help Saylor, whether or not he likes it. But some things need to sit before they become decisions. Forcing my way into this puzzle of tragedy and completing it my way is what a boss would do. Do I want to be Saylor's boss...or something else?

The studio door opens without a knock, which means it's either Margot or someone who has confused my workspace with a public park.

Ugh. It's neither.

Greg walks in like he owns the room. Which, technically, by the parasitic math of our divorce settlement, he partially does. He's wearing a navy suit—Brioni, obviously, because Greg has never met a designer label he didn't want to be seen in—and carrying a tablet with the screen angled toward me like a weapon.

"Celeste. We need to talk about the Q3 projections."

Rina doesn't move from her stool. She doesn't greet Greg. She sips her coffee with the unhurried calm of a woman who has ranked this man on her personal threat assessment and found him somewhere between "mosquito" and "inconvenience."

"I'm in a meeting, Greg."

"It's Rina. *Hi, Rina.*" He barely glances in her direction. "And you're eating a sandwich."

"I'm in a meeting where I'm eating a sandwich. Which, last I checked, is still my prerogative in my own office."

He sets the tablet on my worktable—on top of a swatch, which I clock and file under *more reasons to despise this man*—and crosses his arms. "The fall line is eleven pieces behind. Production is asking questions. The Bergdorf team called my office because they couldn't reach yours. And I've been hearing from multiple people that you've been, let's call it, *distracted*."

"Multiple people?" *Bullshit.* He means Margot who guards personal details about as effectively as a puppy guards its own tail.

Something flickers across his face—the briefest tell, a twitch at the corner of his mouth that confirms what I've suspected for months. Greg has been feeding Margot attention—coffees, compliments, the odd birthday gift—and in return, Margot has been feeding Greg my schedule, my mood, my whereabouts. Not maliciously. Margot doesn't have the strategic capacity for malice. She's simply a woman who responds to kindness with information, which makes her the worst possible person to sit outside my office and the best possible asset for an ex-husband who wants to keep tabs.

"I have sources," Greg says vaguely.

"You have my assistant, who you've been plying with lattes and compliments like she's a parking meter. Don't insult my intelligence."

"The point stands. You're behind on the line. You're burning time on this custody circus—"

"Careful."

"—and frankly, Celeste, the board is going to start asking questions if the spring designs don't materialize. You can't run a company and play house with some manwhore while trying to claim a baby that isn't yours. I mean, what are you going to do with a newborn at your age?"

The room goes very still.

I ignore the manwhore comment. His snide comments about my age are old news. *But a baby that isn't mine?* It's time to roll up my sleeves.

Rina sets down her coffee. I can feel her tensing—not visibly, not in any way Greg would notice, but in the way a woman tenses when she's preparing to either intervene or bear witness, and she's giving me the first right to choose which.

A newborn at my age? Fuck you, Greg.

I look at him. Really look at him. He's wearing the particular arrogance of a man who inherited half a company through fake charm and wit. He desecrated our marriage because women lacking a fully developed prefrontal cortex make him horny. And now he walks into my studio, my space, the room where I create the only thing in my life that has never disappointed me, and tells me I'm distracted? Once again, tells me I'm too old to deserve my life?

"Greg." My voice is level. Controlled. The boardroom voice, the one that means someone has severely miscalculated. "I'm going to say this once, so I'd encourage you to listen with both ears. This company exists because I designed it. Every stitch, every collection, every relationship with every buyer and every mill and every magazine—that's my work. My name. My reputation. You are here because a divorce settlement gave you equity in something you didn't build and couldn't replicate."

Greg rolls his wrist, trying to dismiss my rant. "Celeste—"

"If we go public like you so direly want, and a board of directors sits down to evaluate who is essential to the continued success of this brand, I want you to think very carefully about which one of us they'd consider expendable. Because it's not the woman whose name is on the building." I rise, pick up his tablet from my swatch, and hold it out to him. "And if you ever refer to someone I care about as a manwhore again, or suggest that the baby my best friend entrusted to me isn't mine, I will make that board conversation happen sooner than either of us would like. Are we crystal-fucking-clear about whose house you're in right now?"

Greg takes the tablet. His jaw is tight. His eyes are hard. But he takes it, which means he heard me, and he turns and walks out of the studio without another word. The door closes behind him with a controlled click that somehow sounds louder than a slam.

Silence.

Then Rina, from her stool, both arms extended well above her head like Mario frozen mid-jump, says, "*Hell yes.* That was a long time coming. Oh my God. I did good things in life which is why karma rewarded me by allowing my presence during the most lethal, epic tell-off of all time."

I exhale. The breath comes from somewhere deep—not relief exactly, but release. The feeling of having finally said a thing that's been composting in my chest for months, maybe years.

"He called Saylor a manwhore. It set me off." Partial truth. Partial lie. He doesn't get to badmouth my friend in front of me, but it feels good to know Greg's intimidated by Saylor. He should be. The way Saylor enters a room and can make a woman swoon—it's very intimidating. For all of us.

"I heard."

"Do you think that's what everyone thinks? That I'm a sad old spinster that has resorted to a love life filled with escort-fueled vignettes?"

"Oh stop that. Greg doesn't know what to do with a man who's actually good to you. It short-circuits him. So he diminishes." Rina joins me on the couch, sitting close enough to nudge my knee with hers. "You know, Sean used to do the same thing. Anytime I succeeded at something, he'd find the smallest possible way to make it about luck instead of skill. When I got tenure at Columbia, well it wasn't Harvard, right? It was always 'Right place, right time.' 'The market was favorable.' Never 'you're brilliant and I'm proud of you.' Because a well-read woman is always intimidating to a coward. But a talented, intelligent woman? She is revered by a real man. And the Gregs and Seans of the world will never be real men. They'll just be loud ones."

I sit with that. I sit with the echo of Whitney saying the same thing in different words on a sidewalk outside a fondue restaurant—*he's reminding you that you've expired.* I sit with the image of Saylor in my foyer, paint on his forearm, looking at me like I was the most extraordinary thing he'd ever seen, and not once—*not even once*—making me feel like I was too much, or too old, or too anything.

"Can I ask you something?" Rina says.

"You're going to anyway."

"Fair." She smiles. "I was thinking of booking a spa weekend. Just us. Get out of the city, decompress, drink wine, complain about men, the whole thing. I found this place in Connecticut—hot springs, no cell service, the works. What do you think? This weekend?"

The offer is generous. It's exactly the kind of thing I would have said yes to three weeks ago, before the funeral, before Saylor, before a nursery with *you are so loved* painted on the wall. Three weeks ago, I would have packed a bag and disappeared into eucalyptus steam and silence and called it self-care.

But the woman sitting in this studio right now is not that woman. Or maybe she is, but she wants something different.

"Actually," I say, and I hear the shift in my own voice—something lighter, something almost shy, a register I haven't used in so long that it takes me a moment to recognize it as hope. "I think I want to spend the weekend in Westchester."

Rina raises an eyebrow.

"The renovations aren't done," I add quickly, because I am still Celeste and I still require a logical framework for every emotional decision. "There's the backyard. The guest rooms. Saylor can't do it all alone. I should be there. It's my house."

"It's your house," Rina repeats, and her tone is so carefully blank, it's practically neon. "And that's the reason you want to spend the weekend there. The house."

"Yes."

"Not the Australian."

"The house, Rina."

"The house that the Australian is currently living in. With his mother. While pretending to be your fiancé."

I pick up my iced coffee. Take a long sip. Meet her eyes over the rim.

"I'm going to help with the renovations," I say firmly. "That's all."

"Sure. You of all people, getting your hands dirty."

"Hey!" I scold. But we both know it's the truth.

Rina stands. Collects her bag. Smooths her pantsuit with the practiced gesture of a woman who is about to leave and wants her exit to carry the appropriate weight. She pauses at the door.

"Celeste?"

"What?"

"Bring wine this weekend. You know, to Westchester. Good wine. The kind you drink when you're celebrating something, even if you haven't figured out what it is yet."

She winks, then leaves in the expected Rina fanfare. She's so goofy and yet ethereal, a bizarre combination.

The studio is quiet again. Just me and the copper silk and the dress form and the eleven pieces that are finished and the eleven that aren't and the particular silence of a woman sitting in the mess of an afternoon that contained a work crisis, an unexpected sandwich, a revelation, a long-overdue confrontation, and a decision she's pretending is about a house.

I look at the copper swatch. I rotate it a quarter inch. *It'd help if you had some hips, Patrice!* I rotate it one more quarter inch, and voilà.

For the first time in weeks—not because anything has changed, but because something inside me has shifted, like furniture being rearranged to catch the afternoon light—I see it. The drape. The cascade. The way the fabric wants to move if I just stop fighting it and let it fall.

Newly inspired, I pick up my pencil and start sketching once again.

Chapter 14
Saylor

You know why.

Mum is standing at the kitchen island without her cane.

I notice it the way I notice everything about her mobility—automatically, constantly, the background hum of a brain that's been tracking her pain levels for years. Always hoping for the best, expecting the worst. She's leaning against the granite, both palms flat, the posture of someone who wants to appear casual while doing something that costs her more than she'd ever admit. Her tea is steaming beside her. The morning light through the curtains I found on clearance at Home Depot that Celeste seemed to like anyway.

"This countertop," she says, running her hand across the granite, "is bigger than our kitchen at home."

"The old kitchen or the current kitchen?"

"Both. Combined." She lifts her tea and takes a careful sip. "You know, back in Wollongong, I had exactly one counter and it was also the dining table and also, occasionally, the ironing board. Multi-purpose. Quite efficient." She looks around the kitchen—the new hardware, the scrubbed countertops, the fridge I stocked yesterday with groceries that cost an entire week's worth of bartending tips. "It's strange, isn't it? How people can have all this and just let it sit. Let it rot. Like it's nothing."

"Money does that. When you can replace anything, nothing's

worth maintaining. Money's never worth chasing, in my opinion."

"That's very wise for a boy who grew up chasing chickens."

"I grew up chasing a lot of things, Mum. Chickens were the least of it."

"You were always flirting with some little girl from the neighborhood. From the time you were out of nappies, I knew I was in trouble." She smiles. It's the real one—not the brave one she wears when the pain is bad, not the polite one she gives to strangers who hold doors for her. The real one, the one that makes her whole face change, the one I'd do anything to see more often.

She looks at the window. At the backyard. The tire swing, the garden I've started bringing back, the oak tree that's older than both of us combined. I watch her take it in and I can see the thought forming before she says it—the way her eyes go soft and distant, the way her fingers tighten around the mug.

"I'm sorry I couldn't give you all this," she murmurs.

"Mum—"

"A backyard. A swing. A house with more than two rooms and a shower that didn't take twenty minutes to heat up." She's not looking at me. She's looking at the oak tree like it's a shrine to her failure. "If I'd stayed with your father, maybe we could have—"

"Stop."

The word comes out harder than I intend. She flinches, just barely—a micro-movement that most people wouldn't clock but I've been reading her body like a textbook for years. I soften my tone.

"Mum, listen to me. I had the best childhood. I'm not saying that because I'm supposed to. I'm saying it because I remember." I lean against the counter across from her. "I remember the lunch notes. I remember you running with me in the mornings before the sun came up, both of us half asleep, the roosters going off like we'd beaten them awake or something. I remember you sitting with me at the kitchen table—our one counter—helping me with math even though you hate math. You used to get the answers wrong on purpose so I'd have to correct you, and you'd act shocked every time like I was a genius."

"You are a genius."

"I'm a bloke who can tile a backsplash and barbie a decent steak. But I'm not upset about it. Dad would've given us a bigger house and I would've grown up listening to him scream at you through the walls. You chose small and safe over big and broken. You taught me what a woman should and shouldn't tolerate from a man. Every good instinct I have comes from watching you walk away from the easy life because you knew we deserved a better one."

Her eyes are wet. She blinks it away—Mum doesn't cry in kitchens, she cries in private, at night, when she thinks I'm asleep. I've heard her through thin walls since we moved to our shitty apartment in Alphabet City, and I've never once let her know.

"I'm sorry," I say, and my voice catches on the words in a way I wasn't expecting. "For everything after. For the accident. For the scam. For dragging you across the world and landing us in a fourth-floor apartment with no lift and no plan. You gave me this incredible childhood and I repaid you by—"

"Saylor David Evans."

Full name. She only uses the full name when I've said something she considers profoundly stupid, which, given that she loves me unconditionally, is a high bar.

She pushes off the counter. Her body negotiates the movement—the shift in weight, the careful alignment of her spine, the way she sets her jaw against whatever's firing through her nerve endings. She takes a step. Then another. Then a third. Bold, upright, deliberate—not the shuffling, cautious steps she takes when she thinks I'm watching, but the steps of a woman who has decided that crossing a kitchen is a thing she will do, pain be damned.

She reaches me and wraps her arms around my chest. She's shorter than me by a full head—the way it's been since as long as I can remember. When exactly did I grow past the woman who used to carry me on her hip through the farm with one arm while feeding chickens with the other? Her grip is strong. Stronger than I expect. Like she's holding me together and holding herself together simultaneously, which is probably exactly what she's doing.

"After the accident," she says into my chest, "before the medics got there, when I was on the ground. Do you remember what I said?"

I remember. I remember every second of it. The sound, the glass, the silence after, the way the sky looked from the pavement. I remember finding her and thinking she was gone and feeling the entire world drain of color like someone had pulled a plug.

"You were knocked out, Mum. No way you remember—"

"I do. I was conscious," she says. "For about thirty seconds. Maybe less. And I knew—the way you know things in moments like that, without thinking, without deciding—that I was probably dying. So I prayed. I'm not even religious, Saylor. You know that. But I prayed to anyone listening for one more thing."

My arms tighten around her. I can feel the ridges of her spine through her sweater, mapping the damage that accident left behind.

"What did you pray for?" I ask, even though I think I know. She prayed to live. She prayed for more time. And the cruel cosmic joke is that she got it. She got more time, and every day of that time comes wrapped in pain that would break most people, and she never complains, not once, as if survival itself should earn enough gratitude for a lifetime.

"I prayed that you were okay."

I go very still.

"That's it," she whispers. "Not to live. Not for the pain to stop. I prayed that my son was untouched. Protected. That whatever happened to me, you would walk away from that truck whole, with your whole life ahead of you." She pulls back and looks up at me with eyes that are clear and absolutely certain. "That was my last hope on this earth. And my prayers were answered."

I don't trust my voice. Something has collapsed in my chest—not painfully, not the way the guilt usually collapses things, but like a wall coming down. A wall I built years ago to hold something back, and behind it is a flood of everything I've been trying not to feel since I pulled her out of that wreck and carried her to the shoulder of the road and screamed for help until my throat went raw.

"And now look at you." She reaches up to touch my face. Her hand is warm from the tea. "I get to watch you fall in love. I get to see you build something. Start a family in this beautiful house. My prayers were answered ten times over."

"Mum." I catch her hand against my cheek. "About Celeste. When she gets here today, I need you to not—"

"Not what?"

"Not put pressure on the situation. She's my boss. I'm her contractor. A friend, maybe. I'm helping her get custody of this baby, and that's it. The engagement thing—it's just for the caseworker. None of it's real."

Mum studies me with the expression of a mother who is choosing to let reality correct her son in its own time. "Of course, love. Whatever you say."

"I'm serious. After October, once the baby comes, we'll need to move. This arrangement has an expiration date." I pause, because the next part is harder. "But I was thinking—if I could put some money together—would you want to live somewhere like this? Out of the city. Suburbs. Ground floor. A yard."

Mum barely answers. Her eyes drop to her own body—the crooked posture, the hand that's drifted to her hip where the pain lives, the legs that carried her three steps across a kitchen and are already trembling from the effort. "I hate being this burden on you, Saylor." Her voice is quiet. "You should be planning a future with someone you love. Not your mother."

"You are someone I love, Mum. We're a package deal. Maybe one day some woman will understand that. But for now, one step at a time, yeah?"

She nods. Pats my cheek. Retreats to the counter and her tea with the careful choreography of a woman who has learned to make pain look easy.

I turn back to the stove. There are steaks marinating in the fridge, pasta dough resting under a towel, and a bruschetta situation happening on the cutting board that I'm quietly proud of. I've been cooking since four—not because the meal requires this much time, but because my hands needed something to do besides check my phone for the fifteenth time to see if Celeste has texted that she's on her way.

She texted an hour ago. One word: *Coming.*

I've been marinating in that word ever since. Coming. Present tense. Active. A woman in motion, pointed in my direction.

The doorbell rings and I almost drop the knife.

"She's knocking?" Mum asks from the counter, amused. "On her own front door?"

"Apparently."

I wipe my hands on the towel, check my reflection in the window above the sink. *Why am I checking my reflection?* I never check my reflection. I'm a bloke who invented rugged nonchalance and masked it as style. My hair is unruly like this, not because of gel, it's because I'm a side sleeper.

I open it, and Celeste is standing on her own porch holding a bottle of wine and wearing an expression that's halfway between determination and terror. She's in jeans. I've never seen her in jeans. Every version of Celeste I've encountered has been in structured trousers or blazers or that uppity cream blouse she wore to the caseworker visit. But today it's dark, fitted jeans and a soft gray sweater that falls off one shoulder in a way that might be intentional or might be the sweater's own rebellion against symmetry. Her hair is down. Minimal makeup. Flat shoes.

She looks like a person. Not a CEO, just a person who got in a car and drove forty-five minutes to knock on her own front door because she wanted to be here.

I let my eyes travel the full length of her—slowly, deliberately, not hiding it—from the flat shoes to the jeans to the exposed shoulder to the face that's watching me watch her with an expression that dares me to comment and hopes I will.

"Did you forget the code?" I ask.

"It felt weird to just walk in."

"It's your house."

"I know it's my house. But it doesn't feel like my house anymore. It feels like—" She pauses. Tilts her head. "Your home. I feel like a stranger walking into *your* home."

"Well, we can't have that." I step aside, holding the door wide. "Stay the night. You'll feel less like a stranger after a few hours. I promise."

"Stay the night?" She raises an eyebrow. "Bold opening, Saylor. I'm just here to help...and eat of course. What smells so good?"

"I'm grilling steaks."

"You're grilling steaks."

"Marinated since this morning. Pasta from scratch. Bruschetta that I will humbly describe as life-changing."

"Life-changing bruschetta. That's quite a claim. You know bruschetta is a whole food group to me and I will indeed give you my honest opinion."

"That honest opinion better be, *heavenly, magical, or world wonder.*"

"Oh, no, no, my friend. Deep down, I'm mean-spirited like an undercover food critic. If there isn't garlic confit in the bruschetta, I'll have to remove a star. You're going to have to take it like a man."

"I have no idea what garlic confit is, so I'm going to assume I'm in trouble. But don't worry, I can take it. I'm quite a man."

She rolls her eyes, but I earn a soft chuckle as she steps around me and inside. Suddenly this house—the house that I've been rebuilding for weeks, that I've painted and sanded and wired and furnished—finally feels like what it's been trying to become. Complete. The missing piece just walked through the front door carrying a bottle of wine and wearing what she probably thinks are casual jeans.

Not even an hour later, the kitchen is loud in the best way.

I'm at the stove tending pasta while Celeste leans against the island, a glass of wine in her hand—the one she brought because I was so focused on food, I forgot booze. The steaks are resting on the cutting board. The bruschetta is demolished. Celeste ate four pieces and then accused me of secretly being Italian, which is the highest compliment she's ever given me.

"I don't think my mom or dad ever cooked in this kitchen," she says, and she says it with the slight disbelief of someone who has walked into a house she expected to find in renovation chaos and instead found a man doing very domestic things. "We ate so much takeout growing up."

"Like regular-people takeout—McDonald's, Taco Bell, KFC? Or rich-people takeout?"

She narrows her eyes. "Why does that matter?"

"Being raised on cheap, greasy questionable meat, hurled at you through drive-thru windows paints a very different picture than bags of gourmet meals from high-end restaurants. One a little pathetic, the other a little pretentious."

"So either way, I can't win?"

I laugh. "Let me take a guess."

"Okay, fine. We were a little pretentious. Not at the same echelon of Whit's family or anything, but my parents were also consumed with appearances."

"This is why I wanted to cook," I say, sneaking a sly smile her way. "Because you would have brought something from a restaurant that costs sixty dollars a plate and comes with a foam I'd have to pretend to understand."

"Foam is a legitimate culinary technique."

"Foam is soap that freed itself from the sink and snuck its way onto a plate."

Mum laughs from the kitchen table where she's been watching us with the barely concealed delight of a woman attending a show she bought tickets for months ago. She's settled into the chair I positioned specifically for her—good lumbar support, arms for leverage, close to the table but not boxed in.

"Well it must sound silly to eat out when you can cook like this. You guys are living the dream."

"Oh no, dear, don't be fooled," Mum says. "We don't eat like this every night. Most nights it's whatever he can throw together before he falls asleep on the couch with his boots still on. He's only trying to impress you."

"*Mum.*"

"What? It's charming. Let me enjoy this."

Celeste sets down her wineglass. She looks at my mum with that specific attentiveness that misses nothing—and then she moves.

It's not a big movement. She pushes off from the island, crosses the kitchen in four easy steps, and wraps her arms around my mother.

The hug is careful. Gentle. She minds the spine, the posture, the places where contact could mean pain. But it's not tentative; it's warm and deliberate, the hug of a woman who has made a decision about someone and is communicating it through her arms instead of her words.

"I'm so glad I got to meet you, Ada," Celeste says.

Mum's face does something I will remember for the rest of my life. Her eyes close. Her arms come up and squeeze back with a strength that tells me the hug landed somewhere deep. And she smiles. A real one where joy takes over and moves your muscles for you. The smile I'd move mountains for.

"It's lovely to meet you too, darling. Saylor has told me absolutely nothing about you, which means you're probably very important."

Celeste laughs. It's the unguarded laugh—the one from Tidewater House, the one from the caseworker visit when I told her I'd thought about burning the loveseat. The laugh that tells me she came here tonight, unarmed. Maybe as curious as I am.

I look at the two of them together and for the briefest, most reckless moment, I let myself imagine a life where this makes sense. Where this is permanent. Where Celeste comes home to this kitchen every night and Mum sits at that table with her tea and I cook dinner and the baby is upstairs in the sage-green nursery and the tire swing is getting use and nobody is lying and nobody is leaving.

The moment lasts three seconds. I put it away before it can become a plan.

We eat on the deck. The steaks are good—better than good. The pasta is the recipe Mum taught me when I was fourteen, the one she learned from a neighbor in Wollongong who was actually Italian and actually knew what she was doing, unlike every other Aussie who claims their Bolognese is authentic. The wine Celeste brought is expensive and pairs perfectly, and I pretend to know what "notes of blackcurrant" means when she describes it because I'm learning that being with Celeste would mean learning an entirely new vocabulary.

The evening is warm for the season. The oak tree throws long shadows across the yard. The tire swing hangs motionless in the still air like it's waiting.

"This property has incredible potential," I say, leaning back in my chair. "The guesthouse could be expanded—add a second bedroom, update the bathroom, make it a proper studio or office space. You'd need permits, obviously. And the backyard—there's plenty of room for an outdoor kitchen. Proper barbie, stone countertop, maybe a pizza oven if you're feeling ambitious."

"A pizza oven," Celeste repeats, in the tone of a woman considering a concept from another planet.

"I could build it myself. Stone and mortar. It's not complicated."

"And who would be operating this pizza oven? Because I want to be transparent about my culinary range." She takes a sip of wine. "The last thing I baked was bread and cheese in a toaster oven in a dorm room which led to a small fire that we did eventually get under control."

Mum laughs, then leans forward in her chair. "Sounds like you need someone in your life who can cook, dear."

She beams as if she has been holding her game-winning card all night and finally found the right moment to deploy it. Celeste's cheeks flush. I shoot Mum a look. She returns it with absolute serenity, knowing exactly what she did and she has no regrets.

"More wine?" I ask Celeste, because redirect is the only tool available to me when Mum decides to play matchmaker.

"Please."

I pour. Celeste drinks. The evening settles around us like a blanket—warm, soft, the kind of quiet that doesn't feel empty. Mum tells a story about teaching me to cook when I was twelve. At first, I hated it. Then, she told me cooking was the way to get all the girls and suddenly I was more into it. I burned the first three attempts at scrambled eggs so badly she considered calling the fire department, and Celeste laughs until her eyes water, and Mum glows under the attention, and the deck doesn't creak anymore because I fixed it, every board, with my own hands.

This is what it could be. This is what it could feel like every night.

I put that thought away too. I lock it in a box and throw it into the ocean. It's not easy, but I try to stay present and enjoy the current moment instead of planning the future ones. But that's what keeps me intact. A plan. A promise. Anything to ensure that what I caused won't consume us forever. *Hope.*

At quarter to seven, Mum yawns.

It is the most theatrical, least convincing yawn in the history of human performance. She tilts her head back, opens her mouth to a width that suggests she's trying to swallow the whole sky, and produces a sound that belongs in a community theater production of *Sleeping Beauty.*

"Oh my," she says, pressing the back of her hand to her forehead. "I'm suddenly so terribly exhausted. I think I'll turn in for the night. Don't mind me. You two enjoy the evening."

She rises from the table with a swiftness that is completely inconsistent with a woman who is supposedly exhausted and also has a spinal injury, and retreats into the house with the brisk efficiency of a stagehand clearing props between scenes.

The deck is quiet.

Celeste looks at me. "Does your mom normally go to bed at six forty-five? Or did I scare her off?"

"No." I grin. "She's being my wingwoman and trying to give us privacy."

She lets that music-laughter play again. "Privacy for what, Saylor? Why would you want to be alone with me?"

I look at her. She looks at me. The oak tree holds its breath.

"You know why," I say.

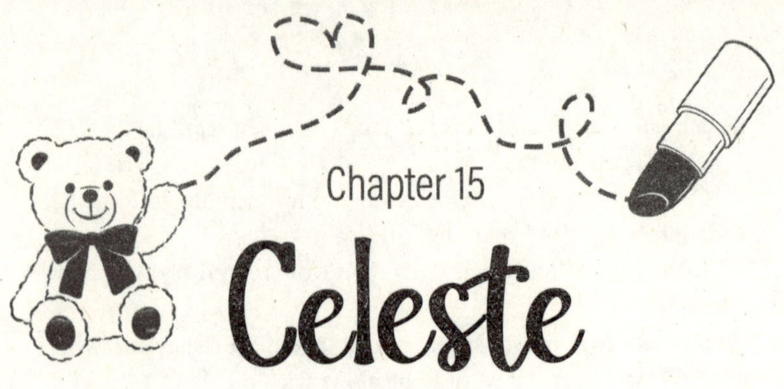

Chapter 15
Celeste

This is like so unexpected.

Do I know why?

Maybe. But it's too hard to admit it.

Even with the wine warm in my stomach, the evening soft around us, and the way this gorgeous man is looking at me with what looks like hunger, I just can't wrap my head around it. We're different species. There's no way I'm anything to Saylor but a conquest. At my age, it's my responsibility to see reason. Saylor gets to live with his head in the clouds, amidst fantasies where we're hot and heavy at night, and a Hallmark family special during the day just isn't happening. And as much as I hate to be the one to burst his bubble, what choice do I have?

I stay silent, testing out words on my tongue before I say them. *Saylor, stop.* Except I don't want him to stop. *We can't do this.* Then to his prior point, why am I here?

"Come on," Saylor says, standing. "I want to show you something."

"Why does that sound a little dangerous?"

He smiles as he holds out his hand. I look at it—callused, broad, paint still under one thumbnail—and I take it, because I've lost the ability to say no to this man and I'm not sure when that happened.

He leads me across the yard toward the guesthouse. It sits

about fifty yards from the main house, tucked behind a hedge that's overgrown but still vaguely architectural. My mother's landscaper used to shape it into something geometric, though it's since returned to its natural state of chaos, which is honestly an improvement.

"I wanted to get in here," Saylor says, nodding at the door. "But it's on a separate keypad and the main code didn't work."

"That's because it's girls only. Boys have to keep out."

He gives me a look of genuine confusion, and something about his face—the furrowed brow, the slight head tilt, like a golden retriever encountering a math problem—makes me laugh before I can explain.

"This was my space. Teenage years, college summers. When I was sixteen, I got so angry at my parents that I moved out here to punish them." The memory surfaces with a bittersweet clarity. The day they missed my school awards ceremony. I told them I won four separate honors and they still didn't bother to show. Nothing was ever good enough to get their attention. "I packed a suitcase, made a dramatic speech about needing independence from their approval, slammed the front door of the main house, and marched across the yard in the rain. Very cinematic. Very sixteen of me."

"How long did the rebellion last?"

"Four years. I lived out here every summer through college." I pause. "The problem was that my parents didn't notice. Or if they did, they considered it a successful transition to self-sufficiency. My mother sent the housekeeper over once a week with fresh towels. That was the extent of the search party."

Something crosses Saylor's face—not pity, thank goodness—but recognition. The look of someone who understands a particular kind of loneliness because he's lived adjacent to it, even if his version had different furniture.

I type the four-digit code that's etched into my memory, and the lock clicks.

"Your code is one-two-three-four?" Saylor scoffs loudly. "That's so lazy I wouldn't even think to try it."

"Mhmm. That's why it's brilliant, right?"

The door opens and the early two thousands hit us like a freight train.

Pink. So much pink. The walls are hot pink, which I chose when I was sixteen because it was the exact opposite of everything in the main house—the creams, the neutrals, the tasteful restraint that my mother treated as a moral philosophy. In here, I was allowed to be loud. And apparently, at sixteen, loud meant pink.

Boy band posters cover one wall. *NSYNC, Backstreet Boys, a Destiny's Child poster that I will defend until death. Movie posters on another—*Legally Blonde*, *Mean Girls*, a *Kill Bill: Vol. 1* print that feels incongruous with the pink but was entirely intentional because I've always had layers. There's a leopard-print beanbag chair in the corner. A lava lamp on the nightstand. Shelves lined with CDs and burned mix-CDs with handwritten labels in purple Sharpie—"Summer Vibes '04," "Songs 4 Driving," "Whit's List," and "HIDE FROM MOM," which I'm assuming was my trap music phase.

It's an eyesore, truly. Everything—the bedspread, the throw pillows, the fuzzy rug—looks like it was purchased during a single, rebellious, transformative trip to Hot Topic.

Saylor gasps. Not a polite intake of breath. A full gasp, the kind that involves his entire chest expanding and his eyes going wide and his mouth forming a shape that is equal parts delight and disbelief.

"Oh my God."

"Don't."

"Celeste."

"Do not say a word."

"This is the most incredible room I've ever seen in my life. Very telling. Your good taste didn't kick in until adulthood, hm?"

I grab the nearest fuzzy pink pillow from the bed and hurl it at his head. He catches it, laughing, and holds it against his chest like a trophy.

"I was sixteen," I defend, trying and failing to suppress my own smile. "Sixteen-year-olds are allowed to have aggressively terrible taste. We grew up with MySpace, okay? It was a different time."

"MySpace?" He quirks a brow.

"It's like talking to a puppy," I grumble. "You really aren't registering our age difference, are you?"

"Know what's so sexy about women your age?" Saylor asks, catching me completely by surprise. "*Nothing*" sounds too self-deprecating, so I don't say it. "They usually have experienced enough that they know what they want. No games. No bullshit. They are so sure of themselves, not because they're arrogant and think they can conquer the world. Simply that they know what's worth conquering within the world. I find that incredibly alluring. The sureness. Like the sureness you've had about Whit and the baby. I really like that. You never stop to question whether you should do the right thing."

Like honey to a dry, achy throat, his compliment soothes me and saves me from all the symptoms of being unseen. Being around Saylor feels like standing in quicksand, waiting for the fantasy to swallow you up whole. But that's the point. *It's a fantasy.* Every romance book, movie, story eventually ends with happily-ever-after because the truth is depressing. Saylor could love me today. But in five years? In ten? When I drop my child off at college, I'll be almost sixty. Is he going to be using words like hot and heavy when my crow's-feet become more noticeable and my hair has more streaks of gray than I can pull out one by one? I trusted a man with that kind of devotion once. With growing old together. But with Greg I didn't grow. I just got older.

"Are you going to whisper sweet nothings in my ear all night, or are you done?"

"Done? Not even close. But I'll pace myself."

I look around the room. Nothing in here is sheeted off. There's a layer of dust, but it's thinner than the main house. The guesthouse is better sealed, smaller, and the memories preserved in here feel less like artifacts and more like friends you haven't seen in a while. I run my hand along the shelf and my fingers leave tracks in the dust, uncovering CD cases and picture frames and a ceramic mug I made in a pottery class that reads "Future Fashion Icon" in crooked letters.

"Care to give me a tour of memory lane?" Saylor asks.

"Sure."

I walk him through. The tiny kitchen where I secretly loved making cheap Top Ramen and mug cakes in the microwave. The bathroom with the mirror I used to practice acceptance speeches in front of—"I'd like to thank the Academy"—because when you're sixteen and lonely, imaginary audiences are better than no audience at all. The closet, which even then was organized by color, because some things are innate.

And then the bookshelf. The bottom shelf, behind a row of YA mystery novels, is a scrapbook. Thick, overstuffed, the binding straining against years of photos and ticket stubs and dried flowers pressed between pages.

I pull it out and sit on the bed. Saylor sits beside me. Close. Our shoulders touching. The scrapbook falls open to the middle—freshman year of college, the year everything changed, the year I met Whitney.

There we are. Eighteen years old, standing in front of our dorm building, arms around each other, grinning like we've just been told the most wonderful secret and are trying to decide whether to keep it. I'm in a skirt I designed myself—asymmetric hem, raw edges, the confident disaster of someone who has talent and no technique. Whitney's in overalls. *Overalls.* Her red curls are enormous. Her freckles are a constellation. She's laughing at something I said, or something I did, or maybe just laughing because that's who Whitney was—a person who found the world funny and beautiful and worth engaging with at full volume.

"I forgot how lonely I was until I met Whit. I used to spend so much time in here by myself. But after Whit, I was never really alone."

I turn the pages slowly. Whit and me at a football game we

attended for the tailgate and left at halftime. Whit and me at a diner at three a.m. studying for finals with textbooks we weren't reading. Whit and me at a Halloween party where I went as Anna Wintour and only about four people understood my costume. They just thought I was well-dressed. *The drunk simpletons*; her bob is iconic and I nailed it. In their defense, I showed up to the party with Whit who went as a crayon because she said she wanted to be "something everybody liked." I would've suggested donuts or a Subway sandwich, but Whitney chose Crayola. We were very confusing as a couples' costume.

I turn another page and stop.

Whitney in her wedding dress. Just a candid, taken by me, the very moment after she said yes to that dress. We rang a bell and everything. She's standing by the window and the light is catching the lace at her shoulders and she's looking at something outside that I can't see. Her expression is calm. Settled. The expression of a woman whose relationship is about to fall apart and doesn't know it yet but looks so beautiful in her certainty that you want to freeze the frame and let her stay there, in the window light, before everything goes sideways.

I wanted to make her dress but she went with Vera Wang in the end, because Eleanor insisted, because Eleanor always insisted. I wasn't good enough yet to design for her daughter. A silent, bitter seed was planted that season. I made a silent vow to out-Vera the entire wedding industry one day.

"She's beautiful," Saylor says quietly. "I didn't know she got married."

"She didn't. About three months before the wedding, she caught him cheating."

"Shame," Saylor says.

"Eleanor begged her not to call off the wedding. Joshua came from a really good family, he was going to law school, dead set on a political career."

"Why would a mother want her daughter to stay with a cheater? All because it looks good on paper?"

I pat his knee. "Now you know the world we come from. Whit's dad died about ten years ago. He cheated on Eleanor and verbally abused her until his dying breath. He probably used his dying breath to call her fat. That's the kind of man Whit learned to run from. Joshua was too much like Whit's father, and she did not want to become her mother."

"She and Eleanor didn't get along, even after her dad passed away?"

I shake my head slowly. "It made it worse. All that pity turned into anger. Whit wanted her mom to be strong. Eleanor chose to endure the abuse because living with pretty things was more important than living, apparently."

"Well, I'm glad Whit didn't stay. Smart girl."

I turn the page and a loose picture falls out. Saylor bends over to pick it up and he's greeted with a photo of me and Greg at senior prom. We're both smiling. Greg's smile is the one I now recognize too well. His smile of overcompensation—too wide, too confident, the smile of a man who is hiding something and practically gleeful he's getting away with it. That night? It was underage booze. Ten years later? Every woman in Tribeca between the ages of twenty-one and twenty-three. My smile is real but small, and I'm not looking at Greg. I'm looking down at the dress. Admiring my own work.

"I wasn't smart. I chose, much like Eleanor, to see what I wanted to, and not what was real. Greg and I were high school sweethearts," I say. I don't know why I'm telling him this. Except I do—because we're sitting on my teenage bed in my pink room and the scrapbook is now closed and Whitney's wedding dress is still behind my eyes and something about this space makes honesty feel safe. "We took a break when we went to different colleges. That's when I met Whit. Two years without Greg were the most creative, most free I've ever felt. Then he graduated, came home, and we got back together. He proposed six months later. I said yes because I thought that's what the story was supposed to be."

"And then?"

"And then fifteen years." I pull my legs up onto the bed, cross them beneath me. "Fifteen years of me building a company instead of a family. Fifteen years of him slowly losing interest in me. Not touching me, not talking to me, not interested in me, silently—and not so silently—telling me every day that I was aging out of my worth. At some point, I started believing him."

Saylor is quiet for a long moment. "He said that to you?"

"Not in those words. Not at first. It started as jokes. 'My vintage wife.' 'The classic model.' Things you laugh off at dinner parties because the alternative is making a scene, and Celeste Prescott doesn't make scenes."

"Prescott?"

"My married name. Don't get confused. Celeste *Brinley* makes all kinds of scenes." I wink at him before taking a breath. "But the point is, it compounds. Year after year, joke after joke, until one day you look in the mirror and you don't see a woman. You see what you had and can never have again. You see an expiration date."

"Celeste." Saylor's fingertips trace my cheekbone so delicately it tickles. I lean into his hand for the extra pressure. "I'll swap out every mirror in this house and the other until you see what I see. Young, old—those are states of mind. But beauty is completely transcendent of numbers."

My jaw drops. "Transcendent of numbers? What the hell, Saylor? Are you picking these lines up from *Bridgerton* or something?"

"What? You've never seen a farm boy pick up a thesaurus to impress a girl he likes?"

"I thought you put on an apron to impress me."

"I did." He widens his eyes. "I'm apparently doing a lot of things to impress you, which is hard to do."

"I'm impressed," I admit.

He leans in closer so I can feel his breath against my ear. "Prove it," he whispers so close it's like he's trying to deposit it directly into my brain. "Do you find me attractive at all, Celeste?

Just put me out of my misery here. Do I have a shot?"

"A shot at what?" I ask. "What exactly are you asking me for?" I lean away and point at his chest. "And don't you dare say 'you know what' because as much as you use that, it's not an actual answer."

"Celeste, look—you feel like a puzzle piece I want to pop into place. I don't know how else to explain this. It just fits. It feels good. I don't want to be some guy you went to Whit's funeral with. Do I want to see you naked? Desperately. But I kind of also want to be there when the courts award you custody of the baby. I want to be there when you bring her home. I want to be the one to teach her how to drive because you should not be imparting your driving knowledge on anyone."

I laugh. "Her?"

"Or him," Saylor says. "I just hate calling the baby an 'it.'"

"I keep picturing a girl too," I muse. "I hope it's a girl because I know nothing about hunting and fishing and..."

Saylor looks at me expectantly. "Did you just run out of boy things?"

"Kind of."

His laugh is deep and rumbly. "Nah, yeah. If the baby's a boy you're definitely screwed. But I don't know..." He hedges, just for a second, then continues. "I'll be here if you want me to be. To teach him more...boy stuff."

"Is that a free offer, or is that conditional?"

"On what?" He stretches out his legs, making the whole bed jostle.

"The seeing-me-naked part."

"*Oh.* No, it wasn't conditional originally, but now that you mention it. I like that. Yes, new terms. I promise to teach your baby all the rugged boy things. Now, take off your shirt."

I laugh, but Saylor's face remains serious, his eyes fixed on mine with the unguarded hunger of a man who's been wandering through a desert and has just spotted water.

"I haven't had sex with anyone but Greg since I was twenty."

The sentence falls out of me like something I've been carrying in my mouth and finally spit onto the floor. Graceless. Unplanned. I can feel the blood rushing to my face and I want to take it back except I don't, because it's true and I'm tired of designing around truths that make me uncomfortable.

"Even before the divorce, we barely—" I wave my hand vaguely, because apparently I can confess celibacy but not describe the actual act. "It's been so long that I've sort of lost the desire for it. You know how when you stop eating sugar, eventually you stop craving it? It's like that. The longer you go without, the less you need it. And honestly, it was never"—I search for the word—"great. It was always a bit awkward. Mechanical. Like we were both following instructions neither of us had read. I know people lose their minds over physical intimacy, but I've always found it kind of...overhyped. All that vulnerability for fifteen minutes of someone else's elbow in your rib. I don't know, Saylor. If you want hot and passionate—I'm not your girl. You're going to be disappointed."

I'm staring at the Destiny's Child poster because I cannot look at Saylor right now. Beyoncé stares back at me with an expression that says: *girl, what are you doing.*

"Celeste." Saylor's voice is different. Lower. Not teasing. "It sounds like you've had terrible sex for the past decade."

"Probably accurate."

"That's genuinely heartbreaking."

"It's not heartbreaking, it's just—"

"It is. Because you're describing a woman who's been told, over and over, that she's past her prime, by a man whose greatest talent was making you feel small. And you believed him. About your worth. About your desirability. About whether you deserve to feel good." He shifts on the bed so he's facing me, and I can feel the heat of him, the proximity, the particular electricity of a body that is very close to mine and very intentional about being there. "Let me tell you something. You deserve to feel great. You deserve a man who watches your eyes to make sure you come first."

"Easy for you to say. You look like a walking wet dream. Not everybody navigates intimacy that easily."

"You think it's easy for me?"

"Isn't it?"

"I was a professional, Celeste. That doesn't mean it was easy. That means I learned how to make someone else feel seen. I'm looking at you and I see the truth." He pauses. "You're not past anything. You're just getting started. *We're* just getting started."

He leans in.

The kiss is not performed. There is no Janet Lundy. There is no leather portfolio. There is no custody case providing an alibi for what's happening.

This kiss is just us.

His mouth meets mine and it's slow. Deliberate. The kind of kiss that asks a question and waits for the answer. His hand comes to my jaw—not grabbing, guiding. Tilting my face toward his with a gentleness that makes my chest ache in a way I didn't know chests could ache. It's nothing like the sofa kiss, which was performance and adrenaline and the blur of a plan being executed. This is specific and calculated and the kiss of a man who doesn't want to stop at kissing.

He pulls back. An inch. His forehead rests against mine.

"How did that feel?" he asks.

"Awkward," I lie.

"Damn, let me try again." He smiles against my mouth. Kisses me again. Deeper this time. His hand slides from my jaw to the back of my neck and something inside me—the mechanism that keeps me upright, that keeps me composed, that has been running on autopilot since my first executive meeting—shuts off. I am not thinking about the fall or spring line. I am not thinking about Greg or Eleanor or the caseworker. I am not thinking about anything except the pressure of his mouth and the warmth of his hand and the fact that my body is doing things it hasn't done in so long I'd forgotten it was capable.

I give in and kiss him back. Not carefully. Not the measured, two-second response I gave him on the burgundy sofa. I kiss him the way fabric falls when you stop fighting it—completely, without reservation, surrendering to the drape.

He pulls me across his lap and I go. I go because his hands are on my hips and his mouth is on my neck and I am thirty-eight years old and I have never in my life been kissed like I am something precious and urgent at the same time. His fingers find the hem of my sweater. Slip beneath it. His palm is warm and rough against my waist, against my ribs, moving upward with a patience that feels like torture and a confidence that feels like permission.

I am on his lap in a bubblegum-pink room surrounded by boy band posters and somehow at thirty-eight I'm living out a teenage dream. It took me two extra decades to get here, but sixteen-year-old Celeste would be thrilled. There is a guy, *a hot guy*, who wants me in that real way. Kissing me in my bedroom, after dark, while all the parents sleep. This place really is a time capsule. And yet this moment feels...timeless. Gliding between past and present, like it doesn't know whether it's a moment or a memory.

His hand cups my breast over the fabric of my bra and I make a sound that I will deny making later under oath. He grins against my mouth—I can feel it, the shape of his smile pressed to my lips—and the grin makes me want to either kill him or climb deeper into his lap. I choose the latter, locking my hips into his, feeling his growing hard-on through his jeans, between my thighs.

I push him backward so he's lying flat on my pink duvet. My hand drops to his waist. Finds the button of his jeans. My fingers graze the hard length of him through the denim and his breath hitches—a sharp, involuntary intake that tells me self-control is a thing of the past. He's said it over and over, time and time again. He wants me. Right now, I'm going to choose to believe it. If he really does want me, tonight, he can have me.

I free his pants button, fingers clamped around his zipper pull when—

A shriek from the main house. Glass shattering. A thud.

We both freeze. The sound cuts through the pink room like a

fire alarm in the silent dead of night—the kind of interruption that evacuates a moment and leaves nothing behind.

Saylor is off the bed before I've processed what I heard. He's out the door, crossing the yard in the dark at a dead sprint, and I'm behind him—sweater twisted, hair disheveled, moving on instinct and adrenaline toward the main house where every light is still on and something has gone terribly wrong.

He's through the patio doors first. I'm three steps behind.

Ada is on the kitchen floor. She's on her side, one hand pressed to the ground, the other clutching her hip. A shattered glass is beside her—water, just water—the shards scattered across the hardwood in a constellation of broken crystal. Her face is white. Not pale—ghost white. The color of pain that has passed through severity and arrived at something beyond it.

"Mum." Saylor is on his knees beside her, his hands hovering, afraid to touch the wrong place. "Mum, I'm here. What happened?"

"I'm so sorry." Ada's voice is small and tight, the voice of a woman who is in agony and is apologizing for it. "I forgot my medicine. The one in the fridge. I thought I could get it myself. Didn't want to bother you two. And I just—the floor was slippery, and I—"

"It's okay. You're okay. Can you sit up?"

She nods. He helps her slowly, carefully, his hands under her arms, lifting with the careful precision of someone who has done this before, in other kitchens, at other hours, hundreds of times. The repetition is in his body. The grief is in his eyes.

And I see it. The thing he carries. The weight that bends him even when he's standing straight. His mother is on the floor, in pain, because she didn't want to interrupt his evening, and now he's kneeling in broken glass with guilt flooding his face like water filling a room.

I move.

I don't think about it. I don't weigh options or calculate appearances or design my response. I move the way you move when someone needs you—immediately, completely, without the luxury of self-consciousness.

"Ada." I'm beside them on the floor. "Let's get you to the couch. Saylor, help me."

We lift her together. Guide her to the living room. I arrange the throw pillows Saylor bought, the ones that made me laugh during the caseworker visit—and help her settle. Ada grips my forearm during the transfer. Her fingers are ice cold and stronger than they should be. I hold on until she lets go.

"Which medicine?" I ask. "It's in the fridge? What does it look like?"

"The small red vial. Second shelf. It should have a yellow label."

I'm in the kitchen. Second shelf, red vial, yellow label. I find it, check the dosage on the label, grab a glass—a plastic one, not crystal—and fill it with water. I bring both to Ada and watch her take the medicine with shaking hands.

"Tea," I say. "I'm putting the kettle on."

I'm back in the kitchen. Kettle on the stove. Saylor is sweeping the glass methodically, thoroughly, his jaw set in that way that means he's not in the kitchen anymore. He's somewhere else. He's in the math of his life—the equation where his happiness always subtracts from his mother's safety, where every moment he spends with me is a moment he's not watching her, where the guilt compounds interest on a debt he'll never believe is paid.

I can read it on his face: this is why he can't have this. Can't have me. Can't have a life. Because his mother will always need him more than any woman will tolerate being needed less.

I think for some odd reason, he's embarrassed. I can't fathom why, but there's the slight hunch of his shoulders, the way he won't meet my eyes, the quiet resignation of a man who has auditioned for happiness and been rejected so many times he's stopped expecting callbacks.

The kettle whistles. I pour Ada's tea. Bring it to her. She wraps her hands around the mug and the color is starting to return to her face. She smiles at me in a way where "thank you" seems redundant. What a special gift. One none of the mothers I knew growing up possessed. How to make someone feel loved with just a look. I squeeze her hand and tell her I'll be right back.

I find Saylor in the kitchen. He's finished sweeping. He's standing at the sink, gripping the edge of the counter, staring out the window at the dark yard.

"I'm going," I tell him.

His head drops. Barely perceptible. An inch of surrender. "Yeah," he says quietly. "I understand."

"No you don't." I wait until he looks at me. His eyes meet mine, bloodshot and weary, like a boxer who's already taken too many hits but knows the final bell hasn't rung yet. "I'm going to the grocery store. There's one about ten minutes up the road. We need popcorn. And wine for me, and mocktails for your mum because she can't drink after taking that medication. I read the bottle." I swipe my keys from the counter. "Can you get the TV connected to Wi-Fi while I'm gone? When I get back, we're doing a movie marathon. All three of us."

He stares at me.

"Is that okay?" I ask.

He stares at me some more. Something is happening behind his eyes—a recalculation, a rewiring, the slow and disbelieving recognition that the thing he expected to happen is not happening.

"That's—" His voice catches. He clears his throat. "That's great. Are you sure?"

"Very sure." I grab my bag, head for the door, but Saylor catches up to me, stopping me with one hand on my shoulder. "Wait. One correction to your plan."

"What's that?"

"I'm coming with you to the store. Then we'll set up the TV together."

"You don't trust me to go to the store by myself?"

"Well, I trust you in the store. It's the getting there part that's a public safety concern. I want to drive you...you know, for the safety and wellbeing of all the other drivers in Westchester who want to live past tonight."

"Hilarious," I deadpan.

His laugh is quiet, rough, the sound of relief disguised as amusement. He grabs his wallet off the counter and follows me to the door.

After assuring us she'll be fine for a while, Ada watches us leave from the couch, tea in her hands, the blanket Saylor chose pulled up to her waist. She looks small in the living room—small and warm and safe in a house that's starting to feel like something more than an unpleasant childhood memory or a stage set or a strategy for impressing a caseworker.

It's starting to feel like what Saylor built it to be.

A home.

"Hey, Saylor?" I say as we walk through the front door.

"Yes?"

"I want to warn you, I'm picky about my brand of popcorn. I don't compromise when it comes to movie theater butter flavor."

"I'd expect nothing less."

"I just want to make that clear in case you want an out now. Popcorn brands matter when you move forward with someone."

Saylor stops dead in his tracks. "What are you saying, Celeste? Because I'll even eat nasty-ass kettle corn if it means moving forward with you."

"You don't like kettle corn?" I balk. "What's wrong with you?"

"Focus, Celeste," he says, taking one step closer to where I'm also frozen in place. Right underneath the stoop of my childhood front porch. "The *forward* part—what does that mean?"

Right when I need her, Whit comes in clutch. Speaking to me through a sisterhood that clearly transcends death. She's gone, yet she's still sending love my way—in the twisted form of this man, who's too young for me to make sense, and her baby, that would only be mine in the worst of circumstances. But it's still...love isn't it? Twisted, messy, new, and shaky. But real.

And then I hear her clear as day. *Lessi, shoot your shot and hit that... Or I will.*

I laugh to myself which must make me look unhinged, but I don't care. *Okay, Whit. Truth or dare. Truth? I want him. The dare? I'm going to do something about it.*

"Saylor, it'd be a good time to ask me out again."

"Oh yeah?" He takes another step closer.

The Westchester night is cool and dark and full of stars you can't see from Manhattan. I feel like I've watched this scene a million times growing up, but I never really saw it. Not until now, with the right cast for what I'm praying is a happily-ever-after.

I fish my keys out of my purse and hold them out. Saylor closes the last sliver of distance between us. Cradles my keys in one hand.

"Celeste Brinley, do you want to go out with me sometime?"

I twirl a loose strand of my hair. "Oh my God, this is like so unexpected," I say in my best impression of *Clueless*.

Saylor smiles with his whole damn face. Forehead crinkled, eyes clamped shut, uncontrollable joy.

"What do you say?" he asks again.

"I'd love to go out with you sometime."

He kisses my forehead and it already feels different. Familiar. Possessive. Like someone can claim you with their lips pressed just below your hairline. How beautifully simple.

We don't have answers tonight. We're eons away from making this make sense, but for right now, with my hand in Saylor's walking toward my car like regular-enough people without a world of guilt and burden on their shoulders, it's enough.

It's more than enough.

It's a start.

Chapter 16
Saylor

I'll relax when I'm dead.

The lobby of Celeste's building has a waterfall. Strange, I didn't notice this the first time I came by. I was too focused on slipping past security.

It's not a decorative trickle or a tabletop fountain. A floor-to-ceiling sheet of water cascading down a slab of black marble behind the reception desk, the kind of architectural statement that exists solely to remind you that some people live in buildings where the lobby has its own water feature and you are not one of those people. There are orchids on the desk. Fresh ones. A concierge in a suit nicer than anything I own. And a security guard whose posture suggests he was either military or a ballet dancer, possibly both.

This time, I stop to give my name at the desk.

"Saylor Evans. I'm here to see Celeste Brinley."

The concierge checks his screen. Types something. And then, without hesitation, without the skeptical once-over I've come to expect in buildings like this: "Of course, Mr. Evans. You're on the permanent guest list. Elevator bank is to your right. Ms. Brinley's floor is forty-seven."

Permanent guest list. Not visitor. Not one-time access. Permanent. Celeste put my name on a list that lives in this building's system, which means somewhere in a database behind that waterfall there is a record that says Saylor Evans belongs here, and the concierge treats this information as unremarkable, as routine, as if men in paint-stained boots walk through this lobby every day to visit the CEO on the forty-seventh floor.

I nod like this is normal for me. Take my visitor badge. Walk toward the elevator bank with the manufactured calm of a man who is not quietly losing his mind over the fact that Celeste Brinley told a building he was permanent.

The lift is mirrored on three sides. I press forty-seven and watch the numbers climb, my reflection staring back at me from three different angles. Boots. Jeans. Flannel rolled to the elbows. The paint that never fully leaves my cuticles no matter how hard I scrub.

The lift stops on fourteen. The doors open and a man steps in.

He looks mid-forties. Tall, sharp-jawed, wearing a suit that fits him so well no doubt it was tailored. Silver watch, little diamonds around the crest. Pocket square folded with geometric precision. The kind of tan that comes from a UV-lit bed, not from actual time in the sun. He carries a tablet in one hand and a coffee in the other, and when he sees me, his eyes perform a full inventory in under two seconds: boots, jeans, flannel, cuticles. The assessment is instantaneous. The verdict, immediate.

I know who he is before he opens his mouth. I've only seen prom photos, but the jaw is the same, the posture is the same, and the smile he's arranging on his face has the same overcompensating wattage I clocked in that picture on Celeste's shelf. The question is...does he know who I am to Celeste? Hell, do *I* know who I am to Celeste?

"Morning," he says, extending his hand. "Greg Prescott. I don't think we've met."

I shake it. His grip is deliberately too firm, the handshake equivalent of a dog marking its territory. I match the pressure without exceeding it because I'm not interested in whatever contest he thinks this is.

"Saylor Evans."

"Saylor." He tastes my name and finds it undercooked. "You're here to see Celeste, I assume?"

"I think you already know the answer to that."

"I do." He sips his coffee. Casual. Practiced. The choreography of a man who rehearses even his spontaneous moments. "I've heard quite a bit about you. Margot's an enthusiastic narrator."

I say nothing. The lift hums between floors. The mirrored walls show me three versions of this moment from three different angles, and in each one Greg is taking up more space than a man holding a coffee needs to.

"I'd prefer if we could be amicable," I say. "For Celeste's sake."

Greg nods. A slow nod to indicate he agrees with the words, while his eyes are constructing something else entirely. The floors tick upward. Twenty-two. Twenty-three. Twenty-four. The silence between us has a texture, like fabric with too much starch. Stiff and deliberate.

The lift reaches forty-six. The doors open. Greg steps out first, then stops. Turns back to me with a smug smile like he's been waiting to say something he's been polishing in his head since the fourteenth floor.

"Word of advice?" He adjusts his pocket square with idle precision. "She's going to get bored of you, Cinderella. I've seen this before. Celeste latches onto projects. Buildings, brands, broken things she thinks she can fix. You got pulled from the streets and put in the palace, but that's temporary. Enjoy the view while it lasts." His eyes drop to my boots. "You don't belong here. You don't belong with her."

The doors begin to close. I catch them with my hand.

"Have a good morning, Greg."

I let the doors shut between us and ascend the final floor toward Celeste's office with Greg's words settling into my chest like coins dropped into a deep well. The problem with cruel people is not that they lie. It's that they aim their cruelty at the exact spot where your own doubt already lives, and then all they have to do is agree with it.

You don't belong here. You don't belong with her.

I've been telling myself some version of that for weeks. Hearing it from the man who spent twenty years diminishing the woman I'm falling for doesn't make it true, but it makes it louder. It gives the doubt a voice that isn't mine, and other people's voices are always harder to argue with.

Margot's desk is empty. Either she's on a coffee run or she's been reassigned or she's in the restroom; all three equally likely given what I know about Margot's professional priorities. I knock on the glass door and Celeste's voice comes through, clipped and distracted.

"Margot, where the hell have you—"

"It's me."

A pause. The sound of a chair rolling back. The door opens and Celeste is standing there in a black pencil skirt and a white silk blouse, sexy glasses on, hair twisted up with a pencil holding it in place, and even stressed and sleep-deprived and clearly mid-crisis, she looks like the kind of woman men write novels about. Which, given her industry, might actually be the point.

"Saylor." She says my name differently than Greg did. Like it belongs here. Like the syllables have weight she wants to hold. "What are you doing? I didn't know you were coming by today. Everything okay?"

"Surprise visit. Wanted to see you." I step inside. The office is immaculate. Clean lines, white walls, the mannequin she calls Patrice standing by the window wearing a half-finished copper gown that's either brilliant or a work in progress depending on the hour. Fabric swatches pinned to the corkboard in clusters that probably mean something to her but look like a mess on a wall to me. "How's the line coming?"

She drops into her chair as if she has been fighting a losing battle against herself. "The line is winning. I had a burst of something last week that felt like a breakthrough, and then it vanished. I keep chasing it and it keeps dissolving, and I'm starting to think the fall collection is going to be eleven inspired pieces and eleven fillers, and Bergdorf will notice the difference even if nobody else does."

"You'll figure it out."

"Will I? Because right now I'm staring at twenty-two dress forms and feeling absolutely nothing. Do you know how terrifying that is? I might actually have to use the uninspired designs Greg's girlfriend is trying to stuff down my throat."

"Well, why do you think you're so blocked? Are you stressed about the custody case?"

"It's not that, I'm worried this is the beginning of the end. Feeling nothing about the thing that defines you? It's like waking up and forgetting your native language. The words are supposed to be there and they're just...not." She pulls the pencil from her hair and the whole thing tumbles around her shoulders. She doesn't notice. "But maybe this is natural selection. I shouldn't be sitting at the head of the table if I can't run this company and design these lines. It's the perfect time to disappear from it all with a baby."

"You don't strike me as a person who runs away from hard things," I tell her.

She scoffs. "You don't know me as well as you think you do, Saylor."

"You're just stressed."

"I'm past stressed. I've lapped stressed, I've overtaken panicked, and I'm now entering a state of creative paralysis that doesn't have a clinical name yet. There should be a German word for it. They have words for everything."

"*Torschlusspanik*," I say.

She blinks at me. "What?"

"It's German. Means the fear that time is running out and doors are closing. Literally translates to 'gate-closing panic.'"

"How do you know that?"

I won't dare tell her a client actually taught me that on a date. Because now that feels like a different life. Before Celeste. Well before I knew what I wanted and decided to go for it.

"Just someone from a past life."

She doesn't question it. She almost smiles. "It's accurate, I'll give you that. Gate-closing panic. That's exactly what this is." She rubs her temples in circles like she can massage her worries away.

"You need to relax."

"I'll relax when I'm dead, Saylor."

"Or," I say, stepping farther into the office, "you could relax right now. For ten minutes. Just long enough to get out of your own head."

"I don't have ten minutes."

"You have all the minutes you decide you have. You own this company. Nobody's checking your timesheet."

"That's not how creative deadlines—"

"It's exactly how creative blocks work. You're gripping too tight. Staring at the design and demanding it speak. Sometimes the best thing you can do is step away and let the idea find you when you stop hunting it."

She leans back in her chair. Arms crossed. The posture of a woman preparing to reject whatever comes next on general principle. "And what exactly do you propose I do for ten minutes that's going to magically cure creative paralysis?"

I look around the office. The glass walls. The corkboard. The mannequin in her copper gown. And on the mannequin's waist, a sash of raw silk tied in a loose knot.

"Does your office have blinds?" I ask.

Celeste squints. "What?"

"Blinds. Privacy blinds. For the windows."

She studies me for a long moment, her expression moving through several phases of comprehension before arriving at something between suspicion and curiosity. Without breaking eye contact, she reaches to her desk and presses a button. A low mechanical hum fills the room as automated blinds descend from the top of every glass wall, rolling down in unison, sealing the office from the open floor plan outside. The light softens. The outside world disappears. It's just us and the mannequin in the corner, watching with what I choose to interpret as approval.

I walk to the door. Lock it. The click is small but fills the room like a punctuation mark at the end of a very long sentence.

"Saylor, what are you—"

"Sit down."

She doesn't sit down. She stands there with her arms crossed, vibrating with the tension of a woman who is never told what to do and isn't entirely sure how she feels about the part of her that wants to listen.

"Please," I add.

She sits. In her office chair, behind her desk, where she's sat a thousand times for a thousand meetings and never once for this. I walk to the mannequin and untie the sash from its waist. The fabric is cool and smooth in my hands, weightless. I don't know what this fabric is, but I like it. It's something I've never felt before, a cross between the luxury of silk and the comfort of cotton. I can learn this stuff. I can learn to speak *Celeste.*

I come around the desk. Celeste watches me with a breathing pattern that has already changed. Quicker. Shallower. Her hands grip the armrests, knuckles going pale, pupils dilating behind those glasses I find unreasonably attractive.

I stop behind her chair. Lean down so my mouth is near her ear. Close enough that she can feel my breath but not my lips. The distinction matters.

"Do you trust me?" I ask.

"That depends on what you're about to do with that tie."

"Close your eyes."

She hesitates. One breath. Two. Her fingers release the armrests one by one, consciously letting go of the controls. Then she removes her glasses and her eyes close. I lay the silk gently across them and tie it at the back of her head. Careful with her hair. Careful with the pressure. The fabric is thin enough to see shadows through but not detail. Not enough to plan or control or design her response. That's the point. For the next few minutes, Celeste Brinley doesn't get to be in control. She just gets to feel.

I move back around to the front of the desk. I don't touch her. Not yet. I let the silence stretch. Let her sit in the anticipation, in the not-knowing, in the space between nerves and need.

"Saylor?" Her tone is pitched differently. Tighter.

"I'm here."

"What are you—"

"Breathe, Celeste. Relax."

I hear her exhale. Not a sigh. A surrender. The sound of an exhausted woman who is still mentally managing crises even as I stand between her thighs, finally breathing out. Choosing to let someone else hold the reins for thirty seconds.

I kneel in front of her chair. My hands find her knees. She flinches at the contact, not from fear but from the voltage of being touched without seeing it coming. I rest my hands there. Still. Just holding her knees through the fabric of her skirt, letting the warmth of my palms communicate before my fingers do.

Then I begin to move. Slowly. My thumbs tracing small circles on the inside of her knees, gradually sliding upward, pushing her skirt higher as I go. Inch by inch. The fabric bunches and rides. Her breathing accelerates with each inch of skin I uncover, the sound filling the quiet office like a metronome set to an increasing tempo.

I reach the lace edge of her underwear. I trace it with one fingertip. Just one. Following the scalloped border where fabric meets skin, from one hip across the front to the other, and the noise she makes through pressed-together lips is so controlled and so desperate that it sends heat straight through my chest and down.

"I have employees," she whispers. "On this floor. Thirty of them."

"You also have a locked door and covered windows."

"The blinds aren't soundproof."

"Then you'll have to be quiet."

I hook my fingers into the waistband and pull downward. She lifts her hips without being asked, which tells me everything about the distance between her protests and her want. Her underwear slides down her thighs, past her knees, over her heels. I set them on the floor beside me. Black lace. I'll be taking those with me.

I don't go straight to where she wants me. That'd be a mistake. The destination only matters if the journey makes you desperate to arrive. So I press my mouth to the inside of her knee. Then higher. Then higher still. Kissing a path up her inner thigh with the patience of a man who has absolutely nowhere else to be, stopping every few inches to let my breath land against her skin so she can feel the heat without the contact. The anticipation does more than the touch. Every pause makes her shift in the chair, angling toward me, seeking something I'm deliberately withholding.

"Saylor." My name comes out like a warning she doesn't mean.

"Mm-hmm."

"If you don't—"

"Don't what?"

She doesn't finish the sentence. She doesn't need to. I can feel the tension in her thighs, the way her muscles are pulled taut, vibrating at a frequency that tells me she's right at the edge of patience. I ghost my mouth over her clit without making contact and she inhales so sharply the chair creaks.

Then I give her what she wants.

My tongue makes first contact with her slick heat and she's already so wet I can taste how badly she's been wanting this. The sound she makes is low and choked and immediately swallowed, her hand clamping over her own mouth with the desperate efficiency of a woman who is trying not to disturb the moment. As if her moans of pleasure would stop me. Wrong. *They energize me.*

I use my tongue with the patience and attention I promised her in the guesthouse. The kind of focus that says I'm not racing toward a finish line. I'm learning a language. I vary the pressure, the rhythm, the angle, reading every shift of her hips, every catch in her breathing, every involuntary movement of the hand that's gripping my hair like a lifeline. I suck her clit between my lips and feel her whole body jerk in response. Her thighs clamp around my head so hard I can barely hear her desperate whimpers.

I want more. I want to see her, taste her, every inch. I hook one of her knees over my shoulder and shift her so she's right at the edge of the chair, her skirt bunched and hiked up around her waist like a ring around a finger. Now she's open in front of me, spread and vulnerable, the blindfold turning her into pure sensation. I press my tongue deeper, flatten it, push past her slick folds and into her. She gasps, the sound completely involuntary this time, a noise of shock and want, and her hands fly to the sides of my head, steadying herself, steadying me, like she's afraid she might fall out of the chair.

She tastes like sweet and salt. Something phantom-like, haunting. A taste I'll chase to the ends of the earth, like the ocean just before a storm. I want to drown in it. I drag my tongue up, circle her clit, playing, teasing, then fuck her with it, plunging in and out, slow and deep. I can hear her fighting so hard not to make noise, her hips rolling against my mouth, her breath going ragged and sharp. It's the most honest I've ever seen her—no armor, no boardroom voice, just the mess of it, the need.

I slide my hands up her thighs, grip her hips, hold her still so I can control the pace, and she gives it up to me, lets me take her apart. I can hear the hum of the air vents, the faint sounds of office life somewhere out there beyond the glass, the slick sound of me lapping at treasure like a starved animal.

"Fuck," she whispers, barely audible, her throat choked with need. "Right there."

When I find the exact combination that makes her thighs tremble, I stay there. I don't change a thing. I suck and lick at her relentlessly, drinking her in like a man dying of thirst. Consistency is its own form of devotion. I slide two fingers inside her, curling them upward, and feel her inner walls clench around me, hot and tight and greedy.

But I don't let her finish. Not yet.

I pull back just as her breathing reaches its peak, withdrawing both my mouth and my fingers. Her hips chase me and find nothing but air. The sound of frustrated protest that escapes her fingers is magnificent—half sob, half curse. Her pussy is glistening, swollen and pink, begging for my return.

"What're you—" She gasps. "You came all the way here just to edge me?"

"So you want me." My smile is wicked.

"I will fire you," she responds flatly, removing her knee from my shoulder, crossing her legs.

"From fixing up your house or eating your pussy?"

She scowls at me. Her eyes are still covered, but I see the way her forehead furrows. "I want you."

"For how long?"

She purses her lips. "Why don't you just tell me the answer you want, Saylor. Will that speed this up?"

"So bossy," I tease before blowing on her center. She shudders as she releases a small gasp. "Give me the honest answer."

"You're holding my orgasm hostage for some big emotional revelation you think I should be sharing. That's manipulative. Big red flag."

I rise, pull up her blindfold for a millisecond so she can see me lick my lips. I adjust the tie so her world goes dark once more. "Sure is. So walk away. I dare you."

I wait. Ten seconds. Fifteen. Letting her body step back from the edge, letting the wave recede just enough that when it builds again it'll be bigger.

"God, maybe it's a good thing I'm blindfolded right now. Look, I want you to really think about what you want, Saylor. Because you're coming on strong and I love it. You treat me like I'm the prize and you're willing to work for it, and that's not fair. Because once you get what you want, you will wake up and realize that you're way too young to worry about getting old. This age gap isn't going to make sense."

"Celeste," I breathe. "I'm already awake. And I know what I want."

I spread her thighs back apart, scoot her to my open mouth.

She's trembling. The chair is trembling. I return to her slowly. Gently at first, rebuilding what I pulled away, and the moan she releases this time is deeper, rawer, the sound of a woman who has been edged and knows what she's owed and is done being polite about it. She finds the back of my head with both hands now, pulling me closer with an authority that has nothing to do with her status and everything to do with a body that is finished asking and has started demanding.

I give her everything.

This time she doesn't even try to control it. Her whole body locks, every muscle in her thighs and stomach tightening so hard she's shaking, and when I push two fingers inside her and curl them, she makes a sound that's not so much a moan as a wail, the kind of noise that would make grown men panic and run toward the source to see if someone is dying. She's coming before she even realizes it, the orgasm ripping through her so fast and sharp she throws her head back and nearly bites through her own hand. I keep my mouth locked to her clit, my tongue unrelenting, my fingers stroking inside her, and she just keeps coming. The release is so intense it's almost violent. Her legs clamp around me, her hips buck, and she lets out a cry that's equal parts agony and relief, like a wound being cauterized.

When she finally collapses, it's not graceful. She just melts, boneless, all pretense of composure gone, slumping into the chair with her skirt bunched around her waist and the blindfold askew. Her chest is heaving, blouse half-untucked, and for what it's worth, despite all the lethally sexy attire and fancy makeup I've seen her wear, this is my favorite look. Celeste...satisfied. Celeste...happy.

I rise and kiss her, slow and gentle, her taste still on my mouth. She kisses back lazily, like she's still not fully in control of motor function. I undo the knot of the blindfold, her hair falling over her eyes as the sash slips away.

She blinks away the intrusive overhead lights. Her pupils are enormous. Her lips are parted. Her hands are still death-gripping the armrests like the chair might eject her into orbit.

"How are those creative blocks feeling now?" I murmur.

She opens her mouth. Closes it. Opens it again.

"I have no thoughts. My brain is completely empty."

"Perfect." I smooth my wrinkled pants and straighten my flannel. Then, she watches me pick up her underwear from the floor and tuck them into my back pocket with the deliberate calm of a man who has just performed a service and is collecting his payment.

"Saylor Evans, give me my underwear back."

"No. Consider them collateral." I lean against her desk. "Now. I need your apartment keys."

She's still gripping the armrests. "My what?"

"Your penthouse keys. I'm planning our first date tonight and I need access to your place. Your other place. Actually, now that we're on the subject, how many places do you have?"

She relaxes back into the Celeste I recognize, shimmying down her skirt, then crossing her arms, looking almost presentable. "In this country or worldwide?"

"*Geez*," I mutter. "Point made."

"Does my money bother you? Do you think I'm spoiled?"

I shake my head. "No. I just feel bad. Maybe I'm a little old-school, but I feel like a gentleman should pick up the check. But I'll never be able to afford the meals you order."

"Well it's a good thing your cooking beats every Michelin-star restaurant I've ever eaten in."

"Don't do that. Don't patronize me." I chuckle softly, playing it off as a joke. But truly...I wish she wouldn't pity me. How can she see anything real with a man she can't respect?

"Everybody has money problems, just the scale is different. But fundamentally, you and I see wealth the same way. Saylor, I had a man who bought me expensive things and took me to fancy places. But he never made me happy. I want a man who can find happiness outside of wealth."

"I've mastered the 'outside of wealth' part. I'm working on

the happiness part. Is that okay? Am I still a contender?"

"Saylor, you're the only contender." I wish I could hold the smile she gives in my pocket forever. It's sweet and girlish. A smile that should be dried and pressed, preserving a perfect moment forever. "So a date," she repeats, in the voice of a woman whose operating system is rebooting in real time. "Tonight."

"Tonight. Dress code is whatever you'd wear to a sleepover in college. I'll handle everything else." I hold out my hand. "Keys."

She stares at my hand. Stares at my face. Stares at my back pocket where her lace is visible above the denim.

"The gold one is the front door," she says, reaching into her purse with hands that haven't fully steadied. "Silver is the elevator override. Alarm code is one-two-three-four."

"Celeste when you've finished the line, and everything has settled with the custody care, you know...when life feels less heavy..."

"Yeah?" she asks. "Then what?"

"We are going through your passwords and passcodes one by one and changing them into something a five-year-old can't hack."

She's laughing as I take her keys. Kiss her forehead, which feels almost comically chaste given what just happened three feet south of that forehead.

I'm at the door when she calls me back.

"Saylor."

I turn back. She's standing by her chair, skirt slightly crooked, hair thoroughly destroyed, the silk sash pooled in her lap like a piece of evidence at a crime scene. She looks like a woman who just experienced something she'll replay in her head for the rest of the day and possibly longer.

"Tonight... Whatever you're planning, it better be good. I promised myself if I ever fell in love again, I'd make sure it was worthwhile. I'd ask for things that I never asked for in the past—fierce loyalty, kindness, soft but strong hands. I'm not going to settle this time. So...bring the magic, okay?"

I salute her. "You've got it, Mrs. Robinson. Magic at six o'clock tonight."

She grimaces. "Seven. I still have a lot of work here to do."

"Seven it is." I nod. "But don't be late."

I walk out of her office. Past Margot's empty desk. Past the open floor plan where thirty-some employees are having a perfectly ordinary Friday afternoon with no idea what just happened behind those privacy blinds. Past the hallway where Greg Prescott told me I didn't belong.

I press the lift button. The doors open. The mirrored walls show me three versions of myself, and in every single one I'm a man with a woman's keys in his hand and her underwear in his pocket and the absolute, unshakable certainty that Greg Prescott has no fucking idea where I belong.

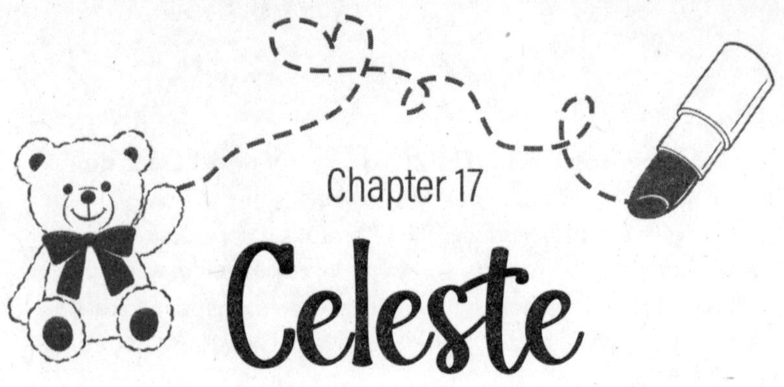

Chapter 17
Celeste

Gummy bears in a Hermès bowl.

I have been useless since two o'clock.

Not creatively useless, which has been my default setting this week. Functionally useless. A woman sitting in a corner office of a building with her name on it, staring at fabric swatches she cannot see because her brain has been wiped clean by a twenty-six-year-old Australian who walked into her office, blindfolded her with her own work in progress, and performed an act on his knees that should be classified as both a workplace violation and a public service.

Every time I close my eyes, I feel his mouth. Not as a memory. As a haunting. The ghost of his tongue, the pressure of his hands on my thighs.

Am I as bad as Greg, getting off in the office? Am I the world's biggest hypocrite now? Hmmm. Feels kind of good.

Perhaps it's time for new rules. Perhaps it's time to *move on.*

At six thirty, I surrender to the uselessness. The copper gown hasn't moved. The swatches haven't spoken. My brain, as Saylor accurately diagnosed, has been reformatted, and whatever creative operating system typically runs this company has been replaced by a screensaver of him kneeling on my office floor with that look in his eyes. That focus. The concentration of a man solving a problem he considers both urgent and sacred.

I pack my bag. Switch to the flats I keep under my desk for the commute. Let my hair down because the pencil holding it up vanished during the incident and I'm not crawling around my office floor searching for it on my hands and knees with no panties. As I leave, I catch sight of Patrice looking naked without her sash.

I glare at her and her unfinished dress. "You just stood there and watched? Quite the voyeur. I always knew you were a bit of a freak, Patrice."

In the elevator, I try to find my reflection in the mirrored walls but the woman staring back is new. Not younger, not prettier, not any of the metrics I've been measuring myself against for twenty years. Just awake. Tapping my toe against the floor impatiently because I have somewhere to be and I'm looking forward to it. Suddenly home doesn't feel like such a rented space.

The car ride home normally takes about twenty minutes. Traffic was forgiving for some reason, which in Manhattan must mean Godzilla is on the way and someone spread the word. I've never seen the streets so uncongested. Instead of twenty minutes, I'm home in ten.

The elevator opens directly into my foyer because penthouses have that privilege, and I stop walking.

My apartment looks like a very stylish hurricane swept through a college dormitory and deposited the wreckage across my living room floor. Every blanket I own, plus several I'm fairly certain were hiding in closets I forgot existed, has been arranged into a sprawling nest between the couch and the television. Pillows everywhere. Snack bowls crowding every flat surface. My television, which I use exclusively for the news and the occasional fashion documentary, is frozen on the opening credits of *Bring It On*.

And in the middle of it all: Saylor. Gray sweatpants. Backward cap. White T-shirt that makes his shoulders and chest look like a problem I'm fully prepared to tackle. He's standing in my pristine apartment like a very handsome squatter who decided to remodel my home into a reincarnation of the year two thousand.

"What is all this?" I ask.

"This is our date."

I look at the sheet face masks stacked on the coffee table that have pictures of animals on them. My collagen masks have gold speckles in it, "guaranteed to give you Korean glass skin." There are gummy bears in a Hermès bowl. I don't tell Saylor he just filled a sixteen-thousand-dollar art piece with Haribo gummy treats. Wine coolers are sweating condensation onto furniture I had custom-made. There's Chinese takeout, still in its containers on the counter. Next to it, unmistakable in its blue-and-yellow packaging: my popcorn. My favorite brand.

"You did all this for me?" My voice does something embarrassing. Cracks, just slightly, around the edges. Like a teacup with a hairline fracture that only shows when you fill it.

I set my bag on the floor and kick off my shoes, letting them ceremoniously skid into the corner by the entrance. I silently apologize to my Manolos because that was kind of rude of me. But I'm giddy and excited, suddenly full of nervous energy that I haven't had since the first time I said "I do."

I pick up a wine cooler and examine it. It's the cheap kind. *The really cheap kind.* Absurdly sugary, like liquid candy. I haven't held one of these in fifteen years. It feels like a time capsule in a bottle. After twisting off the top, I take a big swig.

"Bleh." I swallow, needing air as a chaser.

Saylor chuckles. "That bad? What do those taste like?"

I examine the bottle with a cheesy beach scene on the label. "They taste purple, if that's a thing."

He laughs again until the silence fills the space between us.

"It's obvious I can't compete with money, Celeste." The playfulness leaves his voice. What replaces it isn't sadness or self-pity. It's clarity. Plain and undecorated, the verbal equivalent of showing up in sweatpants and not apologizing for it. "You know that. I'll never book a corner table at whatever French restaurant charges four hundred dollars for a tasting menu. I can't buy you jewelry that comes in a velvet box. I don't know what the opera is actually about and I'll never be convinced that foam belongs on food."

"Saylor—"

"But I can do something I don't think any man has ever done for you." He comes to me, takes the wine cooler from my hand, and sets it on the counter. "I can listen. I can pay attention. I did all this because from everything I've gathered in the couple months I've known you, this was the happiest time of your life. That sacred two years before Greg started suffocating you with his expectations. The two years you had alone with Whit to just enjoy growing up." He gestures at the blanket nest, the snacks, the frozen screen. "I wanted to bring you back to your happy place."

I look at this man. Really look at him. Not like a situation to be solved. But the answer to a question I haven't been brave enough to ask.

When did I give up on love? When did I stop realizing its magnitude? Why did I think I'd want to experience the rest of my life alone?

Maybe until right now, I didn't have another option. But here he is. Seemingly two decades late, but he's here.

"So how'd I do?" he asks tepidly. "Are you feeling at least a little magic?"

I point to the coffee table in my living room. "Are you going to wear those face masks with me?"

"Hell yeah. Dibs on the panda one."

"And what about your mom?"

"Resting, and Forrest has agreed to be on-call if she needs anything at all. We have all night."

"That's sweet of Forrest," I muse.

"He's a good bloke. Great friend. I'm still kind of pissed he got to you first."

I chuckle softly. "Don't be jealous. He didn't get to me. Not like you do."

"Good," he answers. "Keep it that way. I want to be the only man who gets to you. The only one who *gets you.*"

I reach up, his cheeks are in my hands, then my lips soft against his. "I'm going to go change into something worthy of this incredible first date, and when I get back, get ready...it's time."

"For *Bring It On*? Because I've been looking forward to this one. What are the chances you were a cheerleader in high school or college and maybe kept your uniform?"

"Zero. I would've been better suited for the band. But I'm not talking about the movie."

He wets his lips. "Then what's it time for?"

"For us to fall in love." I pick up the wine cooler again and take another long swig, cringing at the sickly sweet syrup that now coats my tongue. I don't actually think there's alcohol in these.

"Go get dressed. Or undressed," Saylor says. "I'll be here. *Ready*."

"Is it supposed to burn a little?" Saylor asks, buried underneath a face mask designed to make it look like he has panda markings around his eyes. We're cuddled up on my oversized chaise lounge, lights dimmed, movie volume low, the faint hint of sweet snacks still lingering on our tongues.

I discarded my Koala mask about ten minutes ago when the smell of grape bubblegum got overwhelming. "How much is a little?"

"Kind of like when you pour alcohol into an open sore."

I widen my eyes at him. "Definitely not. Take that off right now."

I peel it off before he can, pressing against his slightly pink cheeks with two fingers. I put my face in his and pucker, begging for a sweet kiss. He obliges but almost distractedly. "We're missing the movie."

"I've seen it a thousand times."

"*I haven't*," he insists.

Men and media. I swear. Any type of screen is hypnosis,

regardless of the decade they were born in.

I pull off my pale pink sweatshirt that only looks casual. It's part of a set and it matches my nice luggage, but it's big and cozy. The kind of sweatshirt that doubles as a cocoon when I tuck my knees in. Once I toss it aside, I unhook my bra.

After sliding off the straps, shoulder by shoulder, I let the bra dangle from my finger before tossing it into the mound of blankets.

Saylor's pupils blow wide, his attention locked in on me. "You're so—" he starts but loses his sentence. The way his gaze is tracing my body feels like an artist studying a canvas he's about to paint.

I clamber out of our cuddle. The moment my feet hit the ground, I kneel by the loveseat, shins slotting into the plushest spot of the blanket nest. I pat the cushion, indicating where he should sit.

He rises, changes seats, settles into the cushion in front of me, and all the while his eyes never leave my breasts. The last time a man studied me this hard was Greg, shortly before suggesting I get a lift. Instead, Saylor's paralyzed hands reach out, hovering over my chest like he's not sure if he's allowed to touch. I take his hands and put them on me, just under my ribcage where the skin is softest. I breathe in, and his fingers tighten, anchoring me to this moment.

"Do you like this?" I ask, with all sincerity. There's a vulnerability in the question that I can't mask. I'm sure he's used to seeing different bodies. Firmer, fuller, more confident. There's not just underweight and overweight anymore. Women are expected to have bodies that defy physics and gravity. Boobs that stay perched high on their shelves but feel natural. Asses that are bubbly and round, but only if it's paired with thigh gaps and flat stomachs. A size-zero waist, and size-eight hips. We spend so much time thinking about what we should be, we never appreciate what we are.

Saylor seems to be appreciating me exactly as I am. Flat-chested, hip-less, and so desperate for him to still see beauty where

I used to.

"Fuck, Celeste. Do I like this? Right now I feel bad for every woman in the world who doesn't get to wake up and be you."

I bask in the compliment, letting it shower over me, rinsing away all my insecurities. "You think I'm hot?"

"I think you're spellbinding...and yeah, super hot."

"Okay, good. As long as you're into it."

"I'm very into it." His voice goes low and husky. The way he moistens his lips tugs at something well below my navel.

I reach for his waistband, fingers sliding under the elastic of both sweats and briefs, and there's a split-second where he tenses, hissing out a controlled breath like I just grazed his self-destruct button. I pull both down in a single movement and Saylor's dick springs out in a way that's almost comical, cartoonish, like nobody could have ever drawn this up and expected anyone to buy it. I try not to gawk but it's impossible: he's huge, long and thick, with a gentle curve that makes it look like it's perpetually in mid-salute. His skin is smooth, ruddy at the crown and flushed deeper at the base, with a neat, clean line where his hair's trimmed down almost to nothing. At the tip a single bead glistens, clear and obscene, and for a moment I just watch it, tracing the physics of gravity as it clings and then releases, a slow-motion drip onto his thigh.

He looks down at me and his face is all amusement and vulnerability, a silent "well?" that hangs in the air. I take him in my hand, careful at first—there's a pulse to it, a throbbing that makes my palm tingle. I run my thumb over the slick tip and he lets out a soft breath, his chest rising. His cock is heavy and hot, alive. I bring my mouth to him, just the head, and taste him, salt and a little bitter and faintly like skin after sun.

I swirl my tongue around the head, collecting every drop of him, mapping the groove that crowns it, and he shudders so hard I almost lose my grip. I start slow, learning his rhythm—he likes it when I stroke him with one hand, twisting slightly at the end, while flicking my tongue just underneath where the skin is taut and sensitive. I take him deeper, until the tip presses against the roof of my mouth, and the air is full of his soft, shaky moans.

I realize, with a delighted scientist's curiosity, that he really, really likes it when I use my other hand to cup his balls. The reaction is instant: his whole body tightens, his hips jerk up, and his breath turns ragged. So, as a follow-up experiment, I draw one of them into my mouth, gently, and stroke his shaft at the same time.

Saylor groans, louder than I expected, the sound ricocheting around the living room and vibrating through my palms. He's clinging to the cushions, white-knuckled, and for a second I worry he might actually break my bespoke sofa. But it turns me on, the way he surrenders, the way he's so unguarded. I switch it up, using both hands, twisting, squeezing, then taking him as deep as I can go.

I peer up at him through my lashes and he's staring down, eyes glassy and desperate. "Celeste," he says, voice strangled. "You have to stop or—"

I don't stop. I become relentless, a metronome of pressure.

He's saying, "wait, *fuck*, stop, shit, hang on," and then, "don't stop, don't stop, oh my God," and I'm getting drunk on it. On his surrender. It's not a collapse or a defeat, but an offering. Saylor is letting me have him, the whole trembling, pulsing, gasping mess of him, and if this is a power trip then sign me up for the annual convention and let me chair the committee.

My jaw aches a little, but I don't care. I want to give him this. I want to watch him dissolve. I want to be the woman he thinks about, the mouth he remembers, the memory that leaves him stammering and glazed and the next time he sees me across a room I want him to remember the way I'm making him feel right now. I want his release. I make it my mission. I flatten my tongue and take him as deep as I can, letting my spit run down, messy and hungry, and his hands find my hair, gentle at first, then not. He's bucking against my mouth. He's holding on to me like I'm the only thing keeping him from falling into the abyss.

He's close. He's so close. His legs are shaking. He's making noises I've never heard from another human. The way he says my name—Celeste, Celeste, baby, baby, like a mantra—makes something inside me turn liquid and reckless. And I'm oh-so-fucking-close to my victory when Saylor rips out of my mouth. In one fluid motion, he's off the couch, we're both on our feet. He yanks down my pajama shorts and thong like he detests them.

Sitting at the edge of the couch, he spreads his knees, displaying his cock, thick and glistening. I'm entranced by the sight, almost immobile, so he has to guide me between his legs. His hands are rough and greedy on my hips, my ass, my thighs—then, almost ceremonial, he cups my mound, index finger sliding through the slickness there. I'm wetter than I've been in...ever. But it must not be enough for him.

He spits in his palm, rubs it over the head of his cock, and then reaches between my legs, massaging the spit and my own wetness over my clit with slow, deliberate pressure. He doesn't shy from it, doesn't ask if I want it, just moves as if the two of us have been doing this together for years, and now every nerve ending is sparking, every inch of me turned forward and urgent.

He slides a finger inside, then a second, curling up and pressing against the spot that, when touched, turns my whole core to white noise.

I gasp; he grins. "That's it," he says, a coach and a worshipper all at once. He strokes me like he's learning a song by ear, adjusting tempo and pressure until I'm quaking. He guides me onto his lap, my legs draped over his, and continues to play with my clit like it's a stress ball. I could come from this feeling alone, but suddenly I'm empty, his hand gone, and the next sensation is the blunt, hot head of his cock at my entrance.

He holds me there, poised, the tip just nudging in, and I realize he's waiting for permission, or maybe for the satisfaction of watching my face as I take him. I look him in the eye and lower myself, slowly, feeling the stretch, the impossible fullness of him, and then he's all the way in, and I'm all the way gone.

Leaning back, the cushions swallow him, and he takes me

with him, my knees on either side of his hips. He spits in his palm again, messy and determined, and reaches down, slicking the wetness over my clit and his cock at once. It's filthy and perfect and I want him to take me like a drug. I want to know I'm the reason pure ecstasy is speckled in his eyes.

He holds me by the hips, fingers digging deep, and begins to move me. Slow at first, like he's afraid I'll break. I won't break. It's an effort not to laugh with joy as I realize how strong I am, how much of him I can handle, how much I want. I match his rhythm, rocking forward, back, forward, again, until the whole world is just the heat and the slip and the impossibly good friction.

His hands slide up to my waist, then my ribs, then my face, cupping it like I'm precious, and he brings me down for a kiss so tender it almost breaks the spell. *Almost.* But this salacious magic, flesh against flesh, a cocktail of his pleasure and mine, is too deep. Too carnal. This can only end one way, and that's with him spilling into me, stars in our eyes, and no air in our lungs.

We're both sweating and shivering. He's close again but he's fighting it, hard, his jaw clenched, eyes wild. In a low growl, he demands, "Ride me, baby," and I do. I take it as a challenge. I let myself go, chasing it, grinding down and circling my hips until I feel the pressure building behind my pubic bone, the tension so tight I could snap.

Saylor's hands lock on my hips, and for a minute I let him control the pace, the thrust. He's so deep I can feel every pulse, every twitch. He leans back, one arm folded behind his head, the other traveling lazily down my chest, tracing the sweat pooling between my breasts, pinching a nipple until I whimper. I can't decide if I want to ride him into the couch or fall apart right here. I'd be good with either. Both.

Then he sits up, inhumanly fast, and tucks a strand of my hair behind my ear before practically throwing me onto the couch, proving that I'm all but weightless to him.

He buries his face between my legs, hands curling under my thighs to anchor me, and goes at me like he's starving and this is the last meal on Earth. It's nothing like I've had in the past: it's not perfunctory, not something to cross off a list—Saylor eats me out like a worshipper at the altar, like a drowning man clutching the only rope thrown to him. He nuzzles in, tongue strong against my clit, and licks with slow, deliberate strokes, savoring the taste of me like it's a new language he's desperate to pick up.

I fist his hair—his ridiculous, mussed-up hair—and try to steady myself, but he won't let me. His hands pin me open, holding me with so much care that I don't feel exposed; I feel precious. He hums into me, low and deep, the vibration going straight through the center of me, and I whimper, louder this time, not even caring what the neighbors might overhear.

He slides two fingers inside, curling them just right, and my hips buck forward of their own volition, needing more, chasing that ruthless, dizzying pleasure. My vision goes hot around the edges. He pulls back long enough to look up at me, mouth shiny, eyes feral.

"I love the way you look when you're about to come. So fucking beautiful," he praises, voice blown wide open, and then goes right back to it.

He doesn't let up—fingers relentless, tongue circling, lips sealing around my clit until the world telescopes down to that single, throbbing point. I shudder apart and then explode, helpless. The orgasm rips through me so sharp and sudden, I can't breathe. I hear myself cry out, maybe his name, maybe just nonsense, as the contractions roll through my legs and spine and stomach until I'm nothing but a shivering, gasping wreck.

He works me through it, licking and sucking, fingers stroking until I'm whimpering from the unbearable, oversensitive aftershocks. Only then does he slow, easing off, kissing my thighs with an adoration that makes my vision blurry.

He looks up, lips swollen, chin slick, and grins like a man who just found religion before he thrusts into me, sliding inside so deep I arch back and accept my fate. The pleasure swallows me whole; I'm no match. I simply float as Saylor has his way with me.

There's no teasing, no slow build—just raw, glorious fucking, his mouth pressed to mine, his hands under my ass, pulling me up to meet every slam of his hips. The couch is squeaking, the blankets sliding off, but I don't care. He can tear the world apart if it means I get to come with him again.

Eventually, he's gasping, "Celeste, I'm gonna—" and I pull him tighter, wanting to feel it, all of it. He bucks up, hard, then pulls out at the last second, hot pulses striping my stomach, up to my breasts.

He doesn't move. Just stands over me, hands braced on the couch cushions, head bowed, brow furrowed. Sweat drips from his chest, landing on my skin and mingling with the white stripes painting me from navel to sternum. I half expect him to collapse, but he just hovers, staring down at the mess he's made of me with a kind of reverence. Not pride, not embarrassment—something rawer, almost holy.

"Sorry," he says, voice shredded. "I didn't know if you were on anything, and I didn't want to risk—"

I laugh, a little breathless, and run my pinky through the sticky trail on my stomach. "Saylor, I'm thirty-eight. I'm on everything." I swipe a glob up, wipe it idly across my thigh. "You can finish wherever you want."

His gaze flicks up to mine, and for a moment he looks surprised. Then pleased. "Yeah? In you?"

"Yes."

"In your mouth?"

I pause, considering. "Sure." I've never done that for any man, but I don't tell him. I tuck the secret away, a private dare.

But the next thing I know, he's dipping his finger into the pearl on my belly, swiping it up, and holding it to my lips. His eyes glint with mischief, but there's an undercurrent of challenge—will I call his bluff? I part my lips and he slides his finger in. I taste him, salty and alien and strangely electric. He watches, transfixed, as I suck his finger clean, the taste not unpleasant—just strange, like I'm sampling a new cuisine for the first time and trying to place the notes. He grins, triumphant, and wipes the rest off my stomach with a wet paper towel he fetches from the kitchen.

He flops onto his back next to me, which only a couch of this size would allow. Both of us face the ceiling, arms and legs splayed like crime scene outlines. The movie's long since rolled into credits and then into the algorithmic silence that comes when all the suggested content has been exhausted. He's first to break the hush.

He pulls me on top of him, my naked body becoming his blanket. "Hi," he says.

"Hi."

"You okay?"

"I'm so far past okay I might need to invent new vocabulary."

He grins. Presses his forehead to mine. I reach between us, giving his dick a gentle stroke of appreciation and I'm shocked to see he's still hard. Not mildly attentive. Aggressively alert. I know he came...I tasted.

"Did you not get enough?" I ask, genuinely concerned.

"Enough of you? Never." He chuckles as I continue to stroke his length, more out of sheer wonder than anything else. He adds, nonchalant, "This is kind of my superpower."

"And you didn't tell me?" I balk.

"Yeah, and how would that conversation go, Celeste? My super erections are on a need-to-know basis."

Lucky. Fucking. Me.

I smile at him. "Let's do it again."

When he enters me, I close my eyes and make a sound that comes from somewhere behind my lungs. Somewhere underneath my ribs where I keep the things I've never said out loud. Not a performance. An arrival. The sound of a body that spent twenty years believing it was broken discovering it was only misassembled, and the right hands just put everything back where it belongs.

We find our rhythm together again. It's not choreographed. It's imperfect in places, clumsy in others, and infinitely better for every stumble because the stumbles are honest. I wrap my legs around him and his forehead drops to my shoulder and we breathe together in the amber light while the city hums forty-some floors below, a machine that has no idea what's happening up here and wouldn't care if it did.

The second time is slow and I cry at the end. Not from sadness. From the specific overwhelm of a body reclaiming something it believed was lost. He kisses the tears without comment, which is exactly right. No questions. No concern. Just acknowledgment. Just his mouth on my wet cheek saying: I see this. It's okay. Keep going.

The third time is past midnight. We've migrated to my actual bed by then, stumbling through the hallway around eleven, wine-cooler-dizzy and laughing at nothing and bumping into walls because neither of us is willing to stop kissing long enough to navigate properly. It's faster. Hungrier. My teeth on his shoulder. His hands knotted in my hair. The urgent, graceless collision of two people who've stopped negotiating and started claiming. I push him onto his back and ride him and his hands grip my hips and his eyes don't leave mine and I have never in my life felt more powerful and more vulnerable simultaneously. Both at once. Both essential.

I shut my eyes for what feels like mere minutes before gray light begins to press against the windows. Saylor's already awake. He traces the length of my spine with his fingertips. I don't know if this woke me, or he's doing this to specifically wake me. But I shimmy backward, locking my ass into his hips, enjoying being the little spoon. We lie still in the wreckage. Sheets still tangled into modern art. Skyline eventually going gold through the windows as the city wakes up. His chest rises and falls behind my back in a rhythm steady enough to set a clock by. My fingers trace idle shapes on his arm that's draped over my middle, holding me close. His other hand moves through my hair in long, unhurried passes, finding tangles and working through them with a gentleness that belongs in another century.

"I've been thinking about the nursery," I say.

I feel his attentiveness that sharpens without stiffening. Like he's straightening up to pay attention to an important conversation. "What about?"

"The sage green is perfect. You have a genuinely good eye for color."

"Is that surprising?"

"Yes. Because you own three T-shirts and one pair of presentable jeans. I say this with love, but the bar for your aesthetic judgment was not high."

He lays flat on his back, pulling me with him. I shift to my side, head held in one hand, my fingers playing notes onto his bare chest.

"But the color works. I want to keep it. And I want to add a proper rocking chair. Something with a wider seat, so I could fall asleep in it if I needed to, because everything I've read says the first three months are essentially a survival test dressed up as a bonding experience and nobody sleeps in their actual bed."

He laughs. Low, rumbly. It vibrates through his sternum.

"What else have you been reading?"

More than I should admit. Eleven tabs about infants are open on my phone at any given time. I've been reading about feeding schedules and sleep regression and something called the fourth trimester, which sounds invented but is apparently a legitimate developmental stage that nobody warns you about until you're already in it.

"I've been researching formula because I'll have to formula-feed, and the internet has split into two warring factions on this topic: one that treats formula like it was engineered in a villain's laboratory, and another that says fed is best, which seems reasonable but also has the energy of a phrase specifically designed to make formula mothers feel marginally less guilty about a decision that was necessary to make. I mean, shit. I've heard of slut-shaming, but mom-shaming takes it to a whole other level."

"Have you talked to Raven about it? Don't some surrogate moms breastfeed?"

"I could. But I don't want to treat Raven like a dairy cow," I say, and I mean it with every fiber of my being. "She's already growing an entire person inside her body. I am not going to also ask her to produce milk on demand like some kind of human cafeteria. She's a surrogate, not a vending machine. And I'm sure she has a life she wants to get back to. She's young. She doesn't want to be tied down with this baby."

Saylor is quiet for a moment. Not the uncomfortable silence of a man who's lost. The attentive silence of someone who's debating sharing exactly what's on his mind.

I assume his question and force his hand. "Say it."

"Say what?"

"Whatever it is you're holding back at the moment. You're team breast-is-best?"

"I'm young," Saylor says. "Subjectively."

"Objectively," I supply, "but go on. Yes, you're young."

"And I want to be tied down with this baby. Just for the record. You don't have to do this alone."

My eyes close. His heartbeat beneath my ear is steady and slow. I think about the tire swing and whether it needs replacing or just a new coat of sealant. I think about a girl with Whit's red curls reaching for a board book on a low shelf while afternoon light filters through sage-green curtains. I think about sitting in a rocking chair by the window, watching the oak tree, holding a baby who doesn't know yet that she was fought for, that two women went to war in a courtroom so that she could grow up in a house with a tire swing and words painted on a wall that say *you are so loved*. I think about giving that little girl a dad worth calling...Dad.

But is that Saylor? Does he really know what he's signing up for? Hell, do I?

"I'm still picturing a girl," I say, changing the subject so I don't have to force a design that doesn't quite make sense yet. "With Whit's hair."

"Me too. Curly little fire ringlets."

"I want this baby to know she was chosen. Not inherited. Not awarded by a court. *Chosen.* Because the woman her mother trusted most in the world decided, before this baby ever existed, that she was worth fighting for. All I want is to do right by her. To do right by Whit."

"You are, Celeste. You don't have to try so hard to prove yourself. You're already seen. You don't just have a good heart. You have a tireless heart. One that'll never stop beating for the people you love. So relax. Trust yourself, Lessi." Saylor's arm tightens around me. His lips press against the top of my head and rest there for a long moment, like he's sealing something. A promise he hasn't officially made.

We keep talking. About crib mattress firmness and baby monitors with cameras and whether there's a pediatrician in the city that Forrest might recommend. Saylor retells the story about the neighbor's two-year-old who called him "hammer bang-bang man" and whether that little girl could be a future playmate. About whether I should hire a night nurse for the first month or whether that undermines the entire point of choosing this with my own hands.

It dawns on me like diving into ice water. I'm shocked into awareness. Saylor didn't just fall for me. I believe his feelings are genuine. I believe he thoroughly enjoyed our sex marathon over the past twelve hours. But more importantly, Saylor is falling for the idea of a family with me.

Way more permanent. Way more risky. Way too dependent on me being something that I've never been before.

But how can I not take the risk? I always hoped for a man who listens. A man who hears me say popcorn brands matter and drove to three stores. A man who hears me say college was the happiest time of my life and built a time machine in my living room. A man who understands pressure, and how to relieve it. Someone who understands what I need even before I do.

That man is lying next to me. He deserves a chance.

"Hey, Celeste?" Saylor's voice has gone drowsy. Warm and

slow, muffled slightly against my hair.

"Hmm?"

"I'm really happy right now. Fearless, almost. And I haven't felt like this in a very long time."

No poetry, no metaphor, no elaborately constructed declaration. Just a man lying in the dark telling a woman he's happy, and meaning it so completely that the simplicity is what makes it land.

And I love every word.

"Me too," I tell him.

And I am. Not the manufactured happiness of a perfect evening or the manic happiness of something new or the anxious happiness of someone waiting for the other shoe to drop. Just happy. The way a house is warm. The way fabric falls when you stop fighting it. The way a woman feels when she discovers, at thirty-eight, that she was never past anything at all.

She was just getting started.

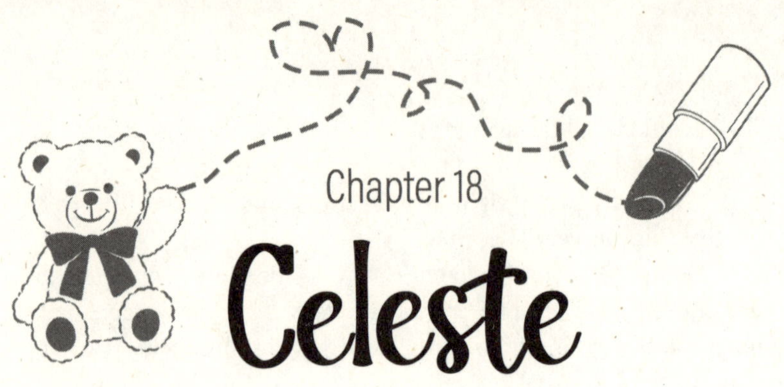

Chapter 18
Celeste

This is not a baby. It's an alligator.

Saylor holds the door for me at the clinic, and for a moment I just stand there on the sidewalk, looking up at the building like I'm about to walk into a cathedral. It's not a cathedral. It's a four-story medical building in Midtown East with a Starbucks on the ground floor and a parking garage that smells like exhaust and orange peels for some reason. But what's inside, on the third floor, behind a reception desk and an ultrasound machine, is the closest thing to sacred that I've encountered since Whitney's funeral.

Today we see the baby.

Not in the abstract. Not in legal documents or custody filings or the imagined version I've been sketching in my head for weeks, the girl with Whit's red curls reaching for books on Montessori shelves. Today we see the actual baby. On a screen. In real time. *Moving.*

My hand finds Saylor's as we walk through the lobby. Not for appearances. Only because we're that nauseating couple that likes to hold hands now. He threads his fingers through mine and squeezes once, and the squeeze says everything his mouth doesn't: *I'm here. This is real. We're doing this together.*

In the elevator, he's quiet. Unusually quiet for a man who once fabricated a bathroom emergency at a funeral. He's wearing a navy button-down that I bought him last week because his flannel and henley collection, while charming in a lumberjack-chic sort of way, is falling apart. He needed new clothes. I snuck in a few upgrades. *Sue me.* He's still rolled the sleeves to the elbow because Saylor Evans cannot exist in a long-sleeved, collared shirt without modifying it to look casual. I've accepted this about him the way you accept weather.

"Thank you," he says, as the elevator passes the second floor.

"For what?"

"For letting me be here. For this. You didn't have to include me."

"Saylor, you painted the nursery. You wrote 'you are so loved' on the wall. You built the new crib and installed a baby monitor. You even bought Dreft."

"It's safer detergent for the baby's skin."

"On what planet do you think I would not include you?"

He looks at the floor. The humble version of him, the one that still can't quite believe he's allowed to want things. "I just know this is your thing. Yours and Whit's. I don't want to overstep."

"You're not overstepping. You're standing exactly where I want you to stand." I squeeze his hand. "Besides, someone has to drive me home afterward because I'll probably be crying too hard to see the road. I could accidentally drive off a bridge."

"Yeah...you're only a terrible driver when you're crying. *Sure.*"

"Hush, you."

The third floor is a women's health practice with soft lighting and abstract art on the walls that's meant to be calming but does not succeed. It's all abstract flowers that are shaped suspiciously like vaginas. Other than the female anatomy art, the waiting room is all muted tones and cushioned chairs and a water dispenser with cucumber slices floating in it, which I find both soothing and pretentious. There's a woman across the room who is approximately eleven months pregnant and reading a magazine with the detached serenity of someone who has moved past anxiety and into acceptance. She knows it. We know it. She will be pregnant forever. That baby will grow a beard in her belly.

"Celeste! Saylor!"

Raven is already here.

She's sitting in the corner chair, the one closest to the outlet because she's charging her phone. Even from her chair, the full scope of her belly can't be hidden. She is magnificently, undeniably, spectacularly pregnant. Twenty-five weeks. Her belly is a small planet. It has its own gravitational field. She's wearing a floral wrap dress that I sent her from the office two weeks ago along with a care package of maternity clothes. Raven's pre-pregnancy wardrobe consisted primarily of crop tops and low-rise jeans, and while I respect her commitment to early-aughts fashion, there are limits to what denim can accommodate.

"You guuuuys." She stands, which is now a multi-phase operation involving a forward lean, a hand on the armrest, and a small grunt of exertion that she tries to disguise as enthusiasm. I meet her halfway and hug her carefully, my arms finding the space above and around the belly, which is warm and firm and startlingly alive. I feel something shift beneath the fabric. A knee, maybe. An elbow. Some small part of Whitney's child rearranging herself inside a body that isn't mine, and the intimacy of that, the proximity to a miracle I have no biological claim to, makes my throat constrict.

I rotate my neck to see Saylor right behind me. "The baby kicked. I felt it."

"More of a roll," Raven says. "This is not a baby, it's an alligator. All day, all night, it rolls. I don't know what it's trying to drown, but it's not working."

Saylor laughs. "May I?" he asks Raven. She nods like it's an obvious question and Saylor replaces my hands on Raven's belly. "Oi, that's good yeah? Active little thing."

"It's good," I assure him before turning my attention back to Raven. "Look at you." I beam, holding her at arm's length. "You're gorgeous."

"I'm enormous. I got stuck in a revolving door last week. An actual revolving door. A security guard had to help me out. It was deeply humiliating and also kind of hilarious." She looks down at the dress. "Thank you so much for all the clothes, by the way. And the books...which I have most definitely been reading."

"Have you?"

"Well, I've been reading the covers. And some of the chapter titles. One of them has a pretty cute font." She grins with the specific charm of a twenty-three-year-old who knows she's being lovingly managed and doesn't entirely mind. "But honestly, the prenatal vitamin guide was actually helpful. I didn't know you weren't supposed to take them on an empty stomach. That explains a lot of mornings."

"Raven, please tell me you've been eating. What did you have for breakfast?"

She looks at her shoes. "Eggs. Fruit. Quinoa."

"Mm-hmm. Now, the truth."

"Flamin' Hot Cheetos," she mumbles.

"So you had heartburn for breakfast?"

"It's a food that I ate in the morning. That's breakfast by definition."

"It's a sodium delivery system disguised as a snack. I'm not asking you to meal prep. I'm asking you to occasionally consume something that grew in the ground, okay?"

"Potatoes grow in the ground. Chips are made of potatoes."

"Cheetos are made from corn, Raven."

"Still a vegetable." She points to Saylor's chest. "And still not helping."

"The point is, do you want me to send you some groceries? I can arrange that," I offer.

"What would I do with groceries?"

"Cook?" Saylor hints, seemingly amused.

Raven laughs, and the sound is bright and young and fearless, like a woman who is growing another human being and treating the experience with the casual competence of someone assembling IKEA furniture. I've never met anyone who wears pregnancy with less pretension. Raven doesn't glow. She doesn't nest. She doesn't post bump photos with captions about sacred journeys. She just shows up, does the work, and eats Flamin' Hot Cheetos for breakfast, and somehow that's more reassuring than every parenting book on my shelf. She makes this look so uncomplicated, even though it's very, very complicated.

"I promise I'll eat real good. Don't worry too much. I promise I'm taking care of little blob just fine."

"I'm sorry. I'm not trying to be controlling," I say.

"You're not." Then her gaze shifts. Looking over my shoulder toward the entrance, her expression changes. Not dramatically. A subtle tightening around the mouth, the way a person's face adjusts when they spot someone they were hoping wouldn't show. "But speaking of controlling," Raven mutters quietly.

I turn.

Eleanor is walking through the waiting room like she owns the building, which, given the scope of her husband's former real estate portfolio, she might. She's in a cream-colored coat and pearl earrings and her hair is blown out to a volume that suggests she came here directly from a salon, which she probably did. Eleanor doesn't go to appointments. She arrives places. She makes appearances.

She looks good. I hate that she looks good. She looks like a woman who has been sleeping well and consulting with an attorney who charges by the hour and winning, or at least believing she's winning, which for Eleanor has always been the same thing.

"Raven," I say carefully, without turning back. "Did you invite Eleanor?"

Raven's voice gets small. "Only because I'm scared of her. She called the office and asked about the appointment and I didn't know how to say no. And she offered to pay for it because this clinic has the 4D ultrasound machine and my insurance only covers the regular one. I'm sorry. I should have told you but I didn't want you to not come."

"It's okay." *It's not okay.* But Raven is twenty-three and pregnant and shouldn't have to navigate the minefield of Eleanor's emotional warfare. That's my job. "Don't worry about it. Go do your thing. I'll handle this."

The nurse appears from the hallway, clipboard in hand, and calls Raven's name. The nurse casts a look at Saylor, then back to Raven's belly. "Dad, you're welcome to come back too. We'll get Mom changed and then you can join for the ultrasound."

The word "Dad" lands in the room like a bird flying into a window. Saylor's eyes bulge. Raven's mouth opens. I watch the misunderstanding form and decide, in real time, to let it stand. Correcting it would require explaining the entire baroque arrangement of surrogacy and custody and fake engagements that brought us to this waiting room, and the nurse has a clipboard and a schedule and does not have time for the novel-length version.

"Go," I tell Saylor. "Make sure Raven's okay. We need a minute."

He looks panicked, eyes darting between me and Eleanor who is now selecting a chair in the waiting room with the careful deliberation of a woman who thinks every chair she sits in is a throne. "Are you sure?" His jaw works. "I can stay."

"I'll be fine. Go."

Once again, I send him off to battle Eleanor alone.

He goes. Not happily. He follows Raven and the nurse down the hallway with the reluctant energy of a man who is leaving a situation he doesn't trust but is choosing to respect the woman who asked him to. The door closes behind them and I am alone in a waiting room with cucumber water and Eleanor and twenty years of history that neither of us has ever resolved.

I sit down across from her. Not beside her. Across. The natural geometry of opposition.

"Eleanor."

"Celeste." She crosses her legs. Folds her hands in her lap. The perched, ready-to-swoop-in-and-attack posture. "You look well. Rested."

"Thank you. I am rested." *Total lie.* Saylor and I have been doing everything except sleeping. The man knows tricks. A lot and lot of tricks that end in blinding pleasure every single time.

"I was being polite, dear. Your crow's-feet are out of control. I have a nice firming cream if the Botox can't quite mend what's broken."

"Eleanor, why are you like this?"

"Like what?"

Bitchy, I say in my head, but don't allow it through my lips. "Never mind. I wanted to tell you that I'm renovating my parents' house in Westchester. It's coming together beautifully. Saylor's done so much work. New kitchen cabinetry, new deck, the nursery is finished." I let that word sit. Nursery. A room that exists, in my home, for this baby. "The home visit went well. Janet has been thorough and fair."

"I'm sure she has."

I force out a deep breath. "Eleanor, I want to be direct with you. I think we're past the point where subtlety serves either of us." I lean forward. "If you stop this, you can still be part of this baby's life. You're her grandmother. That matters. It would've mattered to Whit and it matters to me. I would never take that away from you. But Whitney wrote a will. She was clear about what she wanted. She chose me. Not because she didn't love you, but because she trusted me to raise her child in a way that honored who Whit actually was, not who your family wanted her to be."

Eleanor listens. Her face doesn't move. It's a skill, that stillness. A talent honed over decades of country-club luncheons and charity galas and marriage to a man who screamed at her behind closed doors while the rest of the world saw a philanthropist and his elegant wife. Eleanor learned long ago that the safest face is the one that reveals nothing.

"I'm offering you an important place in this child's life," I continue. "Holidays. Birthdays. Weekends. Whatever arrangement makes sense. But I'm asking you to let go of the custody fight. For the baby's sake. For Whitney's sake."

Eleanor smiles.

Not the polite one. Not the social one. A smile that makes

the hairs on the back of my neck rise. The smile you'd wear in a game of poker when you know without a doubt you're holding the winning hand.

"What are you so happy about?"

"I'm happy because I know your vile little secret, Celeste."

The temperature in the room drops ten degrees. My spine straightens involuntarily, the way it does in boardrooms when someone says something designed to draw blood. I know immediately what she means. I know because there's only one secret that could produce that particular grin on Eleanor's face, and it involves a man in a navy button-down who is currently in an exam room looking at a sonogram of a baby he already loves.

"It doesn't matter how Saylor and I met," I say, and my voice is steady because I've been preparing for this conversation since the caseworker visit, since the moment we lied about being engaged, since the first time I looked at Saylor and knew that his past would eventually become ammunition. "What matters is who he is and what he means to this baby. He's been present every day. He built the nursery with his own hands. He cares about this child not because of obligation, not because of biology, but because he chose to. That's love by choice. No strings. And you should be thrilled that your grandchild has a support system like that before he or she is even born."

Eleanor laughs. The sound is precise and surgical, a scalpel wrapped in cashmere.

"Your little escort-for-hire posing as your future husband?" She waves her hand dismissively. "Don't worry, Celeste. We all see through that and it's pathetic. A prostitute you've rebranded as a fiancé to impress a caseworker. Please. Even Janet Lundy isn't that naïve."

"Don't you dare speak about him like that." My chest tightens. Not because she's wrong about how we met, but because she's reducing Saylor to a transaction, flattening three dimensions into a punchline, and the cruelty of it, the casual cruelty, reminds me so much of Greg that I can feel the connective tissue between them. People who diminish others to feel tall.

"But anyway, dear, that's not why I'm smiling," Eleanor continues. She uncrosses her legs. Leans forward. The distance between us shrinks and the air fills with her perfume, Chanel No. 5, the lavish fragrance I've smelled at every society event for the past twenty years. "I'm smiling because I had a very interesting conversation with Greg recently. Over bourbon. You know how men are after their second glass. Defenses down. Tongues loose. Especially when someone is offering to write a very generous check."

My stomach lurches. "A check for what?"

"An investment, he called it. Into the company. Into you, really. Eleanor Montgomery-Trace investing in Celeste Brinley's fashion empire. A show of good faith. Family supporting family." She pauses for effect, the way a woman who has been rehearsing this moment pauses, savoring the architecture of the reveal. "But Greg didn't need an investment. Greg needed a lifeline. Because your company, Celeste, isn't struggling. *It's drowning.*"

No. *What?* "I don't know what Greg told you, but—"

"He told me everything. He was remarkably forthcoming." Eleanor's voice is level, almost kind, which makes it worse. Cruelty dressed in compassion is her signature. She learned it from her husband. "Your company is functionally bankrupt. The revenue looks adequate on the surface, but underneath, it's been hemorrhaging for years. Mismanaged funds. Overextended lines of credit. Inventory costs that haven't been reconciled since before your divorce."

"That's not true."

"Isn't it?" She tilts her head, the way a teacher does at a student who has given a wrong answer and deserves the courtesy of being corrected gently. "Greg tells me the Q3 projections are catastrophic. That the line he says you're struggling with is your last chance to generate enough revenue to cover operating costs through the winter. That he's been pushing to take the company public because it's the only way to inject enough capital to keep the doors open. And that you've been fighting him on it, because going public means opening the books, and opening the books means everyone sees the rot."

I want to argue. I want to say Eleanor is being manipulated, that Greg is a liar and a cheat and a man who has never operated in good faith in his life. But the words jam in my throat like fabric caught in a machine, because the truth is that Greg has been showing me the evidence for months and I have been looking the other way.

The room tilts. Not physically. The chairs are stable, the floor is solid, the cucumber water sits undisturbed in its glass dispenser. But something inside me shifts, a tectonic plate grinding against another, and the landscape of my life rearranges itself around a truth I should have seen months ago.

Greg storming into my office with tablets and projections and the barely concealed urgency of a man who knows a secret he's weaponizing but also fears. The calls from Bergdorf that I assumed were about timeline but might have been about trust. The Valencia mill contract I missed during my breakdown. A call that wasn't just about the copper silk but about payment terms I haven't reviewed. Greg whispering to Margot in the break room. Greg taking meetings I wasn't invited to. Greg's girlfriend submitting designs I didn't request, as if she was already being positioned as a replacement for a creative director who wouldn't be around much longer.

The fall line isn't just a creative deadline. It's a financial lifeline. And I've been treating it like an artistic challenge while the building burns around me.

"I don't believe you," I say, but the words are hollow. Because I do believe her. Not because Eleanor is trustworthy, but because the evidence was always there, stacked in corners I refused to look at, filed under problems I'd address after the fall line, after the custody ruling, after the baby.

"You don't have to believe me. Believe your own accountants. Or better yet, ask Greg. You've always known him as a trustworthy guy, right?" Her smile twists in the same rotation as the knife jammed into my back. She's reveling in my pain as she pours salt directly into the opening. "The numbers don't lie, Celeste. And when this goes to court, when the judge asks whether you can provide a stable home for this child, I wonder how 'stable' a bankrupt fashion label will look on paper."

The implication settles over me like a weighted blanket made of ice. She's not just telling me my company is failing. She's telling me it's a weapon. That the financial instability will be introduced as evidence. That the custody case I thought was about Whitney's will and home visits and nursery colors is actually about solvency, about the perception of stability, and Eleanor has just acquired the one piece of ammunition I never saw coming.

"You'll have your hands full," Eleanor says, standing. Smoothing her coat. Adjusting her pearls with the mechanical precision of a woman returning to her default settings. "A crumbling company, a fabricated engagement, and an escort's résumé to lean back on. That's quite a lot to explain to a family court judge." She picks up her purse. "I do hope the ultrasound goes well. I genuinely want this baby to be healthy. We disagree about where she belongs, but we agree that she matters."

She walks toward the hallway that leads to the exam rooms, her heels clicking against the tile. She strides with her head held high, as if she just checked a major to-do off her list: *Destroy Celeste's life.* She doesn't look back. She doesn't need to. The damage is done. The information is deployed. Eleanor fights the way her late-husband taught her: aim for the foundation, let the building fall on its own.

I hang back in the waiting room. Alone. The woman who was eleven months pregnant has been called back for her appointment. The cucumber water sweats silently in its dispenser. The abstract art is no longer awkwardly funny. They are simply shapes without meaning, hung on walls to fill space.

My company is bankrupt. Greg has been hiding a ton. Eleanor now has this information. And somewhere down the hallway,

Saylor is sitting next to Raven, looking at a screen that shows the baby I promised Whitney I would raise, in a house I don't know if I can afford anymore, and a pseudo-fiancé whose employment history is about to become a court exhibit.

I think about the copper gown. The one that won't behave. The fabric that went silent weeks ago and only recently started speaking again, only to say things I wasn't ready to hear. I think about gate-closing panic. About doors shutting one by one while I stand in the hallway trying to decide which room to enter.

I think about Whitney. About what she'd say if she were sitting in this chair next to me, in this waiting room, with this mess spread out before us.

She'd say: *Lessi, don't you dare give up. I won't let you. This baby doesn't need money. This baby just needs love. You are its greatest shot at love.*

I stand up. I smooth my skirt. I walk down the hallway toward the exam room where my family is waiting.

The room is dim, lit primarily by the glow of the ultrasound screen and a small lamp in the corner that casts everything in a warm, clinical amber. Raven is on the table in a hospital gown with a blanket draped over her bare legs, her belly exposed, slicked with gel that catches the light. The ultrasound technician is a woman in her fifties with reading glasses and the calm, practiced demeanor of someone who has shown thousands of parents their children for the first time and never tires of the moment.

Eleanor is standing by the far wall. Arms crossed. Watching the screen with an expression that, for the briefest moment, looks like something other than strategy. Something human.

Saylor is in the chair beside the table. He looks up when I enter and his face does the thing it always does when he sees me, the thing I still haven't gotten used to: it opens. Like a door. Like a window. Like something that was closed finding a reason to let the light in.

But then he reads me. He's always been able to read me, from the very first day, from the funeral, from the car ride when I drove too fast and gripped the wheel too tight. He sees whatever Eleanor left on my face and his expression shifts. Concern, sharp and immediate.

I shake my head. Barely perceptible. Not now.

He understands. He reaches for my hand and I take it. I sit beside him and keep my focus on the screen.

The technician moves the wand across Raven's belly and the image adjusts, a shifting landscape of gray and white and shadow, and then there it is.

A profile. Forehead, nose, lips, chin. The curve of a skull that is impossibly small and impossibly complete. The baby's moving. Her hand rises to her face in a gesture that looks like she's waving, or maybe she's covering her mouth the way I do when I'm trying not to say something I'll regret.

"There we go," the technician says. "Measuring right on track. Twenty-five weeks and two days. Strong heart."

The heartbeat fills the room. A rapid, rhythmic pulsing that sounds like a tiny horse galloping through a field made of static. It's the most beautiful and most terrifying sound I've ever heard, because it's evidence of something I can no longer abstract or plan for or manage from a distance. This is a person. A living, moving, heart-beating person who is going to arrive in approximately fifteen weeks and need everything from me, and I am sitting in a chair holding the hand of a man I love while the structural foundation of my life crumbles beneath me like a house built on sand.

"Do we want to know the sex?" the technician asks, looking at Raven, then at me.

"Yes," Eleanor answers from the corner.

"It's up to Celeste," Raven clarifies, speaking directly to the technician. She points at me. "Her."

Everyone stares at me expectantly, but the decision isn't so easy. Once I know, baby girl or baby boy, I'll only get further attached. What if Eleanor wins? What if... What if I actually don't get to take this baby home with me? *What then? What would be left? Whit, what the hell do I do?*

The technician adjusts the wand. The image shifts, rotates, finding the angle. A pause. A small smile.

"Tell us," I finally say, heart pounding fast enough to match the baby's.

"Baby girl. It's a girl."

The room exhales. Every person in it, all at once, releasing something they didn't know they were holding.

Raven lets out a sound that is half laugh, half sob. "I knew it. The kicks were pink. I told you."

The technician smiles. "She's measuring perfectly. Strong bones, good fluid levels. Heart rate is one-forty-two, which is textbook. She's a healthy little girl."

I don't make a sound. I can't. Something has sealed shut in my throat, a valve that won't release, and behind it is everything: the joy, the terror, the grief, the love, the bankruptcy, the custody fight, the weight of a promise I made to a woman who isn't here to see it kept. A girl. Whitney's girl. The daughter Whitney always wanted, the one she talked about in hypotheticals over wine, naming and renaming her, imagining her first steps, her first words, her first day of school. Whitney used to say she'd be the fun mom. The one who lets her daughter eat cake for breakfast on Saturdays and stay up past bedtime to watch shooting stars. The mom Eleanor never was.

And now Whitney's gone, and the daughter is here, and I'm supposed to fill both roles: the responsible guardian and the fun best friend and the mother and the promise-keeper and provider. But that's not even the hardest part. The worst is imagining I might not get the opportunity to do any of that, and it's only right now I realize I want this more than I've wanted anything in my whole life. And Eleanor might take it all away.

I grip Saylor's hand so tightly I must be hurting him, but he doesn't flinch. He grips back. His thumb moves across my knuckles in that small, automatic circle that has become his way of saying I'm here without interrupting whatever I'm feeling.

Eleanor is watching the screen. Her hand has risen to her mouth. To my shock and slight horror, she's tearing up. The involuntary response of a grandmother seeing her granddaughter for the first time, and for one unguarded second, Eleanor Montgomery-Trace looks exactly like what she is: a woman who lost her daughter and is looking at the only piece of her that remains. Her eyes are wet. Her posture has softened. The armor, for just a moment, has a crack, and through that crack I can see the mother who failed Whitney and knows it and is terrified of failing again.

I shouldn't be doing this. I should be spitting on her shoes for the hell she's put me through, but right now, Eleanor and I have more in common than anyone else in the room. She needs me. I need her. I cross the space between us, and like it or fucking not, I wrap her into a hug. "This is for Whit," I mumble into her shoulder. "She wouldn't want us fighting right now. Not during the first time we see her daughter. She's perfect, Eleanor. This baby is perfect."

Eleanor hugs back. That in itself is monumental. But when she rubs my back in slow, small circles, it feels eerily maternal. "I hope she looks just like her mother."

"Me too," I choke out. "Whitney was so beautiful."

"She really was," Eleanor breathes out.

Another second passes. The moment expires. Her hand drops. The armor returns. Eleanor squares her shoulders and adjusts her pearls and becomes, once again, the woman with the strategy and the bourbon-funded intelligence and the smile that cuts.

But I saw it. For one tiny beat, I saw Eleanor resemble something very close to a mom.

The appointment takes another twenty minutes. The technician prints images. Raven asks if the baby has hair yet and the tech explains that it's too early to tell on ultrasound but some babies are born with a full head. Raven says she hopes the baby gets Whit's curls and I say nothing because I can't speak without crying and I've decided that I'm out of tears for today. I have a feeling I need to save them for what's ahead.

In the hallway afterward, Eleanor walks in front. Clicking toward the elevator with all her brisk efficiency like she has big places to be and important things to do. She doesn't say goodbye. She presses the button, waits, steps inside, and vanishes behind closing doors.

Raven hugs me at the entrance. She smells like cocoa butter and Flamin' Hot Cheetos, which is somehow exactly right. "She's beautiful, right?" Raven asks. "The baby?"

"So beautiful."

"I'm going to eat a vegetable tonight. In your honor."

"That's all I ask."

We offer to drive her home, but Raven has friends in the city she wants to see. She walks toward the subway entrance with one hand on her belly and the other on her phone, texting someone, probably her friends that she's on the way, probably with seventeen exclamation points. Twenty-three years old, carrying a miracle, navigating the world with a competence that I envy and a lightness I've forgotten how to carry.

And then it's just us. Saylor and me. Standing on the sidewalk outside a medical building in Midtown East with printed sonogram photos in my purse and the afternoon sun doing that thing it does in Manhattan where it catches the glass on every building and turns the whole city into a chandelier.

Saylor wraps his hand in mine, effortless. The way you grab someone's hand when it's become a reflex rather than a decision.

"So," he says, and his voice has the careful, playful quality of a man who is about to make a joke because he doesn't know what else to do. "Just for the record, I want you to know that I was completely out of the room when Raven was getting changed. Eyes averted. Very trustworthy boyfriend material right here. You can put that on the reference sheet."

I don't laugh. I try. The muscles in my face attempt the configuration of amusement and fail, and what comes out instead is something closer to a wince.

Saylor stops walking.

He turns to face me. His hands find my shoulders. His eyes move across my face with focused attention, like he's reading a blueprint, looking for the flaw, the crack, the place where the structure is compromised.

"What did she say to you? Tell me, so I can explain how she's wrong."

"It's not the time."

"Tell me anyway."

"Saylor, I'm okay."

He studies me for another moment. The way I'm holding my purse too tightly. The way my jaw is clenched. The way I'm standing like I'm holding up a ceiling with the top of my head and cannot afford to relax my posture.

"You don't look okay," he says gently.

"You're right." My voice cracks, just barely, a hairline fracture in the same teacup that cracked when he found my popcorn. "I'm not. But I have to be. I don't have a choice right now."

"You always have a choice."

"Not today." I take a breath. It's shallow and unsatisfying, the kind of breath that tells you your body is managing too many things and oxygen isn't the priority. "Tell me something good. Something happy. Something to distract me right now because if I think about what Eleanor just told me for one more second, I'm going to fall apart on this sidewalk."

Pain crosses Saylor's face. Not his own pain. Mine, reflected. The anguish of a man who can see the woman he cares about hurting and doesn't know why and can't fix it and is being asked to wait. He's not good at waiting. He's a man who builds things with his hands, who fixes what's broken, who drove to three stores for the right popcorn because letting me down wasn't an option. But he looks at me and sees that what I need right now isn't a solution. It's a bridge. Something to carry me from this moment to the next one.

He reaches into his back pocket. Pulls out the sonogram. The one the technician printed. The profile. The nose, the lips, the hand raised to her face.

He holds it up between us. The afternoon sun catches the glossy paper and the image glows, translucent, like a tiny ghost made of light.

"It's a girl," he says. "And she's healthy. That's all that really matters, yeah?"

And I break. Not on the sidewalk. Not publicly. Not in any way that a passerby would notice. I break the way buildings settle: silently, internally, a shifting of weight that changes the structure without altering the facade. My eyes fill but don't spill. My breath catches but doesn't stop. I look at the sonogram of my best friend's daughter and I let the joy exist alongside the terror, because that's what motherhood is, apparently. Holding two opposite truths in the same chest and refusing to let either one win.

"It's a girl. She's healthy. And that's all that matters." I repeat.

Saylor folds me into his arms. Right there on the sidewalk. In Midtown. In the middle of a Tuesday. With a sonogram and a bankrupt company and an ex-husband's betrayal and a grandmother's weaponized grief all pressing against me from every direction.

"We're going to be okay," he says against my hair.

I don't correct him. I don't say that okay is a long way from here, that the distance between this sidewalk and okay is measured in legal battles and financial audits and conversations I'm not ready to have. I don't say any of it.

I just hold on.

Because holding on, maybe for too long, is the only skill I've ever truly mastered, and today, standing on a sidewalk with a picture of someone's daughter pressed between our chests, it's enough.

Someone's daughter.

My daughter.

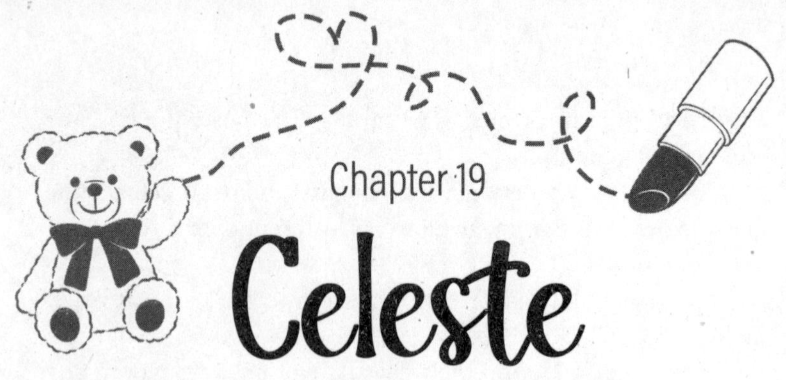

Chapter 19 Celeste

Two futures.

I'm positioned at the head of the boardroom table. A front-row seat to the implosion of my life's work. The numbers are on the screen and they are catastrophic.

The accounting team has been talking for forty minutes. Two women and one man, all of them excellent at their jobs, all of them careful not to look at me directly as they walk through the spreadsheets line by line, column by column, the way a surgeon explains an X-ray to a patient who already suspects the worst but needs to hear it from someone in a white coat.

Greg is at the far end of the table.

He's not talking. He hasn't said a word since the meeting started. He's sitting with his ankle crossed over his knee, his coffee untouched, his face arranged in the expression of a man watching a building he set fire to finally collapse and wanting credit for having predicted the structural failure. I have not looked at him in twenty minutes, but I can feel his presence the way you feel winter through a window—distant, inevitable, cold.

"The short version," Karen, our lead accountant explains, "is that the liabilities exceed assets by a significant margin. We've been operating on credit extensions that were secured against projected revenue from the fall line. Those projections were"—she pauses, choosing her word—"optimistic."

"They were fictional," I say.

Karen doesn't flinch. "The projections were based on assumptions that did not materialize. The Valencia mill contract alone accounts for a payment structure that hasn't been reconciled since before the divorce. There are inventory costs that were logged as assets but functionally represent unsold product in a warehouse in New Jersey. And the lines of credit Greg extended"—she looks at him for the first time—"were done without internal approval, using the intellectual property catalog as collateral."

It's like seeing a car accident seconds before it happens. Blinding lights. Screeching tires. The smell of rubber on road, escalating to smoke in air. But it's too late. There's nothing I can do except take it, hoping I survive the collision. The intellectual property catalog. My fabric names. My patterns. My designs. The language I invented—rusted dawn, coastal bone, mercury drape—pledged against debt I didn't authorize, by a man I was married to, to keep a company running that he was quietly draining from the inside.

"How long?" I ask. My voice is steady because I've spent twenty years making my voice steady when everything behind it is collapsing.

"The irregularities go back at least two years," Karen says. "Possibly longer. A full forensic audit would take six to eight weeks."

"We don't have six to eight weeks."

"No." Karen pulls up the next slide. Two columns. Two paths. "You have, functionally, two options at this point."

My eyes glaze over as Karen explains in great detail the strategy of each plan, but the options as I understand them are clear.

The first: go public. Take on outside investors, open the books, inject capital. The brand survives in name, but I lose creative control. The investors would install their own board, their own creative director, their own vision of what my name means on a label. I'd be a figurehead. A face on a website. The woman who founded the company sitting in a corner office with no authority, watching strangers make decisions for her legacy. The payout would be noteworthy.

The second: declare bankruptcy. Dissolve the company. Sell my intellectual property piece by piece—the designs, the sketches, the contact lists, the name itself if a buyer wants it. Liquidate the remaining inventory. After debts are settled and legal fees are paid, I'd walk away with approximately two hundred thousand dollars cash.

Two hundred thousand. Twenty years of work. A dorm room sketch that became a brand that dressed women for galas and boardrooms and weddings and first dates and funerals. Twenty years of fabric swatches pinned to corkboards and red-eye flights to Milan and fitting rooms where women looked in the mirror and saw, maybe for the first time, someone worth looking at. All of it reduced to a number that wouldn't scratch the surface of enough for retirement.

I stare at the screen. Then blink. But the numbers don't change. Numbers never do—that's the kindness and cruelty of them. They are so concrete. They sit there, indifferent, immune to the story you want to tell. I built an empire and the numbers say it's worthless. The memories have no tangible value.

"Thank you, Karen," I say. "I need the room."

The accounting team files out. Karen squeezes my shoulder as she passes. The door closes.

Greg still doesn't move.

"You knew," I accuse.

"I managed."

"You managed." I stare at him, looking for any sign of remorse in his eyes but they are so empty. "You managed my company into the ground and you sat in this chair and watched me chase a fall line that was never going to save us because you already knew there was nothing left to save."

"The fall line could have worked. If you'd been focused. If you hadn't been distracted by—"

"Choose your next words very carefully, Greg."

He uncrosses his legs. Leans forward. The performance of sincerity, the one I spent decades mistaking for the real thing. "Going public is the smart play, Celeste. I have investors ready. People who believe in the brand. We can restructure, bring in fresh capital—"

"We? There is no we. There hasn't been a we in this company since you decided to leverage my life's work against debts you accrued to fund whatever it is you've been funding. What have you been funding, Greg? Some other venture? The multiple homes I'm sure you're hiding somewhere? The lifestyle you built on my signature?"

He says nothing. The silence is his confession.

"We can rebuild this, Celeste, the same way we built it. *Together.*"

Fool me once, Greg. But only once.

"Get the fuck out of my boardroom."

He stands. Buttons his jacket. Walks to the door, unhurried, believing he'll be back, believing all of this is temporary, believing Celeste Brinley will eventually do what she's always done—absorb the damage, perform the recovery, build something beautiful from the wreckage while Greg Prescott watches from a comfortable distance and takes credit for the view.

The door closes behind him.

I sit alone in the conference room for three minutes. I count them. Three minutes of silence in a room that smells like coffee and the staleness of bad news. I look at the screen. The two columns. The two futures. One where I lose my name. One where I lose everything else.

Then I get up and walk to my office.

Patrice is where I left her. Standing by the window in the half-finished gown, one arm slightly raised because I'd been adjusting the sleeve when Saylor arrived yesterday and I never finished. The silk catches the late-afternoon light and throws it across the wall in a ripple of amber that, in another life, I would stop to admire.

In another life, I would see that light and think: there. That's the color. That's what the collection needs.

Today I look at Patrice and I see two years of talking to a mannequin because I didn't have the person I really wanted to talk to.

I cross the room in three steps and shove her. Hard. Both hands against her torso, the way you'd push a person if you wanted them to feel it. Patrice topples sideways, hits the corkboard, and crashes to the floor. Fabric swatches scatter. The copper gown crumples around her like a body giving up. Pins skid across the hardwood. The arm I was adjusting yesterday snaps off at the shoulder and rolls under my desk.

I stand there, breathing. My hands are shaking. The office is silent except for the sound of a pin still spinning on the floor, a tiny metallic whisper that winds down and stops.

Patrice lies on her side. One-armed. Draped in a ruined dress. Looking, for the first time in fifteen years, like what she actually is—not a creative partner, not a silent witness, not the repository of my best ideas. A mannequin. Fiberglass and cloth. Something I gave a name to because I was lonely.

My rage calming to a gentle simmer, I kneel down and pick her up. It takes effort. She's heavier than she looks, the way grief is heavier than it looks. I set her upright. Smooth the dress. Retrieve her arm from under the desk and reattach it. She stands slightly crooked and wrinkled, the pins gone. I look at her and say, "I'm sorry, Patrice. That was beneath both of us."

Then I straighten my own spine and make a decision.

Not the decision Karen presented. Not the columns on the screen. A different decision, one that has nothing to do with investors or intellectual property or the careful arithmetic of corporate dissolution. A decision about what I want. What I actually want, underneath the brand and the title and the manipulation of the man I once trusted to share my dreams.

None of it matters. The money, the fame, the success. None of it. All I want is my family.

I pick up my bag. I pick up my phone. I call the Thai place on Lexington that does the green curry Saylor likes and the pad see ew Ada asked about last week and the mango sticky rice that I've been craving since the ultrasound, when the stress of Eleanor's revelation manifested as a very specific hunger for coconut and sugar. I order enough for three. I give them the Westchester address for delivery—*yes I know there's a surcharge for the delivery area, I don't care, put it on the card.*

Then I get in my car and drive north.

The house is lit from inside when I pull into the driveway.

Every window is glowing. Saylor must have replaced the porchlight. The old one was a bare bulb, stark and unwelcoming, and this one is warm, amber, the kind of light that makes a front door look like an invitation instead of a barrier. I can see movement through the kitchen window. Two figures. Saylor at the counter, Ada at the table. The ordinary choreography of an evening in a house that works.

I sit in the car for a moment. Engine off. Hands on the wheel. It dawns on me that I've driven more in the past few months than I have in the past ten years. How funny. Even though I still hate driving, it's not as daunting when the destination looks like this. *Like home.* This is why people rush home. This feeling of relief and warmth. A novelty I've always skirted around, but have never really known.

The Thai food is in the passenger seat, the bags warm against the leather. The oak tree is a shadow against the darkening sky. The tire swing hangs motionless. This is so peaceful. How is it that although I've lost everything, I've gained everything as well?

I carry the food to the door. I don't knock and the door is unlocked because Saylor is expecting me. Every night, I belong somewhere now.

"I brought dinner," I announce, rounding the corner into the kitchen.

Saylor looks up from the counter where he's been doing something with a screwdriver and a cabinet hinge. Ada looks up from the table where she's reading a paperback with a shirtless man on the cover, which she makes no attempt to hide. The house smells like sawdust and tea and the lemon cleaner I bought last week that Ada has adopted as her own.

"Thai?" Saylor asks, eyeing the bags.

"Green curry, pad see ew, mango sticky rice."

"The good place?"

"The good place."

He grins. Sets down the screwdriver. Takes the bags from my hands and starts unpacking them on the counter with the efficient care of a man who treats food as a serious matter. Ada marks her page and closes her book. I pull up a chair.

We eat. For twenty minutes, we just eat. Saylor tells a story about the cabinet hinge that involved a YouTube tutorial, a stripped screw, and language Ada pretended not to hear. Ada tells me about the book she's reading. "He's a Scottish duke with a tragic past and enormous...lands. Very large tracts of land." She pumps her eyebrows, thinking her innuendo is cleverly disguised for just us girls. Saylor nearly chokes on his curry. I laugh. That was somewhere between "awww" and "ewww." For twenty minutes I forget to be stressed and distracted. The boardroom doesn't exist. Greg doesn't exist. The numbers on the screen are someone else's problem in someone else's life.

But once the food runs out, the silence that follows is the kind that knows something is coming.

"I need to tell you both something," I say.

Ada sets down her fork. Saylor stops chewing. Two people who love me looking at me across a table, waiting for whatever I'm about to say with the specific stillness of people who have learned, through experience, that bad news doesn't improve with delay.

"A few days ago at the ultrasound, Eleanor cornered me with some insights about my company. Today, I found out she was telling the truth. Celeste, *the company*, is bankrupt." I say it simply because there's no other way. "Greg has been mismanaging funds for a long time. He leveraged property we didn't even have against unauthorized debt. The lines of credit are overextended, the inventory costs haven't been reconciled, and the backers and brands have labeled our accounts as delinquent." I take a steadying breath. "I have two options. Go public and give my company away, or declare bankruptcy and walk away."

"What does walk away mean?" Saylor asks.

"About two hundred thousand dollars cash, in my pocket. Maybe a little less after debts, legal fees, liquidation of assets." I let the number sit. I watch Saylor do the math—the same math I did in the conference room, the math that converts twenty years of a woman's life into a figure that wouldn't buy this house outright. "I think I'm going with bankruptcy. I'm separating from Greg entirely. The brand—" My voice catches. Just once. I clear it. "The brand will be gone. But I'll be free of him. I'm not totally irresponsible. I do have money tucked away for savings. I have personal accounts with investments. There's going to be a lifestyle change, but we're going to be okay. I still have plenty to give this baby."

Ada reaches across the table and covers my hand with hers. Her grip is warm and certain and her eyes are the same clear blue as Saylor's and she doesn't say anything because Ada seems to know that some moments need silence the way wounds need air.

Saylor is very still. He's watching my face. Studying me. Reading me the way he reads everything, with that total attention that makes you feel like the only person in any room he's ever stood in.

"Can you use that money to start another company?" Saylor asks.

"I could," I say. I look at Ada. Then at Saylor. I watch the ripples move through both of them—Ada's hand tightening on mine, Saylor's jaw setting, the kitchen suddenly smaller and quieter than it was thirty seconds ago. I sit up straighter. "But I've already decided how I want to use the cash."

"Use it how?" Saylor asks.

I look at Ada. "Dr. Yassa's procedure. Ada, I want to sponsor your whole treatment. Consult to follow-up. I want to see you walk again, upright and pain free. I want to cheer you on as you run another marathon. Nothing would mean more to me."

Ada's eyes widen. She looks at Saylor. Saylor's face has gone completely still—not calm still, but frozen still. The stillness of a man watching a door open that he'd nailed shut.

"What are you talking about, dear?" Ada asks.

My gaze snaps to Saylor. "You haven't told her yet? Rina told me you and Dr. Yassa were in touch."

"Tell me what?" Ada asks again.

"How do you even know about this?" he asks me accusingly. "So you and Rina just sit around discussing how to solve my problems for me?"

"What? No. Rina mentioned it in passing. She just told me about the accident, and the new surgeon at Mount Sinai. Saylor, I'm offering to help."

"Help? Do you know how much they are estimating?" Saylor asks but it's not a question. It's a demand. He turns to his mom. "Mum, there's a laser procedure that you might be a candidate for but it is approximately a hundred and sixty thousand dollars. It's experimental, so insurance doesn't cover it. I didn't tell you about it because I didn't want to get your hopes up and leave you disappointed. I've been trying to figure out how to raise the money—"

"You just did," I throw in. "I told you—"

"Celeste, your life is getting picked apart like a game of Jenga. I'm not going to be the one who yanks the final block and watches you crumble to the ground. I wanted *you*, not your money. I wanted to fulfill my promises, not have you swoop in like my sugar mama."

"Saylor—"

"No." He pushes back from the table. The chair scrapes against the hardwood. "Mum, I'm so sorry. But...no. We can't."

Ada makes a small sound. Not a word—a breath that carries the weight of a word. She's looking between us, her hand still on the table, her paperback forgotten, her face doing the complicated arithmetic of a mother who has just been offered something impossible by someone she's starting to love only to have it snatched away by her son's decision.

"Saylor," Ada says quietly. "It's not your choice."

"What?" He's standing now. His hand goes to the back of his neck. The gesture I've learned to read as system overload—too many feelings in too small a space, the circuits threatening to blow. "What do you mean it's not my choice?"

"I know that managing my care makes you feel like you're in control of all this, but you're not. The crash was an *accident.* Not destiny. That's all life is, love. Moments followed by other moments. Some good, some bad. But this dream you keep chasing where we have what we once had is killing you. Life is meant to move forward, Saylor. Forward good, or forward bad. What is meant to be, will be. But you micromanaging my life is not to protect me, it's to protect you. You need somewhere to exercise your guilt. But it has to stop. I love you. I would forgive you, but there's nothing to forgive. Listen, love, Celeste is offering me this amazing gift, I intend to take it." She looks at me. "If and when I'm able...I'll pay you back, every penny—"

"Ada, no need."

"Stop!" His voice rises. Not a shout—Saylor doesn't shout—more a sharp escalation.

"Saylor, it's not a big deal—"

"Not a big deal? Do you understand what it's like standing next to you? Every single day in your world is a reminder that I can't provide. I can't pick up the check for dinner at restaurants you love. I can't buy you the things you deserve. I can barely keep this house from falling apart, and every repair I make is on *your* property, with materials bought with *your* money. Sometimes I don't know why you're with me. And now this? You coming in to clean up my life? Not only do I not feel like a man in your world, now I don't feel like one in mine. So, thanks for that."

"Saylor!" Ada scolds.

"I need some air." He grabs his keys from the counter. The sound of metal on granite is sharp and final.

He walks toward the door. Ada stays at the table, wise enough to know that some fights don't need to happen. They can dissolve in fresh air where there's room for angry emotions to swell, explode, then blow away in the night breeze without breaking anything that can't be repaired.

I'm not as wise.

I follow Saylor out of the house. I take hurried steps following his invisible footprints right out the front door. The driveway is dark. The porchlight throws a circle of amber that ends at the gravel. Beyond it, the oak tree and the yard and the shape of the guesthouse in the distance. Saylor is halfway to his truck, keys in hand, moving with the rigid posture of a man who is holding himself together through forward motion.

"Saylor, stop!"

He stops. Doesn't turn around.

"Talk to me," I say. "Don't walk. Talk."

He turns. His face in the porchlight is stripped of every defense I've ever seen him wear—the humor, the charm, the easy confidence that makes him seem like he's never once doubted his place in a room. All of that is gone. What's left is raw and young and furious and terrified.

"You had no right to do that." His tone is lower now but the edges are sharper. "It wasn't your place."

"Not my place? We're sleeping together. You're living in my home. You keep referring to the baby as *ours*. Do I still not have a *place* in your life?"

He flinches. "That's not what I—"

"That is what you said."

"Celeste, this is why relationships rarely work out for me. Why being an escort made sense for a while. I get that my relationship with my mum makes women uncomfortable. They usually do one of two things when we get to this point: they run away or they overstep. No one understands what mum is going through like I do. No one gets what she needs."

"Because you won't let them," I say. "What your mom said earlier...I don't know, Saylor. Do you think you're using your mom's situation to avoid having to grow up?"

"Grow up?" he practically hisses. "Because you know everything about growing up? That's the point you love to make, isn't it? That's the reason you think you know what's best for my mum?"

"Well, are we going to pretend like I'm not older than you? Yes, in this situation, I do believe I know best. You have a shot, take it."

"Been there. Did that. Lost everything."

"But this time, Rina vetted it. I vetted it. You have protection, Saylor. We're not going to let anything bad happen to you or your mom."

He forces out a deep breath. "You know what, Celeste? Stop worrying so much. You're going to be a wonderful mother. You're being one right now. Except I already have a mum. I don't need a second one. What I do need is a woman who respects me and my choices. A woman who trusts me instead of trying to control me by saving the day."

"That's what you think I'm doing? Trying to control you?" I take a step toward him. Then another. Close enough to see the pulse in his throat, the way his hands are trembling at his sides, the way he's looking at me like he's daring me to answer and begging me not to. "What do you need right now?"

"Space." The word comes out rough. Scraped. "Just some space. To clear my head."

"Is this what I can expect from you?" I ask, and the question is quiet but it isn't gentle. "Running away when it gets hard? Because I'm about to go through the hardest year of my life, Saylor. I'm losing my company. I might lose this baby. And I need to know—can I depend on you? Or was this always just a means to an end?" My voice doesn't break but it wants to.

"A means to an end for who? Because I could ask the same

question."

He stares at me. The porchlight catches the wet in his eyes. For three seconds—three seconds that last longer than the three minutes I spent alone in the conference room—he doesn't speak.

Then he crosses the distance between us in two steps and pulls off his jacket, wrapping it around my shoulders. He presses his mouth to mine. Quick. Firm. Not a declaration. A promise condensed to its smallest possible form.

"I'm not running away. Sometimes you need space when you know what you need to say but don't know how to say it yet," he tells me. "That's all. I'm leaving to think." He touches my face. His thumb traces my cheekbone once. "But I'll be right back."

He turns toward the truck. Opens the door. Pauses.

I call after him because the silence is too heavy and the driveway is too dark and I need him to know that even in the middle of a fight, I see him. The man underneath the guilt. The man who is so much more than the worst thing that ever happened to him.

"When did you get so mature?"

He looks over his shoulder. The ghost of a grin. The first break in the storm.

"It comes with age," he says. "You'll get there."

The truck starts. The headlights sweep across the gravel, across the oak tree, across the tire swing that sways once in the draft of his departure. I watch the taillights shrink down the long driveway until they disappear around the bend, and then I'm standing alone in the amber circle of a porchlight he installed, in front of a house he rebuilt, wearing the quiet certainty that he meant what he said.

He'll be right back.

And it almost seems like literally because less than a minute after his brake lights disappear from view, a set of headlights comes up the way. Except it's not Saylor's truck.

It takes a moment for my brain to register Janet Lundy's vehicle. "Oh God," I mutter to myself. "Of course right now."

Janet's sedan rolls to a stop behind my car. The engine cuts. But she doesn't get out right away. She sits there for a beat, both hands on the wheel, and even from fifteen feet away I can see her exhale. A long, deliberate one that indicates she's here with something to say that she is dreading.

When she finally opens the door, she's not carrying her portfolio.

Last time we met she had that leather portfolio tucked under her arm like a precious relic. The pen clipped to the front. The pages tabbed in colored flags. The tools of a woman whose job is to observe and record and never, ever get involved.

Tonight she's carrying nothing. Just her keys and her phone and whatever is sitting behind her eyes that made her drive to Westchester after dark.

"Janet." I pull Saylor's jacket tighter around my shoulders. "If this is the surprise home visit, it's really not a good—"

"It's not a home visit." She stops at the edge of the porchlight. Close enough for me to see her face. She looks tired. Not professionally tired—the kind of tired that comes from caring about something you're not supposed to care about. "Can we sit down?"

There's a bench near the front door. One of Saylor's projects—reclaimed wood, sanded smooth, slightly uneven on the left side because he ran out of shims and used a folded beer coaster instead. I've sat on it a dozen times. It's never felt as cold as it does right now.

We sit. Janet crosses her ankles. Smooths her slacks. Buys herself three seconds of silence before she turns to face me.

"I'm not here in any official capacity," she starts. "I want to be clear about that. This is not protocol. This is not how I do things. In nineteen years I have never once driven to a family's home to deliver information ahead of the court's formal notification, and if anyone asks me whether this conversation happened, I will deny it convincingly and without remorse."

My stomach drops. Not slowly. Not gradually. The way an

elevator drops when the cable snaps—total, instant, irreversible.

"Formal notification?"

"The judge issued a preliminary ruling this afternoon." She says it carefully, the way you set down something breakable. "Guardianship has been awarded to Eleanor."

The truth enters my body but doesn't land anywhere. It floats. It hovers in the space between hearing and understanding, the way a diagnosis floats for those first few seconds before gravity catches it and pulls it down into your bones.

"The will stands," Janet continues. "The judge found that Whitney was of sound mind and the will is valid. But the guardianship clause..." She pauses. Chooses her words. "The court treats guardianship designations as a recommendation. A strong one. But not binding. The judge makes an independent determination based on the child's best interest, and given that Eleanor is family—" She stops herself. Starts again, softer. "Eleanor's team presented a compelling case. Biological grandparent. Stable income. Established home. Aware of the surrogacy and pregnancy. She's actually the one who paid for the surrogacy."

"I had no idea she was so involved." My tone is that of a loser in denial. Grasping onto the final fleeting moments of hope.

I stare at the oak tree as the whole house runs through my mind like a montage. The tire swing. The dark shape of the guesthouse where Saylor and I kissed on my childhood bed. The nursery that doesn't exist yet for a baby who isn't coming here.

"Your attorney will receive the formal ruling tomorrow morning," Janet says. "You'll have the option to appeal. I'm not supposed to tell you any of this."

"Then why are you here?"

She's quiet for a moment. When she speaks, her voice has lost the professional scaffolding.

"Because I've been doing this job for nineteen years, and I have watched a lot of good people lose. People who would have been wonderful parents. People who did everything right and still came up short because the system isn't built to measure what actually matters." She looks at me. "I submitted my report two weeks ago. My recommendation was in your favor. I want you to know that."

Something cracks behind my ribs. Not the dramatic, cinematic kind of breaking—the quiet kind. The hairline fracture that doesn't show on the surface but changes the way the whole structure bears weight.

"You recommended me? But you only saw us once, and I'm guessing you saw through our bullshit."

"The engagement? Yes, bullshit. But the love? That was real. I don't know where Mr. Saylor ran off to, but I assume he's coming back?"

I shrug. "I hope. Does it even matter anymore?"

"Sure it does. Anyone can get a house ready for a baby. But it takes real commitment to get your heart ready for one. That's what I saw during my visit. Two people who were focused on the real changes that mattered." She stands. Brushes off her slacks then picks up her keys from the bench. "The judge weighed my report along with everything else. I'm so sorry it wasn't enough, Celeste. I truly am. But it's never too late to start your own family."

The idea honestly hadn't even crossed my mind. A baby of my own? That was never part of the plan. I was never supposed to be a mom until Whit intervened. And even that didn't come to fruition.

Janet walks to her car. I watch her go too stunned to move. I bid her goodbye with total stillness, total silence, the absolute absence of any useful response. Her headlights sweep across the driveway. The car turns left at the end of the drive. The taillights shrink and vanish and then the road is dark and empty in both directions.

I stay on the bench with Saylor's jacket still draped around my shoulders. The porchlight is humming above me. The house glowing behind me, warm and lit and full of everything I built and everything I'm losing.

Whitney trusted me. She wrote my name in a legal document and trusted me with the most important thing she ever did, and

I wasn't enough. The company wasn't enough. The house wasn't enough. The love wasn't enough. A judge in a courtroom I've never seen looked at the sum of my life and decided it came up short.

My hand moves to my stomach. Instinct. The gesture of a mother, except I'm not one. I'm not going to be one. The nursery Saylor and I whispered about in the dark—the Montessori shelves, the color of the walls, the crib near the window so she could wake up to morning light—all of it dissolving like a dream you try to hold onto after the alarm.

I don't cry. I should. I will. But right now the grief is too new and too large and it hasn't found its shape yet. It's just pressure. Enormous, formless pressure behind my eyes and in my chest and in the place where I was already building a life for a little girl with Whitney's red curls.

Inside, Ada is waiting. She'll need to know. Saylor is somewhere on a dark road, and he'll need to know too. Tomorrow there will be lawyers and appeals and the grim machinery of a system that decided Eleanor Trace's grief outweighed her daughter's wishes.

But right now, I sit on a bench that Saylor built, on the porch of a house we fixed for a family that is unraveling as fast as I can stitch it together.

I hold on to the only thing I have left.

Whit loved me. Whatever a judge says, whatever a court decides, whatever happens next—Whitney chose me.

That has to be enough. For tonight, that has to be enough.

Chapter 20
Saylor

We'll sit in the gray area together.

I drive for forty minutes before I realize I have nowhere to go.

That's the thing about being far away from the place I know as home. No childhood streets to cruise down, no mate's house to show up at unannounced, no bar where the bartender knows my order and doesn't ask questions. I have a borrowed truck, a half-tank of petrol, and a county full of roads I only know because they lead back to the same place.

So I drive in circles. Past the hardware store where I bought the cabinet hinges. Past the farm stand that sells the tomatoes Mum likes. Past the elementary school with the playground where I sat on a bench two weeks ago and watched kids on the swings and thought about what it would feel like to bring our daughter here. To push her on those swings. To be the kind of man whose biggest problem on a Saturday morning is making sure a four-year-old doesn't launch herself into orbit.

Our daughter. The phrase formed so easily, as though she already existed. As though she was already ours.

I pull into a petrol station. Kill the engine. Sit there with my hands on the wheel and my forehead against my knuckles and try to untangle the mess inside my chest.

Celeste offered to pay for Mum's surgery. That's the fact. Everything I said after that—every sharp word, every accusation, the sugar mama comment that I want to claw back out of the air—that was pride. Not the good kind, the quiet kind that holds your spine straight when the world pushes back. The bad kind. The kind that would rather let your mother suffer than admit you can't fix it yourself.

Mum was right. She's usually right. The guilt isn't about protecting her. It's about protecting me. From the truth I've spent four years running from: I was driving. The other bloke had no headlights on, was speeding, and the road was dark. I did everything right according to the book but none of that matters because I was behind the wheel and Mum was in the passenger seat and now she's basically bound to a chair. That's the equation. That's the math I do every morning when I help her from the bed to the bathroom and pretend it doesn't cost me anything.

Celeste sees the cost. That's what terrifies me. She sees all of it, raw, and she stays anyway. She doesn't just stay, she reaches in. She tries to help. And I slapped her hand away because accepting help would mean admitting I've been drowning, and admitting I've been drowning would mean letting go of the only identity I've held onto since I was twenty-two years old.

I fix what I break.

I'm the boy who takes care of his mum.

What if I could be more than that?

What if it's time to do the impossible?

I start the truck and drive straight home.

The house is dark when I pull in. Not the warm, every-window-glowing dark that greeted Celeste a few hours ago. *Dark* dark. The porchlight is off. The kitchen windows are black. The only light comes from a thin line under Mum's bedroom door, which means she's either reading or she's fallen asleep with the lamp on, which she does more often than not.

The kitchen is clean. The Thai containers have been put away. Someone wiped the table down. The normalcy of it hurts more than the mess would have.

Mum's door is cracked open. I push it gently. She's asleep, the paperback tented on her chest, the lamp still on. I ease the book off her, fold the corner of the page she'll scold me for folding, set it on the nightstand. I pull the blanket up to her chin and turn off the lamp, watching shadows reclaim the corners of her room.

She stirs. "Saylor?"

"Yeah, Mum. Go back to sleep."

"Did you apologize?" she asks in the dark.

"Working on it."

"Work faster, love." Within ten seconds her breathing evens out, and I stand there in her doorway and love her so much my ribs ache.

I close her door and walk through the dark house. Celeste's car is still in the driveway, so she's here. But she's not in the kitchen. Not in the living room. Not in my bedroom.

The nursery door is open.

It's the spare room at the end of the hall, the one with the south-facing window and the good morning light. The one Celeste and I talked about at two in the morning with our legs tangled together—Montessori shelves along the far wall, the crib near the window, a reading chair in the corner so she could feed the baby in the sunrise. Pale green walls. A mobile made of fabric scraps from her old collection, the designs that meant the most. We planned it the way you plan something you believe in. Detail by detail. Thread by thread.

Celeste is sitting on the floor beneath the window. Her back against the wall, her knees drawn up, my jacket still around her shoulders. She's not crying. Her face is dry and still. But the stillness isn't calm. It's the kind that comes after the crying stops, or before it starts, or in the space where crying should be but the body has decided it can't afford it.

I know, the second I cross that threshold, that something has broken beyond the fight we had.

"Lessi?"

She looks up. Her eyes find mine in the dark. She holds my gaze for three seconds, and then she says it.

"We lost." Her voice is flat. Quiet. Sanded down to nothing. "The judge ruled. Eleanor gets the baby."

The words hit me in the chest and keep going. Through the ribs, through the lungs, through the place where I'd already started building a room for this child inside myself.

"Janet came by," Celeste says. "Off the record. The will stands, but the guardianship clause was just a recommendation. The judge decided Eleanor was more suitable. Biological grandparent. Stable finances. She even paid for the surrogacy, Saylor. Did you know that?"

I shake my head.

"So." She exhales and stares at the empty room. "No more baby. You're off the hook."

The hook. As though this were an obligation. As though I were here under contract, fulfilling a role, playing house until the arrangement expired. She doesn't mean it that way—or maybe she does, a little, because the woman I love is sitting on the floor of an empty room that was supposed to hold a crib and she's hurting in ways I can't reach. I know better than anyone, severe pain makes people admit things in the dark they'd never say in the light.

I don't answer right away. Instead I look at the dresser against the far wall. The one I sanded and repainted two weekends ago, the one I was going to mount a mirror above once I found one the right size. There's a black marker on top of it. A Sharpie. I'd been using it to mark the wall for picture hooks—measuring the spacing, penciling dots, then tracing them in marker so I wouldn't lose them.

I pick up the marker. Pop the cap. Walk over and sit down on the floor next to her. The hardwood is cold through my jeans. Our shoulders almost touch. The window above us lets in a thin wash of moonlight that turns the empty room silver.

"Give me your hand," I say.

She looks at me. Suspicious. Exhausted. Wanting to trust me and too tired to verify.

She gives me her hand and I hold it steady.

I uncap the Sharpie and draw a thin black line around her left ring finger. Slow, careful, the way you'd handle something irreplaceable. I complete the circle. Then, on top, where a stone would sit, I draw a small heart. It's not a good heart. It's lopsided, slightly too large, the kind of heart a kid would draw on a Valentine's card for their mum. But it's there. A ring made of ink on the hand of the woman I love, in an empty nursery, on the worst night of her life.

"Do you know the story about the man in the flood?" I ask.

She stares at her finger. At the wobbly heart. She doesn't speak.

"There's this bloke, yeah? Devout man. Prays every day. One day, a flood comes, water's rising, he climbs up on his roof and he prays. 'God, save me.' Within the hour, a rowboat comes by. Bloke in the boat says, 'Hop in, I'll take you to safety.' The man on the roof says, 'No thanks. God will save me.' So, the water keeps rising and the guy keeps praying. After a bit, a motorboat comes. Same thing. 'Hop in.' He says, 'No thanks, God will save me.' Water's up to his chest now. A boat won't do. This time, a helicopter flies over, drops a ladder. 'Grab on!' they call. Once again the bloke says, 'No thanks. My God will save me. He's coming.'"

I pause. Celeste is watching me. Still holding her hand out, the marker ring drying on her skin.

"Who saves him then?"

"No one. The man drowns. Dies. Gets to heaven. Stands in front of God, furious. He shakes his fist at him and says, 'What good are You? I prayed every day! I believed in You! Why didn't You save me?' And God looks at him and says, 'Mate, I sent you two boats and a helicopter.'"

The corner of her mouth twitches. Not a smile. The muscle memory of one.

"Cute story." She nods, defeated.

"Celeste, the point is, I've been the idiot on the roof," I admit. "Praying for a way to fix Mum's surgery. Praying to feel like I'm enough. Praying for someone to make me believe I deserve more than guilt and a toolbox. And you, Celeste. You're my boat. You've been my boat this whole time, and I've been standing on the roof telling you I don't need a ride because I'd rather drown than admit I can't swim."

Her breath catches. A small, involuntary sound. The crack before the dam.

"I'm not rich," I say. "I can't buy you a ring yet. I can't buy much of anything, honestly, and that used to be the thing that kept me up at night—all the ways I couldn't match your life. But you know what? I am wealthy in the things that count. Like how much I love you. Like how certain I am that this"—I gesture at the dark room, the empty walls, the two of us on the floor—"is exactly where I'm supposed to be."

I lift her hand. The marker heart is dry now, slightly smudged at the edges. Permanent enough to last a few days. Temporary enough to fade.

"That'll eventually wash off," I say, "But I'll keep drawing it until I can find a real one. A small one, but real. I don't know how. I'll figure it out. But that's my promise to you."

She looks at the ring. Turns her hand in the moonlight. The heart catches the pale glow and holds it.

"I'm so sorry about Whit," I say. "And the baby. Fuck, I'm so sorry, Celeste. I want to reach inside and hold your heart because I know it's about to break apart. But try to remember it doesn't erase what we've built. And it doesn't change what's ahead. If you want to be a mum—" I turn to face her fully. My hand on her knee. My eyes on hers. "Then let's do it. You and me. Our own family. Not because someone wrote it in a will. Because we chose it. With each other."

She's quiet for a long time. The house settles around us. Somewhere down the hall, Mum shifts in her sleep and the bedframe creaks—a small, domestic sound, proof that we're not alone even when it feels like it.

"Do you actually want this?" Celeste's tone is careful. Guarded. Protecting something she can't afford to lose again.

"Or do you just pity me? Because from where I'm sitting, I'm an older woman whose company just imploded, whose best friend is gone, who just lost a custody case, and who is—by any objective measure—the saddest person you've ever met. You don't have to save me, Saylor. That's the whole point of what you said tonight. You don't want to be saved and neither do I. So if this is a rescue mission, tell me now."

"It's not pity." I say it simply because simple is all I have left. "And it's not a rescue. It's destiny, Celeste. You're my boat. But here's the part I didn't say before." I take her other hand so I'm holding both. "I'm your boat too. That's how it works. We don't just save each other. We refuse to let the other one drown."

She looks at me. At the marker on her finger. At the empty room that was supposed to hold a baby and now holds only us and the quiet wreckage of a plan that fell apart and the first, fragile scaffolding of a new one.

I kiss her. Slow this time. Not the quick peck from the driveway, the compressed promise between two people mid-fight. This one is unhurried. Tender. The kind of kiss that doesn't demand anything, that just says: I'm here. I'll be here tomorrow. And the day after that, and the one after that, for as many days as you'll let me.

When I pull back, her forehead rests against mine.

"Tomorrow is going to be hard," I say.

"I know."

"And the day after."

"I know that too."

"But tonight, you're not doing any of it alone. Yeah? We'll sit in the gray area together."

"Gray area?" she asks.

"Something my mum used to say. The gray area is when you're at the end of something awful breaking apart, but you're also on the cusp of something beautiful coming together. All you can do is sit with it. That's hard for a lot of people, to have hope when everything seems bleak."

Celeste looks at me like she's looking into my soul. Weighing something, sizing me up. A kiss on the cheek tells me she finds me more than worthy to be by her side. "The gray area isn't so bleak if you're sitting in it with the right person."

I nod. "Exactly." Her hand tightens around mine. The marker heart presses between our palms—a ring drawn in the dark, a promise made on the floor, a future sketched in Sharpie that will fade from her skin long before it fades from her heart.

We sit there. Two people on the floor of an empty room, holding hands in the moonlight, letting the worst day end the only way it can.

Together.

Chapter 21

Saylor

Like trying to pat your head and rub your stomach at the same time, except naked and with higher stakes.

Look away, *NSYNC. This is about to get inappropriate.

Justin Timberlake stares down at me from the poster on the guesthouse wall with his frosted tips and his denim-on-denim commitment, and I would apologize for what he's about to witness except I'm too busy kissing Celeste's neck at six in the morning in her childhood bed while the sunrise turns the bubblegum-pink walls the color of a blush.

She's half asleep. Or she was, until I started tracing my mouth along the curve of her shoulder, down the line of her collarbone, across the soft skin just above her breast. She shifts against me, arching into the contact with the drowsy instinct of a body that has spent the past few weeks remembering what touch is for.

Celeste hasn't been going to the office. She needs time and space, so she's home—here in Westchester. And there's not much to do in Westchester...except fuck. All hours of the night and day. And somehow, even during one of the most tumultuous times in our lives, it's a little slice of paradise.

"Saylor." Her voice is thick with sleep. "It's before seven."

"I'm aware."

"The sun isn't even fully up."

"It's getting there. So am I."

She laughs. The sound vibrates through her ribs and into my mouth where it's pressed against her sternum. I slide lower, kissing the valley between her breasts, the plane of her stomach, the ridge of her hip. She threads her fingers into my hair and tugs gently, not to stop me but to hold on, the way you grip the bar on a ride that's just starting to move.

"Come here," she says.

"I am here."

"No, come *here*." She tugs harder. Pulls me up and kisses me deep, morning breath and all, which is the kind of intimacy that means more than any silk-draped penthouse encounter because it means she's comfortable with me. She rolls me onto my back and climbs over me, settling her weight across my hips with a confidence she didn't have a month ago. Her hair falls around us like curtains closing on a stage.

"I want to try something," she says.

"Handcuffs? Whips? Butt plugs?"

She narrows her eyes at me.

"Okay, sorry. I'm listening."

"You know that thing where..." She pauses, squinting one eye, looking adorably bashful. "Where both people are...you know... going down on each other...simultaneously..."

"Sixty-nine?"

"Don't say it like that."

"Like what? It's a number, Celeste."

"It's a very loaded number." She sits up, still straddling me, and pushes her hair out of her face. "I've never done that. It always seemed so logistically complicated. Like trying to pat your head and rub your stomach at the same time, except naked and with higher stakes."

"It's not complicated."

"There are angles to consider. Breathing logistics. The question of where one's knees go. And the whole thing seems very..." She waves her hand in a circle, searching. "Gen Z."

I laugh so hard she bounces on my chest. "Gen Z? Sixty-nine has been around since the invention of two bodies and a flat surface. The Romans were doing this, Celeste. It predates democracy."

"Well, I wouldn't know. I missed that class during my sexual education. Honestly, my past sex life consisted of Greg Prescott and twenty or so years of missionary with the lights off. I'm working from a limited dataset."

"Well, baby. I'm your professor now." I sit up, bringing her with me, my hands on her hips. "Here's the deal. You turn around. I lie back. You focus on what you're doing and I focus on what I'm doing, and if at any point you feel like you can't concentrate, just stop and enjoy it. Don't worry. Your performance will not be graded."

"I hate that you just made a school metaphor about oral sex."

"Would you prefer a construction metaphor? Because I've got those too. Something about excavating your desire, or hammering in my point."

"Dear Lord, *stop*."

She stares at me. I stare at her. JC Chasez stares at both of us from the poster, frozen in a choreography move that now feels uncomfortably relevant.

"Fine, let's do it," she says. "But if this is awkward, we never speak of it again."

She turns around. There's a moment of negotiation that is, admittedly, less graceful than either of us would prefer. Knees reposition. Elbows find purchase. She hovers above me and I can feel her self-consciousness radiating through her thighs, the tension saying she's trying something unfamiliar and bracing for failure.

I press my mouth to her and the self-consciousness evaporates in approximately two seconds.

Her skin is already hot and slick when I spread her thighs in my hands, the taste of her familiar and urgent. I press my mouth to her, tongue working in slow, circular strokes, and she melts downward, her hips riding the wave of contact. I'm greedy for her—there's so much more of her from this angle, so much more to explore. I plunge deeper, sucking her clit into my mouth and drawing out a gasp that vibrates through her whole body and, by extension, into mine.

She's trying to focus, I can tell—her tongue flickers over the head of my cock, tentative, then more bold when she feels me shudder in response. For a second, I lose track of which of us is making which sound, the pleasure ricocheting back and forth until it's all just one bright, shared current. Her hands clutch my thighs, fingers digging in, and I counter by holding her hips fast, refusing to let her escape the intensity building between us. I want her to know how good she tastes. How much I want to consume her whole.

She whimpers and writhes and I don't let up, not even when I hear her breath catch and her movements stutter. I drag my tongue higher, tease the tight ring of muscle above, and her whole body jolts—the shock of it making her clamp down on me, burying her face in my lap as if she could crawl inside the sensation to hide from it. I work her with my mouth, alternating pressure and speed, and she loses all sense of self-consciousness, moaning shamelessly into my skin.

Celeste slides her lips down to the base, swallowing me so deep I see static behind my eyes. She's ravenous suddenly, devouring me with a hunger I didn't know she had, and I'd like to say I'm still in control but I'm not—she's running the show now, her hand twisting and pumping in perfect sync with the suction of her mouth. The wet heat of her tongue, the clutch of her palm, the velvet clamp of her throat—it's all too much, and I'm right there at the edge with no hope of rescue.

I double down, desperate to drag her with me. I suck her clit, gentle at first, then harder, and when I slip a finger inside her, she goes taut, every muscle in her body straining as if she's about to snap in half. She sobs around my cock, the sound vibrating through my whole body, and then she's coming, gushing, shaking so hard she has to steady herself with both hands on my thighs.

The taste of her floods my mouth and I drink it like I've never tasted anything sweeter, my own climax hitting me at exactly the same moment.

She doesn't stop. She sucks every drop from me, her lips sealed tight, her tongue cradling the head, and when I finally collapse back against the pillows, she swallows, licks her lips, and laughs—this disbelieving, delighted little sound, as if surprised by her own animal ferocity.

We collapse in a tangled, backwards heap. Her feet are near my pillow. My head is somewhere near the foot of the bed. Lance Bass observes us from the wall with an expression of patient tolerance.

"Verdict?" I ask the ceiling.

She's quiet for a moment. Catching her breath. "I understand the hype."

"Not overhyped?"

"Not even slightly. But I do have a question."

"Shoot."

"How does anyone concentrate? I kept forgetting what I was doing because of what you were doing. It's like trying to read while someone plays the piano. Hard to strategize."

"You strategize while you're giving me head?"

"Always."

"Woman, if it's the last thing I do, I will find a way to get you to relax."

She crawls back up the bed and settles against my chest. "I'm relaxed."

We lie there for a few minutes, tangled together in a twin bed that was built for a teenager and is barely containing two adults, while the pink walls turn gold in the sunrise and the *NSYNC poster bears silent witness to things no boy band should ever have to see.

Then the sound hits.

A truck. Not just any truck. The rattling, diesel-throated growl of a vehicle that sounds like it's been arguing with its own engine for the past hundred thousand miles. It rumbles up the driveway, loud enough to vibrate the guesthouse windows, and comes to a stop somewhere near the main house with a shudder and a hiss that suggest the brakes are having a philosophical disagreement with the wheels.

Celeste sits up. "Is that your truck?"

"My truck doesn't sound like that."

"Your truck sounds exactly like that. Saylor, is someone stealing your rental? How much are you paying for that thing, anyway?"

"Enough that I should own it by now." I pull on my jeans and a T-shirt. "But that's not my truck."

"Then whose—"

"Stay here. Get dressed. Meet me out front in ten minutes." I kiss the side of her temple, quick and warm. "I have a surprise."

"The last time you surprised me, I ended up blindfolded in my own office."

"This one's better. *Eh*," I correct myself. "*Comparable*. This surprise is comparable."

I cross the yard barefoot. The grass is cold with dew and the morning air smells like cut wood and the end of summer. The main house is quiet. Mum will be awake soon, but for now the kitchen windows are dark and the only sound is birdsong and the ticking of the truck engine cooling in the driveway.

The truck is a Ford. Old, green, mud-caked on the wheel wells, with a livestock rack in the bed and a bumper sticker that reads HEELER MOM in peeling letters. The driver's door opens and a man steps out. Mid-fifties, sun-weathered, wearing a canvas jacket and boots that have seen actual farms. He's got a crate in one hand.

"Saylor Evans?"

"That's me."

"Dave Kendrick. Meadow Ridge Farm, up in Dutchess County. Got your heeler." He sets the crate on the tailgate and unlatches the door. "Eight weeks old. Female. Dam's a working dog, sire's a champion agility runner. This one's the runt, but don't let that fool you. She's got more engine than her siblings."

He reaches into the crate and pulls out a puppy.

She's small and compact and the color of a thunderstorm. Blue-gray speckled coat with rust patches above her eyes and on her chest, ears too big for her head, paws too big for her body. She blinks at the morning light and immediately starts wriggling, not with fear but with the full-body enthusiasm of an animal that has decided the entire world is happening right now and she needs to participate in every part of it simultaneously.

Dave hands her to me. She weighs nothing. I bet less than eight pounds. She fits in one hand, though she immediately tries to climb out of it, scrambling up my forearm with uncoordinated determination like she has no concept of her own limitations.

"She's perfect," I say.

"She's work," Dave corrects. "But the good kind. Heelers need a job. Keep her busy and she'll be your best mate. Let her get bored and she'll eat your furniture."

"Yeah, I got it. We know heelers well."

I sign the paperwork on the tailgate while the puppy chews on my shirt collar. Dave gives me a bag of food, a vaccination schedule, and the breeder's number. He shakes my hand, gets back in the truck, and rumbles down the driveway in a cloud of diesel and dust.

I stand in the driveway holding a puppy.

For three weeks I've been trying to figure out how to tell my mother that the surgery might happen. That Celeste offered. That the money exists and the surgeon is real and the possibility of Mum running again is not a fantasy I constructed out of guilt and desperation. But every time I tried to form the words, they got stuck behind the same wall they always get stuck behind: the fear that hope is just disappointment wearing a costume.

The puppy licks my chin. Her tongue is warm and her breath smells like milk and she has absolutely no idea that she's a metaphor. She's just a dog, happy to be outside, thrilled to be held, unaware that the man holding her is about to use her tiny body to make a promise he's terrified to break.

I carry her inside.

Mum is in the kitchen, awake now. She's already made tea, already dressed in the soft cotton trousers and the blue cardigan she wears when her joints are cooperative. She's standing at the counter, weight distributed carefully, one hand on the granite for balance. She hears me come in and starts to turn.

"Saylor, did I hear a truck? What on Earth was that noi—"

She stops. Her eyes land on the puppy.

The puppy's eyes land on her.

For a moment nobody moves. The kitchen is silent except for the kettle cooling on the stove and the small, breathy panting of an eight-week-old heeler who has just discovered a new person and is vibrating with the need to investigate.

"Saylor." Mum's voice is barely above a whisper. "What did you do?"

"Mum, this is your dog."

"My dog."

"A heeler from a farm Upstate." I step closer, holding the puppy out where Mum can see her clearly. The rust patches. The speckled coat. The ears that are actively trying to evolve into satellite dishes.

Mum hasn't taken her eyes off the puppy. Her hand is still on the counter. Her tea is still steaming beside her. She's not moving because Mum doesn't react to surprises until she's decided how she feels about them, and right now she's still deciding.

"I've been afraid," I say. "For years. Afraid to let you hope because I thought if I let you hope and it didn't work out, it would break something in you that I couldn't fix. So I managed everything. Controlled everything. Decided what you were allowed to want and when you were allowed to want it, because if I kept the walls tight enough, nothing could get in and hurt you."

The puppy squirms in my hands. She wants down. She wants to explore. She wants to do everything her breed was built for, and being held still is an affront to her engineering.

"But Celeste has helped me see something. Guilt is a bigger shield than pain." I take a breath. "I'm done managing you, Mum. I'm done deciding what you're allowed to hope for. This puppy is a promise. Not that the surgery will work, or that everything will be fine, or that I can fix what happened. But that we're going to do things differently. Instead of sulking over what we lost, we're going to find joy in what we have. And maybe, just maybe one day, you can run with this little girl the way you used to run with Red."

Mum's chin trembles. Just once. A single crack in the composure she's maintained through years of pain and thousands of miles from home and every indignity that comes with a body that stopped cooperating at its peak.

"Oh, Saylor. Come here, you," she says. But not to me. To the puppy.

I set the dog in her arms, and what happens next is something I will hold in my memory for the rest of my life.

Ada Evans, who walks with a cane and sits with a wince and hasn't lifted anything heavier than a kettle in three years, wraps both arms around this puppy and raises her to her chest. It's not a casual lift. I can see what it costs her. The muscles in her arms shake. She clenches her teeth. Her shoulders bunch against the effort, and her spine protests in ways I can read as clearly as print on a page. But she does it. She lifts this five-pound bundle of fur and holds her against her chest and closes her eyes and the tears that Mum never cries fall down her cheeks in two straight lines.

The puppy, oblivious to the magnitude of the moment, licks the tears off her face.

Mum laughs. A wet, broken, beautiful sound. She opens her eyes and looks at me and I can see everything in them: the gratitude, the fear, the hope she wasn't sure she was still allowed to carry. And underneath all of it, the particular love of a mother looking at her son and recognizing, maybe for the first time, that he's grown into something she didn't have to build alone.

"I forgive myself, Mum. The accident... I never meant to hurt you. It happened. And I hate it. But now, I'm letting the past go, because I'm ready for the future now."

"She's perfect," Mum says.

"She's trouble. The breeder made that very clear."

"Not the puppy, love. Celeste. She's perfect for you."

Right on cue, Celeste appears in the kitchen doorway. She's dressed, hair pulled back, cheeks still flushed from the guesthouse. She takes one look at Mum holding a puppy and her whole face opens up. Her heavy thoughts go airy for a moment at the sight of something so sweet. For a flash, there's pure, uncomplicated delight in her eyes.

"Oh my gosh," Celeste breathes. "Saylor."

"Surprise."

"That's a puppy."

"Excellent observation. Your fashion eye extends to zoology."

She crosses the kitchen and stands beside Mum, reaching out to scratch behind the puppy's ears. The dog responds by attempting to climb from Ada's arms onto Celeste's head, which requires an intervention from both of us and results in a three-person, one-dog pile-up that dissolves into laughter.

For twenty minutes, the kitchen is chaos in the best way. The puppy explores every corner with frantic energy, sniffing cabinet doors and skidding on the hardwood and attempting to befriend the table leg. Mum watches from her chair with the kind of focused joy I haven't seen on her face since Wollongong. Celeste sits on the floor, cross-legged, letting the puppy climb over her lap, and every time the dog licks her hand she makes a sound that is completely at odds with her professional reputation.

"She needs a name," Ada says.

"Not yet," I say. "Let her tell us. Heelers are opinionated. She'll let us know who she is."

"Spoken like a true dog dad," Celeste says.

"Dog brother. She's Mum's."

"I think she belongs to all of us," Mum says quietly, and the words land heavier than she intended, because "all of us" means something different now than it did a week ago. All of us means a family. Fractured and improbable and held together with marker-ink promises and borrowed trucks and a love that nobody planned for, but a family nonetheless.

The puppy falls asleep in Mum's lap. Just drops mid-exploration, the way puppies do, from full speed to unconscious in the space of a breath. Mum strokes her ears with fingers that are steadier than they've been in months, and the kitchen goes quiet, and the morning fills the room with the kind of light that makes everything look possible.

I'm watching Celeste watch Mum when I notice the shift.

It's small. After a small *ding*, Celeste pulls her phone out of her pocket. The screen is lit up with a notification. She reads, her face contorting just a beat before she recomposes herself. The warmth in the room drains by a degree. Her jaw sets, just slightly. Her thumb hovers over the screen as if she's reading the message twice to make sure she understood it correctly.

"Everything okay?" I ask.

She looks up. The smile she gives me is real, but it's braced. Reinforced at the corners, the way you shore up a wall you know is about to take weight.

"Everything's fine." She slips the phone into her back pocket. Then she stands, brushes off her jeans, and bends to kiss the puppy on the head. She kisses Mum on the cheek and congratulates her on the new puppy. She crosses to me and holds my face in both hands and kisses me on the mouth, quick but firm, right in front of my mother, in the morning light, with no hesitation at all.

"Enjoy the puppy," she says. "Both of you. I have something I need to take care of."

"Now?"

"It can't wait." She's already reaching for her keys on the counter. Her bag is by the door. "I'll be back. I just need to handle something."

"Celeste."

She stops at the doorway. Turns back. Her eyes meet mine and

I search them for a clue, for the content of that text, for whatever just pulled her out of the best morning we've had in weeks. But Celeste Brinley has spent twenty years learning to keep her face still when the ground moves beneath her. She gives me nothing.

"Trust me," she says. "I'll explain when I get back."

She's gone before I can answer. The front door closes. A moment later, her car starts in the driveway. The engine fades down the road and the house goes quiet except for the puppy snoring in Mum's lap and the kettle clicking as it cools.

Mum looks at me. "That wasn't nothing."

"No," I agree. "It wasn't."

The puppy sighs in her sleep. Mum's hand rests on the small gray body, protective and steady. I stand at the kitchen window and watch the empty driveway and tell myself that Celeste said 'trust me,' and that trusting her is the one thing I've learned to do this summer that doesn't scare me anymore.

But the driveway stays empty. And the morning, which started with laughter and boy bands and a woman in my arms, ends with a silence that has teeth.

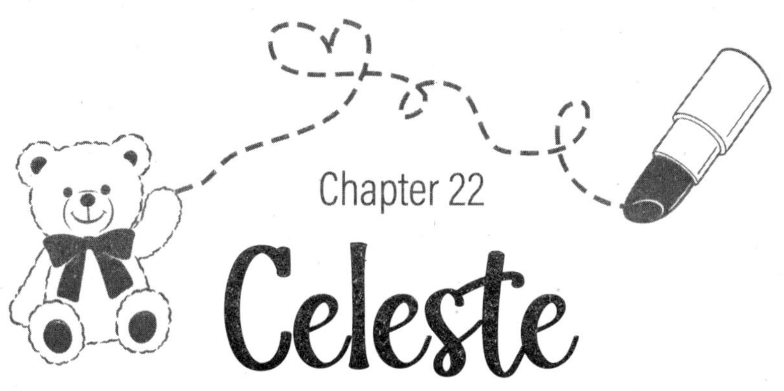

Chapter 22

Celeste

Eleanor looks a lot like a boat right now.

The cemetery is beautiful, which feels like a contradiction.

It shouldn't be beautiful. It's a place for grief, not for aesthetics. But the Hamptons don't know how to be anything other than curated, so even the dead get ocean views and landscape architecture. The headstones are spaced generously across rolling green, shaded by old elms and bordered by hedgerows that someone trims on a schedule. There are benches placed at tasteful intervals, stone paths winding between the plots, and in the distance, the gray shimmer of the Atlantic visible through a gap in the tree line. It's the kind of place where wealthy people come to rest and their families come to grieve in a setting that suggests death is simply another venue requiring appropriate attire.

I am wearing the wrong shoes.

My Louboutins were the right choice for the drive. Black patent, four-inch heel, the pair I wear when I mean business. But the cemetery path turned to grass three minutes ago, and the grass turned to soft earth near the newer plots, and my stilettos are now punching into the ground with every step like tiny aggressive shovels, sinking two inches deep and requiring excavation each time I try to move forward.

I stop walking. Look down. My left shoe is buried to the sole in dark cemetery dirt. I yank it free with a sound that is deeply undignified.

"I'm sorry," I say to the shoe. "You don't deserve this. Neither of us planned for terrain."

I take them off. Both of them. Holding my shoes by the straps in one hand, I continue barefoot across the cold grass, feeling the chill climb through my feet and into my ankles and not caring, because dignity has limits and mine ended at the second sinkhole.

I find Eleanor at the far end of the newer section, standing in front of a white marble headstone with roses carved into the border. The stone is clean. Polished recently, probably this morning, probably by Eleanor herself. Fresh flowers sit in a small stone vase at the base. Not the kind from a florist. These are garden roses, slightly imperfect, the kind you cut yourself from a bush you've been tending.

Whitney Anette Trace. Beloved daughter, loyal friend, brave heart.

I stand beside Eleanor. She doesn't turn to acknowledge my arrival. Her eyes stay fixed on the headstone, her posture rigid, her hands clasped in front of her like a vigilant soldier, guarding whatever moment she's lost in.

"I guess you had to unblock me to text me," I say.

Eleanor's jaw twitches into something akin to a smile. Her eyes never leave the stone. "It was time."

We stand in silence. The wind picks up from the east, carrying salt and the distant sound of waves and the coolness of a coastline that's preparing for winter. I look at Whitney's name carved into marble and try to feel something specific, but what I feel is everything at once, and everything at once has no shape.

"Have you been out here?" Eleanor asks. "To visit her?"

I hang my head. The honest answer costs me. "No, actually."

Eleanor's chin lifts a fraction.

"Not out of disrespect," I say quickly. "I miss her constantly, but that's not news. I've missed her for years. I hear her sometimes. Not literally, but her opinions. Her reactions. The things she'd say if she were standing next to me, which would mostly be inappropriate but always brilliant." I press my hand flat against my chest. "She's never far."

Eleanor is quiet for a long time. When she speaks, her voice has lost the polished edge I've heard at every prior encounter. What's underneath is rougher. Older. Tired in ways that have nothing to do with sleep.

"I envy that," she tells me. "I don't hear her at all. I come out here every day and I stand where you're standing and I wait. For a sign, a feeling, something. Anything that tells me she's still close." Her throat moves around a swallow. "I told you at the funeral there's no apologizing to someone who's gone. And yet here I am. Every morning. Trying to find the words."

The wind shifts. A leaf skitters across the base of the headstone. I watch it catch against the stone vase and hold.

"Why did you want to meet, Eleanor? Because if this is just to gloat over your victory, speed it up. I have a long drive home and a crumbling life to get back to."

Eleanor reaches into her purse. Not the portfolio-sized designer bag she carried at the ultrasound. A smaller one, practical, the kind of purse you carry when you're not performing wealth. She pulls out an envelope, opens it, then hands me a check.

I look at the number. Then I look again, because the first time my brain rejected it as a misprint.

"What is this?"

"What does it look like? A very large check, dear. Made out to you."

I stare at her. The check is trembling slightly in my hand, which I'm going to attribute to the wind. "Are you out of your mind? What is this? You're paying me to go away? The judge already ruled. I can't contest your guardianship."

"I sold two commercial resort properties in Fort Lauderdale." Eleanor says this with the flat efficiency of someone reporting a transaction, not a sacrifice. "Prime waterfront. My husband acquired them in the eighties. They've appreciated substantially. I sold them twenty percent under market value for cash offers because I needed the money liquid and I needed it now." She nods at the check. "That should be more than enough to cover your corporate debt. The unauthorized lines of credit, the inventory reconciliation, whatever Greg left you holding. Keep the company private. I'll be your angel investor. Don't worry, very favorable terms. Now, speaking as an investor, how long would you need to get the business back up and running?"

The question is so practical, so completely detached from the emotional earthquake happening inside my chest, that I almost laugh. "Eleanor. Why are you doing this? Guilt?"

"No."

"Then what?"

Eleanor turns to face me for the first time since I arrived. Her eyes are clear and hard and certain, the way they always are, except that now I can see what the hardness is built over: something broken. Something that broke a long time ago, long before Whit died, maybe as far back as the marriage she stayed in and the daughter she couldn't reach and the decades of choosing image over honesty until the image was all that was left.

"I'm not going to let my granddaughter grow up underneath a bridge," she says. "I want this child well taken care of. You need a job to do that."

"What are you talking about? You won, Eleanor."

"I thought I did." Her gaze drifts back to the headstone. The roses carved in marble, the calligraphic W that looks more like a symbol than a letter. "I'll admit it. Last week I was so sure things were exactly as they should be. I drove out here to tell Whitney the news, promise her that I'd take good care of her daughter, and that I was sorry. For letting her down as a mother. For all the ways I pushed instead of listened. I told her this baby was going to be my second chance. My apology to her, made flesh. I was going to do motherhood again, the right way this time."

She pauses. The wind fills the silence.

"But once I got out here," Eleanor continues, "in the quiet, do you know what I realized?"

I shake my head.

"My biggest mistake with Whitney was never that I pushed her or challenged her. It wasn't that I had expectations or specific dreams for her life. Every mother has those." Her voice catches on the word *mother*, a hairline fracture that she does not address or repair. "My biggest mistake was that I didn't know my own daughter. I never listened. I spent thirty-some years talking at Whitney and not once did I sit down and ask her who she was and what she actually wanted, and then respect the answer."

The tears start. Not dramatically and not with a sound. They track down Eleanor's face in two clean lines she doesn't wipe away. She doesn't acknowledge them at all, as if crying is something happening to her body that she has elected not to participate in.

"And it dawned on me," she says, "standing right here, that that's why she chose you. Not because you'd be the better mother. You might be, you might not. That's not the point." She turns back to me. Her eyes are wet and her bottom lip is quivering, yet her voice is steady despite everything happening on her face. "Whitney chose you because you knew her. Because you can help her daughter get to know her. Not the version I built. Not the version I wanted. The real Whitney. The woman you had the privilege of knowing, and yet I failed to. I've hated you, Celeste, because you were the friend she loved more than she loved her own mother and I have to live with that, and I do live with that, every single day. But now I see it differently. Thank God she had you."

She takes a breath. Holds it. Lets it go.

I try to say the right things—that I'm not blameless. That there were times I didn't listen to Whit when I should have. But the words tangle in my throat like Christmas lights fresh out of storage, knotted and impossible to unravel in the moment.

"The last thing I can do for my daughter is finally listen to what she wanted. And respect it."

The cemetery is silent. The wind has dropped. The Atlantic has gone quiet in the distance, as if even the ocean knows that something irreversible just happened between two women standing at a grave.

"I'm relinquishing my guardianship rights. I'll recommend you for adoption. All you need to do is apply. You'll have my full support, in writing, with my attorneys."

I look at the check in my hand. The number stares back at me with the blankness of figures on paper, offering nothing beyond their face value, demanding nothing beyond a decision. My fingers itch to tear it in half. The pride that Greg installed in me, the armor that says accepting help is admitting defeat, rises up my throat like bile.

And then I hear Saylor's voice. Clear as if he were standing beside me in the cold grass. *I've been the idiot on the roof. You're my boat.*

I look at Eleanor. Standing in a cemetery in the Hamptons, offering me a check that represents the sale of her dead husband's legacy, asking nothing in return except that I raise her granddaughter the way her daughter would have wanted. Eleanor looks a lot like a boat right now.

"I won't let you down," I say. "I promise."

Eleanor nods. Once. Sharp. A nod that says: *Better not.*

"And I want you to be part of this," I continue. "Every birthday, every holiday. First steps, first words, first day of school. My home is your home, Eleanor. This child is going to know her grandmother."

Something shifts in Eleanor's face. The hardness doesn't leave, exactly. It rearranges. The wall doesn't come down, but a door appears in it that wasn't there before, and through that door I can see the woman Eleanor might have been if she'd left her misogynist husband at thirty and raised Whitney alone. What if she had let herself be soft in all the places she decided softness was a liability—would she have had a happier life?

Eleanor steps forward. Wraps her arms around me.

The hug is stiff at first. Eleanor usually shakes hands, or air-kisses at charity events. She maintains a perimeter of personal space that could be measured in city blocks. But right now her arms tighten. Her head drops against my shoulder. And for five seconds that stretch into something longer, two women who spent months on opposite sides of an emotional war hold each other in front of the grave of the person they both loved and failed and are trying, too late and imperfectly, to honor.

When she pulls back, her composure is restored. The tears have been processed and filed. She smooths her coat. Adjusts her collar. Returns to herself the way a building settles after a tremor, same structure, slightly different alignment.

"Shall we say goodbye?" Eleanor asks, looking at the headstone.

We stand together. Side by side. Between us the carved name of a girl who loved us both in different ways and trusted us both with different things and somehow, from wherever she is, engineered this exact moment.

"Bye, Whit," I say quietly. "I'll come back soon. I can't wait for you to meet your daughter."

Eleanor mutters something inaudible underneath her breath. Then a little louder, "Bye, sweetheart. Rest now. I'll visit soon."

We turn and walk back toward the path. I'm still carrying my Louboutins by their straps. I've apparently given up on pretentiousness and find it liberating. Eleanor walks beside me at a measured pace, her heels navigating the soft ground with a competence that makes me wonder if she practices cemetery walking the way some people practice yoga.

"Celeste."

"Hmm?"

"Why are you barefoot?"

"Because this cemetery is an obstacle course disguised as a memorial garden, and my shoes weren't designed for cross-country."

"Those are Louboutins."

"I'm aware."

"You're carrying four-thousand-dollar shoes through a graveyard like a pair of flip-flops."

"They'll recover. They've survived worse. I once wore them to a sample sale."

Eleanor shakes her head. The disapproval is familiar but the edges have softened into something closer to exasperation, the kind a mother directs at a daughter she can't quite control but has stopped trying to redesign. We walk a few more steps in silence before Eleanor speaks again.

"Now, have you given any thought to names for the baby?"

"A little but nothing finite."

"Well, names require lead time. You can't name a child under pressure. That's how people end up with children called Nevaeh or Brinleigh."

"Jokes on you." I grunt as I nearly roll my ankle on an unexpected hill. "I like those names."

"What about something classic? Margaret. Catherine. Elizabeth."

"Those are queen names, Eleanor."

"Queens are excellent. Queens endure."

"I was thinking something more personal. Something connected to Whitney."

Eleanor is quiet for a moment. "Whitney's middle name was Anette."

"Which she hated," I remind Eleanor. "No offense."

We reach the parking lot. My car is on one side, Eleanor's on the other. The check is in my purse, folded once, the crease sharp and deliberate because even in emotional upheaval I fold things properly. Eleanor stops beside her car and turns to face me.

"My attorneys will have the paperwork drafted by Friday," she says. "I'll need your lawyer's information."

"I'll send the contact. Since we can text now and all."

"Good. And Celeste?"

"Yes?"

"The fall and spring line. Is it salvageable?"

"With that check? It's more than salvageable. It's funded."

"Then fund it. Build something beautiful. Show that ex-husband of yours what happens when you bet against Celeste Brinley."

She gets in her car, starts the engine, but then pauses with the window down.

"One more thing."

"Of course there is."

"The young man. The Australian."

"Saylor."

"Is he staying?"

I think about a marker ring drawn in moonlight, a flood parable told on the floor of an empty nursery, a puppy delivered at dawn as a promise that hope is allowed to exist even when everything suggests it shouldn't.

"He's staying," I say.

Eleanor nods. A single, crisp nod. "Good. He seems sturdy."

"Sturdy. Sure."

"It's a compliment." She rolls her eyes before putting on her sunglasses. "Sturdy men don't leave. Flashy men do. I married flashy. I recommend sturdy."

She rolls up the window. I watch her go and stand in the parking lot in bare feet on cold asphalt, holding my shoes, feeling the wind off the ocean, and trying to process the fact that the woman I've been fighting for six months just handed me everything I lost and asked for nothing but a seat at the table.

I get in my car and go through the motions. I set my shoes on the passenger side floorboard. Put the key in the ignition. Check my mirrors.

Then I sit there.

Whit's grave is fifty yards behind me. The ocean is a gray line on the horizon. The check is in my purse. The phone in my pocket holds a thread of messages from Saylor that I haven't answered, the last one reading simply: *Everything okay? Don't be mad but the puppy found one of your shoes.*

I'll answer him. I'll drive back to Westchester and walk into the kitchen and find Ada with a dog in her lap and Saylor pulling a sock out of a puppy's mouth and I'll tell them what happened. All of it. The cemetery, the check, the custody, the fact that Eleanor showed up at her daughter's grave and did the one thing she never did while Whitney was alive.

She listened.

But first I sit in the car and close my eyes and let myself feel the size of what just happened. The company is funded. The baby is mine. Saylor is home. Ada is family. A puppy is destroying footwear in my kitchen. My best friend is buried in a beautiful cemetery with roses on her headstone and a mother who finally heard her. And the life I thought was falling apart has, while I wasn't watching, quietly rebuilt itself into something I didn't know I was allowed to want.

I open my eyes. Pull down the visor mirror. Look at myself.

My mascara migrated during the hug. My hair is doing something unacceptable in the wind. And I'm smiling because as always, with perfect timing, I feel Whit near.

She's probably having a good laugh up there. Celeste Brinley, barefoot in a graveyard, inheriting a baby and a grandmother in the same conversation.

I love you, I tell her. *And I'll make sure she loves you too. She'll know who you were. The real you.*

I start the car and pull out of the lot with extra caution. I've got big things to live for now. I turn left toward the highway, toward Westchester, toward the house where everything started and nothing has finished and the gray area is narrowing, day by day, into something that looks less like uncertainty and more like a life.

The road stretches ahead. The ocean disappears in the rearview mirror. Whit stays where she is, under marble and roses, resting in the knowledge that the two women she loved most in the world finally stopped fighting over her legacy and started building something together.

Chapter 23
Saylor

See you on the other side, Lessi.

12 weeks later.

We're running.

Not the casual jog of two people who left the house late. The full-sprint, adrenaline-fueled, dodging-a-man-in-a-wheelchair sprint of two people who have been waiting twelve weeks for a phone call and got it forty-five minutes ago on the Saw Mill River Parkway, while Celeste was driving, which means we're lucky to be alive and at the hospital instead of in one.

"Elevator!" Celeste shouts, stabbing the button with her index finger. Then again. Then a third time, because Celeste believes that urgency can be communicated to machinery through repetition.

The number above the door doesn't move.

"Stairs," I say.

"I'm in heels."

"Then take them off."

"These are Valentino."

"Celeste, your daughter is being born on the fourth floor. Take off the shoes or I will haul you over my shoulder like a sack of taters."

She kicks them off without breaking stride and we hit the stairwell at a pace that would concern a cardiologist. She takes the steps two at a time, barefoot, one hand on the railing and the other clutching her phone where Raven's text still glows on the screen: *She's coming. Right now. Bring snacks.*

We did not bring snacks. There was no time.

Three flights up, my lungs are burning and Celeste is somehow ahead of me, which I'm going to attribute to sheer maternal willpower rather than any deficiency in my cardio. She hits the fourth-floor door with both hands and bursts into the labor and delivery ward like she's the doctor and she needs to save a life.

"Raven Pecker," she announces to the nurse at the station. "She's in labor. Where is she?"

The nurse, a sturdy woman in floral scrubs who has clearly weathered decades of frantic almost-parents, doesn't flinch. She consults her screen with the calm of someone checking a lunch reservation. "What's your name?"

"Brinley. *Celeste Brinley.* That's my baby she's having. Wait—no, that came out wrong. She's a surrogate."

The nurse's face transforms into several opinions before she checks her screen again. "You're on the guest list, Ms. Brinley. Drews Pecker is in room three-sixteen A. Down the hall, second left."

Celeste takes three steps. Four. She realizes I'm not beside her and turns back. "Saylor, come on!"

I'm standing in the middle of the L & D ward with both hands on my chest, shoulders shaking.

"Drews Pecker," I mutter. "That's still hilarious."

"Saylor."

"What? It's funny. Do you ever say the full name out loud? Because Drews Pecker is—"

"A perfectly lovely name belonging to the woman who is currently delivering our child. Move. Your. Feet."

"It's just—the nurse said it so seriously—"

"Men," Celeste grumbles, and the word contains the exhaustion of every woman who has ever watched a man find something funny at the worst possible time. "I swear to God."

She grabs my hand and pulls me down the hall. Room 316A has a closed door and the muffled sounds of controlled chaos behind it. Celeste stops. Smooths her hair. Straightens her blouse. Takes one breath. Then she turns to me.

"This is it."

I smile. "See you on the other side, Lessi."

Raven only wants Celeste in the room which was a relief to me. As supportive as I want to be, there are a lot of bodily fluids in that room, and Raven's a good bro. I think seeing her expel a human being from her body might ruin the friendship.

"I'll tell her you love her."

"And I'll tell her again ten minutes later once she's bundled and they get the goo off her."

"Don't say 'goo' when you're talking about our baby," Celeste scolds.

She kisses me. Quick, firm, the compressed version of everything she doesn't have time to say. Then she knocks twice on the door, slips inside, and is gone.

The door closes. The hallway is suddenly very quiet.

I wander down the hall a little aimlessly until a voice reaches me from the waiting area around the corner.

"Saylor."

Eleanor is seated in a row of chairs near the window. She's in a navy dress, low heels, a strand of pearls that probably predate my birth. Her posture is perfect, her hands folded in her lap, her expression composed. She looks like she's waiting for a board meeting, not a baby.

"Eleanor." I walk over. Sit down in the chair beside her, leaving one empty seat between us...for safety. A snake loves to strike when your back is turned. Celeste has warmed up to Eleanor. I need a little more convincing. "You got banished too?"

"Banished? No." She adjusts a pearl. "I chose to wait out here. Raven was very generous with the invitation, but I have never been good with...squishy things."

"Squishy things."

"Yes, I've had a child, remember? I know the mess that's made in there." She crosses her ankles. "Thank goodness Celeste is here. She has a stronger stomach than I do."

I lean forward, elbows on my knees, thumbs twiddling against each other. The nervous energy that was propelling me up four flights of stairs has nowhere to go now. It's pooling in my hands, my feet, the base of my spine. I bounce my right knee. Stop. Start again.

"Stop fidgeting. You're making me anxious."

"I can't."

"You can. You simply choose not to."

"Eleanor, give it a rest. My kid is being born twenty meters from where I'm sitting and I don't know what to do with my hands. *My kid.*" I say it like I'm testing the integrity of the word. A baby is one thing. *My baby* is a whole other thing.

She looks at me. Something moves behind her eyes, something warmer than I've seen from her before. Not soft, exactly. Eleanor doesn't do soft. But the hardness rearranges into something adjacent to tenderness, the way a winter sky can look almost gentle just before dawn.

"You're going to be a good father, Saylor." She says it with certainty, as if the matter has already been settled and she's merely informing me of the outcome. "Don't worry too much. Children are resilient. They forgive the mistakes you make as long as you show up for the moments that matter." She pauses. "This is one of those moments. You're here. That's enough."

I look at her. This woman who fought us for months, who deployed lawyers and legal strategies and every weapon in her arsenal to claim this baby. This woman who then stood at her daughter's grave and chose to let go. Who sold two properties and wrote a check and surrendered her rights because she finally heard what her daughter was saying.

"Thank you, Eleanor."

"For what?"

"For being here. For all of it."

She nods but doesn't elaborate. Eleanor does not require gratitude to be expanded upon. She accepts it the way she accepts a coat check ticket: efficiently, without sentiment, and with the expectation that the interaction is now complete.

We sit in silence. The hospital hums around us. Nurses pass in soft-soled shoes. A phone rings somewhere down the hall. The clock on the wall ticks through minutes that feel like geological eras. Eleanor reads a magazine she brought from home. I stare at the floor tiles and count them because my brain needs a task or it's going to implode.

Thirty-seven tiles between my chair and the nurses' station. I count them twice. The number doesn't change, but the exercise keeps my hands from shaking.

Then, finally, after two trips down to the cafeteria, three loo breaks, and failing to finish two different Sudokus, the door opens.

A nurse steps into the hallway. Young, smiling, tired in the good way. She looks at me, then at Eleanor, and the smile widens.

"Family for Drews Pecker?"

I don't laugh this time. I'm too far past laughter. I'm in the territory beyond it, where everything is sharp and bright and the air tastes different.

"Baby girl is here," the nurse says. "Healthy. Strong lungs. Mom and mom and baby are ready for you."

When I stand, my legs feel borrowed. Eleanor rises beside me with considerably more grace, smoothing her dress, touching her pearls, preparing to meet her granddaughter the way she prepares for everything: with composure and an unshakable belief that presentation matters even when the world is falling apart. Or coming together.

The walk to 316A takes ten seconds and ten years.

I push open the door.

Celeste is in the chair beside the bed, and she's holding a baby.

The room is quiet now. The chaos of delivery has settled into the particular hush that follows arrival, the reverent silence of a space that just witnessed something impossible become ordinary. Raven is propped up in the bed, sweaty and wrecked and grinning with the satisfied exhaustion of an athlete who just finished a race she trained nine months for. Medical equipment beeps softly. The afternoon light comes through the window and lands on the bundle in Celeste's arms, and the bundle has hair.

Red hair. A full head of it. Bright copper, curling already at the temples, catching the light the way only that specific shade of red can. Whitney's hair. Whitney's daughter.

Celeste looks up at me. Her eyes are wet and her face is open and there is nothing guarded, nothing designed, nothing held back. She is, in this moment, the most undefended version of herself I have ever seen.

"Come here," she says.

I cross the room. Celeste stands, careful, slow, cradling the baby against her chest with natural confidence, like she's been rehearsing this hold in her imagination for months. She transfers the baby into my arms and the weight is nothing. Six pounds, maybe seven. A whole person who weighs less than the puppy did at eight weeks but carries the gravity of everything we've built and lost and rebuilt to get here.

"Meet our daughter," Celeste says.

Our daughter.

I look down. She's sleeping. Her face is scrunched and pink and impossibly small. Her fingers are curled into fists, each one the size of a grape, and she has the serious brow of someone who arrived with opinions. The red hair fans across her forehead in wisps that are already unruly, already refusing to cooperate, already Whitney's.

I look at Raven. She's watching us from the bed with glassy, exhausted eyes. Her hair is matted to her forehead. Her hospital gown is twisted sideways. She looks like she's been through a war, and she has.

"Good on ya, kid," I say. "You did amazing."

Raven laughs, a hoarse, relieved sound. "Oh dear God, thank you. I can officially drink again."

I kiss the baby's forehead. Her skin is warm and impossibly soft, and she smells like something brand new, like a room that's just been painted, like a future that hasn't been touched yet.

"Thank you," I say to Raven. "For carrying her. For delivering her into our lives. *Thank you.*"

Raven waves me off, but her eyes are wet.

I turn to Eleanor, who is standing in the doorway. She hasn't come fully into the room yet. She's holding her purse in front of her with both hands, and her composure is intact, but her chin has the faintest tremor, and her eyes are bright in a way that has nothing to do with the fluorescent lighting.

"Thank you," I say. "For listening. For letting her come home to us."

Eleanor nods once. She steps forward and I place the baby in her arms and watch Eleanor Montgomery-Trace meet her granddaughter.

The composure cracks. Not dramatically. Not with sound. But Eleanor's face does something I have never seen it do before. It melts at the sight of this little person. Completely, utterly, as if every wall she ever built was made of ice and this baby is the sun. She looks down at the red hair and the scrunched face and the tiny fists, and a tear falls. Just one. It lands on the baby's blanket and Eleanor doesn't wipe it away, doesn't acknowledge it, just stands there holding this child and letting the weight of what she chose settle into her arms.

"She looks like Whitney," Eleanor whispers.

"She does," Celeste says.

"No, I mean she looks *exactly* like Whitney. The day she was born. It's like déjà vu."

Nobody speaks for a moment. The room holds its breath. Whitney is here, in the copper hair and the serious brow and the unruly curl that refuses to lie flat. She is here in the silence between people who loved her, standing around the baby she planned for and trusted to the right hands and never got to meet.

Eleanor transfers the baby back to Celeste. Gently, precisely, the way you hand someone something priceless. Then she excuses herself to the hallway, and I know it's because Eleanor does not cry in front of people and she's about to cry in a way that her composure cannot contain.

Celeste settles back into the chair with the baby against her chest. I stand beside her, my hand on her shoulder. My eyes on the red hair and the tiny fingers and the small, steady rise and fall of breathing that has only existed for twenty minutes and already feels like the most important sound in the world.

"Look at you," I say to Celeste. And I mean all of it. Everything. This woman who was told she was past her prime. Who was told her worth had an expiration date. Who lost her company and her best friend and a custody battle, all in the span of a summer, and rebuilt from the wreckage something no one predicted. She is full of youth. Full of life. Brave enough to start over as many times as life requires it.

She was never too old. It was never too late. She was just waiting for her story to begin.

Celeste

The room is quiet.

Raven is asleep, her breathing deep and even, her body finally surrendered to the rest it earned. Eleanor has gone to the cafeteria. Saylor stepped out to call Ada, and I could hear his voice cracking through the phone even from the hallway. "She's here, Mum. She's got red hair. She's perfect."

It's just me and the baby.

She's awake. Eyes open, unfocused, staring at nothing and everything with the bewildered calm of someone who has just arrived in a world they don't understand yet but has no choice but to trust. *I've got you, baby girl. I'm here.*

Her eyes are slate blue, the way all newborns' eyes are, but I already know they'll change. They'll become green, maybe. Or brown. Or something entirely her own.

I hold her against my chest and breathe her in. Lavender. Everything in this hospital room smells like lavender, the lotion, the blankets, the wipes. It's in her hair and on her skin and I know this scent will be tattooed on my memory for the rest of my life. The smell of the first hour. The smell of pure joy.

I lean down. Close enough that my lips brush the peach fuzz on her temple. Close enough that she can hear my heartbeat and my voice at the same time.

"Know what, sweetie?" I whisper. "I think we're finally out of the gray area. We've been hoping and waiting. Healing from the tragedy while waiting for joy. Sitting in the aftermath of the storm, eyes fixed on the rainbow above. You, baby girl, are our rainbow. You are the magic. You're all the colors we've been waiting for."

Her fist uncurls against my collarbone. Five tiny fingers spreading open, then closing again, grasping at fabric, at air, at the newness of having hands.

"I love you, sweet girl. And so did your mama," I say. "Her name was Whitney, and she was the best person in the whole world. She had red hair just like yours. And a laugh that could fill an entire room. And she loved you before you were even possible. She planned for you. She fought for you. She trusted me with you, which is either the smartest or the craziest thing she ever did, and knowing Whit, it was both."

Baby girl blinks. Yawns. A whole-body yawn that scrunches her face and curls her toes and makes her look so much like Whit that my chest cracks open in the best possible way.

Saylor appears in the doorway. He doesn't come in right away. He leans against the frame and watches us, and the look on his face is one I'll keep alongside the lavender and the red hair and the weight of her in my arms.

"How ya goin'?" he whispers.

I smile. "I'm good. Just obsessed with holding her."

He comes to my side and kneels beside the chair. His hand finds my knee and rests there, warm and steady.

"What are you thinking about?" he asks.

"A name. I think I've got it."

"Yeah?"

"Wren."

He's quiet for a moment. "Is that significant?"

"It was Whit's pen name. She used it to publish a few short stories in college. Published all her articles in the literary magazine under the name Wren Tracie. She always loved the bird because she said wrens were such a contradiction. They sing beautifully, but too loud. They were small, but fierce. Whit loved their idiosyncrasies, like they couldn't help but be exactly what they were. She always loved the name." I look at the baby. At the red hair and the serious brow and the fists that are already clenched with purpose. "If it was good enough for Whit, it's good enough for her. Small, but mighty."

"Wren," Saylor repeats. He reaches out and touches the baby's hand with one finger. She grabs it and holds on with all her might.

"Welcome to the world, baby Wren," he says. "We've all been waiting for you."

He lifts her from my arms. Gently, carefully, like he's handling the most important thing he's ever held. He cradles her against his chest and her head fits perfectly in the hollow below his collarbone, and she settles there as if she's known him longer than an hour. As if she's been listening to his voice through months of walls and waiting rooms and the particular acoustics of hope.

I watch them together. My daughter in the arms of the man I love. And I have one more conversation.

Thank you, Whit. For the greatest gift anyone has ever given me. Not the baby, though she's everything. Your trust. Your whole heart. You looked at me when the world told me I was finished, and you said: not yet. You're just getting started.

I'll make sure she knows you. Every story, every photo, every terrible joke. She'll know about the overalls and the crayon costume and the red curls and your perfect laugh. She'll know her mother loved her before she existed and chose the people who'd love her after.

We will never forget.

The hospital room is quiet. The lavender is everywhere. Saylor is humming something to Wren that sounds like a lullaby he's inventing in real time, and she's asleep against his chest, and the afternoon light is turning everything gold, and I am thirty-nine years old and I have never been more alive.

Not too old. Not too late. Just right on time.

THE END

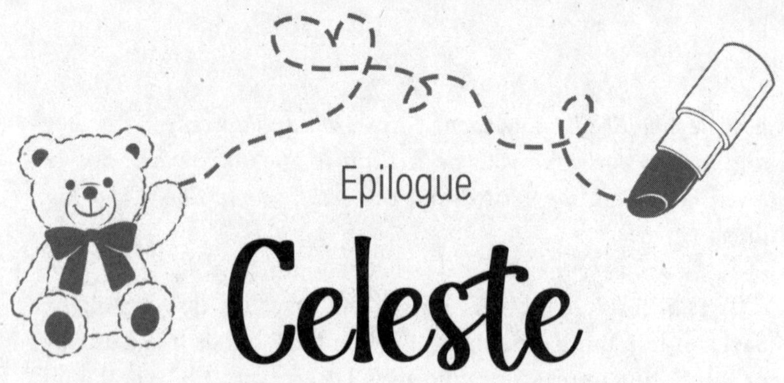

Epilogue
Celeste

You planned this, didn't you, Whit? You absolute menace.

About one year later.

Patrice looks magnificent.

She's standing in the corner of my office in a floor-length gown that catches the afternoon light and throws it back in shards of violet and gold, the silk shimmering with the kind of depth that only happens when you get the dye ratio exactly right. I spent three weeks on that color. Three weeks of samples and rejections and one very dramatic argument with my textile supplier in Milan who insisted the shade I wanted didn't exist, to which I replied that it would exist when I was finished inventing it. He sent me fourteen test swatches. I rejected thirteen. The fourteenth was close enough that I could work with it, and what I built from that starting point is now draped across Patrice's fiberglass shoulders like a second skin made of crushed amethyst.

I'm calling the color Regal Plum. Not because it's regal or particularly plum-like, but because the name sounds like something a woman would wear to a gala where she intends to be remembered, and that's exactly the customer I designed it for. The gown is the centerpiece of the new fall collection, and it's the first piece I've created since the relaunch that made me stand in front of the mirror in my office and think: *there she is.* The designer I used to be, before Greg hollowed out the company and my confidence in the same slow, methodical stroke.

Patrice wears it well. She always does. Fifteen years of standing in this corner, absorbing my best and worst ideas without complaint, and she's never once asked for a raise. Employee of the century.

I ease down into my desk chair, one hand bracing against the armrest, my five-months-pregnant belly requiring a new choreography for even the simplest movements. My hand goes to my belly, where the bump is now undeniable, the kind of round that strangers feel entitled to comment on and touch, both of which I've discouraged through a combination of no direct eye contact and the specific tone of voice I reserve for people who reach for me without invitation.

My phone chimes from my desk, bursting with excitement. *Celeste! Another message you're too busy to respond to!*

Raven, who became one of the most unexpectedly important people in my life, who texts me photos of Wren's birthday gift options with the chaotic enthusiasm of a favorite aunt who has no concept of age-appropriate presents.

I pick up my phone. Her latest text arrived an hour ago: a photo of a tortoise at a pet store with the caption: *Wren would love this. Please say yes.*

Her most recent message is just a slurry of question marks.

We are absolutely not giving a one-year-old a tortoise, Raven.

Her reply is immediate.

Raven

Turtles are educational.

Perhaps. But what you're looking at is a tortoise and a possible EIGHTY YEAR commitment. She already has a dog... That eats my shoes.

Raven

See? Dogs eat shoes. Turtles eat lettuce. Seems like an upgrade.

Sorry.

I mean tortoise. Just consider it!

I set the phone down and make a mental note to have Saylor intercept whatever package Raven brings to the party, because I know with absolute certainty that this woman is going to show up in two weeks with a tortoise in a box and a grin on her face, and Wren is going to lose her mind with joy. Powerless, I'm going to end up with a reptile in my kitchen and no one to blame but myself for befriending a woman whose approach to gift-giving mirrors her approach to surrogacy: excessive, generous, and completely impossible to refuse.

Heels strike the hallway floor outside my office—deliberate, rhythmic, unmistakable—the sound of someone who walks as if each footfall is punctuation at the end of a sentence. I know that walk. I've been hearing it for eleven months, ever since the woman attached to it signed the paperwork that made her my business partner. I have come to associate the sound with a very specific emotional blend of gratitude, affection, and the urge to hide under my desk.

Eleanor sweeps through the office door without knocking.

She never knocks. Knocking implies that the person on

the other side has the option of saying no, and Eleanor has not recognized the word "no" as a valid response since approximately nineteen eighty-seven. She's in a cream blazer with sharp shoulders, tapered trousers, and a silk blouse in a shade of ivory I have yet to name. But I will. Her hair is blown out with so much hairspray it has the architectural integrity of someone who considers her stylist a structural engineer. Her reading glasses hang from a gold chain around her neck, and she's carrying a leather folio that I've learned to interpret as a warning sign, because the folio means she has notes, and Eleanor's notes are never brief.

"The board meeting went well, I think," she announces, settling into the chair across from my desk as if she owns half the furniture in this building. Which, technically, she does.

When Eleanor bought out Greg's stake in the company, she gave him a choice that I will treasure for the rest of my professional life. He could accept a modest severance and walk away clean, or he could stay on in a newly created position she'd designed specifically for him: mailroom coordinator, reporting to a twenty-three-year-old named Benji who had been with the company for six months and already understood more about operations than Greg had absorbed in fifteen years.

Greg took the cash. He left the building in under an hour, and I watched him go from this window, and I didn't feel triumph or vindication or any of the dramatic emotions you'd expect. I felt the same thing you feel when you finally remove a splinter that's been embedded so long you forgot it was there. Relief. And the faint surprise of remembering what it feels like when something stops hurting.

"The members seemed quite pleased," Eleanor continues, crossing her legs and opening the folio. "The quarterly projections exceeded expectations. The fall collection pre-orders are strong. And the department heads presented with confidence, which tells me morale is healthy." She looks at me over her reading glasses. "You've done incredible work, Celeste. One year. This company was on life support, and you brought it back. I want you to know that I'm proud of you."

The words land in a place I didn't know was still tender. Eleanor says "I'm proud of you" the way other people say "it's a nice day out"—factually, without fanfare, as though the information is self-evident and she's merely confirming it for the record. But the fact that she says it at all, this woman who spent the first three months of our partnership communicating primarily through margin notes and disapproving sighs, means something I'm not equipped to process without my eyes doing something embarrassing.

"Thank you, Eleanor. That means a lot."

"Of course it does." She adjusts her glasses. "Now. About Wren's birthday."

And just like that, the sweet moment evaporates like morning dew on a hot dashboard.

"The catering," Eleanor says, consulting the folio as though the birthday party of a one-year-old requires the same logistical framework as a corporate merger. "I want to revisit the menu."

"The menu is set, Eleanor."

"Is it? Because the invitation mentioned hot dogs, hamburgers, and fried cheese."

"You know the invitation said mozzarella sticks."

"I'm choosing to call them what they are, which is fried cheese. And I have concerns." She pulls a printed page from the folio—printed, with bullet points, because Eleanor brings supporting documents to party-planning disputes—and sets it on my desk. "I've taken the liberty of drafting an alternative. The truffle brie bites would be far more suitable for a gathering of this caliber."

"This caliber? It's a one-year-old's birthday party. Wren is going to eat cake with her hands and then try to befriend a balloon. The caliber is 'sticky.'"

"All the more reason to elevate the adult experience. The parents will be there. The neighbors. Your business associates."

"I'm not inviting business associates to my daughter's first birthday party."

"You should. It's called networking, Celeste. Birthdays are an untapped professional resource."

"They are not. *They are birthdays.* And the mozzarella sticks are staying." I lean back in my chair and rest both hands on my belly, a gesture that has become my default punctuation mark in arguments. The bump makes an excellent period at the end of a firm sentence. "Besides, the mozzarella sticks are more for Saylor than Wren, and if I remove them from the menu, I'll have a mutiny on my hands."

Eleanor purses her lips in the specific way that means she's lost this round but intends to revisit the issue from a different angle at a later date. I've learned to read her tactical retreats the way meteorologists read pressure systems—the calm before the next front moves in.

"Fine," she states, in a tone that does not mean fine. "While we're on the subject, I know the Westchester house is finished with renovations, but there's a last-minute opening at the country club for that Saturday, and I thought—"

"No."

"The grounds are impeccable this time of year—"

"No, Eleanor."

"There's a children's garden with a fountain—"

"The party is at our house. In our backyard. Under the oak tree that Saylor strung lights through last weekend." I fold my arms above my belly. "This is casual. Come in jeans, for God's sake."

Eleanor looks at me as though I've suggested she arrive in a swimsuit. "I don't own jeans."

"Buy some."

"I'm sixty-three years old. I haven't worn denim since the Carter administration."

"Then you're overdue. As a matter of fact, buy the stretchy kind. They're a revelation." I hook my thumb under the waistband of my own maternity jeans and pull, demonstrating the elastic with the enthusiasm of an infomercial host. "See this? Pregnancy pants. No zipper, no button, just faith and elastic. These jeans have changed my relationship with food, with sitting, and with the entire concept of waistlines. I may never go back."

Eleanor stares at the elastic waistband with an expression that suggests I've shown her something medically concerning. "That's not fashion, Celeste. That's surrender."

"It's comfort. And comfort is the ultimate luxury. I should embroider that on a throw pillow."

"Well, don't put that pillow in my house."

"You sure? The furniture in your ice castle is so stiff. A pillow could help."

"Ha. Ha." There's not even the ghost of a smile on her face.

She closes the folio, which is her version of a white flag, and folds her hands in her lap. The combative energy softens. She looks at my belly, and the look that crosses her face is the one I've come to recognize as the *other* Eleanor. The human one who lives underneath the blazers and the bullet points and the relentless opinions about party menus. The one who is, against all odds and against her own expectations, becoming a grandmother for the second time.

"How are you feeling?" she asks, and her voice has dropped the boardroom register. It's quieter. Almost careful.

"Nothing remotely worth complaining about," I say. "The nausea is persistent and creative in its timing, and I've developed a relationship with saltines that borders on romantic. But Wren is getting a sister, and I'm thrilled."

"Me too," Eleanor says. Two words. No elaboration. But her eyes stay on my belly for a beat longer than necessary, and I can see the math she's doing. It's the same math she did standing in front of Whit's grave a year ago, recalculating what family means and where she fits inside it. *She fits.* It took us both a while to build the door, but she walked through it, and she's not leaving.

She stands, smooths her trousers, and begins a slow tour of my office that I've come to recognize as her post-meeting wind-down ritual. She straightens a frame on the credenza. Adjusts the angle of a vase on the windowsill. Runs her finger along the edge of my bookshelf and inspects it for dust, which she finds, and addresses with a look of personal betrayal directed at my cleaning service.

"You know," she says, pausing at Patrice, "this gown is extraordinary."

"Thank you."

"The color is exceptional."

"It's Regal Plum."

Eleanor tilts her head, considering. "That's not bad. I might have gone with Imperial Amethyst, but Regal Plum has a certain accessibility."

"Imperial Amethyst? Damn, Eleanor." I hand over nothing but air. "Here's the crown. Consider me humbled. That's a great name. But no, we're going with Regal Plum."

"Why?"

"Because I want this to feel approachable. I want women to feel like they can wear it, not like the dress is going to wear them."

"Is it all finished?"

"Yes, except for pockets. We're working that into the final production."

"Pockets?"

I look at her very seriously. "Yes, pockets. Like Target dresses."

Eleanor nods like I just insulted her religion. She touches the sleeve of the gown the way I've seen her touch Whitney's headstone—with reverence, with grief, with the quiet understanding that beautiful things are worth protecting even when they can't protect you back.

She finally bores of the gown and continues through my office to investigate the imperfections. I have a conversation with my best friend that takes place entirely inside my chest.

You planned this, didn't you, Whit? You absolute menace. You knew leaving me with Wren would shackle me to your mother until the end of time.

I can almost hear her laughing. That big, room-filling laugh that made strangers turn and stare and waiters bring extra bread because they wanted to be near whatever was making someone that happy.

I love her, Whit. She drives me insane, but I love her. And she loves Wren in a way that would make you cry, the good kind, the kind where you're not sad but your body needs to do something with all that feeling so it picks crying because it's the only release valve big enough.

I hope you can see this. I hope wherever you are, you can see that the people you loved figured it out. It took a cemetery, a bankruptcy, a fake engagement, a real one, a marker ring, an Australian, a puppy, a caseworker named Janet, a check written in a cemetery, and one deeply unfortunate conversation about mozzarella sticks, but we figured it out.

I miss you. Every day. But I'm not sad anymore. I'm just grateful. For the trust. For the time we had. For the little girl with your red hair who is about to come through that door any second now because I can hear her father's boots in the hallway and she's probably chewing on his collar.

Right on cue, the office door opens and Saylor walks in with Wren on his hip.

She's gotten so big. A year of growing has transformed her from the scrunched, fist-clenching bundle I held in the hospital into a bright-eyed, copper-haired tornado of opinions and motion. She's wearing a yellow dress that Ada picked out and tiny white shoes that she's already kicked off, because Wren has inherited her mother's hair, her godmother's stubbornness, and apparently Whit's feelings about uncomfortable footwear.

"Look who it is, sweetie," Saylor coos, bouncing her gently on his hip. "Mummy and Grandma."

Wren's face splits into a grin that takes up her entire head. She reaches for me with both arms, fingers opening and closing in the universal toddler signal for *give me to that person immediately or face consequences.*

Saylor sets her in my lap, careful to protect my belly. She settles against my belly with a comfort reserved only for mama.

I've been her pillow, couch, and bed for so long, this little girl has a permanent butt print in my lap. I never thought I was a cuddly person. When I met Saylor, I realized I was wrong. When we met Wren, I realized I was *very* wrong. She pats the bump twice with her palm, which she's been doing for weeks, not because she understands what's inside but because she's noticed the bump is new and she's conducting an ongoing investigation.

Saylor leans down and kisses my temple, and the warmth of his mouth lingers on my skin the way it always does—not fading so much as settling in, becoming part of the ambient temperature of my life.

"How'd the run go?" I ask.

"Sixteen-minute mile, but Mum ran the whole time." He grins, and the pride in his face is luminous, the kind that can't be performed or manufactured. "The whole thing, Celeste. Start to finish. No cane, no stops. Doc Yassa said her mobility has improved forty percent since the surgery. She cried after. I cried after. Ruby cried after, but I think that's because she wanted a treat."

Ruby, our red heeler, who has grown from a five-pound bundle of chaos into a thirty-pound bundle of slightly more organized chaos, probably ran the mile twice, because heelers don't understand pacing and Ruby in particular doesn't understand the concept of "enough." Ada named her Ruby in the second week much to Saylor's protest who wanted Roxanne. Ada calmly explained that she loved him, but this was her puppy, and Saylor could suck it.

"Forty percent," I repeat. "Saylor, that's incredible."

"*She's* incredible. I just drive her to the appointments." He's being modest, which is his default setting when it comes to anything he's done for Ada. The truth is that Saylor has attended every session, every follow-up, every grueling hour of physical therapy where his mother gritted her teeth and pushed through pain that would flatten most people. He built a set of parallel bars in the backyard so she could practice walking between them, and he lined the path with flat stones so she wouldn't trip, and he never once told her to slow down or be careful, because he learned, finally, that managing her was never the same as loving her.

"Are you ready for lunch?" Saylor asks. "What are you craving?"

I know the answer before the question is finished. The craving has been building since ten this morning, escalating through the board meeting, reaching its peak during Eleanor's truffle brie offensive, and now sitting in my chest like a neon sign that will not be dimmed or reasoned with.

"Flamin' Hot Cheetos," I say.

Saylor and Eleanor produce identical eye-rolls in perfect synchronization, which is the only thing I've ever seen them agree on without negotiation.

"Those aren't food," Eleanor says.

"Those are chemical warfare in a bag," Saylor adds.

"Those are what this baby wants, and this baby gets what this baby wants, and if either of you has a problem with that, you can take it up with my uterus, which is currently running this operation and has overruled both of you."

Wren, sensing the energy shift, slaps my belly again and says something that sounds like "chee," which I'm choosing to interpret as solidarity.

"See?" I say. "Wren agrees."

"Wren agrees with everything that involves food," Saylor points out. "She agreed with Ruby's breakfast this morning. Literally. She tried to eat it."

He scoops Wren off my lap, hoists her onto his hip, and extends his free hand to help me out of the chair, which I accept because I've reached the stage of pregnancy where standing up from a seated position requires either assistance or a small crane. He pulls me to my feet and keeps holding my hand, his thumb running across the diamond on my ring finger with the absent, habitual tenderness of someone who touches it every time our hands connect, not because he's checking if it's still there but because the feel of it reminds him of a promise he made on the floor of an empty nursery with a Sharpie and a lopsided heart. He wants to get married before the baby comes. I say, what does it matter? We've been destiny since the beginning. Time doesn't need to rush us now.

Eleanor is already at the door, folio tucked under her arm, prepared to lead us to lunch, clearly considering herself in charge of all outings regardless of whether she's been appointed to the role.

"I'll drive," I say.

"You will not," they argue in unison.

"Celeste, you drive like you're being chased," Eleanor adds.

"I've gotten better," I protest.

"Yeah, but...not by that much, baby." Saylor grimaces.

We file out of the office, past Patrice in her Regal Plum, past the corkboard where new fabric swatches hang in clusters that make sense only to me, past the window where I once watched Greg leave the building for the last time and felt a splinter slide free.

Saylor walks ahead with Wren on his hip, pointing out things through the hallway windows—birds, cars, a cloud that looks like a dog—and Wren responds to each one with the wide-eyed amazement of someone who has been alive for twelve months and is still not over the fact that the world exists. Eleanor walks beside me, matching my slower pace without comment, which is her way of accommodating my pregnancy without acknowledging it as a limitation. Eleanor does not believe in limitations, not for herself and not for the women she's chosen to invest in.

The elevator arrives. We step in, all four of us—five, if you count the bump, and I do. Saylor presses the lobby button. Wren grabs for the panel and manages to hit three additional floors before anyone can stop her, which means we'll be making scenic stops on nine, five, and two, and Saylor will apologize to every confused person who watches the doors open on an elevator containing a laughing toddler, a pregnant woman, an impeccably dressed grandmother, and a man in work boots who is clearly outnumbered and wouldn't have it any other way.

The doors close. The elevator begins its descent. I catch my reflection in the polished metal wall—blurred, imprecise, more impression than portrait. I can see the shape of my belly and the fall of my hair and the ring on my finger and the people standing beside me, and the image is distorted but the feeling is clear.

This is my life. Not the one I planned. Not the one I designed on a mood board or pitched to investors or sketched on a napkin at twenty-two with a girl in overalls who believed I could build an empire out of thread and nerve.

This life is better. It's messier and louder and full of mozzarella sticks and elastic waistbands and a toddler who just pressed buttons willy-nilly in the elevator. It's full of people I didn't expect and couldn't have predicted and wouldn't trade for any version of the future I once thought I wanted.

Not too old. Not too late. Just right on time.

The elevator stops at the second floor. The doors open. A man in a suit looks at our full, chaotic car with visible confusion.

"Going down?" he asks.

"Eventually," Saylor says, grinning. "We're taking the scenic route."

The doors close. Wren laughs. Eleanor sighs. And I ride down with my family, floor by unnecessary floor, in no rush to arrive, because the destination was never the point.

The point was always the people in the car.

Lessi & Whit's Road Trip Bangers - 2007

"Pieces of Me" — Ashlee Simpson

"Fighter" — Christina Aguilera

"Since U Been Gone" — Kelly Clarkson

"Hollaback Girl" — Gwen Stefani

"Toxic" — Britney Spears

"Unwritten" — Natasha Bedingfield

"Pon de Replay" — Rihanna

"Leave (Get Out)" — JoJo

"Stickwitu" — Pussycat Dolls

"Promiscuous" — Nelly Furtado ft. Timbaland

"Bye Bye Bye" — *NSYNC

"My Happy Ending"— Avril Lavigne

"Before He Cheats "— Carrie Underwood

"Misery Business" — Paramore

"So Yesterday "— Hilary Duff

Acknowledgements

To Mr. Cove, for being my boat. And the other boat. And the helicopter. Because I'm pretty stubborn. When it feels like the world is against me, you always encourage me to just write another world. Thank you for helping me escape into our lives in the absolute best way.

To Michelle, for loving this story from your bones. For being the constant cheerleader in my head at every moment of doubt and questioning. You are the only person who knows when I'm creatively blocked or just a little hangry, and I am forever grateful. I will treasure our adventures in creating just the perfect amount of *Aussie*.

To Page, for reminding me to stay delulu, hopeful, and happy. You're right, my friend. The grass is so much greener on this side and the stories here are endless. I'll keep writing words. You keep making magic. I am forever in your debt.

To Brooke, for my daily starshine voice memos. Thank you for reminding me to touch grass, breathe air, believe in myself, and most importantly for reminding me that while I'm always the last to the trends and the Gen Z lingo, and my bedtime is basically eight at night, I'm still pretty cool.

To Valentine, my passionate agent, for talking me off the ledge for the thousandth time this month (okay fine, the thousandth time today). Every time I tell you I've got nothing left, you remind me that that's probably BS. Thank you for dreaming big with me. Cheers to the long, twisty, and rewarding road ahead.

To Aga, for continuing to inspire me with your art. Thank you for taking such good care of my characters every single time. Your talent is unrivaled.

To my real life version of Whit, my ride-or-die, my person who finishes my sentences, is fantastic at the bombastic side-eye, and once upon a time taught me to drink wine like a real New Yorker. I love you, bestie. Also, it's been too long since I've seen you, and I'm back to wine coolers, so we may have work to do.

About the Author

Kay Cove, a Korean American, *USA Today* and Amazon bestselling author, known for Camera Shy, is a wife, boy mom, and accidental entrepreneur. After (surviving) a career in HR she ultimately decided to pursue her dream of becoming a published author. She writes contemporary romances filled with angsty characters, green flag MMCs, and witty banter.

She currently resides in Georgia with her husband and two sweet—albeit rambunctious—little boys. When she's not writing she can be found drinking copious amounts of coffee and watching true crime documentaries—all while keeping her tiny humans alive.

Some of her works include the Lessons in Love, PALADIN, Real Life, Real Love, and Off the Books series.

Also by Kay Cove

Lessons in Love
Camera Shy
Snapshot
Selfie

Real Life, Real Love
Paint Me Perfect
Rewrite the Rules
Owe Me One
Sing Your Secrets
First Comes Forever

Paladin
Whistleblower
Tattletale
Snitch - Coming 2026
Canary - TBD

Off the Books
Role Play
Paper Hearts
Gray Area - Coming 2026
Sweet Spot - Coming 2026

kaycove.com

PAGE
&
VINE